NIGHTBLADE'S
HONOR

ALSO BY RYAN KIRK

Blades of the Fallen

Nightblade's Vengeance

The Nightblade Series

Nightblade
World's Edge
The Wind and the Void

The Primal Series

Primal Dawn
Primal Darkness
Primal Destiny

NIGHTBLADE'S HONOR

BLADES OF THE FALLEN
BOOK 2

RYAN KIRK

Published by 47North, Seattle

www.apub.com

Amazon, the Amazon logo, and 47North are trademarks of Amazon.com, Inc., or its affiliates.

ISBN-13: 9781503953154
ISBN-10: 1503953157

Cover design by Zlatina Zareva

Printed in the United States of America

For Mackenzie

Chapter 1

Koji's sword cut down, its song clear to his ears in the crisp early morning air. The cut was close to perfect, the melody of the steel reflecting none of the indecision that plagued him.

What did it mean to be honorable in a world that seemed to care so little for honor?

A simple question, but one that Koji struggled with from sunrise to sunset.

His blade cut sideways as he executed a sharp quarter turn, his imagination creating enemies and their attacks.

Those acquainted with Koji often first believed his thoughts came slow. He heard the whispers, saw the sympathy in their eyes, even if no one dared speak the sentiment to his face.

He was a ponderous thinker—that much was true—but not stupid. He worked on problems one step at a time, making sure each step was perfect before moving on, just like the stonemasons made sure each stone fit perfectly with its neighbors before building any higher. His master, Minori, was entirely the opposite, his mind leaping forward and making connections far before others.

Koji took his time to work through problems. Once people got to know him well enough, they saw the process for themselves and gave him the time he needed.

With a sword in hand, however, he was an entirely different person. Fighting was something he *understood*. He was sense-gifted, able to feel an incoming strike moments before it happened, but his skill went deeper than that, an intuition for combat not shared even by other nightblades. Koji hadn't been beaten in a duel for many cycles.

Sometimes he tried to clarify his thinking by practicing with his sword. He took a problem, like that of honor in a dishonorable world, and held it in his mind as he began practicing. Sometimes the method worked, and when his morning routine was done, he had an answer in his head. Other times the method failed, but Koji had learned patience, a necessary skill for a man often considered slow.

Koji was camped in a small grove of trees several leagues away from the emergency shelters that had been set up for the residents fleeing from Haven. Though it was early in the season, the trees were already changing colors, and a thin layer of snow covered patches of exposed grass. Although he was tempted to approach the shelters, wisdom dictated he keep to himself. Blamed for the burning of Haven and the attempted murder of King Shin, both nightblade warriors and dayblade healers were being hunted by roving groups of citizens and soldiers.

So he practiced in a clearing in the grove, largely hidden from the rest of the world, trying to solve the problems that confronted him.

The one he was most focused on was the problem of his master, Minori.

Was Minori still his master?

The question was the first Koji needed to answer, and as his blade sliced through the morning air, his mind worked on the solution.

Minori had offered to release Koji from his service, but Koji had never given an official answer. Instead, he continued serving Minori, burning down the king's palace and killing Lord Juro.

With an upward cut, Koji understood that he was asking the wrong question. Whether or not Minori was his master didn't matter.

What mattered was that Koji owed the elder blade a life debt. Koji had been scheduled to be executed when Minori broke him out of prison. Master or not, Koji didn't believe he had repaid his debt yet.

One piece of the puzzle settled into place. His body was starting to warm up from his practice, his breath visible in the sunlight.

Koji had donned the clothes of a peasant to watch Minori's trial. The old nightblade, deeply wounded and barely able to walk without assistance, faced a litany of charges: the burning of the palace, the burning of Haven, the attempted murder of King Shin. Perhaps most serious, he was charged with leading a coup to overthrow the rightful government of the Kingdom and replace it with one led by blades.

The trial had been held outdoors in a large depression, the ground sunken as though the bottom had fallen out from below, less than a league away from the ruins of Haven. The natural amphitheater held thousands, which suited King Shin's plans perfectly. Many of the displaced and homeless had come to attend the trial and let their anger be known.

From Koji's perspective, the proceedings had been a fascinating mixture of truth and lies. As Minori's closest aide, Koji, perhaps better than anyone else, knew what had actually happened. Some of the accusations were true. Minori had burned the palace, but on Shin's orders. That detail didn't make the trial, and Koji often wondered why Minori didn't protest more strongly against the lies told of him.

Koji wasn't sure about the burning of Haven. He had been outside the city when the event happened, but the action didn't seem like one Minori would take. Koji had little doubt his master had tried to kill the king. Minori had served Shin when the politician was still a lord, only to be betrayed once the lord became king. Revenge was a reasonable response.

The heart of the problem, though, was the supposed coup. Koji knew Minori worked toward the strengthening of the blades. He had admitted as much directly to Koji. But there had been no coup attempt. If there had been, Koji would have been one of the first to know.

Minori had been sentenced to death, the execution scheduled for the next morning. No one in the streets or tent city doubted the verdict. Only the method of punishment had been open to speculation, and as Koji had walked through the crowds of humanity gathered for the trial, he heard decent citizens discussing punishments so heinous his stomach churned.

If Koji still owed Minori, the next question was how to repay his debt. Two responsibilities conflicted with one another. Koji struck downward with his sword, trying to find some way to untangle the issue. He was a nightblade, sworn to protect the Kingdom even if the Kingdom didn't want his protection. Shin was the king, and doing anything to disobey the king was dishonorable and thus detestable to Koji.

But Koji owed this exact debt to Minori. He, too, had been sentenced to death by the previous monarch, and Minori had rescued him. Koji's honor hadn't mattered much to him when he had been wrongfully accused, as Minori was now.

Koji spun in the shallow layer of snow that covered the ground, the remnant of an early autumn snowstorm. With one final cut, he sheathed his sword, sweat streaming down his face. Honor to the man who had saved his life or honor to the Kingdom?

A thought wiggled into his mind. To the best of his knowledge, Minori had never lied to him. The older man had certainly withheld information, but Koji couldn't think of a single deception.

Shin lied, as did the Kingdom by extension. Minori hadn't launched a coup. Perhaps the blade was guilty of some crimes, but justice could never be served by liars.

The next step of his reasoning fell into place. Honor was due to one who acted with honor, and Minori's case was clearly superior.

Koji tested his conclusion. He owed Minori, and Minori's honor was less tarnished than that of Shin and the Kingdom. The chain of thought was short but solid, every link acceptable to Koji.

His decision was clear. He would save Minori's life, no matter the cost.

———

Rescuing Minori turned out to be more challenging than Koji expected. The young blade knew he had only until the following morning to find and free his master, but the task was proving impossible. Minori's place of imprisonment was the best-kept secret in the Kingdom, and every method Koji tried to determine his location was met with blank stares and dead ends.

Koji tried drinking with a group of off-duty soldiers, but even with their tongues loosened by alcohol, they said nothing about the traitorous nightblade. He wandered as close as he dared to the barracks, but his sense couldn't find another blade anywhere nearby. By the time the sun began to set, Koji despaired of ever finding his master.

Then it occurred to him that he didn't need to search. He knew where the sentence was going to be carried out in the morning. They had built a platform for the execution halfway between the encampment of Shin's army and the refugee camp, about two leagues from the smoldering remains of Haven. The location was ideal, the ground flat prairie for hundreds of paces in all directions, not even a single tree present to block line of sight. Shin intended to make the execution a spectacle.

Koji could arrive early and allow the soldiers to bring Minori to him. The escape would be difficult, but he had already accepted that his mission would be almost impossible. His attempt was less about success and more about satisfying his honor. He couldn't think of a reason why the rescue needed to happen that moment. Tomorrow would work just as well.

Koji retired for the evening, determined to get his rest for a challenging day ahead.

He rose before the morning sun and went through his traditional practice, the sword barely visible in the soft glow of the moon. Koji felt, rather than saw, the quality of his cuts. He would never be more ready. To pass unnoticed, he strapped his sword to his back and covered himself with the rags of a poor man. He emptied his mind of thoughts and went to the location of the execution.

Koji was surprised to find he wasn't among the first to arrive. Minori's execution was at dawn, and though only the first pinks of sunrise were casting dim light on the proceedings, a significant crowd had already gathered. A ring of soldiers maintained a perimeter around the platform where the execution would occur.

The citizens milled about, and Koji could feel the simmering rage, barely contained even in the peaceful early morning stillness. He tried to understand their perspective. So many had lost everything to the fires. Minori, through Shin's manipulations, had become the target of all that anger. Koji heard snippets of conversation as he moved closer to the platform.

". . . kill all the nightblades in the city . . ."

"Any death is too kind for a man so evil . . ."

". . . heard that Shin actually defeated him in single combat . . ."

Koji soaked in the conversations, allowing himself to feel the mood of the crowd without allowing the comments to affect him. His purpose was clear, the conversations nothing but empty noise.

He was distracted by the smell of those gathered. Several days had passed since Haven burned, and water was a scarce resource. No one wasted it on bathing. In small groups the smell died in the cold autumn air, but with all the warm bodies pressed together, the stench of unwashed flesh was overwhelming.

The smell wasn't just from the bodies. He saw that several citizens had come prepared for the day. Some were carrying manure, others rotten food, and some held stones loosely in their hands. Many seemed ready to inflict additional suffering on Minori if the opportunity was presented. Koji frowned. Minori was far from perfect, but he didn't deserve the level of hatred heaped upon him.

In time, Koji worked his way close to the front of the crowd, his progress halted by a line of guards. He took their measure in a moment. Their dark red uniforms indicated they were members of Shin's armies, but Koji didn't see any individual threat. The danger would only come when they swarmed him.

Soon, Koji got his first glimpse of his master, and his plans, simple as they were, were thrown into disarray. A ragged cheer came up from the edges of the crowd, a roar full of anger and loss. Only Minori would deserve such a greeting. But a cheer? Koji's unspoken question was answered when his master came into view, already nailed to a post and being carried none too gently by a group of eight guards.

Koji recognized the number instantly, his instincts confirmed by the spears strapped to their backs. Minori was being carried by the nightblade hunting unit that had first captured him.

Koji's plan, such as it was, had been to kill the guards before they could begin the execution and then attempt an escape. That plan was no longer feasible. Minori was already a living dead man. Even if the younger blade killed the guards, the two would never be able to escape. Minori couldn't run, and Koji couldn't carry him fast enough. Add to that complication a unit of men specifically trained to kill blades, and his mission had become even more of a suicide than before.

Another cheer rose from the crowd, as different from the first as night was to day. This was the cheer given to a savior. In a few moments, Koji saw the shout was for Shin, the new king.

Koji's hand immediately went to his sword. More than anyone present, Shin was the one guilty of the pain and suffering the populace had experienced. He had ordered the palace burned, and Koji suspected he was the one who had ordered the burning of Haven. If one knew Minori wasn't the culprit, few other likely candidates offered themselves. Shin deserved Minori's fate far more than Minori did.

Koji heard a cry of agony, the sound coming from a throat that had known nothing but screams in the past few days. Koji's attention focused on Minori once again. The anguish lasted for a few heartbeats and then died with a long, low croaking sound. The post had been placed in a hole in the platform designed to accept it, and Minori now hung vertically on the wooden device. Koji wanted to turn away, but he forced himself to watch. Minori deserved at least one person who would witness his suffering with pity in his eyes.

Koji had never seen an execution before. The punishment wasn't levied often, reserved only for those criminals for whom labor or confinement was considered too lenient. He would have been happy never seeing such an act.

Shin stepped up to the platform, and the crowd quieted to listen to their king, the man who held their hopes in his hand.

"Friends. Today we take the first step in pursuing the justice the Kingdom requires. For too long we have lived in fear of the blades. Once, perhaps, they were our protectors, but now they seek to rule us. Today I have given the order that all blades turn themselves in to the local authorities. If they don't, they shall be executed immediately for their treason!"

The crowd cheered again, but Koji was already losing interest in the speech. Shin continued, and Koji watched as the crowd responded with excitement to every word he uttered.

Nothing was right. Minori didn't deserve the suffering that burned through his body as Koji debated his actions. Even worse was Shin, basking in the adulation of the crowd only paces away.

Something inside Koji broke. The part of him responsible for self-preservation went silent, and Koji's determination to right the wrongs he saw took control. He scanned the scene in front of him with new eyes.

Most of the soldiers he could safely ignore. One-on-one they stood no chance against him, and he wouldn't stay still long enough for any of them to gather and pose a threat. The true threat were the eight guards who'd carried Minori in. They now surrounded Shin, protecting their liege and dooming anyone who got caught within their circle. But Koji saw a weakness in their positioning, for they were spread too thin around the platform.

Koji didn't put any more thought into his actions. His course wasn't rational, but it was correct, and that mattered far more to him. He shoved forward, every sense he possessed coming fully alive as he leapt toward the guards at the front line.

To their credit, the soldiers reacted quickly, spotting him even as he approached. Their swift reactions didn't matter. Koji's sword jumped from its sheath, cutting through the two closest guards with lightning-fast cuts. He walked through the perimeter.

Koji's actions sparked a wildfire of chaos. The young man's sense, open to the world, felt everything. He felt Minori's attention focus on him, a distraction from the unrelenting pain. He sensed Shin start to look for an escape. The guards around Koji reacted, each in a different way. Some drew swords, the aggression clear in their intent. Others hesitated, confused as to why guard duty had suddenly become more than crowd control.

Behind Koji, a ripple ran through the assembly. They had come to see an execution, not a fight. Those within reach of the blade stepped backward, trying to find a safe distance. Those farther away pulled back their arms, ready to throw their stones and protect their king.

He had to act quickly. The chaos he unleashed would turn on him in a few moments. His primary problem was the eight spears in front of him. If he gave them a chance to work together, he would have little hope of surviving.

Four of the spears were in front of the platform, and two were on each side. They didn't guard the rear of the structure, but Koji hadn't thought of sneaking around.

The spearpoints came down in an attempt to block Koji, but he still had room to move. He sensed where each of the spears was going to be and knew exactly where an open space was going to be in just a heartbeat. He stepped toward the space, entering it the very moment an opening appeared. His blade flashed in the early morning sunlight, and two of the eight spears were down.

For the first time he spotted a direct line between him and Shin. The king saw the open path as well and backed away toward Minori.

The remaining spears from the front of the platform struck out at Koji. He deflected their strikes, deciding whether to return their attack or pursue Shin.

Instinct told him to eliminate more of the guards before approaching the usurper. Six working in tandem could still trap him.

Koji slapped away a half-hearted stab attempt and lunged forward. The two spears retreated, keeping him out of sword reach with their longer weapons. For a moment, Koji thought of Asa and wished he had her skill with throwing blades.

He didn't have the time for a drawn-out fight. Every heartbeat gave his enemies a chance to gather, a chance to overpower him. That couldn't happen.

Not until he'd killed Shin.

Koji lunged again, but as the spears came up to defend, the blade went low. He shoved the spears up with the side of his sword. He was inside their guard, just where he needed to be. Killing strikes would take too long, but he cut at their legs, crippling them.

Everything came down to time, the one resource he was quickly running out of. The spears on either side of the platform were coming around to the front, but Koji knew if he engaged them, he wouldn't escape alive. Four down would have to do. He turned and pulled himself up on top of the platform.

Time slowed. Koji saw and sensed everything. Shin couldn't get away. He knew the truth, and the fear on his face was absolute, his features twisted into a grotesque visage. Koji savored the fear and held his sword back for just a moment, to give Shin another few heartbeats of pure terror.

Off to the sides, Shin's guards were trying to react. If Koji had given them more time, they might have had a chance to be effective. One guard, desperate to delay the inevitable, drew back his arm to throw his spear. Koji sensed the movement and stepped back, allowing the spear to pass harmlessly in front of him.

The extra pace gave Shin enough time to form a coherent sentence. "If you do this, the Kingdom will burn!"

Koji glanced toward where Haven had once stood, the great metropolis now only marked by hollowed-out ruins and thin wisps of smoke rising into the autumn air. The only structure that remained was the city's stone wall. He met Shin's frightened stare with his own, cold and remorseless as the steel he held in his hands.

"You started the fire."

Shin's face contorted once again, and Koji held his sword just long enough for the king to realize he had no hope of living, no hope of surviving this encounter. When he saw that Shin understood, the blade's sword came across in one quick cut, drawing a thick red line across exposed neck.

Shin collapsed, but Koji could still feel the life inside of the king. Koji's cut had been fatal, but not instantly. He let the sense of failure haunt the doomed monarch for a few moments longer, stepping over the prone man to stand in front of his master.

Koji's actions had bought him a few moments of confusion. The guards were momentarily stunned, unsure how to react now that their king was dead. The nightblade knew the indecision wouldn't last long.

Minori's eyes were bright and danced with pleasure despite his pain. Koji already knew the answer, but he studied his master to see if there was any chance of escaping with the older man.

There wasn't. The physical damage Minori had suffered was incredible, and the only possible way to escape would be to pull out all the nails and carry his fellow blade. The likelihood of either warrior living through the attempt was zero, and Koji saw that Minori knew the truth as well.

Minori glared at the young man he had once rescued from prison. "Kill me. Now."

Koji hesitated for a moment. He could give Minori a warrior's death, a death worthy of the man, and he would.

"Do you have any last words?"

Minori's voice held no hesitation, and although the effort must have caused him impressive physical pain, his voice was strong and clear.

"Protect the blades. Protect the Kingdom."

Koji nodded and raised his steel. The cut was at an awkward angle, and he wanted to make sure his aim was true.

"And Koji," Minori rasped.

"Yes?"

"Thank you."

Koji gave Minori a small bow of respect. He would have given a deeper bow, but the guards were clambering onto the platform, and his time was short. Koji saw a path out. He would have to fight, of course, but he was certain he could escape.

Koji's and Minori's eyes met one last time, and then Minori raised his head, looking up to the sky, exposing his neck. Koji took one deep breath and swung.

His cut was perfect.

Chapter 2

Despite her better judgment, Asa remained around the ruins of Haven for Minori's trial. After burning the bodies of Kiyoshi and the real king, Masaki, Asa had planned on wandering the Kingdom. But she had felt that watching the trial would close the book on everything that had happened in the past few moons.

That was what she wanted: to put her entire past behind her, to start new and fresh as though she still had her entire life on the horizon.

Yet as she listened to the accusations made against Minori, her haunted memories replayed themselves in her mind. She couldn't forget the blade who had come to their home to inform her family of her father's murder, or the cycles she'd spent training and tracking down the murderer, an enigmatic nightblade named Osamu.

More than those memories, though, she wanted to forget the stabbing betrayal she'd felt when she discovered Osamu was Kiyoshi, King Masaki's closest adviser and friend, and a powerful dayblade.

She had tracked him across the plains, only a few dozen leagues from where she now sat, watching this farce of a trial. Then she had killed him.

At least Asa wished the final battle had been that simple. She had dealt Kiyoshi a serious blow, one that might have been fatal in the open expanse of the prairie they had fought in. But Kiyoshi had also wounded her fatally. In the end, he had used his energy to save her, dooming himself in the process. Remembering it now still threatened to conjure tears.

Despite her life's work being completed, Asa felt as though something was missing. So she remained here, thinking Minori's trial would tie up the loose ends of her story. She had no doubt her fellow night-blade would be found guilty and Shin would solidify his power over the throne. The question of the blades was an open one, but she suspected once Shin's hold on the throne was firm, he would ease up on his anti-blade rhetoric and eventually the world would return to normal.

Asa listened half-heartedly to the trial. She didn't believe any truths would come to the surface. Politicians were rarely trustworthy, and she had seen little in the past cycle to shake her from that notion. Minori's trial was a sham, but no one seemed to think so. The trial was all anyone talked about, and as Asa walked through the crowds, she was surprised by the amount of frustration and anger heaped on Minori.

The anger saddened her. People's homes were destroyed, their livelihoods a mere memory. They should be focusing on the future instead of seeking to place blame for the past.

Asa pushed through the crowds day after day. She couldn't extend her sense more than a few paces. Any more would have overwhelmed her mind and sent her crashing to the ground. Unlike those surrounding her, she was dressed in warmer winter robes. She had left Haven with all her possessions days before the burning.

That made her more fortunate than most. The city had been evacuated hastily, and people had left with the clothes on their backs and little else. The autumn was too cold for the garments the people wore, and the masses huddled together for heat, their arms clenched tightly around themselves as they shivered constantly. Many wore nothing but thin bed robes when they left their tents. They darted from group to group, always keeping close to others for warmth.

Despite the shame of being so poorly dressed in public and for the freezing weather, citizens were still out day after day, ready to heap their rage on the nightblades, represented by Minori.

On the morning of Minori's execution, Asa promised herself she would leave that evening. There was no point in remaining any longer. If Minori's death didn't close the chasm inside her, the only other option she could think of was to give herself time to heal.

Asa didn't try to push anywhere near the front of the crowd. She was disguised as a commoner, but hatred for the blades was as high as it had ever been, and she didn't feel the need to attract any attention. Instead, she remained near the back of the crowd, making sure an escape route was always nearby. As more people pushed into the crowd to see the execution, Asa drifted backward, keeping to the loose collections of people in the rear.

Minori was brought out and placed into position. As she watched, she was disappointed. This moment was supposed to have brought her closure, but after looking at the broken figure of the nightblade, once so proud, she felt overwhelming sorrow. For all the scheming and effort Minori and Kiyoshi had put into opposing each other, their reward was the same: a premature journey to the Great Cycle. They had both worked so diligently to secure a future for the blades, but in the end, the blades were more hated than ever before.

Shin was speaking to the audience, but Asa couldn't hear his words from her position in the crowd. She wouldn't have listened if she could.

The emptiness in her that had once been an annoyance, an itch to be scratched, had just become deeper, more troublesome.

Seeing the conclusion to her story was supposed to close her wounds, but watching Minori hang from the post tore open a hole in her heart almost as deep as the day she learned her father was dead.

Kiyoshi's life and Minori's life. Both had been meaningless.

And her revenge had been meaningless. Her actions hadn't brought her any peace. She woke up feeling no different than she had two moons ago or two cycles ago.

Asa wanted to cry, to scream into the sky, to beat the snow-covered ground with her fists.

Instead, she stood as still as a statue, staring at Shin as he spoke.

Her anguish was such that she needed a few moments to realize something was happening up front. Eventually, as her focus clawed its way into the present moment, she saw that the platform was under attack from a single individual.

Asa knew who the attacker was even before she saw him. Only one person would try.

She watched as Koji dodged a spear. Watched as he hesitated, just a few moments, before killing Shin. Watched as he gave Minori a warrior's death.

Through it all, she didn't care.

She didn't care that Shin was dead or that Minori hadn't experienced his true punishment.

She didn't even care that Koji was still alive.

The crowd panicked, a reaction Asa didn't understand. They were in no danger. Onlookers trampled over one another in an attempt to get as far away from the platform as possible, as though Koji was somehow out for each of their lives. The uncrowded rear of the gathering was suddenly slammed with people trying to escape.

For several heartbeats, Asa stood there, the crowd parting around her as though she was a rock in a powerful river. Her eyes were on the platform far ahead but remained unfocused, staring off into space.

Finally, the more rational part of her mind inserted itself and reminded her it would be wise to leave with the crowd. She turned slowly around and walked away, feeling meaningless against the power of the Great Cycle.

———

Asa returned to the tent she had been calling home for several days. She had plenty of money, enough to rent a room at an inn even with the vastly inflated prices chaos brought. However, she believed the money was going to have to last her a long time, so she kept her purse strings tied and pretended to be a refugee from Haven.

Asa carried little, living most of her life on the road. Her only possessions of any worth were her weapons, and those remained on her at almost all times. Small but deadly throwing knives were in sheaths wrapped around both of her forearms. A longer knife with a thin hilt rode in a sheath on her inner left thigh. Her two short swords, her primary weapons, had different homes depending on her circumstances. As she was in hiding, today they were tied to her back between her shoulder blades, underneath her clothing. She packed what little remained in the tent and took one last look before departing.

Her overwhelming desire at that moment was to be away from the ruins of Haven. Not only had she not found closure, but Shin's death would spark a war. Asa was as certain of that as she was of the sun rising tomorrow morning.

The events of the past two moons had sent armies from each of the three great houses hurtling toward Haven. Shin's actions had stopped that conflict from happening, but all three armies were still camped around the area, each about a full day's march away. Now that he was dead, no one stood between the masses of soldiers.

A few steps away from her tent, Asa was confronted with another problem. She didn't know where to go next. The obvious answer was to go back to Starfall and report to Hajimi, the head of the Council of the Blades. But when she thought the plan through, she realized there would be little benefit.

Hajimi would learn enough of what happened through his other sources. Asa didn't feel the need to dishonor the name Kiyoshi had made for himself in his second life. Beyond that, the leader of the blades had far more important matters to worry about.

She could turn herself in, as poster after poster suggested she do. But she was nobody's fool and recognized a death sentence when she saw one.

A stiff breeze blew through the refugee camp. Asa wasn't certain if the weather was a fluke or if winter was truly coming early this year. Either way, the cold was a real danger to the thousands who had no more substantial shelter than the tents.

The thought of the cold made Asa think of the mountains, and just like that, her decision was made. She had always wanted to spend more time in the mountains, a terrain she rarely traveled through. The best place for high, breathtaking peaks was in the late Lord Juro's kingdom. Lacking any better options, the impulse was enough to act as her guide. Asa turned toward the northeast and walked away from the camp.

Eventually the crush of people lessened. The outskirts of the refugee camp were far less crowded than the center, and Asa got a glimpse of the impending chaos. Supply wagons were halted outside of the makeshift city, stopped by a lack of direction. Asa observed some wagons, fully loaded with needed supplies, leaving the area. A tentative peace hung over the camp, but it wasn't the relaxing peace of a slow summer evening; rather, it was the absolute stillness before a storm crashed over the plains.

Shin had been the one who set up the refugee camp and provided supplies. Now that he was dead, uncertainty reigned. Asa shook her head in worry. Not only would battle soon be joined, but this camp, which had supported those who had lost their homes, would be a site of chaos as people struggled to find food. Disaster was right in front of everyone, yet no one was taking the time to avert it.

If Kiyoshi had still been alive, he would have done something. Asa was convinced of that. The thought caused her to pause. Was there something she could do?

As quickly as the thought came, it left, and Asa continued on her way. She wasn't Kiyoshi, and all his efforts had come to nothing. She couldn't save the refugee city, and the truth was she didn't much care.

She was on the edges of the camp when she came across a family trying to leave via wagon. One of the wagon's wheels had come off, and the vehicle had tipped, spilling the family's possessions across the ground.

Without thinking, Asa moved to help the family. She set down her own bag and collected a few of the spilled items, handing them to the wife as she loaded the cart. The woman gave her a short bow.

Asa had collected several loads when everything went wrong. A moment of carelessness gave her away. Instead of squatting down to pick up a sack of rice, she bent at the waist. Asa didn't see the glance, but when she stood back up, the bag of rice in hand, she noticed the look of terror on the woman's face.

She didn't need to be told what had happened. The only women who carried swords in the Kingdom were blades.

The wife screamed, "Nightblade!" and the entire world sped up.

Asa threw out her sense, contained for so long among the crowds. Only a handful of people were nearby, but one group of four was running toward them almost in formation. A quick glance over her shoulder confirmed they were soldiers.

Her sense picked up another motion. The husband, the man who had been working on repairing the wagon, stood up and pulled a scythe from the family goods. She saw the combination of anger and fright on the man's face, but he still stepped forward, his anger at the blades overpowering his fear of their abilities. In a moment all her help toward his family had been forgotten.

Asa could have killed them. Even the soldiers moved like standard infantry. Against the speed of her blade, no one stood a chance. But she didn't want to spill any more blood. Asa tossed the bag of rice at the husband, turned, and grabbed her own bag, sprinting away.

She sensed the pursuit behind her and felt a lone archer pulling his bowstring back to his cheek. His aim was true, but Asa knew the moment he released the string. She stopped in her tracks, and the arrow split the air in front of her.

Her biggest problem was that there was no place to hide. They were in the rolling plains of the south, and there weren't many ways to lose her pursuers. She had to outdistance them until they lost interest.

Asa ran, her lungs starting to burn. She was well conditioned for the intensity of battle but not for long-distance runs. She would have given anything for a horse at just that moment.

The anger driving her pursuers was intense. Asa felt as though they should have turned back long ago, but they kept coming after her, unwilling to let her out of their sight.

Asa wasn't sure how long she ran. When the pursuit finally gave up, she continued running until she was out of sight over a small rise.

Finally she was able to stop and take a breath, exhausted and beaten. Yet she'd have to continue walking. In her mind's eye she attempted to imagine a map of where she was. Finding a place to camp for the night would be challenging, but she would go until she found one.

Asa was a nightblade, and she knew she would be endlessly hunted by everyone who discovered her identity.

Chapter 3

Mari meditated before the makeshift shrine, her breath entering and leaving her body in deep, regular intervals. The sounds from below her room in the inn kept pulling her away from the practice, but after every distraction she returned her focus to her breath. As a child she had abhorred the practice of meditation, hating having to sit still and focus on such a natural process.

Instead of meditating, she had always loved to read, her vivid imagination making the pages of stories come alive. When her face wasn't pressed up against books, she tried to sneak into the martial training sessions her brothers daily engaged in. Time and time again she had been told that fighting wasn't for women, and especially not for noblewomen. No one had ever given her a satisfactory reason why, though, so she kept observing her brothers and mimicking their moves in the shadows.

As she had gotten older and more responsibilities were given to her, she began to understand more clearly the purpose of meditation. By the time she had seen fifteen cycles, meditation was the island in the middle of the storm-tossed sea that was her life. Now she sought out the practice daily.

Mari didn't meditate for any specific length of time. Some days her mind wandered too much to control, and a short session was all she could manage. Other days focus came easily, and she would sit for half the morning. Either way, there was always a point when she knew she had gone as far as was beneficial, her mind and focus turning slightly away from the practice.

The shrine helped her. The world around her seemed to be falling more into chaos every day, but here, kneeling in front of the shrine, she felt at peace.

The shrine was to her late brother Juro, killed less than a moon ago, supposedly by a nightblade. The offering was simple, as her brother had been. The centerpiece was his sword, a piece of steel that their father had gifted to Juro the day he had abdicated his seat as the lord of House Kita. Their father's health had been failing even then, and Mari remembered with clarity the look of solemn responsibility on Juro's face when he had taken the oath making him lord. The memory brought a hint of a smile to her face.

Underneath the sword were two pieces of paper, tokens that would have turned Juro red with embarrassment had he known his younger sister still kept them. Both had been gifts. The first paper had only Mari's name on it but had been given to her by Juro when she had just started to learn how to write. Because of that paper, Mari had learned how to write her name and developed an insatiable appetite for reading and writing. Their father had been old-fashioned and didn't see why Mari wanted to be literate, but in his way he had always been kind and indulged Mari's passion with a personal tutor.

The second piece of paper was the one that really would have tormented Juro—a poem he wrote to her before he went off on his first patrol. Like all the children, Juro had grown up with the tales of the heroes of old, and at some point he had learned that several of his favorite warriors were poets as well. The young future lord had practiced, gifting his sister his first attempts. Mari chuckled at the bittersweet memory of her brother leaving for the first time.

As far as shrines went, this one was small and almost so barren as to be offensive. But Juro had been a simple man with few possessions. He hadn't left much behind.

Mari had thought on this after the initial wave of grief had passed over her upon learning of her older brother's death. When their father had died, the impact had been tremendous. He had known his journey to the Great Cycle was coming, of course, and had taken steps to reduce the impact on his house. He had elevated Juro and guided him as well as he was able. But he lived a life of excess in most things, and their castle at Stonekeep was still filled to the brim with items they would never use again. Their father had made a dent in this world that would take some time to erase.

Juro was almost the opposite. He shunned material wealth, obsessed as he was with the way of the warrior. His only prized possession had been his sword. In the fabric of the world, Juro hadn't made an impression. He had come and gone with barely a trace.

When Mari had first realized that truth, it had filled her eyes with tears. She wanted her brother to leave a legacy, even if it was only in the form of excess possessions. Now, though, she saw her brother's focus as a positive trait. Inspired, she had been quietly shedding herself of material objects in the hope she would gain some of her brother's clarity of purpose.

The technique had worked. Mari had regularly nurtured ambitions and plans, and unlike most women she knew, she wasn't afraid to figure out how to make those ambitions come to fruition. In the moon since her brother's death, she had found a new level of clarity and understanding.

Mari bowed deeply to the shrine, thanking her brother once again for everything he had given to her, both in life and in death. She vowed to always honor his memory, and she was a woman who kept her vows.

Standing up, Mari walked over to her simple desk, where papers were neatly organized. The vast majority of them were in her own hand, written in an invented language only she knew. There was no key, although she expected the Kingdom's best codebreakers might be able to decipher the language based on patterns.

Mari's eyes flicked over the different piles as she considered her next actions. The papers were sorted by a system also known only to Mari, each one labeled with one or more words in the top corners, allowing her to sort and organize information on a whim.

She was convinced that information was the key to success and power. The reason the nightblades wielded such strength was because their sense gave them more information than anyone else. That bit of extra knowledge made them legendary warriors, but it didn't make them better people.

Mari couldn't deal in force. Her father might have been generous, but outside of simple self-defense lessons, he was far too old-fashioned to train his daughter in the ways of war. Mari walked with a thin blade strapped on her inner thigh, and she knew how to use it, but that wasn't any thanks to her sire.

So Mari focused on the strings that connected them all. Interdependence was a teaching she believed deeply in, and by exerting what influence she could in the places she could, she slowly worked her will in the world. Perhaps her ways weren't as simple as cutting through opponents with a sword, but they were still effective.

Several documents in particular attracted much of her attention these days. These papers were some of the few not written in her own hand, and her very possession of them was dangerous. But the ideas contained within were necessary to consider, the risk unavoidable.

They were the collected teachings of a man who had lived in the west of the Kingdom, a man named Takashi, and Mari was certain they would change the fate of the world.

Her musings were interrupted by a soft knock on the door to her chambers. Without hurry, she hid the offending papers within the stack she had found them in. She stood and walked gracefully to the door, even though no one was there to watch.

One of her shadows was at the door. Money was one tool Mari had no shortage of, and a fair amount of her wealth went to developing a shadow network that rivaled any in the Kingdom. The shadow didn't waste time with unnecessary greetings. He passed a sealed note to Mari and left down the hallway.

She opened the note and read it quickly, a frown growing on her face. She reread the short missive, just to ensure her understanding was complete, then threw it in the small fire keeping her room at the inn warm. Once she was certain the paper was nothing but ashes, she turned from the fire and considered her options.

She had been preparing for this moment for almost a half moon now. She had hoped, of course, that it would never come to this, but circumstances couldn't be controlled.

Her impulse was to rush out and sprint toward her younger brother's room, but she restrained herself. Her mind raced as she forced her body into complete stillness. A stranger walking into the room at just that moment might have thought her a statue if not for the gentle rise and fall of her chest.

In the heart of chaos lay the greatest opportunities. Her study of history told her that much. There was an opportunity here; she just needed to find and exploit it.

The answer came to her. She tested the solution, turning it back and forth in her mind, seeing if it held up to reasonable objections. She nodded to herself. Her plan could work. Making it work would be her responsibility.

She stepped forward, moving from stillness to motion with the balance of a dancer, which she had trained as for many cycles. Her father, frustrated with his inability to keep his daughter from more physical pursuits, had compromised by allowing her the practice.

Their forces had rented an entire inn outside of Haven for their quarters. Both she and her brother had accompanied the army. Perhaps "rented" wasn't accurate. After all, they had an army at their command. The innkeeper was receiving only a small recompense for hosting them. Her brother, stingy as always, hated to part with coin when he didn't need to.

Mari stepped out of her room and went toward her brother's. The guards at the door bowed to her and permitted her knock.

The door was opened by a guard on the other side, who let her in the room without a word. Her brother was there, surrounded by his advisers, his war council.

If one was detached enough, the scene in front of her could be read as humorous. Even though they had taken over the entire inn, the commanders had decided that the common room on the first floor was too accessible for their secret war councils. Instead, they used her brother's room, setting up a large table with maps in a space far too small. The generals and the lord were squeezed around it, one general in particular struggling to find room to stand, constantly grabbing the edge of the table to prevent himself from falling into the bed that had been pushed into the corner of the space. Mari contained a smile, wholly inappropriate for the situation.

Hiromi was no Juro. The brothers were separated by more than just the cycles between them. Juro had never wanted to be head of the family and wanted only to soldier. He hadn't been the best lord, but he had been honest and straightforward. Not a politician, not even a leader suited for the responsibilities he faced, but a good man. He had guided them well enough.

Hiromi didn't have Juro's build. Like Juro, Hiromi had trained in the arts of war but never took to them the way his older brother had. Hiromi, the youngest of the three siblings, only had eyes to become lord of House Kita. Mari believed his ambition was rooted in the natural instinct to want that which you couldn't possess.

If not for the seriousness of the situation, the irony would have almost made Mari laugh. Hiromi hadn't been present in the days leading up to Juro's coronation. Juro had approached their father on bended knee, begging to have the crown taken from him. He wanted nothing more than to go back and command his men in the army.

Their father had been torn by the request but finally said, "The true mark of a ruler is the desire not to rule. My decision stands."

Juro hadn't fought his sire, too driven by honor to protest. But Mari had watched him clench and unclench his fists as he left the room all those cycles ago.

In contrast, Hiromi had fought and schemed for cycles, trying to win a race where he was the only competitor.

Now circumstances had given him that which he had coveted, and Mari admitted that in time, Hiromi could become a much better lord than Juro had been. Hiromi didn't understand war and was blinded by his greed for greater power, but he understood people. Channeled properly, Hiromi could reshape the Kingdom. Such was Mari's goal.

Hiromi noted her entrance, but the commanders didn't stop the meeting. Mari's place in the house was somewhat unique. She had been one of Juro's closest advisers, and for that alone she was allowed into the meeting chambers. Unfortunately, she could do no more. Juro had understood that good advice came from all quarters, but that understanding wasn't shared by the men in the room. If she dared to speak her mind, she'd be ejected completely from the meetings.

Hiromi's generals were briefing him on the movements of the troops of the other houses. Mari noted their attitude made the others sound like enemies. They weren't at war yet, but the commanders seemed to believe conflict was a foregone conclusion.

Mari's note had informed her of Shin's death that morning. In response, Lord Isamu's troops had moved closer to the refugee encampment. Because of that, Shin's armies, now led by his younger brother Katashi, had closed ranks in defensive formation. All this Mari already knew. After a few moments in the meeting, she was almost certain the armies were going to collide.

The generals were highlighting hills to where they thought Hiromi should move their army. They had estimated the location of the upcoming conflict and believed higher terrain placed them in the most advantageous position.

When there was a break in the conversation, Mari shuffled her feet, drawing the room's attention to her. She bowed deeply, a mock apology for her minor disruption.

"I am terribly sorry, generals, but I have just heard news of King Shin's death. I know time is essential, but may I have a few moments in private with my brother to grieve over another royal death so soon after Masaki rejoined the Great Cycle?"

The excuse was flimsy, and Mari didn't doubt that everyone in the room saw through her ploy, but Mari didn't think she had time for more subtlety. The decision to go to war would be made at this meeting. Regardless, decorum was clear, and they had little choice but to acquiesce. They agreed, begrudgingly giving Mari and her brother a few moments together.

Hiromi wasn't pleased by the interruption. Mari wasn't surprised. He hated the idea that his generals believed he took advice from his older sister. Like Juro, he recognized her wisdom, and looked up to her as an older sibling, but he would never acknowledge so in public.

"Sister," he said, the edge in his voice apparent.

"I'm sorry for my actions, but you need to pause and reconsider."

Hiromi sighed, expressing resignation. "Let's not dance, Sister. State your case and leave."

Her eyes pointed at his feet, Mari listed what she had come up with in her room. "First, you do not know the reasons for the advances."

Hiromi interrupted her, his impatience showing. "Shin died! We fight for the throne."

Mari glanced up, the steel in her gaze causing Hiromi to falter. "Or Isamu's troops thought Katashi's could use help calming the populace. This is his house's land, after all. It is not wise to jump before you know how deep the stream is."

Hiromi looked as though he was about to argue, but he wasn't foolish. He knew his sister spoke truly.

"Second, although military strategy isn't my strength, isn't it better to wait out the first battle? If the other houses do become our enemies, they weaken themselves by attacking each other. Then, if we must fight, our opponents are already bloody."

She risked a glance up at Hiromi to see he was considering her point. She continued. "Third, we still don't know what's happening with the blades."

"They are being hunted whenever they are found."

Mari contained her grimace. Hiromi still tended to accept stories at face value. "Perhaps. Or perhaps the story is a ploy by House Amari."

Hiromi looked as though he had never considered the option.

"The point is that the blades are an unknown. If even a dozen nightblades have aligned with one of the other houses, the entire course of the battle would be changed. By sitting out, you learn whether or not the other houses have blades or if the pronouncements are true."

"Is that all?"

Mari nodded. She hated that she was forced to rationalize with Hiromi, but there wasn't any other way forward. She saw, though, that he understood her logic. His mind was working quickly, but Mari had grown up with the young lord, and she knew she had convinced him. She breathed a sigh of relief. At best, her maneuver had bought her time, but with any luck, that time would be enough to unveil her plans.

She turned and stepped out of the room, bowing deeply to the generals outside. "I apologize once again, generals. Thank you for your generosity in allowing us a moment of private grief for one we were close to."

As the door closed behind her, she heard her younger brother speak, a tone of command in his voice. "Generals, in my time of grief with my sister, I've developed a new strategy for victory."

Mari hid her relief from the guards as the door swung shut. She had never cared about credit. Only results. The time had come to set her plans into motion, whether she was ready or not.

———

Mari approached the battlefield with a mixture of trepidation and excitement. She had never seen a battle before, and her natural curiosity was excited by the prospect of a new experience. Guilt flooded over her, but that didn't make her interest less real.

When she tried to rationalize her interest, she told herself that her actions, even behind the scenes, could very well lead to the death of others. She wasn't sure that in the chaos of their age, the consequence could be avoided, and she didn't want to ignore the unpleasant truths of power. If she couldn't face the results of her decisions, she had no right making those decisions in the first place.

Yet, she would be lying if she claimed she wasn't afraid. She didn't consider herself delicate, but she feared watching the battle would test her mettle. What if she found herself wanting?

Mari vehemently pushed the thoughts from her mind. There couldn't be any room for doubt. Only strength and action. She certainly couldn't show any weakness in front of the assembled generals.

Mari, Hiromi, and their generals and attendants settled on a rise overlooking the site of the battle between Lord Isamu's House Fujita and Lord Katashi's House Amari. In the past few days, the armies had crept closer, today's battle inevitable.

Mari's shadows had been able to provide some information about the prelude to the battle, but it was far too little for her liking. She couldn't understand why this battle needed to happen. Her shadows indicated neither side wanted to fight, but both seemed committed to their course of action. Mari felt as though the Great Cycle itself was in control, as if a giant boulder had been pushed down a hill and now couldn't be stopped.

Both parties were guilty and stubborn. After Shin's death, the throne technically passed to Katashi, but the boy had only seen nineteen cycles, and Shin had only been king for less than a moon. Neither Isamu nor Hiromi had acknowledged the boy's claim. Katashi seemed willing to settle the matter by force, and if Mari's reports were any indication, his well-trained troops would easily overrun Isamu's disorganized forces.

Isamu had also claimed the throne after Shin's death. He argued that since he was the most experienced and longest serving lord, he was the obvious choice. His claim had been greeted by silence from the other two houses.

If Hiromi had allied with either of the other houses, the matter might have been settled. But he had no interest in bowing to another lord. Mari had considered the matter carefully, and although her heart desired peace, she couldn't bring herself to support anyone besides Hiromi. Isamu was a weak leader, evidenced by the quality of his forces. Katashi had potential, but he was even younger and more inexperienced than Hiromi. In the limited exchanges Mari had with Shin's son, she had distrusted him. Thus she had counseled that diplomacy begin with the other lords accepting Hiromi as king.

If the circumstances or leaders had been different, perhaps they might have been able to negotiate. Instead, civil war loomed on the horizon.

They had learned from their shadows that Katashi planned on attacking this morning, and Hiromi had insisted on observing "to better understand the nature of the opponents they faced."

The reason was a thin one, but no one acknowledged the truth. Like Mari, Hiromi had never seen two full armies meet in combat. Unlike her, he felt little trepidation. He believed wars to be glorious and honorable, a time when men tested their skill against one another. When he had been a boy, he devoured stories of heroes and blades, and while he had never shown Juro's martial mastery, it didn't make the pull of warfare any less attractive to him.

Mari feared the impending fight would only whet his appetite further. The sensations she experienced were hard to understand. She and her brother were safe and at a distance. House Kita banners flew proudly in the early morning breeze, and no army would dare attack them. Hiromi would see the battle and the maneuvers but wouldn't witness the blood and suffering. Their servants even carried a picnic lunch for the day.

The party came to their vantage point and dismounted. Mari looked over the battlefield as the sun rose. The prairie here wasn't completely flat, but gently rolling, providing some troops the illusion of safety. As Mari looked over the field, she saw the battle would be everything she had feared. There was no cover and little protection. This would be a battle of force against force. Flanking maneuvers would be seen far in the distance, and the terrain offered little in terms of strategic advantage for either side.

She suspected that had been Katashi's intention all along. All their reports said his troops were better trained and disciplined. By eliminating terrain advantages, he had reduced the chance of a brilliant but lucky maneuver by one of Isamu's generals succeeding. The strategy would be costly in terms of lives but, if her understanding was correct, virtually guaranteed a victory.

There was a beauty to the stillness before the charge. Mari was impressed by the organization and the courage shown by everyone present. Banners snapped in the wind as it picked up, and Mari held her clothes tighter. She had worn heavy blue robes over her daily silk ones, but still she shivered. The weather had insisted on being surprisingly cold this past moon.

Part of Mari urged her to run down onto the battlefield, to stand between the two lines and make a heroic plea for peace. She silenced her foolishness.

A yell erupted from one of the lines, and Katashi's forces began to advance. Mari wasn't overly familiar with military strategy, but she saw that the lines stayed organized as they advanced, and once they were in range, they let loose with flights of arrows that darkened the sky.

From a distance it was easy to get entranced by the beautiful arcing flights of the shafts, shot up hundreds at a time. If one could ignore the death that marked the end of their flight, Mari would have almost called the display one of the most impressive sights she had seen.

Here the first difference between the forces became apparent. Katashi's launched wave after wave of arrows, an endless rain of horror on an enemy whose return fire was sporadic at best.

She glanced over at her younger brother, almost enraptured by the sight in front of him. More than any other behavior, that look on his face scared her. He was a smart man, but his childhood fascination with war could lead him to make horrible decisions.

The lines met with a roar and the cold clanging of steel on steel. From the outset the battle was a rout. As soon as the lines met, Isamu's forces seemed to disintegrate as though they were paper placed in a rushing stream. Even at a distance Mari could see how Katashi's forces remained coherent, piercing through the thin shell of order that held together Isamu's army.

Her heart sank as she watched the calm precision Katashi's army maintained. Their own military was well trained, and in the mountainous lands of their house, no force was better. But she had never seen the order of Katashi's forces.

The morning wore on, and Mari forced herself to watch the entire ordeal. From her perspective the battle had been over almost as soon as it began, but there were still thousands of men on the battlefield. Even a rout took time. Hiromi was fascinated throughout, holding hushed discussions with his generals as they ate an early lunch. Mari found herself without an appetite.

For a while, when the sun was highest in the sky, Isamu's forces looked as though they might be rallying. They had gathered around one of their last remaining banners and pushed the opposing army back dozens of paces.

The surge was too little too late. Katashi's forces bent but never came close to breaking. They pressed harder, and not long after, the fight was over.

Mari watched as soldiers roamed the battlefield, swords stabbing into those enemies still alive but wounded. Healers carried off and tried to save those they could of their own forces. She wanted to look away but couldn't tear her eyes away from the efficiency with which Katashi's men worked, even after the battle. Bile rose in her throat, but she kept it down. Never in front of her brother and his advisers.

As they rode back, Hiromi was as gleeful as she had ever seen him. He kept discussing moments with his commanders, sounding more and more like he had watched an epic battle, a titanic struggle between two noble forces. All that Mari heard was that he wished he had been there, in the heart of the conflict. She couldn't bring herself to respond, but she understood her future task would be that much harder.

Mari agreed with her brother on one thing: she didn't think the battle would be remembered because of how well the opposing sides had fought. The entire affair had been one-sided from the beginning. But the battle would be remembered as the start of the Kingdom's civil war.

Chapter 4

Koji's escape had been easier than he expected. The guards immediately surrounding Shin had been strong, but those farther away from the platform had fallen to his sword, a series of single cuts dispatching an entire unit. He had sown enough confusion and fear that he was easily able to slip into the crowd gathered to watch the execution and disappear.

He had almost been disappointed. Shin was the king, and if even two nightblades had been present, Koji never would have gotten to him in time. Shin wanted to see what the Kingdom was like without the protection of the blades and had been the first to find out.

Koji's path was clear to him. His personal vendetta and honor had been satisfied. His next task was to see how he stood among the blades. He would have to be careful. Officially, he was still under a death sentence from Kiyoshi's judgment made many moons ago. Minori had hidden him, but with both of the old men now gone, Koji wasn't sure if the judgment still held any weight.

He also wasn't sure how his killing of Shin would affect his future with his people. If the situation was as bad as Shin claimed, Koji might be welcomed as a hero for killing the blades' greatest enemy. If the dead king had been exaggerating for political gain, Koji would be sentenced to death again by his own.

Either way, the easiest way to find out was to journey to the nearest way station for blades. Given the nomadic life most blades lived, a system of way stations had been established that served both as a hub for messages and a place to stay. Most were simple single buildings with a few places to put a bedroll and train. With Haven burned to the ground, he believed the nearest one was a village called River's End, about a nine days' walk away. Koji was already carrying all his belongings, so he had immediately left.

The road was packed with people trying to escape the chaos they knew was coming. Koji let himself be carried along the wave of humanity, halting the use of his sense so as not to be overwhelmed by the refugees or detected by any blades who might be searching for him. Giving up his gift, even for a while, made him feel as vulnerable as a child, but his rational mind suspected he was safer without it among the crowds.

The fear felt palpable to him. Many families didn't know where to find food, shelter, or safety. Koji, who was competent in finding all three no matter his circumstances, had a difficult time understanding the waves of panic that swept over the line of people escaping the ruins of Haven.

At times Koji stopped to help where he could. He held a cart while a farmer replaced a wheel. He picked up a young child who was about to be trampled by people unaware of their surroundings in the rush to leave. The blade found the grateful mother a few moments later. His duty, as he saw it, was still to the people of the Kingdom.

At night Koji left the road and wandered far afield until he was certain he was alone. His sense would protect him while he slept, warning him of anyone coming near.

Koji slept under the stars, his heavy robes and training enough to keep him warm through the increasingly frosty nights. If the weather continued getting colder, he would soon be forced to find shelter or risk nightly fires.

The next day the crowds along the road were even more agitated. Meals were scarce, shelter even more so. Rumors were spreading about an impending civil war, and Koji saw more violence as citizens fought one another for food or tents. He saw one man punch another for nothing more than a bite of an apple. The outbursts were occasional, but if something wasn't done soon, the road wouldn't be safe even for one as strong as he.

That night Koji wondered for the first time whether his actions had been correct. His honor and duty had been satisfied, but he hadn't considered that Shin might be the very person holding the Kingdom together.

Koji wrestled with the problem. He was trapped in a web of conflicting duties. Duty to Minori and his memory. Duty to the blades and duty to the Kingdom. How did he decide which duty took precedence when they warred with one another? The question was troubling, and Koji didn't have an answer by the time he drifted off.

The next day dawned like any other. Koji woke and practiced his forms empty-handed. After a light breakfast he went back to the road, where he immediately knew something was wrong. Koji didn't bother asking anyone; he simply continued walking, listening to the conversations as he passed. The same word was on everybody's lips.

War.

He wasn't sure how much credence to give the news, but the panic on the road became almost physical in its overwhelming hold on the people. Families jogged, fathers holding their children in their arms. Farmers tried to push their animals faster, and those who couldn't move faster watched warily as people charged by them. Koji briefly debated trying to help somehow, but every idea he had involved him revealing that he was a nightblade. Instead, he left the road, feeling guilty that he was running away from the problems and people he was supposed to protect.

———

Koji wasn't the only person who had the idea to leave the road, but there weren't many who left the illusion of safety the road provided. He typically found that those who left the path were those who had the skills to survive on their own. Men who made their living by hunting and trapping. Former soldiers and their families.

Off the road there seemed to be an unspoken agreement. Everyone gave others safe distance, and for two days Koji didn't speak with another living soul. He didn't mind the opportunity to reflect on his actions, but he wouldn't have minded a friendly face.

He thought he was only about two days away from the way station when his sense alerted him to the presence of two other blades off in the distance. Cautious, Koji crept toward them, discovering the gift was coming from a small farmhouse.

Koji observed the structure from a distance before approaching. He wasn't sure where he stood with the blades and didn't understand why there would be blades in a farmhouse in the middle of nowhere.

He waited for most of a day, watching the farm and studying the terrain. The house wasn't very defensible. He didn't understand why blades were here, of all places. The only worthwhile quality it possessed was that there was no way to approach the house without being spotted.

There were more than two people in the farmhouse, but Koji was far enough away that he couldn't make out the individual lives. The only reason he'd even noticed the farmhouse was the distinct sense of other gifted ones. Koji looked in the direction of the way station, then in the direction of the farmhouse. With an almost imperceptible shrug of his shoulders, he walked toward the farmhouse.

His reasoning wasn't complicated. The way station would still be present later, but an opportunity to speak with two blades away from many civilians was too good to pass up. With luck he'd get an idea of what was happening in the world of the blades and see where he stood.

As Koji approached the house, the two nightblades he had sensed stepped out, taking up positions side by side about twenty paces in front of the door. One, who Koji decided was the leader, was smaller, one corner of his mouth turned up in a perpetual grin. The other was a large man, head shaved bald. They stood guard, still as any statue, giving the house an almost menacing appearance.

Koji stopped fifteen paces away. He didn't want to present any threat. He kept his arms hanging loosely at his sides, away from the sword on his back. The two blades were dressed in their traditional garb, heavy black robes rustling gently in the breeze. Koji noted the detail. These two weren't afraid of being identified as nightblades.

He tried to gauge their strength, a habit he had picked up many cycles ago, a process almost as automatic as breathing for him. They both appeared to be strong, their stances solid. Koji was confident enough to fight two nightblades if the situation required, and he didn't see anything that alarmed him here. The other warriors would undoubtedly be skilled, but not invincible.

He was sure they were doing the same evaluation, confident their numerical advantage would lead them to underestimating him.

The nightblade on Koji's right spoke first. "Greetings, brother. You are welcome here."

Koji gave a slight bow. "Your hospitality is appreciated."

The blades shifted their weight, and the moment of tension between strangers in a chaotic world passed. Koji also relaxed, although his sense was active, prepared for any surprise. The blade who spoke turned and led the way, while the bald man waited to follow Koji in.

Koji hadn't been in a farmhouse for cycles, and this one was large. From his glances around, little seemed out of the ordinary. He noticed a small, tasteful shrine to the Great Cycle, the traditional three concentric circles drawn by a confident hand, a well-equipped kitchen, one large room for dining and gathering, and what appeared to be plenty of bedrooms. The home was well maintained and clean, both the wooden floors and tatami mats spotless.

The furniture was old and clearly used frequently but taken care of. There were no holes in the paper walls, and the doors slid open and closed with ease. Not a rich family, perhaps, but one that took pride in their living quarters. Koji noticed it all but said nothing.

He could sense the other lives in the building, but they weren't to be seen. He thought about asking about them, but an internal warning held him back. Koji hadn't observed anything that worried him, but still, something didn't feel right.

The young nightblade's silence didn't bother his two hosts. They finished their tour in the living room. The space was large, clearly intended to be the center of activity in the house. Today it was empty except for the three blades.

Koji was invited to sit. The nightblade who had done all the speaking on the tour, the one who had greeted him outside, rang a small bell. Moments later Koji heard the sounds of footsteps approaching. A young woman came in and bowed demurely.

"We have a guest. Would you be kind enough to prepare us some tea?"

She bowed again and left the room without saying a word. Although her expression didn't give any indication of discontent, something in her bearing made Koji believe she was carrying a heavy burden.

The blade who had made the request saw the question flicker through Koji's eyes. He gave a reassuring smile. "She is one of the farmer's daughters. When we arrived we made an agreement. We offered to protect the grounds if they would serve us while we were here. It has been beneficial for everyone."

Koji heard the tone of voice, the half truth present in the statement, but he didn't ask any questions. His instincts warned him that the less he said, the safer he was in this new world of conflicting loyalties.

"While we wait, let us properly introduce ourselves. My name is Ryo, and my more silent companion is Hiroki. I am Hiroki's master, although in my opinion he is more than ready to take the trials."

The fact was yet another one to add to his growing list. Blades, once they had finished their training as children, had one of two ranks: master or apprentice. There were a series of tests one needed to pass to become an apprentice. You were given three chances, and if you failed, you were no longer considered a blade. Those became the people who served the blades, carrying messages, maintaining the way stations, and completing other necessary but distasteful tasks.

If you became an apprentice, you gained your first freedoms. You were assigned to a master and traveled the lands under her or his supervision. The only real restriction on your behavior was that you had to obey your master. Many blades spent much of their lives as apprentices, fighting or healing side by side with their masters.

The tests to become a master were of a different sort. Skill was, of course, a consideration and an important one, but just as important was one's judgment and wisdom. Becoming a master meant traveling on your own, with no guidance except the occasional command from the Council of the Blades. The trials, therefore, were no small task, and only two attempts were allowed in a lifetime.

Koji bowed to the duo upon learning their names. He considered lying about his identity but dismissed the idea. There was every chance they knew who he was, and he didn't want to lose their trust. "My name is Koji. It is a pleasure to meet you."

Koji received their bows in return, and the tea was prepared. He studied the daughter carefully and saw the slight tremble in her fingers as she served. Her eyes darted around the room, as though looking for the nearest exit. He kept his expression perfectly neutral, well aware of Ryo's constant gaze.

After the daughter departed, her footsteps quicker than when she had entered, Koji turned to Ryo and asked his most burning question.

"I must apologize for my rudeness, but I have been in the wilds for several days now. My plan was to travel to the nearest way station and see what news could be had."

He was interrupted by Ryo's laughter. "If you mean River's End, I can save you the trouble. The way station was burned to the ground two days ago when word of Shin's death arrived."

Koji tried to shut his jaw but failed. "By whom?"

"The citizens of the town. I'm not sure, but I heard the keeper died in the fire. Brother, I'm glad you found us first. If you had gone to River's End, your life would be in great danger."

Koji didn't reply.

"I don't know how much you've heard, but several days ago, King Shin was killed by a nightblade," Ryo said. "Since then we've heard that civil war has broken out among the houses. The Kingdom can't agree on much these days, but there is one truth everyone agrees on: everyone hates the blades."

Koji digested this information while he sipped his tea, a hard knot forming in his stomach. Civil war? The blades despised by everyone?

The fear that controlled his mind was that everything was his fault. If he hadn't killed Shin, the war would never have happened. The blades would have eventually returned to their former status. The weight of his actions crashed on him, and the thought he kept returning to was that he should simply take his own life. He couldn't live if so many deaths were on his shoulders.

He didn't hear Ryo at first. The blade spoke louder and dislodged Koji from his thoughts.

"I asked if you are all right. You turned very pale for a moment."

With an almost physical effort, Koji turned his mind back toward the present. "Yes, I'm sorry. I didn't realize the situation had become so horrible. Your news is appreciated, but . . . devastating to hear."

The room was silent as the two blades gave Koji time to come to terms with the news. Koji tried to break the cycle that dominated his thoughts, but to no success. Overwhelming guilt tore at his heart.

His actions had been honorable, hadn't they?

Ryo's voice again broke into his awareness. Koji stopped himself from glaring angrily.

"I am sorry that the news has disturbed you so. We will all retire for the evening soon, but first, I must ask you a question."

Koji looked up and focused on the other nightblade.

"These are difficult times, and our safety is important. You are familiar with Kiyoshi and Minori, are you not?"

Koji almost burst out laughing. Although he had only met Kiyoshi in person once, he was certain he had known the two old blades far better than anyone else in the room. Instead, he nodded.

"You are familiar with the philosophies they both espoused?"

He nodded again.

"Although they have both rejoined the Great Cycle, whose philosophies do you agree with?"

Koji saw the heart of the question. It was strange, he reflected, that for all his experience with the two dead blades, he had never thought of his loyalty in such terms. Both men had wanted the blades to serve the Kingdom, although Minori would have them rule the land while Kiyoshi would have them be slaves to its people.

He knew the answer the blades in front of him wanted. The character of his hosts had become obvious with the question posed.

Koji considered his response, his guilt still tearing him apart.

He could feel his silence increasing the tension in the room. The men in front of him expected the answer to be easy. They needed an answer soon.

Koji gave them his most disarming smile. "I am sorry. My former master once told me that I wasn't a very fast thinker, and I have never had the question asked before."

Some of the tension seeped from the room, but not much. Hiroki looked as though he was about to draw his sword. Koji didn't sense any violent intention from the blade, but that could change in a moment.

"I agree with Minori's philosophies," Koji lied.

His hosts visibly relaxed.

"I am glad to hear it, brother. I am sorry I had to ask, but surely you can understand why I must in these days," Ryo said.

"Certainly."

"Very good." Ryo looked outside at the sunset and turned to their guest. "The day is coming to a close, and I'm sure you must be exhausted from your time on the road. Hiroki and I have our evening training session, but I will ensure you receive a meal and a bath before you retire."

Koji bowed his head in acknowledgment of the kindness, and after the appropriate farewells were exchanged, Koji found himself alone in the giant space, unsure of everything he had once believed.

———

Koji had never been great at meditating. The practice had been pushed on him as a child, but sitting still and trying to let go of his thoughts had rarely worked for him. He far preferred the peace that came from sword practice, the blending of the mental and the physical. But such active meditations weren't available at times.

He sat in his room, a plain area without decoration, trying to calm the tempest of his thoughts. He couldn't shake the belief that he was responsible for the tumult happening in the Kingdom.

The thought was foolish and prideful. Perhaps he had contributed, but the lords had reacted, driven by thoughts of power and greed. He told himself he was nothing but part of the problem. Yet if he hadn't killed Shin, none of the horrors of the past few days would have come to pass.

Koji forced his limbs into stillness, fought the urge to get up and move, to pace the room. The farmhouse, for all its size, was still small, and every action he took would be noted by the other blades.

His dilemma was postponed by a bath and a meal, the best he had eaten in many days. The food was simple, nothing more than rice with fish from a nearby stream. But he held every bite in his mouth, allowing the flavors to wash over his tongue.

On the road he survived by hunting and harvesting what food could be found. The sustenance was enough to live off, and sometimes the freshest meat, killed just that day, was excellent. But often only dried meat, nuts, and berries sustained him. The chance to eat fresh fish and hot cooked rice was an incomparable pleasure, his mouth watering long after the food was gone.

He returned to his room and his tormented thoughts, eventually giving up as the moon rose over the horizon. He turned in for the night, sleep coming with surprising ease.

His sense warned him of life nearby, and he came awake with practiced ease, his hand flying to the hilt of his sword, ready to draw. As his awareness returned, he saw the farmer's daughter, Hana, silently closing the door to his room. The young blade held his draw. The girl posed no threat to him.

She finished closing the door, knelt before him, and bowed. "I'm sorry to disturb you, master. I didn't realize you had already fallen asleep. I hope you're not angry with me."

Her voice was soft, but still it quavered, and Koji thought he saw her shoulders shaking gently in the dim light of the moon. His mind, still clouded with sleep, was slow to understand what was happening.

Koji didn't respond, confused, as Hana began disrobing in front of him. Her movements were quick and jerky, lacking the grace such movements usually enjoyed in the brothels he had visited. In a few heartbeats she knelt before him, naked and shivering although the room was warm enough. Her arms were crossed over her chest, although they were too thin to do much good.

Still slightly dazed, all Koji could think was that everything happening was wrong. He couldn't rationalize his discomfort. She was certainly old enough, a young woman by all accounts. He hadn't done anything dishonorable, and his manhood was reminding him it had been many moons since he'd had the pleasure of a woman's company. Yet everything was wrong.

Instinctively he reached toward her. She flinched away from him, then moved toward him, surprised when he reached past her, pulled her clothes off the floor, and draped them over her.

"Master, what are you doing?"

Koji scooted backward, putting some space between them. "I'm not your master."

The uncertainty on Hana's face saddened Koji. "But they told me to come to you tonight. Are you not with them?"

His faculties returned to him. He pieced together what he should have understood much earlier. Now he understood why she was here.

His anger flared. To test him this way was beyond reason, and indicated the weakness inherent in Minori's beliefs. Blades shouldn't be able to command such actions, but if they placed themselves above the law, similar commands would be inevitable. Greater power was only useful if greater control was exercised over it. The blades were no better at controlling their weaknesses than any other person. Combined with their strength, situations like this would become common.

"I am no more with them than you," he answered.

A new determination came across Hana's face, her shoulders set and square at him. She disrobed again, but still Koji saw her discomfort in the action.

He reached over to clothe her again, but she stopped him and pulled him close.

Koji pulled away. "What are you doing?"

Her voice shook as she whispered, "I need to do what they say. Otherwise they will hurt or kill my family. My father already can barely walk because he stood up to them."

She leaned in toward him, and Koji wrestled with temptation. His mind screamed that this was wrong, but he hadn't been with a woman for a very long time.

She kissed his cheek, and he almost turned his face to kiss her lips. Trying desperately to hold on to the hate he felt for the other blades, he pushed her aside.

"I will not."

Relief and fear crossed her face. "But I must."

Koji hated Ryo and Hiroki. Minori would be disgusted by the men who claimed to work for his memory.

"You've been to them?"

She nodded, tears in her eyes.

The thought occurred to Koji that there was another choice. He didn't need to play their game. He didn't need to curse either Hana or himself.

"You don't need to do this. I will confront them." Koji reached for his sword.

The young woman grabbed him again. "Please don't. They sleep in the same room as my younger sister."

Koji was disgusted, but Hana shook her head. "It's not like that. They sleep there so that if we try anything, she is the first to die. You can't confront them now."

"Very well. I shall do it in the morning. Return to your room."

The woman hesitated. "May I stay here? Then I can act as though I obeyed, and my family will be safe."

He almost told her it wouldn't matter. Inside the farmhouse they would be able to sense everything that happened, and they would know Koji hadn't slept with her. They would know he failed their test of his beliefs. But when he saw the terror in her eyes, he relented.

Without hesitation Hana climbed into his bed and laid her head on the pillow. Unsure of what to do, Koji reached out and ran his hands through her hair, letting her cry. As he did, his mind was plodding along, considering the different outcomes of his actions and the story he would need to tell.

He didn't notice when she fell asleep, but eventually he realized that her breathing had become slow and steady. What had she been through in the past few days? Had he caused her suffering, or would it have happened anyway?

The questions troubled him, but a new thought formed in his mind, a new purpose for him to pursue.

Eventually Koji fell asleep, his heart set on rectifying his biggest mistake.

Chapter 5

She had only been traveling a few days, but Asa was already tired of looking over her shoulder. For some time the populace had been wary of the blades, but now Asa and her kind were being hunted, an accident of birth making them targets.

She had gotten used to the suspicious looks, the fear on the faces of those she passed. Where once fellow travelers may have welcomed her and given her food, now she was greeted with quick glares. No one shared, and no one spoke to outsiders, blade or not. She was always on edge, always waiting to be attacked. She replayed the incident on the road over and over. One moment she had been a helpful stranger, the next an enemy worth risking one's life to kill. The shift didn't seem possible in so short a time.

Asa was tired. The constant vigilance was more than she was used to, and it wore her down, like a grindstone wearing down a once sharp knife.

For two days Asa had wandered away from the road, always keeping to the northeast. Unfortunately, necessity required her to return to the populated paths. She didn't know the territory well enough to wander it without a guide. She needed to stay close to the road, as much as she detested the idea.

At times she wondered if being attacked would ease the constant pressure. She itched for the chance to practice her forms, but there was no chance of that now. If anyone saw her, she would be pursued relentlessly.

Despite her wariness, no one attacked her as she journeyed. She blended in with the sea of humanity heading away from Haven, away from war.

She barely noticed the sign for River's End, knocked over along the side of the road. Someone had nailed another sign to the same broken post proclaiming "No Food—No Room." The letters were painted with a bright red color that pierced even Asa's exhausted awareness.

Asa didn't need food or shelter, but she did vaguely remember that there was a way station for blades at River's End. If her hazy memory served, the small village was only about a half-day's walk from the road.

She decided to change her course. The mountains of the northeast would still be there later, but Asa saw a chance for a place to rest. The way station would have bunks and food. She could practice her forms without fear of being hunted. The offer was too good to pass up.

The road to the village was almost completely abandoned, and Asa decided to stick to it, seeing no reason to get lost in unfamiliar territory.

When she first came into sight of River's End, her heart sank. The ruins of the way station were no different than the ruins of Haven, smoldering days after they'd been burned. She didn't have to ask what had happened. Although the village numbered less than a hundred people, it seemed each person glowered at the ruins as they passed, as though by their stares alone they could reignite the blaze.

The remains of the way station were a startling contrast to the natural beauty of the town. Most of the houses near the city center were two stories tall, opulent by most standards. Asa's eyes followed the river, and she assumed that though the village was small, its residents lived well off the trade coming from upstream.

If not for the burned remains of the way station, the village had an idyllic quality. River's End lacked the noise and bustle of a city like

Haven, but its shops were well supplied with food and spices. In the background, the soft sounds of the running river relaxed and soothed.

Asa sat down next to the river that ran through the town, utterly exhausted. All that was left was a bleak, seemingly endless trek. She didn't want to live like this.

Her head was cradled in her hands when she heard a friendly voice behind her. "Excuse me, ma'am, but do you need a place to stay?"

Asa looked up and saw an older man, who had seen maybe fifty cycles, looking at her with a face filled with concern. He was dressed in common clothes: a loose-fitting robe that had been patched countless times, sandals, and a wide hat. At first glance he appeared entirely nondescript, but as she studied him, she realized he held himself well, almost with the balance of a swordsman.

She almost said yes, but memories of her encounter with the family by the road stopped her. "It's a very kind offer, but I'll be fine, thank you."

The gray-haired man had a vitality about him that belied his age. His gaze was piercing, and he smiled as though Asa was simply trying to be polite.

"Nonsense. I know the look of a weary traveler when I see one. We're well stocked on food and have a comfortable room for guests with my son gone to serve in the army. I won't take no for an answer."

Asa should have said no. But the man's energy and kindness were impossible to resist. And she was tired. Too tired to pass up even an offer that she was sure wouldn't end well.

Asa sighed and bowed. "Thank you very much. I'm very grateful."

The older man led her to his house on the outskirts of the village, which wasn't saying much. The entire town could be walked in less time than it took to cook rice.

The man quickly told her about himself. His name was Daiki, and he was both a farmer and a merchant. He sold furniture as well as some of the crops he grew. He lived at home with his wife, Ayano. Their only child, Akihiro, was part of Isamu's army, and although his eyes hungered for knowledge of his boy, there was nothing Asa could tell him. She was woefully out of touch with the news of the day.

Their home was small, but behind it was a beautiful workshop, clearly Daiki's pride. The outside of the house was unremarkable, but the tables and tools inside were wonderfully worked. The carvings on the legs of the table were ornate, and the wood was polished until Asa could see her reflected face. She could barely discern a single joint in the work. The blade gazed in amazement. This man, apparently of no great wealth, built furniture lords would be jealous of.

Ayano fixed Daiki with a stare that could have melted stone when he entered with Asa. The woman was large and strong, no stranger to hard work. Although her anger was apparent, it was quickly defused by Daiki's easy humility.

"I know you don't want guests, but she has been on the road for days without a place to rest. She looked like she was about to fall asleep in the street. I couldn't help but let her stay the night."

Ayano's glare softened, and Daiki took the opportunity to excuse himself. He claimed to have a piece he needed to finish before the sun fell. As Asa watched the couple, she felt as though she was watching a play the performers had acted out a hundred times.

Almost as soon as Daiki left the room, Ayano sighed as she looked at Asa. "He's a good man. Perhaps too good for the times that are coming, if the rumors we hear on the wind are to be believed."

Asa bowed, careful not to dip too low and reveal the blade hidden on her back. She wouldn't make that mistake again. "Thank you for opening your doors to me. I am very grateful."

Ayano looked Asa over carefully. "You're welcome. How did you come to be on the road by yourself?"

Asa had known this question was coming—the unspoken suspicion. She had dealt with it throughout her life as a woman traveling the roads alone, incognito in her role as a blade. The lie came easily to her, a lifetime of practice allowing her to not miss a beat.

"My family's home burned down in Haven. I tried to find them in the camps but failed. I heard rumors they had traveled northeast. When I saw the sign for the town, I decided to try my luck."

Ayano's eyes narrowed. "I'm sorry to hear of your loss. What did your family do?"

"My father was a blacksmith."

The older woman's gaze relaxed. "A good profession. Hard work is always rewarded. How old are you?"

"I've seen nineteen cycles." Another lie, but if she told the truth, Ayano would wonder why she wasn't married. She could pass as nineteen, barely.

"You look older." Ayano's tone was flat.

Asa tried to disarm the suspicious woman with a smile. "My father always said I looked older than I was."

"Why aren't you married?"

The question was beyond rude. Ayano would have been shunned from polite company for moons had she asked such a question in public. Asa got the impression the woman would have asked anyway. She was direct, as straight and unbending as stone.

Asa looked down at the ground, as she expected an unmarried girl of nineteen would. She spoke softly. "My father was searching for a good match when the troubles started in Haven. He said he had found someone promising, but he is missing, too."

Asa held her head down, using her sense instead of her sight to judge Ayano's reaction. The woman's weight shifted, and she suddenly threw her arms around Asa in an embrace. Asa panicked for a moment but realized she still had her knapsack strapped to her back, protecting her blades from unwanted discovery.

"You are welcome in our house. There's some water in the back if you'd like to clean yourself. You look dirty."

Just like that, Asa became part of the family. She bowed to Ayano for her kindness and went to the back to bathe.

That night Asa ate a meal unlike any she had tasted for more than a moon. The three dined on beef and vegetables with strong wine. Asa was only allowed one cup on account of her age, but the entire dinner was delicious. Ayano was a superb cook.

Afterward they sat around, bellies full. Daiki regaled them with stories from his time in Isamu's military. Despite her exhaustion, Asa was pulled in by her own curiosity. Daiki had been a typical infantryman, and his perspective was one Asa had never heard. Since the most his former unit generally worried about were skirmishes, the bulk of Daiki's stories revolved around pranks and superior commanders who were bores.

She had never really thought about war and combat from the perspective of those closest to it. Had conflict broken out during Daiki's service, there was every chance he would have been among the first to die. Asa, as a nightblade, would have been used with care and caution by any sensible commander, while Daiki would have been thrown into the thick of battle with no regard for his individual life.

There was a fascinating difference between the stories he told and the tone he used to tell them. The stories made his time in Isamu's army sound terrible: endless bureaucratic infighting, more regulations than one could count, and the ever-present knowledge that you might be called to battle at any moment. Despite this, Daiki spoke as though he were talking about a long-lost friend. Asa was curious enough to ask him about the difference.

Daiki laughed. "You're right. The thing is, every day of my service was probably terrible. If I had to relive those days, I'm sure I'd complain endlessly, just as we all did back then. But there were good memories, too, and time softens the edges of all pain."

For the first time in what felt like forever, Asa found herself relaxing. Perhaps the wine was responsible, or perhaps it was the company.

Daiki and Ayano couldn't have been much more different, but the strength of the bond between them was obvious in even the short time Asa had spent in their company.

Asa had occasionally thought about a home and family. Up until a moon ago, her entire life had been driven by thoughts of revenge. Now that she had killed her father's murderer, she had the space. She had never been tempted before, but sitting here with this couple, she began to see the appeal. Was this next for her?

Her thoughts wandered briefly to Koji. Of all the people she had met recently, he was the one she was most curious about. He had killed a king. No small feat, that. She expected he had escaped. He was far too strong to be easily captured.

Too late she realized a question had been asked of her. She startled, her eyes focusing on Daiki's grinning face. "I'm sorry, what was that?"

Daiki waved the question away. "No apology needed. It was rude of us to go on for so long. It's been some time since we've had guests, and I forgot that you must be exhausted from your journey."

"No, you've both been very kind. I'm sorry, but it's been a while since I've felt so relaxed. You have my sincere gratitude."

Asa complimented Ayano again on the food, and after an endless farewell, she retired to her room and fell asleep the moment her head hit the pillow.

———

The next morning Asa woke up to a silent house. She suspected a trap, almost leaping out of her bed. As she became aware of her sense, though, she felt Daiki outside, working in his space behind the house. She didn't feel Ayano anywhere near.

After her initial panic, Asa took her time getting ready for the day. She supposed she should continue on to Starfall, but it was hard to summon the energy or desire for the task. Her night had been peaceful, uninterrupted. Right now, that was about all she wanted.

The nightblade took the time to check each of her weapons in the privacy of her room. As expected, all were in perfect condition, but better to be sure than dead. She hid them on her body in the accustomed places and went out to speak with Daiki.

Her host had developed quite a sweat by the time she made it out to his large workspace. For a while she watched him. Tools hung on the walls in a precise order, handsaws in various shapes and sizes, hammers and mallets, chisels, and plenty of other items Asa didn't recognize. He was building a low table as near as Asa could tell. She had never seen a master woodworker in action, but her curiosity was instantly piqued.

Daiki didn't acknowledge her presence, although Asa had deliberately made noise on her approach so as not to startle him. He had to know she was there, but his focus was on his craft.

He was cutting wood in half, his saw moving back and forth in smooth, even strokes. Afterward he worked on cleaning the edges of the board, straightening and smoothing them out. In no time at all, Asa was looking at a board ready to be added to the table.

Before her eyes he had taken raw material and shaped it into something someone could use every day. She watched as he joined the board he had made to another, his cuts and techniques simply but beautifully holding the two pieces together.

She had probably been standing there for most of the morning when he looked up, his eyes gazing at her as though he had just woken up from a dream.

"You're very patient for a young person. My son would have run off a dozen times by now. I'm sorry for my rudeness, but when I get into the middle of something, I find it hard to stop."

Asa didn't mind at all and said as much. "What you do is fascinating."

"Yes. I know that my time in the military doesn't sound too exciting, but the entire time I served, all I could think about was what I might have to destroy to do my duty. Fortunately, I only saw combat once, which was enough for me. When I came back, I helped my father with this farm, but I always wanted to do more. I always wanted to create."

Asa looked over the piece in progress. "You're very good."

"Thank you. I've been trying to improve for many cycles now."

Daiki must have seen Asa's eyes wandering over his tools. "Would you like to help?"

Asa surprised herself by agreeing. Together they went to work on the table, the day passing them by. Daiki was a patient teacher, emphasizing detail and care over speed and completion. Asa lost herself in the practice, a moving meditation.

The sun was setting when Ayano called them in for supper. Asa had been so distracted with helping Daiki she hadn't noticed when Ayano returned home. Even more surprising was the realization she wasn't even bothered by her lack of awareness.

That evening was almost a repeat of the night before. Daiki and Ayano told stories, and Asa listened with rapt attention. As before, she was exhausted before them, her shoulders, back, and arms sore from the day of physical labor.

The next morning she was up early, breaking her fast with the couple. Ayano left and went to a neighbor's house, a routine Asa guessed was daily. Daiki led her to the workspace, and together they returned to work on the table.

By early afternoon the project was finished. Asa stepped back and admired her work, a deep sense of satisfaction filling her bones. There was something about making a physical thing that held meaning. She lightly ran her fingers over the surface, smiling.

She hadn't done much. Most of the toil had still been Daiki's. But she had helped make a table.

Daiki looked at her and smiled. "It's perfect. Thank you."

He shuffled around the workspace, putting his tools away, clearly done for the day. An overwhelming feeling of being lost suddenly descended on Asa. What would she do for the rest of the day? Should she even remain?

Daiki's movement caught her attention, and she focused on the older man. In his hands he was holding two wonderfully crafted wooden swords. He handed one to her.

"Perhaps you'd do me the honor of a short sparring match?"

Asa's mind raced, confused by the sudden shift. She tensed up as she realized that somehow he knew what she was.

His chuckle only confused her more. "I'm sorry. Yes, I know that you're a nightblade, but you don't need to worry. Your secret is safe with me."

"How did you know?"

"Well, it is unusual for a woman to be traveling alone, but not so much in these times. I was watching you when you came into town. What gave you away was when you glanced at one of my neighbors before he'd even turned the corner, before you could see him. You have the gift of the sense, and I was once enough of a swordsman to recognize skill when I see it, which means you're a nightblade."

"Why did you invite me in if you knew?"

Daiki sighed. "There's a lot of gossip going around about the blades. I don't know what's true and what isn't. But everyone always talks about the blades like they are one big group that all act and think the same. They forget there will be good blades and bad blades, just like there are good people and bad people. You are definitely a blade, but you seemed to have a noble spirit, and I'm always willing to try to help righteous people. Was I wrong about you?"

Asa stared down at the floor, ashamed by such simple belief. "I'm really not sure."

Daiki's gentle chuckle caused her to look up. "Only a good person would be unsure, so you can take it from me, at least."

He stepped away from her and assumed a fighting stance, one that was remarkably solid. "Ever since I was in the army, I wanted the chance to fight a blade. Now, for the very first time, I have that chance. Will you?"

Asa hadn't caught up yet, still shocked that her secret was known. But she liked Daiki, and any combat practice felt better than none. She agreed.

She waited for him to attack, but he seemed content to let her make the first strike. That was fine. She stepped in, attacking with a basic pattern anyone with training would be able to avoid. The move was a test. Daiki looked almost hurt she had tried something so simple. Before he could complain, she attacked again, trying to pressure him backward.

Daiki held his ground and more. Asa was surprised by the older man's agility. He might have gray hair, but his movements were as strong as a warrior with far fewer cycles. Asa could still sense every move, but the fight was markedly better than she expected.

Twice she got inside his guard, delivering soft strikes each time. She pulled away, but he pressed his attack again, a large smile on his face. He looked like a child receiving the birthday gift he'd waited an entire cycle for.

He struck out with a series of cuts that kept Asa on the defensive. The attack culminated in a thrust aimed at her heart, clearly a move he'd practiced dozens of times. The combination was a good one, designed to get the opponent's sword in a bad position against a thrusting strike. Against any other warrior it might have worked. Unfortunately for Daiki's hopes, Asa sensed the attack and easily evaded, tapping her own sword against his neck in response.

Even though he lost, Daiki laughed, a deep hearty bellow Asa had never heard before. His enthusiasm was contagious, and Asa couldn't help but let out a small chuckle herself. It had been too long since she'd practiced.

When Daiki caught his breath, he bowed deeply to her. "Thank you! When I was younger I drilled that last attack every night, thinking I had discovered how to defeat even a mighty nightblade! I'm fortunate that I never had the chance to try with real steel."

Asa returned Daiki's bow. "The attack was well designed, but it is not sufficient to defeat one gifted with the sense."

"Will you grant me another favor?"

"If I can."

"May I see one of your forms?"

Asa agreed, pulling out her swords from their sheaths on her back. Without introduction, she launched into her forms. She focused on her foot placement as the sword cut down and then immediately came up and around in an overhand block. She stabbed the air, then twisted and sliced low. Practice felt good, muscles releasing from a tension she hadn't even realized was there. As always, she began slowly, adding speed as her focus settled. By the time she was finished, her blades were kicking up sawdust as they passed close to the ground.

She sheathed her swords, glad for the opportunity to practice but afraid of how Daiki might react. She needn't have worried. If it was possible, his smile had gotten even wider to better match his eyes.

He shook his head slowly in disbelief. "I have, of course, heard the stories of the skill blades possess, but I have never seen anything like that in my life. How good are you?"

"Better than many, but far from the best," she replied. Telling the truth also felt good. She was tired of hiding and lying just to stay safe.

Asa helped her host clean up the workspace, sweeping up the sawdust and putting away the tools. As they finished Daiki stopped her from leaving.

"Do you have plans?"

"No. I had thought to go to Starfall to see what the situation was, but the truth is, I want no part of what seems to be coming."

Daiki thought for a moment before he spoke. "I will, of course, need to speak to Ayano before I am certain of this, but you are welcome to stay here for as long as you like. I'm grateful for your help, and I can see how much it means to you to have a place to practice. My space back here isn't large, but it looks to be just large enough for you to have a place out of sight."

Asa was more grateful than she would have imagined. A question stopped her in her tracks, though. "Does Ayano know as well?"

Daiki shook his head, the sorrow evident in his bearing. "She does not. My wife is a very good woman, concerned only with the safety of our home and our son. But with him gone, she is easily swayed by the news coming from Haven. She would happily poison you if she knew the truth."

Asa wasn't upset by this, yet she didn't understand. To say she did would go too far. But she did have sympathy for the woman. Her son was at war, fated to a future that grew more uncertain every day. Most people only came across blades a few times in their lives and then only for moments or an evening at most. With the gift, so mysterious to those who didn't possess it, the blades were the easy and obvious target. Shin had been right in that, at least.

"I understand. If my presence would be a cause of discord between you two, I would leave."

"Nonsense. You hide your skill well, and I have no doubt she won't discover you. She's not the type to pry, at least not beyond her questioning. You look like you could use a rest, and I'm happy to have some help."

"I'm very grateful." Asa bowed again. "Thank you very much."

"You're welcome. My question is, will you allow me to continue watching you practice?"

Asa nodded, a rare smile coming to her face at the thought of more nights of uninterrupted sleep.

Chapter 6

The candles were burning low, and if Mari had any wisdom, she'd already be preparing for bed. But she couldn't dismiss the feeling that her brother was leading their house toward a cliff.

Isamu's army had been utterly destroyed by Katashi's. Fortunately for the defeated lord, he hadn't been captured or killed, but his claim to the throne was looking weaker than ever. Katashi's forces had immediately wheeled around and marched toward Hiromi's, but no battle had yet taken place. If Mari had anything to do with it, the battle never would take place.

She pressed her hands against her eyes, trying to ease away the exhaustion. All day long she had read and reread through all the information at hand. One of her shadows, a serving woman in Katashi's court, had provided her an insight into the young lord's mind.

Katashi hadn't celebrated after his victory. Mari's shadow had brought him wine, and he had refused it. She claimed he was studying maps with a frightening intensity. Mari would have paid her weight in gold to know exactly what those maps showed, but Katashi's intent was clear enough.

He was focused on destroying the military might of both Isamu and Hiromi.

Mari sighed. Men always focused on their displays of strength, thinking power descended from might and that contests could only be decided on the battlefield. Unfortunately, Hiromi believed the same.

Her brother, under the influence of his generals, was preparing his forces for battle. Mari wasn't a general, but she had seen how well organized Katashi's troops were. Those of her house were also disciplined, but she didn't think they would win.

But she had no authority to stop the fight. Hiromi was determined, his pride demanding that he attack and win the throne with one clean victory. His generals whispered in his ear, telling him that every day he delayed was another day he allowed his enemy to rest and prepare.

And what did a woman know when it came to such matters, Mari thought bitterly. They had been at the same battle and seemed to have seen two entirely different conflicts. Even if Hiromi and his generals were right and they could win, what good would it do? Hundreds, if not thousands, of their men would die. And even if they won, for Hiromi to become king, Isamu and Katashi needed to acknowledge him.

Mari searched for a way out, combing through her letters and correspondence from shadows scattered throughout the Kingdom. The lords were all thinking of their own lands and people. But no one was thinking about the health of the Kingdom anymore.

Their last council meeting was in the morning, and Mari knew they would make the decision to go to war. She had asked repeatedly for Hiromi to come to her or to accept an audience, but all her missives had gone unanswered, and she herself had been turned away by his guards. He'd have no private conversations with her, and if she spoke out at the council, she risked losing what small influence she had.

She pounded her forehead softly against the table, disorganizing her papers. No use in bemoaning her difficulties. She still had time. If Hiromi set them upon this path, turning around wouldn't be an option. The houses would go to war, and the land would be devastated. She had to stop her brother.

Mari felt a gentle touch on her shoulder. She started awake, her head immediately pounding from the quick movement. She opened her eyes and quickly shut them, cursing herself for falling asleep at her writing table again.

She peered at Takahiro, the head of her personal guard and a close friend to her and the entire family. Takahiro had seen a few more cycles than Juro and was one of the best swords in their entire house. He had been the head of Mari's guard for at least ten cycles and was the closest person in the world to her now that Juro had rejoined the Great Cycle.

"Sorry to wake you, but the council is going to start shortly."

Mari didn't rush. Takahiro was the type of man who knew how much time she needed to get prepared and would have given her just enough.

She almost didn't move at all. No solution had come to her last night. She didn't know what to do. She didn't know how to proceed. They were going to war.

But she couldn't let that stop her. She would try, and if she failed she would try again. Hiromi would listen to her, even if it meant her giving up what little power she still had left.

Takahiro noticed her hesitation. "What troubles you?"

"Hiromi will destroy this house if he goes to war. But no one seems to believe that."

Desperate, Mari turned to Takahiro. "Do you believe me?"

Takahiro wouldn't lie to her, and he thought his answer through carefully. "I am not privy to the discussions of the commanders, so this is an incomplete answer. However, my understanding is that one of the reasons peace has always been maintained is because the houses have close to the same strength. In that case, decisive victory is challenging, if not impossible."

"So how would you stop disaster from happening?"

Takahiro frowned. "I do not know. My role in life has always been to take orders. I do not know how to manipulate the opinions of others."

Disappointed but undeterred, Mari dismissed Takahiro as she prepared for the day. She didn't know what she would do, but perhaps an opportunity would present itself. She would be ready.

The council hadn't yet started when Mari arrived, which she was grateful for. She knelt on the floor in the corner, waiting for the rest of the generals to arrive.

When the council began, talk started immediately on the preparations for war. Mari was taken aback. She didn't realize how far the discussion had already come. Everyone in the room spoke as though the decision to fight had already been made. All that was left was to create and execute their best plan.

Mari needed to speak to Hiromi alone. She cleared her throat and attempted the same stunt that had worked before, but a stern glance from her younger brother made it obvious such behavior wouldn't be tolerated. Mari felt as though she was trapped in an invisible cage that was slowly shrinking.

The understanding, when it came to her, was crushing. Her cage was very real, and it was being filled with sand, suffocating her and rendering her helpless. She couldn't do anything. Nothing would make a difference. She fought the urge to cry, curse, and scream.

She knew the action was unwise, but she couldn't allow the conversation to continue without her voice. "My lord."

At the sound of Mari's voice, every eye in the room turned on her, not a friendly one among them. She knew how they saw her—a woman who had been given too much voice by her older brother. Her presence was an annoyance at best and a threat at worst. The hardest eyes in the room were Hiromi's. Mari had used up whatever influence she had over him. Tears threatened to stream down her face when she realized she had been foolish to believe she held any power over these men. Still, she wouldn't give them the satisfaction.

"I understand it isn't my place to speak, but you are all being fools. There is no chance that we win the throne by force. Any victory would destroy us as certainly as our opponents. Pride and honor need to be balanced by our duty to our people. Stop this madness and find another way! For our people, please!"

Mari had much more to say, but her brother had motioned for the guards. She played her last card, certain it wouldn't work but determined anyway.

"Hiromi, you know this is wrong! You have to know there is no way to win once you bring our house into this war. You know Juro would have agreed with me."

Hiromi's eyes hardened against her even more, turning from rock to steel in an instant. "Juro is dead. My dear sister, your presence is no longer required at the council. Thank you for your service."

Mari almost fought against the guards, but if nothing else, she could hold on to her dignity.

The door slammed on Mari's face, and once she was out of sight of the generals, she allowed her tears the freedom they desired. All she could think about was her people and the suffering they were about to endure because their lord wanted to be king.

Mari wiped her tears and swore at the door. She would find a way to save her people.

———

Mari focused on her breath and pulled the bowstring back toward her face, her hand resting comfortably underneath her ear. She focused on her breath and the position of her body, her mind empty of any distraction except for her arrow. Her release was smooth, the shaft digging into the heart of the target.

Takahiro laughed. "I don't know why you insist on bringing me out every moon to repeat this game. We both know you're a far better archer, and I'm not getting any better."

Mari stepped away from the line, satisfied with her shot. She had been aiming a little higher, but her shot had been true. In battle, her arrow would have killed the enemy, and that was all that mattered.

"Take the shot. Maybe you'll get lucky."

Takahiro drew the bow, and Mari automatically critiqued his form in her head. His body was too tense, lacking stability, and she could see the tip of his arrow moving back and forth as her guard aimed. His release was good enough, but the shot was low, digging into the target several hands below Mari's.

As a soldier, Takahiro had been trained in both sword and bow, but his skill with steel far surpassed his proficiency with a bow. "It seems I've been proven right once again."

The tone of his voice indicated resignation, but Mari knew he enjoyed these outings as much as she did. He practiced every day with his sword, and Mari practiced as often as she could with a bow. He had as much of a chance beating her in an archery competition as she did beating him in a sword fight.

Growing up, Mari always wanted to train with Juro and Hiromi. Their father would have none of it. Swords were for men, and no daughter of his would train in such a way. However, he did relent when the subject was archery, and Mari had thrown herself into the practice. She rapidly outpaced the boys, becoming the best archer in the family. The feat had always been a point of pride for her, even if her brothers refused to acknowledge it.

As Mari had grown into a young woman, Juro had her trained in the art of knife fighting. His rationale had been simple and direct, much like he had been. The world was a dangerous place, especially for women. Guards wouldn't always be enough. The knife could kill an opponent or even oneself if the situation was dire enough. Mari had taken to that training with equal eagerness.

Between the knife and the bow, Mari had grown confident in her own physical skills. She recognized her limitations but also knew she was far more dangerous than most women. Opponents would underestimate her, and on some days she longed to use that to her advantage.

She had hoped an outing with Takahiro would clear her mind, but at best it distracted her for a time. The decision had been made to attack Katashi. Even as Mari and the head of her guards enjoyed a lazy afternoon of archery, their men were gathering and preparing for the assault. If she let herself think about the situation too much, she was liable to make herself mad.

An idea had been forming in the back of her mind, which was the real reason she had invited Takahiro out. He always advised her honestly, a gift far too rare in their house.

Mari debated all afternoon whether to bring up her idea. But if nothing was risked, nothing was gained, and their time was coming to a close.

"Takahiro, I would like your guidance."

Her guard looked up from unstringing his bow, his face giving nothing away.

"I have been considering traveling to Starfall."

Takahiro didn't react, testament both to his skill at cards and his long service with her. He continued packing his bow as if nothing had happened.

Mari wanted to say more, but she wanted his initial reaction as well. He didn't make her wait long.

"Such a decision certainly seems unwise."

The statement was made without much emotion, and she gave him credit. Right now, going to Starfall was more than unwise. It was foolish, at best. Mari was grasping at whatever chances were open to her.

"What makes you believe such a trip is worth the risk?"

Mari chose her words with care. If she couldn't convince Takahiro, a man who had gladly served her for cycles, her idea truly was foolish.

"If there is any hope for peace now that my brother has decided to march to war, it must rest with the blades. The public sentiment may be against them, but we cannot ignore their power. Every path to peace I've imagined involves them, whether it be an alliance with a single house or a moderating influence on all three."

Takahiro's face dropped, and Mari wondered what saddened him.

"My lady, you've always understood the actions of the houses much better than I. But if I may say, you don't understand your subjects as well as I do. The public sentiment isn't just against the blades. They *hate* the blades. People have always feared and respected the power they possess, but the brilliance of Lord Shin was to push that fear one step further into anger. He started a fire that will burn long after the ruins of Haven have stopped smoldering."

Mari was ashamed to admit this was news to her. "Are you certain?"

His voice was firm. "Mari, they've burned dayblades alive. Dayblades who were in their villages to heal. They've rejected soldiers wearing swords simply because they suspected the soldier might be a nightblade. The blades have been blamed for everything from famines to mysterious illnesses. The stories almost defy belief, but I've heard them firsthand from the soldiers returning from patrols. If you have any plan that hinges on the blades, I would urge you to reconsider."

"But what if they are absolutely necessary?"

Takahiro shook his head. "Then I fear we are doomed."

Furious, Mari stomped back toward her bow, picking it up and restringing it. In a single motion, she nocked an arrow, brought the bow up and the string back, and released the arrow into the heart of her target.

"Takahiro, I don't see any other choice. None of the houses has a clear dominance over the others. Katashi has won an early victory, but he doesn't have the troops or resources to conquer and hold the entire Kingdom."

Her guard agreed. "Winter is also setting in. I imagine he is hoping both Isamu and Hiromi will capitulate if he defeats your brother. But even if he wins against us, he can't launch a large-scale campaign. He'll need to prepare for a spring offensive, but by then we'll be dug in. We would be looking at a prolonged war."

Nothing worried Mari more. "We need the blades, Takahiro. Even hated, their strength will be necessary to bring this conflict to an end."

She watched the battle of thoughts cross his face as clear as day. He didn't want to enlist the aid of the blades, but he had seen enough battlefields to know the disaster a prolonged war would bring. The question was, which was the lesser of two evils for him? Mari was certain of her answer, but in her mind, Takahiro represented the people. If he chose the certain destruction of war, all her planning would be for nothing.

He made his decision and met her gaze. "So how are we going to sneak out of here in the middle of battle preparations in order to get to Starfall?"

Chapter 7

Koji's sword sliced through the thick air of the barn behind the farm-house. Even though the autumn weather insisted on remaining chillier than usual, Koji was shirtless in the stench of the barn. Between the sweat of his own frustrated practice and the heat given off by the animals, he was plenty warm.

Koji cut and cut again, feet, arms, and sword all extensions of his heart. He had long ago finished his forms and was now fighting wave after wave of imaginary foes. His hands were slick on the hilt of his steel, but he wouldn't stop. He couldn't stop until he was exhausted.

The barn was one of the greatest gifts the farmhouse had to offer. Traveling incognito meant not practicing in the early morning hours, and Koji always felt wrong when he missed his practice, as though the day that followed wasn't quite real to him. His forms grounded him, kept him attached to the present moment.

He made an angry cut, imagining Ryo's little grin as though the other blade was always laughing at a joke no one else understood. In his mind his following cuts sliced through Hiroki, the large man astonished at his own mortality.

Koji wanted to speed up his practice, to move faster, near the edges of his limits. He didn't dare, though. Ryo and Hiroki had become foes in his mind. Whether he was sure that fact was true or not, he didn't want to risk displaying his full strength. Better to be underestimated.

He had meant to confront them the morning after Hana came to him. That morning, Ryo had eaten breakfast with him. Hiroki didn't join them, remaining near the family's younger daughter.

Ryo had fixed him with a stare over the table. "You didn't sleep with the girl last night." The comment was half a statement and half an accusation.

Koji met the other nightblade's gaze. He couldn't act, not with Hiroki in another room. He needed to bide his time, wait to get the two of them together. Then he could confront them and fight if the confrontation turned violent. Until then, he had to play along as well as he could. He wasn't a man skilled at deception.

"She wasn't to my liking."

Ryo nodded slowly, and Koji got the distinct feeling the older nightblade was unraveling his statement and looking straight to the truth of the matter. Neither was sure of the other. Each was suspicious, but neither was willing to shed blood, not yet.

Since that breakfast Koji's two hosts had never been together. One was always with a family member, the other going about a variety of daily tasks. Ryo, in particular, seemed a man of letters, with a constant stream of correspondence coming and going. The farmer's family made for excellent couriers.

As the days passed, Koji met the members of the family whose house he now slept in. The father, a man who was just starting to get the first hints of gray in his hair, walked with a noticeable limp. His wife was a plain-looking woman who cooked some of the best food he'd ever tasted. Both tended to avoid him, and he caught only glimpses of the couple.

Koji saw more of the four children. The older son was often dispatched with Ryo's letters, but sometimes they sent the older daughter, a cycle or two younger than the son. The two younger children, also a son and a daughter, most often performed chores around the house.

None of them spoke much to Koji, turning the other way when he came into the same room or hallway. Occasionally the older daughter would make eye contact, but he otherwise felt as though he was living in a house of ghosts.

The more time Koji spent with the two other blades, the more he began to believe they were involved in something larger. The correspondence was the biggest clue. Couriers arrived throughout the day, and from a glance, Koji got the impression they were as willing to perform their duties as the farmer's family. The volume indicated the messages couldn't be going too far. Koji was consumed by curiosity, but he kept his own counsel.

Every morning when he woke up, Koji hoped the day would be the one when he could confront his hosts about their behavior. He sensed their actions at night, and it was all he could do not to crash out of his room. But wasn't silence better than the loss of life? Every night he gritted his teeth and contained his anger.

Ryo, at least, was clever. The two never slipped up, were never together anywhere except near a hostage, and Koji might as well have been tied to a chair for all the good he could do. His only outlet was his morning practice, as unsatisfying as that was.

Koji sensed Ryo approaching the barn but didn't stop his practice. He switched to a standard form, one taught to all nightblades when they were young. His sword came up above his head over his right shoulder, and he pivoted around, stepped backward, and cut down. He stepped forward as he brought his sword back up, his body easily remembering the form he had worked through a thousand times. Even if Ryo observed him, he would learn little from the practice.

Ryo watched as Koji finished the form, then nodded approvingly. "It's vital to practice the basics. Hiroki could learn something from your dedication. How long have you held the status of master?"

"Almost two cycles." Koji couldn't help but feel a flush of pride in his chest. He had been one of the youngest nightblades ever to complete the trials of mastery.

Ryo agreed. "You were young." The nightblade seemed like he was about to say something more but stopped. Koji could guess, though. Passing the trials at such an early age indicated a level of skill Koji hadn't yet displayed. His limited practice was further proof he didn't trust Ryo.

Koji wanted to interrupt Ryo's thoughts before they got too far. If he was going to help the family, he needed to stay in Ryo's good graces. "Can I help you?"

Ryo came out of his trance and looked at Koji. "Yes, as a matter of fact. This evening there is a gathering of blades. I'd like you to join me."

"Is Hiroki going?"

Ryo shook his head. "He would like to, but someone needs to stay here to make sure the family doesn't try to spread more unfounded rumors about us. He wanted me to ask you to stay, but we both decided it was more important for you to meet some of the people at this gathering."

Koji considered the offer. He couldn't decline, not really. The meeting was either a test of his loyalty or a trap. Perhaps both. But Ryo confirmed what Koji had suspected—other blades were in the area. Koji wanted to go to the meeting, regardless of its purpose. He was afraid to leave the family alone with Hiroki but didn't see a better option.

"It would be a pleasure to meet other blades. Thank you for your invitation."

Ryo bowed slightly and departed.

———

Koji left the farmhouse with a strange mixture of trepidation and excitement. The day had passed like his last few. He trained and tried to meditate while Ryo and Hiroki went about their daily tasks. Koji remained alert for any break in his hosts' routine. He found none.

The sun had fallen when the two warriors left the farmhouse. Koji was impressed by how cold the weather had become. Winter wasn't for another moon, but the snow crunched under his feet as they walked. He realized it would be almost impossible for him to go anywhere without leaving tracks.

He followed Ryo, who seemed to know the land intimately. They proceeded without hesitation, even in the dark snow, toward some unknown destination. Their walk was silent, Koji extended his sense farther than usual to catch any possible traps.

He sensed the blades just before he saw another farmhouse. Surprising, considering they were out in the plains. The sight should have traveled farther. Only after they crested a small hill did Koji realize Ryo had approached the farmhouse keeping the rise between them and their destination. Koji wasn't certain, but they apparently hadn't taken the most direct route. Had the blades here made traps to protect the farm? The sense wasn't much good against a sharpened stake in the ground in the middle of the night.

More blades were in the farmhouse than Koji expected. If he had to guess, he would have said that most of the blades who had once been stationed in Haven were here. At least two dozen were present.

Koji wasn't expecting what he discovered when he stepped inside. Not only was the farmhouse filled with blades, but the mood was almost boisterous. The gifted passed cups of drink around freely, and the room was filled with laughter and shouts.

His stomach sank. As much as inebriation sounded appealing to him, he was disgusted by what he saw. Some of the blades were completely drunk, their faces red and voices out of control. Others were more subdued, but they were in the minority. Koji remembered that outside these walls, the Kingdom was falling into civil war. His anger was intense, and it took all his willpower to keep his rage contained. Ryo watched him carefully.

Koji took the first drink that was offered. No harm in one, and if drinking helped allay Ryo's suspicions, so much the better.

They imbibed and socialized, and as they did, more blades trickled into the farmhouse. Koji recognized a number of them. In his role as Minori's aide, one of his first tasks had been to go to the gathering places of the blades in Haven. He had sought out the leaders or blades most prone to spreading rumors. Then he would tell his story about being sentenced to death for doing his duty. Minori had rescued him, and Koji's work was to let the blades know that his master stood up for their rights. Because of that work, Koji recognized several people, and several recognized him as well.

Fortunately, his name was known far more than his appearance. Most who recognized him saw him just as he saw them, a face they had seen in the inns and teahouses around Haven. One or two knew his name, but he did his best to keep what distance he could from them in the small hall.

The door to the room opened one more time, and a silence slowly descended upon the crowd. Koji turned, his stomach sinking even farther into his bowels when he saw who had entered.

Koji knew her all too well, and she knew him, too. Her name was Akane, a tempestuous nightblade who had been willing to watch the world burn back when it was still standing. Most of the places Koji had gone to as an aide had been sympathetic to his story. Akane had been willing to go to the streets and attack the lords that night.

Koji wished he knew more about her. She was fierce and believed the blades needed to have more authority in the Kingdom. Akane was clearly the leader of this contingent of blades, a group strong enough to change the course of events. He suspected he already knew what her goals were.

Akane recognized him, and her face lit up. She shouted, even though the room had largely fallen silent upon her entrance. "Brothers and sisters! What a great day this is! Do you know who we have in the room with us? It's Koji, once Minori's right hand and the man who killed King Shin!"

Koji's heart missed several beats as he swore repeatedly in his mind, a fake grin plastered on his face. How had she known? She must have been close enough to the stand to have seen him. Maybe she'd even had the same idea, and he'd just beaten her to it.

None of that mattered. Everyone in the room was looking at him, and he was afraid they would be able to see through his grin, see the dilemma eating him up within.

They didn't. Their smiles grew wider, and what Koji observed was a horror he had never thought to live through. He was their hero. Several blades were bowing deeply to him, and the rest were nodding and cheering even though he couldn't hear anything. Cup after cup was brought to him, and he drank them all freely, hoping to find solace and peace wherever he might. He had killed a king. He had killed their king. And they were celebrating him.

He was given the seat of honor at Akane's right side. The meeting began, and Koji still couldn't work through what had just happened. Sound slowly returned to his awareness, and he realized his nightmares were coming true. They discussed recruiting more members, of growing their ranks so they could fight against the armies of the lords.

Koji's attention fully returned when he heard a name he'd heard once before. Akane was continuing a monologue. "Takashi, one of our greatest commanders, taught us that this new world was coming, a world in which every person was free to choose their own path."

The leader of the group was waving a small book. Koji caught the writing on the front, which read simply, "The teachings of Takashi."

Where had he heard that name? The memory came, particularly potent in his current company. He remembered drinking with Asa the night they had dueled. She had told him her story, which had begun with an assassination she had completed for the Council of the Blades.

Takashi had been the man she had killed, the man who'd been her father's commander at the massacre of Two Falls.

The world was a large place, but sometimes it didn't seem that way, the threads of people's lives constantly twisting and knotting up. So the man she had killed had teachings that were spreading through the land? He wondered if she would find that as funny as he did right now. Minori, Kiyoshi, and now Takashi. The blades of the present couldn't look beyond the blades of the past.

His attention returned to Akane's rising voice. "I see a day, not long in the future, when blades are able to decide their own destiny! A day in which our power and our abilities are respected for the gifts they are!"

She finished her speech by pounding her cup on the table and drinking deeply. She was joined by many around the room. Koji studied the group. Akane had obviously enthusiastic supporters, but Koji had no doubt that even those who didn't shout agreed quietly with her words.

After Akane finished, Ryo spoke next. Koji took note. The other nightblade must be high up in whatever passed for a hierarchy here.

"Our leader speaks truly. She has the vision, and it is up to each of us to put it into practice. Our numbers grow day by day, but we are reaching a point where there are not many more blades in the immediate area. Akane and I have spoken, and we believe it is time to move to the next steps in our plan."

"The idea of staying in farmhouses was a good one. We were able to spread out and recruit many of the blades traveling between Haven and Starfall."

That was new to Koji. He thought he had just stumbled upon the first farmhouse through pure chance. But if everyone here was also occupying farmhouses off the road that led between the two cities, they would catch all the blades trying to make it to Starfall for guidance. A smart plan and a simple one.

"Unfortunately, we are gathering fewer and fewer blades. That is to be expected. We assumed most would head to Starfall, and there are few left in the area surrounding us. Now the distance between us is no longer a strength but a weakness. We must remain in a small area to be better able to protect ourselves."

Koji saw the logic behind the idea. If the blades were discovered now, armies could isolate the farmhouses and pick them off two or three at a time. All together, overwhelming force would be required to dislodge them.

"After much debate, we would like to propose River's End as our new location." Ryo held up his hand to still the argument that instantly sprang up around the table. "We'll have a chance to discuss the decision, but here are our reasons: First, we sent a shadow to the village several days ago. It's well stocked with food for the winter, which promises to be a cold one. Second, because of the river access, we'll be able to get messages and news much faster than overland. Third, they burned our way station. They have no love lost for the blades, and it's worth teaching them the mistake in that."

The assembled blades started a vigorous debate, voices rising in disbelief and anger. Koji thought their plan sounded a lot like that of the blades who had lived at Two Falls, and he was one of the few who knew how that had actually turned out. More than twenty cycles had passed since that group of blades had tried to break away from the authority of the Kingdom, and each and every one of them had rejoined the Great Cycle for their efforts. But he didn't reveal that history, content instead to listen to the arguments. They seemed to fall into two categories.

Some felt that River's End was too small. If they wanted to grow, they were going to need more space and more houses. Others seemed to feel uncomfortable gathering at all. Spread out they were more vulnerable individually, but their movement was safer. There was no way for one military maneuver to destroy them.

Despite his anger at what he saw, Koji also observed hints of what life could be like under Akane's direction. All blades with something to say had their turn to speak. Whether dealing with the logistics of running a village or mulling over the ethics of their actions, everyone with a concern spoke, and every concern was discussed with equal merit. Koji had never seen anything like it, and at times, he almost forgot the context and was impressed by Akane's leadership. The downside was that the meeting lasted long into the night. It was far faster to tell others what to do than to convince them all of a course of action.

At least that was what Koji thought initially. As an outsider, perhaps his experience was just different. What he noticed as he watched was that, although there was a place for disagreement to be voiced, there was never any doubt of what would actually happen. The details might change, but the larger mission never would. No doubt, no misgiving, no matter how valid, would change Akane's mind. She wanted River's End, and they were going to take it. First, though, they were going to talk.

The meeting was just another facade. Another illusion of power. Most of the blades around the table had no more say than they had when they were taking commands from the Council of the Blades. They had merely traded one master for another.

Now that Koji had a bit of alcohol flowing through him, he couldn't summon the anger he had earlier that evening. Now he was just saddened. The monks devoted to the teachings of the Great Cycle had it right. History always repeated, an endless cycle no one knew how to break.

The moon was past its midpoint when the meeting finally finished. As Koji had expected, the decision had been made to attack River's End. To their credit, the blades moved fast, deciding to attack the day after next.

Everyone was about to disband when Akane made one final announcement. "Brothers and sisters, remember we can't leave witnesses behind when our movement is so young. Make sure when you leave the farmhouses, no one is around who can speak of our plans or slander our reputation."

Even inebriated, Koji was shocked. The command was met by the others with silent acceptance.

His anger, even smothered by drink, flared back, his rage and frustration as hot as ever. These blades had trained their entire lives to protect the people they were now talking about killing! And they didn't even object. Koji was disgusted to be among them.

He kept his emotions in check, just barely. Before, he wasn't sure what he was going to do, but now he was committed.

———

One benefit to the frigid air was that it sobered Koji up quickly. He and Ryo had only been walking for a little while, but Koji's head already felt clear, and small tests of his reflexes let him know most of his speed was still present.

Ryo had been silent after the meeting, probably thinking through the details of the attack. Koji had the feeling that Ryo was the man who took care of details. Akane was the woman who provided the leadership, the figure whom warriors were willing to follow.

Eventually Ryo's attention turned to Koji. "What did you think of the meeting, king-killer?"

Koji hated the title, given to him by a few of the blades who had been present. The question was weighted with meaning, but Koji had decided on his course of action. He would never get Ryo and Hiroki away from the family, not the way events were transpiring. Soon he wouldn't have any more chances.

"I think you are all fools."

Ryo stopped in his tracks, his hand coming down to his blade. Koji didn't care. He had never had a chance to see Ryo fight, but he had been observing his host for days. He was certain he didn't have to fear the other blade's skill.

"Say that again."

"None of you know that you are doomed to failure. Some of your ideas have merit, but you live without honor."

Ryo drew his sword at that. Koji still didn't act. It felt good to get his feelings off his chest. If such expression made Ryo too angry to fight well, so much the better.

"Yes, I killed the king. I felt it was a debt of honor to the man who saved my life. But now that I see the results of my actions, I regret what I did. The Kingdom needs us more than ever, and all you seek is to tear it apart for your own ends."

Ryo attacked, the final insult too much for his pride to handle. The strike was obvious, an overhand cut even a civilian would have seen coming. Koji easily sidestepped, the steel passing harmlessly on his right side. He drove his fist into Ryo's stomach, knocking the wind out of him and dropping him to the snow-covered ground.

The older blade coughed and gasped, clawing at his stomach as though he could force it open and let air in. Koji drew his own sword and waited. Ryo's next attack would be better, but Koji wanted him to feel as helpless as he had made the farmer's family feel.

Koji took a deep breath and looked around. A few trees were visible in the moonlight. Many leaves remained attached, the snows falling before the trees could complete their preparation for a new season. He exhaled, watching his breath freeze in the still air.

His host attacked sooner than he expected, bringing his sword up and trying to cut him from below. Koji sensed the strike coming and stepped back, allowing the tip of the blade to pass just a hand's breadth in front of him. Although he knew an opening was there, he didn't attack.

Ryo got to his feet and launched a series of cuts, fast and strong, but Koji found himself disappointed. He expected better from a nightblade. This fight would be far too easy.

Koji watched as the fire left Ryo's eyes as each strike missed. No matter what the older nightblade did, he couldn't bring his steel anywhere near Koji.

He deflected a cut and stepped inside Ryo's guard, bringing his elbow to the man's face. Koji felt a satisfying crunch as Ryo's nose collapsed from the blow.

Ryo dropped to the ground again, clutching at his bloody face. He looked up at Koji with hatred in his eyes.

"You can't stop what's coming, Koji. You're trying to have it both ways. Are you going to side with blades or with those who hate you? You'll need to decide. A war's coming."

The other nightblade must have thought that he was distracting Koji, because he tried another cut. Koji met his steel with his own, pushing aside the weak strike and slicing through Ryo's neck. His host collapsed, his life spurting out of him in pulses.

Koji bent down so that he was the last thing Ryo saw. "The war is already here, fool."

———

Koji returned to the farmhouse before the sun started to rise over the horizon. He had been careful in his battle with Ryo not to get any blood on himself. His sword was clean, and there was no evidence he had been in a fight.

If one of his two hosts was going to cause him trouble, it would be Hiroki. The man was large and moved with the grace of a cat. He had clearly been the muscle of the partnership. Koji wasn't frightened. He was certain of his skills. He was looking forward to fighting the other blade.

He entered the farmhouse and took off his sandals. There was no hurry in his action. He tried to move as though he was tired from a long night, even though nothing could be further from the truth.

As he had hoped, Hiroki came out into the common room to meet him. He brought the younger daughter with him, but he didn't look to be on his guard. "Where's Ryo?"

"The meeting went long, and he is planning on staying for a while with Akane to discuss plans. We're going to attack River's End in a few days."

Koji spoke nonchalantly, watching as Hiroki worked his way through the new information. He would never have a better time to attack. Hiroki was distracted and wouldn't have time to draw on the girl before Koji reached him.

Koji sprinted at the other nightblade. Hiroki was fast. Even distracted, his hand was drawing his sword out of the scabbard by the time Koji reached him. Koji might have gotten in a first cut, but the only thought in his mind was getting Hiroki away from the family. He lowered his shoulder and crashed into Hiroki before the man's steel could clear its sheath.

Hiroki's sword slammed back into its scabbard, and the two of them crashed through one of the paper walls dividing the rooms. Remarkably, Hiroki kept his balance, even as he stepped backward over the waking form of the farmer's older daughter.

Koji also stepped over her, driving his legs hard, pushing the large man through another wall into an empty room. He tried driving his fist into Hiroki's stomach to knock the wind from him like he had Ryo, but he couldn't bring his fist back far enough to generate sufficient power, and when he did punch, his hand felt like it had crashed against a brick.

Koji gave one final shove, and both warriors drew. Koji was faster, but Hiroki's hand had started far closer to his blade. Koji deflected Hiroki's cut, but it was a close affair.

He hadn't expected Hiroki to be as fast as he was. The downfall of most physically strong sword fighters was that they had a tendency to rely on their strength in the heat of combat. Hiroki didn't make that mistake, and their swords crossed three times before they broke apart.

Koji expected a short break, but Hiroki wasn't giving him one. The massive nightblade used the extra space to bring his sword over to Koji's weak side and launch a powerful attack. Koji blocked it as Hiroki pivoted on his foot, trying to get behind the younger blade.

Koji let him, certain that Hiroki was used to fighting nongifted civilians or soldiers. If a warrior gets behind a civilian, the fight is over. The civilian doesn't know what's happening and dies. But a nightblade can easily sense attacks from behind. When Koji sensed the cut coming, he dodged low and spun.

Hiroki was fast even if he was caught by surprise. Koji's cut sliced through the bigger man's robes and into his stomach.

The duel continued, Hiroki becoming more cautious. The cut had to be painful, but his face gave off no expression. They slowly circled, Koji trying to keep his foe from the rest of the household. He could sense others moving behind him, gathering to watch the fight for their lives.

The sun was just coming up, lighting the blade's fight just enough for the family to see what was happening. Koji was at a slight disadvantage because he had to keep them safe. Hiroki figured this out and started trying to angle toward the family.

This had to end. Hiroki wasn't like Ryo. Koji wouldn't be able to get him to die in fear the same way he had with his master. Koji needed to just kill him.

He took a deep breath and lunged forward. Steel met steel in the predawn light. It took five moves for Koji to get inside Hiroki's guard, but he was too fast for the bigger man. One cut opened up the nightblade's arm, but the killing blow was a stab into the heart. When Hiroki died, his face was as expressionless as it had ever been.

Despite the knowledge he had done the right thing, Koji felt his own heart tear at his actions. It still seemed wrong to fight and kill his brothers and sisters.

Koji sensed the movement behind him but didn't react. The family would be safe now. He would help move the body and then leave. He wasn't sure how he could save River's End on his own, but he had to try. If he died then, at least his problems would be over.

He felt the blow coming, but he had let the farmer get too close, thinking he posed no threat and being distracted by the future. Koji started to spin around, but his world went black in an instant.

———

Koji's first sensation was pain. His second was more pain.

He came awake with a gasp, his head immediately flaring in agony. He blinked away the stars in his vision threatening to black him out again.

Once or twice, when he had been younger, he had been hit in the head, but he couldn't remember any incident in recent memory. The pain was excruciating. Every time he moved his head, the pain came back with a fresh vengeance.

Koji forced himself to remain still. He tried to bring his hand to feel the knot on the back of his head, only to realize he was tied down to something.

He groaned. At that moment, he didn't care why he was restrained. He didn't care about who captured him or where he was. All he felt at that moment was an overwhelming desire for a strong bottle of sake.

His memories returned quickly to him. He remembered the meeting and slaying Ryo and Hiroki. He remembered the farmer coming up behind him in the dark. Then he remembered that the blades were going to attack a village soon.

Koji struggled against his bonds, sending another wave of agony traveling from his head down his back. Whoever had restrained him had done so well. Time would be needed to escape, the one thing he didn't know if he had. How long had he been unconscious?

The door slid open, and Koji watched with some degree of disbelief as the farmer and his entire family came into the room. Everyone appeared. The farmer and his wife first, the older son and Hana next, the younger son and daughter trickling in behind. They stood there for a moment, and if it didn't hurt to move, Koji would have laughed at how absurd the situation seemed.

The farmer spoke first. "I'm sorry for the pain that I caused you. I saw a chance to free my family, and I wasn't sure if you were any better than the others. Had it been up to me, I would have killed you, but Hana claims that you helped her."

Koji glanced at his bonds.

The farmer continued, "Although I trust my daughter, you must understand: the safety of my family was at stake. I felt this was my only choice until we spoke."

Koji didn't care. The family was safe, so his duty here was complete. There was only one subject he cared about now. "How long was I out?"

"Most of the day. It's almost evening."

Koji swore. "How far is it from here to River's End?"

"A day and a half on foot perhaps. Why?"

Koji swore again, unconcerned about his language even in the presence of the younger girl.

"Are there any horses nearby?"

The farmer frowned, apparently confused by the questions, but he still deferred to the authority of the blades, answering Koji's inquiries without debate. "Some of the wealthier farmers nearby had some, but they've all been captured by blades."

The farmer seemed to realize after giving his answer that he was the one who was supposed to be in control. He tried to direct the questions. "Are you a danger to my family?"

Koji shook his head. "That doesn't matter now." His mind was racing.

On a horse, a day and a half would become less than half a day. He could still reach River's End in time. He would need to get to the nearest farm with a horse and kill the blades there before they left. A difficult task, but if he left now, perhaps there was still a chance he would make it.

First he needed to get out of the house. The farmer was about to ask another question, but Koji stared daggers into him. "Let me go, now. I need directions to the nearest farmhouse with a horse."

The farmer was taken aback. He looked around the room for guidance, and Hana nodded. Still the farmer hesitated.

"Come on, old man! I don't have time for this. The other blades are gathering to launch an attack on River's End. There's still time for me to stop them, but I need to hurry."

Something he said snapped the farmer out of his indecision. He moved quickly to untie Koji, giving him directions to the nearest horse. "I can come with you."

"Can you run the entire way?"

The farmer shook his head.

"Then you're just holding me back. Stay here and protect your family."

Koji sat up, a wave of nausea passing over him. The farmer had hit him hard. He tentatively reached out with the sense, grateful that he could use the ability without more pain.

Forcing his discomfort aside, Koji stood up and grabbed his weapons piled in the corner.

The farmer's directions had been clear. Koji ran, seeing every landmark described to him. He raced across the fields, his legs carrying him as fast as they could. The moment he saw the farmhouse, though, he knew the truth. He didn't sense anyone.

The farm was as dark to his sense as it was to his sight. Because he wasn't sure what else to do, Koji entered anyway, disgusted at the sight of the corpses left scattered on the floor.

The blades who'd made this house their home hadn't treated the bodies with respect. They didn't give the family a warrior's death.

Bodies were bruised, stabbed, and sliced, but nowhere did he find a body with the single clean fatal cut most blades prided themselves on.

Koji didn't even bother with the barn. He would have been able to sense the horses. Instead, nothing.

He went out into the fields, taking a deep breath and fighting the frustration and anger welling up. These blades, led by Akane, were a disgrace to everything he'd been taught.

With no horse, Koji started running.

Chapter 8

Asa had grown up on a farm. Many of her earliest memories were of the time she spent in the fields, planting and harvesting rice. The work had always been a torment to her, but every hand was needed, and those early years certainly helped to give her the strength she currently possessed, shaping her physically and mentally.

When she had begun training as a nightblade, she had never thought to return to farming. The work was difficult, and the reward was small. She remembered thinking on the day she left, her mother waving goodbye and crying, that she would never work on a farm again. That day it had been the only happy thought she'd had.

Now, cycles later, she was working on a farm willingly. It was too late in the season to harvest many crops, but there was still some work to be done, work she had long been familiar with.

She was surprised how quickly she allowed herself to fall into a routine. She had been with the couple less than a quarter moon, but already a definite pattern to her days had emerged. There was a beautiful and rugged simplicity to the life. The three were up early every morning, Asa helping with the chores that she could. Rice harvesting was her primary responsibility. She cut the remaining stalks and hung them out to dry. Then she'd thresh the rice and toss it, watching the husks fly away in the breeze. The harvest she could do with little supervision. At other times she helped Daiki in his woodshop, learning and assisting.

Ayano had tried to recruit her in more womanly duties, such as laundry and cooking, but she quickly discovered it was faster to do the tasks on her own than supervise Asa. The younger woman's basic inabilities had confused Ayano, who seemed to think Asa would never find a husband without the most fundamental of skills.

Daiki, at least, enjoyed his wife's confusion. He had no doubt Ayano was evaluating Asa as a match for their son, and Asa's clear discomfort at this thought seemed to be one of his greatest joys.

Despite the occasional awkwardness of the situation, Asa felt more at peace than she had since she'd been a young child. Every day was filled with things to do, and she fell asleep fatigued every night. Life was hard but simple.

One morning Asa came across Daiki kneeling in front of the family's small shrine to the Great Cycle. She was surprised. Most mornings he gave the shrine a perfunctory bow but nothing more. Driven by her own curiosity, she knelt beside him.

When he finished, he looked at her. "Most days I am able to go about my life as though nothing out of the ordinary is happening. I clean my tools and build new creations in my shed. I can lose myself in the work. More than anything, having something to do with my hands, something to focus on, allows me to forget the outside world."

Asa understood the sentiment well enough. She felt the same way about practicing with her sword.

"But there are also days," Daiki continued, "when I'm doing everything I can just to maintain a sense of calm. Days where all I can think about is how desperately I miss Akihiro. We worked hard to raise him and give him a future.

"I was proud of my military service. I was a decent sword, and at the time, the military gave me the order and purpose I so desperately needed as a young man. When it came time to send my son into service, I was glad, thinking he would have the same experience I had."

Asa wasn't sure what to say. She had never been good at consoling others. Her own childhood had taken that ability away from her. Regardless, seeing Daiki this vulnerable made her at least want to try.

"There is every chance that he still lives."

"Perhaps. Perhaps not. Part of me wants only to know the truth. Is my son alive or not? But another part of me says that it's better not to know. Now at least, I can pretend he's still alive. Some days the illusion even works."

Asa gestured toward the shrine. "Does it help?"

"Sometimes. It provides hope, at least."

Daiki glanced at her as though he was unsure whether to ask his question or not. "It is said you nightblades know more about death than anyone."

Asa nodded. She threw out her sense to make sure Ayano wasn't in the house. When she was certain they wouldn't be overheard, she spoke softly. "I don't know for sure what happens when we die. No one does. But you know what the sense actually is, I assume?"

Daiki looked at her as though she was asking him if he knew what wood was. "You sense the energy from living creatures."

A simple explanation, but accurate enough. "Yes. I also know that when people die, their energy doesn't disappear. Instead, it dissipates and merges into the life surrounding us. Although I can't say what the experience is like, I can say for certain that some part of us goes on after the body is dead."

Daiki turned to her and bowed deeply, his gratitude unspoken.

They stood up, and Asa thought Daiki looked a bit older than he had before, his limbs a little less mobile than they had been yesterday. He took one last look at the shrine.

"I so desperately want my son to be alive. I want to embrace him tightly, even if he tries to break away. My desire is so real, sometimes when you walk into the room, I think for a moment you are him. But I've heard the same rumors everyone else has. The houses are at war, and it's likely my son is dead."

Asa stopped him. "You can't think that way. You need to keep up your hopes."

Daiki shook his head back and forth slowly. "No. Perhaps in front of my wife I can keep up pretenses, but I've always believed that it's important to see things as they are, not as we wish them to be."

Asa didn't have a reply to that. She agreed with Daiki and could bring no comfort to him.

He looked up at her and smiled, an expression that communicated a deeper sadness than any tear ever could.

"Come, we have work to do."

———

Asa awoke with a start. The first hints of sunlight were just beginning to crawl through the window, and her room felt bitterly cold.

Her gut told her something was wrong. Something had startled her from sleep, but she wasn't sure what. She gently extended her sense. Ayano and Daiki were sleeping in the next room. Outside, everything was quiet. From her bed, Asa could see the sky, perfectly clear and cloudless. All in all, a perfect, if chilly, autumn day was promised by the rising sun.

But she had learned to trust her instincts, and something had awoken her. She sat up and took another glance out the window. Everything was just as it had first appeared. The world outside was quiet, even the animals not yet awake.

A feeling of unease grew in Asa's stomach, twisting it tightly. Her gift of the sense was average at best. If something had awoken her with a start, something big was wrong.

Asa took a deep breath and threw her sense out wide. When she discovered the truth, she felt as though she had been stabbed deep in the chest. For a few moments, she struggled to breathe.

River's End was surrounded. Asa couldn't sense the blades, but she could sense their gifts, like hers, spread wide like a net across the village.

Asa cursed. She couldn't make out the number, but there had to be more than a dozen. Why would so many blades be here? In her heart, she knew that such a large gathering of blades couldn't portend anything good.

She raced through her options. There wasn't any escape from the village. She could sense the gifts of the others all around her.

She could go out and talk to her peers, reason with them. The idea had some merit, but Asa didn't think it would work. If the blades had been peaceful, they wouldn't have surrounded the village. She tried to think of a benevolent reason they would be in such a formation, but none came to her.

She could fight, but a strong enough nightblade would kill her in a duel. There was no chance she could take on more than a dozen.

Asa swore. They might spare her, but she wasn't the one she cared about. Her thoughts focused on Daiki and Ayano, waiting to see their son again. Could she escape with them in the confusion of the attack?

Her only option, as little as she liked it, was to go out and speak with the attackers. She didn't think she had a hope of succeeding, but even the slimmest chance was better than where she stood otherwise.

Asa strapped on all her weapons, worried that she would need them again for the first time in what felt like forever.

She snuck quietly out of the house and beyond the outskirts of River's End. A small rise overlooked the village to the south, and she imagined that if this raid had a commander, she would find that person there.

Asa wasn't disappointed. As she crested the rise, she came upon a line of blades, almost all nightblades. But Asa saw two who wore the white robes of the dayblades. Her sense and sight confirmed that the situation was worse than she had thought. More than two dozen blades surrounded the village.

Asa was soon greeted by another nightblade, a woman who stood at least a head taller than she. Asa looked up and gave her a short bow, a courtesy among peers. The bow wasn't returned.

"What business do you have in River's End?" Asa asked.

The question sounded hollow, even to her. Whatever the taller nightblade's business was, she had the power to make it happen. With the number of blades apparently at her command, she could attack and hold a city.

The other woman didn't respond to Asa's question. "I could ask you the same thing. What is a blade doing surrounded by civilians?"

The inquiry struck Asa as being incredibly odd. There weren't that many blades in the world, and almost all of them spent most of their time being surrounded by civilians. The question was a glimpse into the mind of the woman, and Asa didn't like what she saw.

"I have taken refuge from the storm of hatred pursuing us. There is a kind old couple who have sheltered me for many days."

"They know you are a nightblade?"

Asa nodded. It was a half truth at least.

Asa had hoped that perhaps her statement would elicit some sort of positive response, but she was disappointed.

"Good, then they will be willing servants once we move in."

Asa had suspected the group's plan, but the woman's comment confirmed her fears. The nightblades were trying to take over a village and make it their own. Asa couldn't help but think of her time with Kiyoshi and her knowledge of the massacre at Two Falls. That had been a horrible day for the Kingdom, and this didn't seem to be any different.

Looking at the stern faces she was flanked by, Asa realized that her only hope of surviving, her only hope of saving the couple she had come to care for, was deception.

She didn't mind. Honor meant little to her.

"If you're planning on taking over the village, I can give you whatever information you like. I know where they store their food and which villagers might pose a problem."

The other woman looked at her coldly. "We already have all the information we need. And none of the villagers are going to give us a problem."

The woman's tone of voice was clear. She planned on killing all the villagers. She wanted their property, not their lives.

Asa was careful to keep her face as blank as a stone. If there was any chance of saving Ayano and Daiki, she needed to take part in the attack.

The woman didn't seem like she was going to offer, so Asa was forced to ask. "If you are setting up a place for us to live, I would like to join you. My name is Asa."

The woman's stare was cooler than the morning air, but eventually she nodded. "Very well. We'll talk more after our work here is done. My name is Akane, and I lead this band of blades."

Asa understood she was only a distraction, so she left and joined the loose ring of blades that circled the town. She studied each one, trying to measure their strength. After a few, though, she gave up. Saving Daiki and Ayano was almost hopeless. But still, her determination was as sharp as her swords. If she wasn't willing to fight here, she was worthless.

In the few moments before the charge into the village began, Asa felt herself completely relax. There was nothing else for her to do. She would either save her hosts or die in the trying. Her life had quickly become very simple.

Akane drew her sword, and the ring of blades around Asa screamed a battle cry. Asa joined in, but she felt as though her voice was empty.

The small village of River's End came alive quickly. Some residents poked their heads outside in confusion, but as soon as the first alarm was raised, villagers started stumbling out with scythes and homemade spears. Their eyes were bleary with sleep, their reactions dulled. She saw a glimpse of steel in the small gathering crowd and wondered if Daiki was there, holding a sword. What would he think when his home was attacked by blades and the one he had hosted for almost a quarter moon was gone?

Asa shoved the thought out of her mind as she charged with the rest of the blades. There wasn't any plan or strategy that she could discern, the attack more a slaughter than a battle.

She almost cut down the blade next to her the moment they entered the village. The two were out of sight from the others, and the temptation was strong. She held her swords back, though. She was only going to have one moment to betray her fellow blades, and she wanted to make the best of it.

Around her, the raid began. Asa didn't partake, working her way through the chaos toward the other edge of town to Daiki's house. One villager took a swing at her with a scythe that she easily ducked under.

She could sense what was happening. The ring was closing on River's End, cutting off all escape. The blades were working methodically, advancing slowly from the edges of the village into the center. Asa needed to get to the other edge of the village before the blades on that side of the ring made it through her new home.

She sprinted through the center of the village, surrounded by citizens who screamed for her blood. Those who didn't tried to stay as far away from her as possible.

Some weren't so wise. One old farmer stabbed at her with a homemade spear. She sidestepped the attack easily and sprinted past him, almost running headfirst into a young man with fire in his eyes.

The youth was unarmed, but he threw a punch at her with all his strength. Asa didn't have the space to dodge but deflected his blow and pushed against the back of his head, sending him hurtling beyond her.

Asa crashed through the front door of Daiki's house, certain she'd made it just a few moments before anyone else. Her sense warned her of danger, and she stepped back as a huge kettle swung in front of her face. Ayano was behind the attack, and when she saw Asa, a look of confusion came across her face.

"Asa, what's happening?" The voice was childlike, weak and scared.

"Your village is being attacked. We need to get you out of here while we still can."

As Asa finished speaking, Daiki came out of the couple's bedroom. Despite the chaos, despite everything that had happened, the sight of him brought a smile to Asa's face. He was wearing an old military uniform. The outfit, once a bright blue, had faded to a sky blue over the cycles. At his side was a sword. If the condition of the hilt and scabbard was any indication, the steel was plenty sharp. Daiki was a warrior, even if he wouldn't call himself one.

They shared a look that communicated everything they needed to know. Asa breathed a little easier knowing that he had never doubted her.

Ayano, however, was a different problem. She noticed for the first time Asa's swords, hanging outside her clothes in almost a moon. Understanding dawned on her brow, and she lunged, attempting to claw at Asa's face. "You dare to come into our house! You ate my food!"

Avoiding Ayano in the small space of the house was no easy feat, but Asa managed. Daiki grabbed his wife, and although the anger in her eyes burned as hot as it ever had, she didn't strike. Asa would need to be careful. She knew if she gave Ayano the chance, one of Asa's own daggers might find its way into her back.

Asa stepped forward, hoping the action would get their attention. "Stop!"

They both paused, fear instinctively taking control. Asa used the moment to her advantage.

"We don't have any time for this. Blades are attacking the village and killing everyone. We need to get you out."

Just as Asa finished speaking, two more blades stepped into the house.

Confusion was the order of the day. The other warriors could sense that Asa was a nightblade, but they didn't recognize her. They hadn't observed the exchange with Akane on the other side of the village.

Asa drew her sword and sprinted at the two, surprise her only advantage.

The warrior closer to her reacted too slowly, his movement slowed by confusion. Her steel opened up his thigh and sword arm in quick succession, sending blood spraying across the spotless room and the priceless woodworking.

His partner didn't have the same problem. She was fast, although not quite as fast as Asa. She was a taller woman with long arms, and her sword held Asa at bay as her mind tried to comprehend what had just happened.

Asa didn't have the time to wait for an opening. Every blade in the village would have sensed one of their own dying, the gift winking out like a candle in the dark. They would be drawn to the event, knowing someone was strong enough to kill one of their own.

Daiki stepped in and made a cut at the enemy blade. The tall woman deflected the strike without a problem, but the move left her in a vulnerable position. Asa stepped in, her short sword keeping the woman's longer one away just long enough for her to reach with a dagger and thrust it repeatedly into the woman's stomach. She collapsed, her insides threatening to spill out on the floor.

Asa felt sick bringing such violence to the house where she had found a temporary measure of peace. But there was no time. Already she could feel the flames of the other sense-gifted approaching the house.

As a complaint died on the older woman's lips, Asa grabbed Ayano and dragged her out of the house into the open. She used a precious moment to look around and confirm what she had sensed. The rout of the village had happened even more quickly than she had expected. The few survivors were being slaughtered in a small open space in the center of River's End. Most of the blades had turned their attention to the house, upset that two of their own had rejoined the Great Cycle.

Asa saw Akane and knew they were doomed. With a yell, Akane summoned the attention of all the blades and pointed at Asa. "Kill the betrayer!"

A savage shout came up from the assembled blades. Asa glanced back and saw that there was no one between them and the rest of the world. Unintentionally, the trio had broken through the advancing ring of blades. She stared at Daiki as she pushed the two of them away out into the fields that surrounded the village. "Run, now! There might be horses nearby."

Her two hosts were silent and still as statues, and Asa pushed even harder. None of them had time for indecision. "You need to leave! I'll try to hold them back for as long as I can."

The reality of their situation finally seemed to sink in, and both spun toward the open fields. Daiki turned around and looked at her once as they ran. She bowed low to him and whirled to face the incoming wave of blades, her death certain at the hands of those she'd once trained with.

Steel met steel, and the sound of battle rang throughout the village. Asa used her left hand to fling throwing knives, trying to deflect the wall of steel coming toward her. For one pass she held them off. Then for a second pass. On the third, her sword was knocked from her hands. She heard a commanding voice—Akane's. "Don't kill her but teach her, friends."

With that, Asa's life became a living nightmare. Flashes of steel cut into her. Once she lost her balance and fell, kicks rained down on her. She felt the blood pouring from her nose, and stars lit her vision as a toe caught her directly under the eye. At first she tried to get back up, tried to give Ayano and Daiki a few more moments, but a series of brutal kicks rendered her useless.

The blows subsided, but Asa couldn't move, couldn't open her eyes to see what was happening. She tried to push past the pain and focus on her sense, but her mind was too disjointed. Blinded in every way that mattered, Asa lay there, waiting helplessly to see what would happen next.

Asa was startled by a crunch of snow right in front of her. Two strong hands lifted her head up, causing unimaginable agony. Why couldn't they just let her die? Why torture her anymore?

Asa's arms were grabbed by two more people, and she was lifted off the ground. She wanted to kick out at whoever was holding her, but her body wouldn't respond to her commands.

The same strong hands that had first grabbed her head rubbed their thumbs against her eyes, removing freshly crusted blood. Asa found that she could open her eyes. When she did, she saw Akane looming over her, a triumphant grin on the commander's face.

Asa wanted to spit or scream or kick, but she was dead on her feet.

Akane leaned close. "I will kill you, young blade. Don't worry. But I want you to rejoin the Great Cycle understanding what is going to happen, not just here, but to the Kingdom. The blades are going to take their rightful place as rulers of this land. Those who fight against us will be taught lessons they will never forget. You will learn a lesson that will follow you in whatever future awaits you."

There was a commotion off to the side, and Ayano and Daiki were thrown down in front of her. Daiki was clutching his right arm, and Asa saw that his hand had been cut off at the wrist. Like her, he was dead, but his body just hadn't realized it yet. Ayano was covered in blood, but Asa couldn't tell how much of it was hers and how much was Daiki's.

A despair of a kind she had never known washed over her.

Akane looked at her. "I will give you a choice, young blade. You fought to protect these two, killing some of my warriors. But resistance against us is helpless. You can't fight the storm any more than you can fight what's coming to the Kingdom. Either you can kill them yourself, as quickly as you like, or you can watch them die, very slowly and painfully."

Asa felt as though all her emotions had been wrung from her, leaving only a deep sorrow, a sadness that had no bottom, no place to try to get up from. No right choice materialized, no action that wouldn't haunt her dreams in the future.

A glance at Daiki made the decision for her. He was a warrior who deserved a warrior's death. These blades would never give him one. Their eyes met, and an understanding passed between them. He actually smiled at her, bowing his head slightly in her direction.

She wasn't sure that she was strong enough to make the cuts.

"I will kill them."

Ayano spat into the ground, leaving yet another bloody streak in the snow. She didn't fully understand what was happening, and Asa didn't think she'd have the time to explain. That was regrettable but better than the alternative. Either way, Ayano would die hating her. Asa might as well show her what mercy she could.

Akane nodded at the two blades holding Asa, and they gently released her. She was still hemmed in by swords, and Asa knew there was no escape. Akane grabbed the short sword Asa had used against the blades from the snow and tossed it to her. Asa managed to grab the weapon in midair, although the effort took almost everything she had.

She shuffled slowly toward the couple who had opened their home to her, to the man who had opened his heart to her, a complete stranger. She moved as slowly as she could.

Akane called after her, "If you kill yourself instead, I'll still torture them, Asa."

Stopping a few steps away, she spoke softly, her voice barely carrying in the crisp morning air. "Do you care who is first?"

Daiki spoke, his voice strong. "Ayano, please."

Ayano looked at her husband with hate and fear in her eyes. "How could you?"

Tears fell down Daiki's face. "I don't want you to have to see me die."

Hate turned to compassion in a moment on Ayano's face. "Daiki." Her voice was full of love, the love that Asa had observed hidden beneath the bickering that happened every day.

Gently, Asa pushed down Ayano's head. For the first time since she had met the strong woman, Ayano was submissive, providing no resistance. Asa stood between the couple so that Daiki couldn't see what was about to happen.

Asa's cut was clean.

She turned to Daiki. Words seemed like dry leaves, too brittle to matter, but she had to say something. "I am sorry. I hope that someday, a long time from now, you meet your son again."

Daiki's teardrops froze in the snow. He bowed before her, exposing his neck. "Thank you, Asa."

Her cut was clean.

Chapter 9

Leaving camp had taken a fair amount of effort, but Mari thought the price was worth paying. For one, she was away from the daily life she found so taxing. She recognized that her power came through her network of shadows and her wealth, but all the same, she found those parts of her life the least interesting. Those were her duties, not her pleasures.

There were days when she longed for the simplicity of the life of a common woman. The cares of raising a child and maintaining a household, while no doubt difficult, often seemed preferable to the matters of state she involved herself in.

Regardless, she enjoyed the chance for fresh air. She had been cooped up in the inn they had secured as a command post for almost a moon, and the breeze, biting as it was, was still far preferable to the stuffy air of her room. Out here, the reports from her shadows couldn't reach her as they had in the inn, but the small sacrifice was necessary. Much better to be out here riding than analyzing the same news over and over.

Beside her rode Takahiro, who alternated between the joy of being out in the world and depression over his ward traveling with so little protection.

For Mari, the logistics of the journey had been easy to decide. Her palanquin, the method of travel Takahiro would have preferred her to take, would have drawn far too much attention. Her shadows had been clear in their messages: the Kingdom was ripping apart at the seams. If she displayed her wealth for all to see, she would be targeted instantly.

Riding a horse was still a clear indicator of resources, but it was a sight better than the palanquin. It was also much faster. Mari had argued that they should walk, and the horse had been their compromise.

As they left Haven and moved out along the roads to Starfall, Mari began to realize just how dire the situation in the Kingdom was. Each of the lords, her brother included, was so focused on conflict, they ignored the plight of the common people. With the impending war, more and more demands were made, and winter showed every sign of being one of the most difficult in memory. Prices for basic staples were several times higher than they had any right to be. Fields full of rice were dying in the freezing nights. The evidence was everywhere that thousands were at risk of dying during a harsh season.

Small, local militias with limited training and weapons were doing everything they could to keep the peace, but their efforts were insignificant.

In one village a farmer's cart had been overturned, citizens stealing their neighbor's food. Mari was tempted to judge them, but there was little point. If she was hungry and had a family to feed, she'd probably do the same. Regardless, if the lords didn't attempt to restore normal order soon, the task would be almost impossible.

The longer they rode, the more troubling scenes they encountered. A small group of bandits was scared away by Takahiro's sword and confidence. Families huddled along the side of the road, not sure where to go, begged for aid. At first, Mari wanted to stop, but soon the enormity of the mission dawned on her. If she wanted to save the greatest number of people, she needed to complete her task. As much as the act pained her, she passed by the people on the road, focusing instead on reaching Starfall as soon as possible.

Eventually Mari and Takahiro seemed to pass the worst of the troubles. The number of people on the side of the road diminished, and the fields became emptier. Mari understood. They were getting closer to Starfall, a city no one wanted to go near anymore.

She wondered how the blades would be reacting to this sudden change in their status. They certainly hadn't been without blame in the conflict among the lords. One of them had killed her brother, something she wasn't likely to forget anytime soon. But they had kept the order in the land for generations. Their absence from their usual duties was as much to blame for the chaos in the land as the lords' infighting.

Mari tried to remember the last time she had met Hajimi, the head of the Council of the Blades; it had to have been several cycles ago at the least. She hadn't spent much time with him, forced to rely instead on her impressions, which hadn't been positive. He had seemed to be a conniving man, a man she wouldn't want to trust.

Even though she wanted to keep pushing forward, Takahiro made her stop at an inn about a half-day's ride from Starfall. They were so close, but the night fell rapidly, and Takahiro didn't trust his ability to protect her in the dark. They had argued, but her guard had been adamant, and eventually Mari acquiesced. The idea of a bed was tempting, even if she didn't want to admit it.

The inn was almost empty. The brown wooden building was large, three floors tall, with plenty of rooms on every floor. Inside, the simple furnishings were well maintained, the tables wiped clean, the tatami floors spotless. Mari imagined that in other times, the inn would be bustling. The keeper tried to charge them an exorbitant amount, but Takahiro, using a combination of threats and more threats, managed to negotiate the price down to one that was almost reasonable.

Staying in an inn where it was just them and one other traveler got underneath Mari's skin. She was used to crowded places, the loud laughter of men who had too much to drink. Instead, she and Takahiro sat at one table in one corner, and the lone traveler, a man, took a table in the corner farthest from them. Mari and Takahiro spoke in whispers, as though afraid to disturb the silence that shrouded the building.

When Takahiro offered to pay the innkeeper for a drink, the man sat down and shared the news of the area with them. Unfortunately, it was no more than they expected. No one traveled to Starfall anymore. The expectation, unspoken unless one had too much to drink, was that the Kingdom would be invading the city soon.

The only people who had passed by were blades, and they tended to shun the inn. They preferred to stay out in the cold, where their sense would warn them of potential attack.

The two spoke with the innkeeper for a while longer before retiring to their rooms. The next day they would reach Starfall, and their real work would begin.

———

Mari had only been to the city once before, when she had been a young girl. Their father had taken the entire family on a trip there. Juro was at the age where he was obsessed with the stories of nightblades, and their father had thought it best for the future head of the house to observe reality instead of just relying on the legends. At the thought, Mari almost gave a sad laugh. Juro, more than any of them, had learned the bitter truths underlining the existence of the blades.

Starfall was a walled city, one of the few in the Kingdom. Mari studied the smooth stone walls carefully, admiring the handiwork involved in their creation. She had always been fascinated by masonry and the ability to fit stones together in such a way that they stood even when under attack. What most amazed Mari was that nothing held the rocks together. The big ones formed most of the wall, with smaller stones inserted between the larger ones to keep everything in place. The walls were sturdy, but not nearly so thick or tall as the walls that had surrounded Haven.

For what good that did the city, she reminded herself. Walls were a tool for blocking invaders. They did nothing when your world was crumbling from the inside out.

Their first challenge was gaining admittance to the city. Mari was no lord and, in truth, had no real standing or power. The older sister of a lord counted for next to nothing in the world. But she was rich. The mines in the mountains of her house's land provided most of the gold for the Kingdom, and not all the precious metal went into circulation.

Mari wished they lived in a world where money didn't matter as much as it did. But the blades had stopped receiving their payments from all three houses, and even a fraction of her wealth could go a long way toward convincing the blades to help. That, at least, was the best offer she had for Hajimi.

They came to the main gate, which was closed to traffic. When Mari and Takahiro rode up, they were the only two on the road. For the entire morning, Mari had felt like the Kingdom had already ended and everybody had perished. They hadn't seen a single person since leaving the inn.

The two nightblades who stood guard at the gate had a relaxed posture. Mari and Takahiro pulled up their horses a safe distance away and dismounted, walking until they were a few paces away. Mari studied the sentries.

For a moment, she was surprised. Both were women. Mari's experience with the blades was limited, and she'd forgotten how much power women were granted in the culture of the blades. She reminded herself that they all lived in the same Kingdom, but the blades moved in a very different world than her own.

"Who are you, and what do you want?" the woman on Mari's right asked. Although the two guards were of similar stature, the one on the right kept her hair cut very short, and the one on the left kept hers long, hanging down almost to her waist.

"My name is Mari. I'm a representative of House Kita." The lie was subtle. Her trip certainly hadn't been sanctioned by her house, but that was a problem for another day. "I've come to see Hajimi and the Council of the Blades, if I may."

The two women studied her, clearly dubious. They might live in a world that accepted them almost as equals, but they had traveled in the Kingdom enough to know that a female representative of a house was no true representative at all.

The short-haired nightblade replied, "Starfall is closed to guests at the moment. Please turn around and leave."

Mari had hoped entry would be easier, but she wasn't surprised. She turned to her horse and grabbed one of the bags from her saddle. She did her best not to struggle with the weight of the bag, not in front of these two warriors.

She opened the flap, showing the pile of gold inside. "I come bearing substantial gifts."

The two blades glanced at each other, uncertainty dancing across their faces. Mari wondered just how much authority the guards at the gate were given.

The short-haired warrior came to a decision. "Very well. News of your arrival will be brought to Hajimi. The council has been busy as of late, so it may take a few days to reply, but you may stay in Starfall until such time as a decision is reached."

Starfall operated differently than most cities, with no free trade in the area. Merchants were paid directly by the Council of the Blades, and goods were exchanged without gold inside the city walls. Mari didn't understand the entire system, but she knew that the city was structured around the blades being able to practice their skills to the exclusion of almost all else. They didn't need to worry about shelter, food, or any of the other necessities that made daily living a constant challenge.

For Mari and Takahiro, it meant they didn't have to pay for an inn. One was provided for them, the same inn Mari had stayed at so many cycles ago. She was fairly certain it was the only one for outsiders in Starfall.

Mari and Takahiro were escorted through the streets by the longer-haired nightblade. The other sentry had remained at the gate with a replacement. Mari's eyes wandered around the city, taking in the home of the blades with adult eyes for the first time.

Starfall had a certain stark beauty, but Mari imagined not everyone would agree. The blades, as a whole, gave little thought to aesthetics in construction. Most of the buildings the three passed were plain wooden structures, designed as temporary resting places for visiting blades. A few homes were for the permanent residents of Starfall, but even they were plain by the standards of the rest of the Kingdom.

Everyone could agree on the cleanliness of the city. As unadorned as the buildings were, they all sported paint that had been applied in the past cycle or two. Not a single piece of refuse could be found on the streets, and no injured or lame begged for money on the corners. Walking through Starfall was like walking through a plain but idyllic mirror image of a normal city.

Their escort seemed friendlier than the blade they had spoken to at the gate, so Mari used the opportunity to get more information. "How are things in Starfall? The streets are busy."

Mari was surprised by the number of blades in the city. On her last visit, the streets had been almost empty, but they now contained many people in both black and white robes. If the land surrounding Starfall was empty, it seemed as though that was because the city had sucked everyone nearby inside its walls. Like most people, Mari had only occasional glimpses of blades in her daily life. To see so many in one place was disconcerting. One forgot that even though the blades made up only a small fraction of the number of people in the Kingdom, thousands of them still existed. Their strength, if directed to any particular end, would be tremendous.

Their guide replied, "Yes. With all the uncertainty from Shin's proclamation and subsequent events, most blades have returned to Starfall. There's safety in numbers here. Also, if the council ever makes any decisions, most want to be present to help carry out those decisions."

Mari wasn't surprised so many blades would seek to return to Starfall. That was natural. She was interested to learn that the Council of the Blades hadn't come to any decision yet about what actions they would take in response to events in the Kingdom. Perhaps there was still hope for her mission.

"If you don't mind me asking, how are the blades reacting to everything happening in the Kingdom?" Mari saw that her question raised the woman's suspicions, and she immediately tried to defuse them. "Our lords are always focused so much on their own houses, no one ever stops to ask about how the blades feel."

The nightblade seemed uncertain, but eventually she answered. "It's tough to say. Many times, civilians like you think of the blades as one group that thinks the same way. But we're as different as you and just as divided. Many of us are depressed by recent events. We were happy to serve the Kingdom and did the best we could with our gifts. Most of us would be delighted if things could return to the way they were.

"There are plenty of others, though, who feel differently. Maintaining a warrior's mind-set can be difficult if you are born with the gift. It is easy to think you are somehow better than civilians. Even I fall into that trap on occasion." The woman's voice carried off as she was lost in thought.

Mari turned the woman's information over in her mind. Everything she was hearing confirmed what her shadows had relayed. She wondered if she was taking the right approach. The woman clearly believed in serving the Kingdom, so Mari pressed her a little harder.

"I am here to see if there is a way for us to work together toward peace. Do you think the council will hear me?"

The blade gave her a quick cynical smile. "With the amount of gold you flashed at the gate? Yes, the council will hear you. Whether they cooperate is another matter entirely."

"If I can convince the council to work together for peace, how will the blades respond?"

The question was one the nightblade hadn't considered before. They walked in silence for two blocks before she responded. "I would like to think that most would back the council. If I am being hopelessly optimistic, I would tell you that we'd all throw our strength behind you, but I'm not sure that's true. Just as the Kingdom is on the brink of civil war, the blades are as well. If we're going to survive, I fear we must purge our ranks."

The answer was far bolder and more insightful than Mari had expected.

They arrived at the inn. Mari bowed deeply to the guard. "Thank you, both for your escort and your thoughts. I will meditate deeply on what you have said."

———

As predicted, Mari received her invitation to the council, but it took several days. The time between her arrival and her invitation was filled with frustration and angst. Every day she and Takahiro waited, the situation in the Kingdom got worse. Every day, Mari knew that people were suffering and dying. She didn't know what could be more important for the council, and in her darker moments, she imagined them sitting and doing nothing, making her wait for the sheer joy of lording their authority.

When she wasn't in her room, pacing in frustration, she was going over her arguments again and again. She anticipated objections and rehearsed answers. If the council could be swayed by logic, she'd succeed. She had to be sure of that.

Eventually the summons came, and Mari went immediately to the council, forcing her nerves down. The way that Takahiro looked at her sometimes, as though she was a willfully foolish child he was exasperated with, made her feel like she was wrong in coming here. She felt like she should have returned to the palace and let the world go the way it would. But he believed in her enough not to voice his objections. He followed her to the chambers, giving his ward one last nod of encouragement before they went in.

When Mari was announced in the council chambers, her courage and commitment almost left her. She blamed the cycles of learning of the greatness of the blades. Their culture was filled with stories of heroism and sacrifice and amazing deeds. Even she struggled not to look at a blade and think of being in the presence of a living legend. Now she was here, in front of seven of their strongest and wisest. She had no place here.

But she did, she reminded herself. There were three women on the council. Even though her status didn't count for much in the Kingdom, she was still the sister of a lord and the owner of tremendous wealth. Her voice would be heard.

The hall of the council was filled with blades. The council sat in front of her, but the walls to each side were packed three deep with blades who had come to hear her speak. She hadn't considered that she'd have an audience. But she remembered her lessons. The council was generally open to all, and with the lack of outside contact as of late, her presence was likely one of the most interesting events happening in the city.

She bowed deeply, and the man she believed to be Hajimi spoke. Her memory of him was vague, dulled by the passage of time. He looked much older than she remembered, his hair gray and brown eyes restless. Perhaps he had just aged poorly. Perhaps the events of the past cycle had made him this way. Either way, he didn't look the part of the strong leader that Mari had expected.

"Greetings, Lady Mari. If my memory serves, we have met before."

"We have, Master Hajimi. I am pleased you remember."

"Thank you for your patience and for your efforts in coming before this council. What brings you before us today?"

Mari noted the shift in language. Traditionally, a person before the council was asked how the blades could serve them. Hajimi's language was an ominous start to the meeting.

She pressed forward. "I come to beg for your assistance in maintaining peace in the Kingdom."

Hajimi frowned. "There is little peace left to be kept, my lady."

113

"Making what remains far more precious than gold. The people of the Kingdom are suffering, and the lords do not see it. I am convinced the only way peace may be attained is through the intervention of the blades."

Mari's eyes traveled over the room to see what effect her words were having. There were several who seemed interested in what she had to say. Her shadows were fairly certain no other house had come before the blades since Shin's proclamations. If nothing else, Mari provided the only way for the blades to legitimately come back into the life of the Kingdom.

Hajimi ran his fingers through his long gray beard. "I agree that the people of the Kingdom are suffering, which pains this council greatly, but I am not sure I see how even our strength can stem the flow of events overrunning the land at the moment."

Mari had considered her offer carefully. At first, she had thought to bring the blades in as a neutral fourth party. Perhaps their strength could keep the houses at bay long enough for a peace to be negotiated. Yet the more she had considered the idea, the more she had rejected it. The blades were too divided to be useful in that capacity, and the risk they ran to themselves was too high. The three houses could use their combined might against the blades, destroying them completely.

"I understand how this offer sounds, but I come before you today to request you align with House Kita."

There was a collective intake of breath around the table. What Mari was proposing went against countless cycles of tradition.

Hajimi shook his head. "You know as well as anyone the blades cannot align with any of the great houses."

"If there were another way, you can be certain I would propose it. But there is no other way, and you yourself have set precedent. My information indicates that your liaison to the king, Minori, supported Shin in his rise to the throne."

Hajimi snapped, "A decision, not passed by this council, that has placed us in the situation we are in today!"

Mari eyed the leader of the blades. His outburst was the first real emotion she had seen from him today, and it confirmed what Juro's last letter to her had said. Perhaps the council hadn't explicitly backed Shin, but Hajimi had given Minori the freedom to do whatever he cared to. The council may not have been guilty, but they certainly weren't free from blame, either.

"The past is now behind us. There's nothing we can do to change what has already happened. I seek only to protect the future. Alone, the blades cannot effect the change needed in the Kingdom. It is too likely the houses would band together against them. However, with a house and the blades aligned, we have a chance of ending this civil war before it truly tears us apart."

A woman beside Hajimi spoke up. Her white robes indicated she was a dayblade. "*If* you are right"—Mari noticed the distinct emphasis in the question—"why should we align with House Kita?"

Mari bowed. "I know what you would expect me to say. I could talk about the riches of my house and how we could continue to support your people. I could talk about how we've given you this land to build your home on. Perhaps I could make an argument about how my house has the Kingdom's best interests at heart. These statements, I believe, are true. But all the same, I would rather you side with any house than remain neutral or stand alone. Better a peace under the rule of another house than war."

The blade who had asked the question gave Mari a bow herself. "I commend you for your honesty and your values. Such beliefs are rare in this age."

Mari felt a flush of pride but ignored it. This couldn't be about her.

Hajimi's next question made her wince. "I agree. Your ideals are rare and a jewel in these tough times. But would your brother agree? It seems unlikely that you are here on his command."

Mari grimaced. She knew the question was going to come up, and she had debated long and hard how to address it. Finally, she had decided to tell the truth. Blades didn't have any magical ability to detect lies, but they were trained to be more observant, and their gifts gave them the ability to better understand others. Besides, lying would only be more harmful in the long run. A successful mission based on deceit was built on shifting sand.

"I do not know what my brother would think. I have been excluded from his councils."

The statement had the effect she had dreaded. The council, which had been leaning forward in their chairs, interested in the discussion, suddenly leaned back, and their eyes wandered. Surrounding them, Mari could hear the whispered muttering of the gathered blades.

Mari cursed to herself. She couldn't lose the council. They had been interested.

"Masters! I realize how my plea must look, but you must take action. I am certain that if you approached my brother, he would see reason. The only wrong decision here is to do nothing. The Kingdom needs you now more than ever! At the very least, send out the day-blades in disguise to heal those who need their care."

The hall burst out in shouts, some in agreement, some in anger. Mari wasn't prepared to be assaulted by the uproar. Hajimi stood up, causing silence to descend almost instantly. When he spoke, his voice was hard.

"Lady Mari. Your character is obvious to this council. You have brought us a proposal, and we will consider it." He held up his hand for silence, Mari's words dying before they could leave her lips.

"You have my word on this matter. I do not say this to rid ourselves of you. This council will hear arguments on both sides, and we will summon you within the next day to inform you of our decision."

Mari knew she wasn't going to get any better than that. She got down on her knees before the council and bowed her head all the way to the floor. In all her life, she had only done so once before, on the day that Juro took over as head of their house. Someday soon, she would do so for Hiromi, but they hadn't yet had time to prepare a formal ceremony. She was still a lady of the Kingdom, and there were few who commanded such respect.

She held the pose for longer than she was comfortable with, and the entire room was silent, recognizing her display. She felt tremendously uncomfortable and exposed, but still she held the position.

Finally, she stood up, turned, and left the hall of the council, Takahiro falling in behind her. Hopefully her words and actions had been enough.

———

Mari was tempted to speculate endlessly on what the council's judgment was going to be. She ran over her plea time and time again, satisfied that she had done everything that was in her power to do. The day wore on as Mari wore a path across the floor of her room.

Takahiro had grown impatient with her pacing and left the inn. He'd received an invitation to join young nightblades in training and been itching to go since they'd first arrived. Mari had finally convinced him there was no place she was safer than in Starfall. By itself, the argument wouldn't have compelled him, but he needed space as well after the audience with the council.

As promised, Mari was summoned the next morning. Her escort gave her no indication of what the council's decision had been. The debate had been public until sundown, and then the council had retired to their private chambers to continue debating the matter. All her escort knew was that they hadn't left until the moon was high in the sky.

That, at least, was a positive sign. Mari was grateful that her proposal had started a discussion. Whether or not it had turned to her favor, she was less certain. All she could do now was hope.

The hall was even more crowded than yesterday. Blades were milling about outside, and inside the standing space was as packed as possible. Had the building chosen that moment to catch on fire, a healthy portion of the blades would have been wiped out.

Mari took her position in front of the council. Hajimi patiently waited for silence and then spoke.

"First, Lady Mari, I must again make clear that the council was impressed by your character. We have decreed that no matter what happens, we will always offer you sanctuary here. Our doors will always be open to you."

Mari's heart sank.

"This council has debated long and hard, my lady, but despite your heartfelt plea, we cannot do as you ask. The situation is too volatile, and the safety of our people must come first in our minds. As much as we are impressed with your character, without some guarantees from your brother, we fear that any action on our part will only deepen the problem that we currently find ourselves in. I know this is not what you wanted to hear, but we believe this is best for everyone."

The room exploded in an uproar that washed over Mari. Even guessing the worst was coming, she wasn't prepared. Hajimi had been her last hope.

A flicker of hate stirred deep in her gut, but it was quickly overwhelmed by despair.

A memory came unbidden to her mind, drowning out the angry shouts on both sides of Mari. She had been a child who had stolen one of Hiromi's toys after being beaten at a game. Hiromi had cheated to win, and Mari had thought to teach him a lesson.

Hiromi had told on her, of course, and the resulting argument led to them both being sent to their father, the most severe punishment available. The complete truth had come out, and they had both been sentenced to strict punishments by their father, whom they didn't dare disobey. But Hiromi had been dismissed from their father's side, and Mari had been told to stay. Mari didn't remember her punishment anymore, but she remembered, as clear as yesterday, what he had said.

"Mari, what Hiromi did was wrong. But what you did, in my mind, was even worse."

Mari had stopped crying long enough to ask why.

"It is easy to be nice to people when they are nice to you. But your quality is only truly displayed when others cheat you, betray you, and disappoint you. If you can act with honor in those moments, I will have done well as your father."

Mari swallowed her despair. If ever there was a moment to impress the blades, this was it. She took three determined steps forward, and the uproar in the room was cut off with the sharpness of a legendary sword. Hajimi looked at her, confusion in his eyes.

Mari's voice was stronger, stronger even than it had been presenting her case the day before.

"I understand your fear, even if it has led you down the path of cowardice."

Mari didn't need to be a blade to sense the barely unrestrained anger in the room. She delivered her final blow.

"Despite this, I came to your gates offering funds to support the blades. In honor of your past service to the Kingdom, I will leave all the wealth I carried here, except enough to bring me home again." Mari bowed deeply, turned, and left before Hajimi could respond.

The gesture would probably mean more to the blades than it meant to her. The gold she had brought was a small fraction of what she possessed, but it was still no small sum.

She walked quickly back to the inn, trying to hold back the tears that threatened to pour down her face. No one was willing to stand for the Kingdom. No one was willing to stand for anything besides themselves. Maybe the Kingdom deserved to implode for becoming too weak, lacking any heart.

At the inn, she immediately busied herself with a bottle of wine, quickly giving herself to the blissful, uncaring state of inebriation. She fell asleep in the early afternoon and didn't wake until the middle of the night. She heard Takahiro pacing the room next to hers and went over.

When she entered, the relief on his face was palpable. "My lady, I heard the news! I was worried for you."

She managed an unconvincing smile. Her head was pounding. "We've done all we could. We'll leave in the morning. How was your training?"

The shift caught her guard off-balance. "It was wonderful, but that hardly matters now. The entire city is talking of your actions in the hall of the council. Is it true that you gave away the gold we came with, even though they refused to help?"

Mari nodded. "Whether or not they realize it, the blades are the only hope for the Kingdom. The money will support them while the war rages on, but more importantly, the gift will hopefully remind them the Kingdom is still worth fighting for."

Takahiro looked as though something was bothering him, and after the silence had stretched out long enough, he spoke. "Mari, I'm afraid I've underestimated you. I didn't think coming here was a good idea, but you've made a name for yourself among these warriors in just a few days. My sword is yours, no matter what comes."

Mari bowed at her guard, a gesture of honor he wouldn't have expected. "Thank you, Takahiro."

The next morning dawned cloudy and gray, omens of another storm. Mari bitterly thought that if the blades wouldn't try to stop this war, at least the weather might try.

The two left their rooms, surprised when they came upon a group of blades waiting in the common space. The inn had been empty their entire stay, and even if the locale had guests, the visitors would be civilians, not blades. About a dozen of them, including four women, sat in the room. As Mari entered, they all stood and bowed.

A man who had probably seen about forty cycles stepped forward. "Greetings, my lady. I'm sorry to startle you, but my name is Jun." He gestured toward his robes. "As you can see, I'm a dayblade."

Mari returned the bow. "I'm pleased to meet you, Master Jun." She tried to figure out what was happening. Was she in danger?

Jun spoke softly. "I was among many who saw both your appearances in front of the council. To say we were impressed, well, wouldn't be saying enough. There are those of us who believe in the Kingdom, and we have decided you are worthy of our service. If you will accept us, we will join you on your journeys."

Mari needed a few moments to understand, but once she did, possibilities suddenly opened in front of her. She had been planning on returning to her ancestral castle at Stonekeep, to sit and wait for the war to end, if it ever would. Now she had options that came with risk. She had no doubt this help wasn't sanctioned by the council, and Shin's proclamation still made the blades criminals.

Her hesitation was momentary. The benefits far outweighed the risk. Also, she thought with a mischievous grin, Hajimi had declared she could return to Starfall for shelter. She suspected he had never predicted this.

"I would be grateful. Do you have the uniforms of our house? I fear that outside these walls, our options would be limited if your skills were obvious."

Jun nodded. "We anticipated the request and are prepared to leave whenever you are."

Despite the failure in front of the council, Mari grinned.

Chapter 10

Koji stumbled in the late afternoon sunlight, catching himself on his hands, which immediately reminded him that snow was cold and he wasn't prepared for the weather. He could never remember being this tired, this sore. He had run since leaving the farmhouse, realizing too late that he should have paced himself better.

The last time he had run for a distance was cycles ago, when he was training as a nightblade. Although his strength was excellent, he had lost the skill of distance running. Still, he pushed on, moving as fast as his weary legs would carry him.

He passed several other farms on his journey. All had been devoid of life. Although Koji didn't check, he was certain what he would find if he did. Corpses, brutally murdered as they had been at the first farm he had checked. The actions of his fellow blades drove him. They couldn't be allowed to have a village.

Koji sensed River's End before he saw it, telling him that he was too late. There were too many present with the gift.

Koji collapsed to his knees. He was so tired, but there was nothing to be done. Too late, he saw the smoke rising from River's End, and although he couldn't see what was burning, he was certain it was the corpses of the villagers.

As his knees froze in the shallow snow, Koji wrestled with his anger. He wanted to attack, but the idea was beyond foolish. Perfectly rested, he would still be slain by such a force of blades. As he was, he would be just as successful if he fell on his own sword.

In the distance, two shapes crested the hill. Koji cursed. In his exhaustion, he had forgotten that if he could sense them, they likely could sense him as well. So much for the element of surprise. He thought about drawing his sword, but then thought better of it. His arm would barely respond to his commands.

The two shapes solidified, and he heard one of them yell his name. Of course, he thought, they remember me from their meeting.

Koji attempted to stand to greet them, but his legs gave out from under him and he collapsed, his last vision of the white snow fading to black.

———

When Koji came to, he was warm, and his bed was soft. He awoke slowly, looking over at the fire that kept the cold at bay. As his awareness returned, he sensed another with him, and he turned his head to see Akane's concerned face.

"We were worried about you, Koji. When you, Ryo, and Hiroki didn't meet at the gathering point, we feared the worst but couldn't delay our attack. Our scouts brought you in, but we couldn't figure out why you had passed out. The dayblades' best guess was that it was a case of exhaustion, pure and simple."

Koji tried to sit up, both to see how he felt and to give himself time to think. The truth would get him killed, but lies were slow in coming.

Fortunately, Akane's concern overwhelmed any suspicions she might have held. She leaned over and put her hand on his shoulder. "Rest, please. There's no hurry now. You're safe among friends."

Her words had an unintended effect, spurring his imagination to a story.

"I needed to hurry. As we left the farmhouse, we were ambushed by two nightblades. They were strong, and in the ensuing battle, they killed Ryo and Hiroki. I killed them, but I feared they were part of a larger party. I sought a horse, but none were nearby. I ran as fast as I could to come and warn you of the possible danger."

To his relief, Akane nodded as though his story was perfectly reasonable. "As always, Koji, you are an inspiration to us. That was no small journey you undertook. I had hoped for more time, but the council has shadows everywhere. No doubt they hope to stop our movement before our ideas can spread like wildfire. I will prepare our blades and double the number of our scouts. We will not be caught by surprise!"

After making sure Koji was cared for, Akane went about her work, and he realized just how misguided she was. She saw conspiracies where there were none, and in her mind, he could do no wrong because he had killed a king. Koji was sickened by all the blades, but none so much as her.

Not long after, he fell back asleep. Koji was exhausted, and he knew that even if his story was doubted, someone would need at least a full day of riding to get to the farmhouse and back. He had the time to rest, and the soft lapping sounds of the river against the bank outside his house soothed him to sleep.

When he came to again, he was able to take his feet with ease. He stretched his body out, pleased that everything seemed to be in order. His muscles were still sore from the demands he had placed on them, but they reacted with their usual speed. If he needed to fight, he would be at his full strength.

Hearing Koji was awake, Akane came to give him a tour of River's End. She showed him a well-equipped woodshed, a stable for their horses, and the river access that gave the village its name. But the highlight of the tour was the center of the village. A post had been buried in the ground, and tied tightly to it was Asa.

Akane saw Koji's flash of recognition. "You've seen this nightblade before?"

He nodded. "Yes. She tried to kill me twice." The statement was true, even if it didn't tell the whole story. But Koji was learning about Akane, and his statement confirmed everything she already believed.

"I'm not surprised. She's a foolish one. She fought against us all in an effort to protect the villagers. As punishment, I made her kill the two she had tried to help escape. She's been out here all day, and I expect she'll die from exposure soon enough." The pride was evident in her voice.

Asa reacted to the conversation about her, and her eyes met Koji's. Koji saw the hate and resignation and hoped desperately that Asa wouldn't say anything foolish. As it was, he'd never had more respect for her than he did now. They had been on opposite sides of a battle, and now Koji realized he might have been on the wrong side. She was a blade who acted with honor.

Koji resisted the urge to cut down Akane. He needed to know more about the layout of the village and where the blades were stationed. But his new path was clear. As Akane turned around to continue the tour, Koji gave Asa an almost imperceptible nod.

He studied Asa, both with his sense and with his vision. Her scalp had several cuts that had bled down her face, and one eye looked as though it had swollen shut. He saw she had been cut deeply at least twice. The blood had clotted, but who knew what damage was beneath the surface? His sense told him that her energy was strong considering all she had been through, but he could also feel it waning. She had some time, but not much.

He kept his face neutral through the rest of the tour, nodding appreciatively when he thought the gesture was expected of him. While his face was steady, his mind was working through the escape. Akane was a decent commander. The patrols around the village were consistent, and Koji knew that the gifts of those patrols overlapped, casting an impenetrable net over the village. As soon as he acted, the alarm would be raised.

Too many blades were present for him to fight alone. He was good, but he wasn't sure anyone was that good. From experience, he knew patience would be rewarded, so he allowed his mind to continue working on the problem.

Koji waited until most of the blades were asleep before he wandered from the home he had been given. The patrols were still out, but Koji paid them no mind. They were a problem for later. First, he went to the stables and saddled a horse with supplies. It would be ready for him when he returned for it. Others would sense him. So long as the blades didn't act right away, he should be fine. He didn't need much time.

As Koji approached the center of the village, he noticed that a few people were still awake and following him closely with their sense. Koji ignored them. He expected Akane to be suspicious. If she acted before he could, he would deal with her.

Extending his sense, Koji felt Asa's energy, weaker than earlier today but still strong. That was good. If she didn't have the strength, he wasn't sure escape was possible.

He walked straight to her. In a village where everyone could sense your moves, there was no point in delaying.

Her good eye opened as he approached. He wasn't sure if she'd gotten his reassurance earlier, so he wasn't sure how she'd react. He was fortunate. Her whisper was hoarse. No doubt she hadn't been given water. "I thought you were with them."

Koji didn't bother replying. His actions were answer enough. He could sense the blades coming behind him, but he could ignore them for a few more moments. "Can you stand? Can you escape?"

Her eye narrowed in anger, which Koji took to be an affirmation. "Let's go, then. Start working your way toward the stables." He drew his sword and cut her bonds. She fell to her knees, and for a moment, Koji wasn't sure she'd be able to move. But slowly, she stood up.

"What are you doing?"

The voice came from behind, and Koji recognized it as Akane's. He turned around, eager for the chance to fight. Diplomacy and subtlety were not his ways. He excelled with a sword, and it was time to remain true to that.

"I'm leaving."

Akane laughed. She had only brought two other blades with her, and all had their steel drawn. Already the village was stirring, and if he and Asa were to have any hope of escape, they needed to leave now.

Akane began to lecture him. "If you think you can leave . . ."

Koji didn't let her finish the thought.

He darted toward the blade farthest to his right. The blade reacted, but too slowly. Koji swung with strength, backed up by the full power of his short sprint. His opponent managed to get his blade up to defend, but Koji's swing knocked the other warrior's sword far off-center. Koji followed with a stab, piercing the heart of the nightblade.

Akane had already turned her sword to face Koji. They passed twice, but Koji's speed was far superior to her own. Koji sliced cleanly through her neck and moved on to the final blade. The duel was almost too easy. He dodged the first cut, but the blade didn't dodge Koji's.

Asa pointed to a pile of weapons not far away. "Would you grab my weapons?"

Koji did, then half supported, half carried Asa to the stables. Shouts rose behind him, but Koji was relying on a few moments of confusion. Killing Akane had been a bonus. If Ryo had been her second, that meant he had killed most of the rebel blades' leadership.

The two mounted the horse, Asa grunting with the effort. Koji was worried about her. He was fairly certain they would escape the village, but she was weaker than he had surmised. No matter. The only way was forward. Koji cut the ropes holding the others' horses in place and screamed as loudly as he could. The animals were spooked, and Koji and Asa rode out in the midst of a small stampede.

As soon as they could, Koji turned away from the village and in the direction of Starfall. The seat of the blades seemed their best option.

The council needed to know what was happening and take action to stop the rogue blades.

One of the patrolling blades tried to catch them, but Koji kicked his boots into the horse's side and pulled easily away. They rode into the night, Koji enjoying the feel of the wind in his face, his boiling blood cooled.

Not long after their escape, Koji sensed life behind him. Two blades were in pursuit, their horses gaining on his own. No surprise. His horse had to carry two. Confident they were far enough away from the village not to be interrupted, Koji brought the horse to a stop and dismounted. He was a decent sword mounted but didn't dare risk their horse.

The pursuing blades never paused. They attempted to ride Koji down, one on each side of him. Koji smiled, his memories of training coming back to him. He and his fellow students had even practiced this exact scenario. He had been the only one who "survived."

As the riders approached, Koji ran at them, hoping that he could throw off their timing. At the perfect moment, Koji cut to his left. To the rider, it must have looked as though Koji had stepped right in front of her horse.

Koji just managed to avoid the charging beast, feeling the reverberations of the hooves in his feet, the snort of air that blew at his hair. His sword flashed, slicing deep into the thigh of the rider, a lethal cut if given enough time.

The rider turned, but Koji knew the battle was over for the blade. Without saying anything, the woman kicked the horse with her good leg and rode back toward the village, no doubt hoping she would make it to a dayblade before she lost too much blood. Koji didn't rank her chances high.

The second rider had turned and dismounted. A fire blazed in his eyes, and Koji assumed the blade thought he was better off a horse than on. Koji sympathized. He felt the same way.

The exchange was over in two passes, and Koji was cleaning his sword.

He extended his sense, trying to feel if there was any more pursuit heading their way. It didn't seem so. Between the confusion and the defeat of the pursuers, he imagined he and Asa had an open road ahead of them. If not, his steel was still sharp.

———

Koji's worry was on the edge of becoming panic. Asa was fading quickly. He was no dayblade, but he assumed that her internal injuries were even worse than her external ones. He could do nothing but ride faster.

As evening turned to morning, a storm came upon them with unexpected ferocity. Koji fought off the biting cold as well as he could, but he was losing a battle as well. Asa had been unconscious for most of the night, and Koji had tied a rope around both of them so she wouldn't fall off the horse.

If the weather hadn't been so dangerous, Koji might have found it beautiful. He imagined watching the storm from the shelter of a house, a fire warming the inside. Flakes dashed against his face, tiny freezing pinpricks that gradually sucked the feeling from his skin. He had covered as much of himself as possible, but it wasn't nearly enough.

The road markers were his only guide. He would find one pile of stones and then desperately seek the next one. Marker by marker, the two made their way toward Starfall. The going was slow, and Koji was becoming more certain they wouldn't make it.

His options were terrible. He could leave Asa behind as she was already dying. Better one of them survive than neither. But his spirit rebelled against the idea. He had risked his life to save hers. He wasn't going to give up simply because the task became more difficult. Killing the horse could potentially give them shelter, but that was

Koji's last option. Once they went down that path, he was certain they would have to wait for rescue, and the road to Starfall didn't seem too crowded.

More than that, Koji couldn't allow himself to fail. Not with Asa's life at stake.

Her presence brought back memories of their duel, in particular the day Koji had killed Juro.

Asa had known there was no way for her to win that fight, but she had fought anyway. Knowing what had resulted from his actions, he knew she had been in the right that day.

He had wronged her then. But not today. Koji refused to fail her.

Koji pushed forward, desperate to find shelter.

When he saw the lights off in the distance, he thought he was imagining safety. Who else was on the road to Starfall, trapped in this storm? He rode toward the lights, hoping there might be shelter and help available.

He came upon a well-provisioned camp, with a large, sturdy tent built up against the wind. Even more surprising, Koji's sense informed him that the tent was filled mostly with blades, with two civilians inside. After his most recent experiences, he was wary, but he and Asa needed shelter and aid. Beggars could hardly afford to be choosy.

Koji reined the horse to a halt on the outskirts of the camp. He gently untied Asa from him and the mount, then began the complicated process of getting her off. He leaned her body forward, hoping she would remain balanced long enough for him to dismount.

He half slid, half fell to the ground, his feet shooting needles of pain up through his legs as they recovered from disuse. Asa, fortunately, remained on top of the horse. He pulled her down and caught her. She seemed too light.

The two were greeted outside the tent by a pair of nightblades who had doubtlessly sensed their arrival. They gave Koji a shallow bow when he stopped short of them, shallower than would be expected of blades meeting on the road.

The two blades looked relaxed, but their hands rested near their swords. Despite their advantage in numbers, they were nervous. Given everything happening in the Kingdom, Koji understood.

"She needs help," Koji said, his voice cracking from disuse.

They glanced at each other and nodded, pulling back the door of the tent so he could bring her inside.

The inside of the tent was plain, with several sleeping pads laid out and a small table currently used for a small game of strategy between a dayblade and one of the two civilians, a man clearly in the military. Despite the simplicity of the tent, its warmth immediately brought hope and new energy to Koji.

Koji was surprised when the civilian woman approached him. "Greetings, stranger. My name is Mari. What brings you on this road?"

Koji thought her wording unusual, but his mind caught up quickly. She hadn't offered aid but instead asked his purpose. The dayblade and the civilian were still playing chess, while all other eyes were on him and Asa. Several of the nightblades were ready to draw on him if Mari gave the word. They were nervous, too, and under the command of a civilian woman. Who was she?

He offered as much of the truth as he thought was wise. "We were attacked by nightblades. I killed them, but my friend was beaten. We were on our way to Starfall to seek healing." Koji glanced around the room again and took another risk. "We were going to inform the council that there are rogue blades taking over villages."

The tension in the room eased considerably, and Koji knew his guess had been right. These were loyalists, dedicated to the Kingdom. First, Koji felt a weight come off his shoulders. Just to know he wasn't alone was a relief greater than he'd imagined. Second, he wondered why this group, if they were loyalists, were so nervous.

The woman seemed to understand his thoughts. "I'm afraid you'll find no help in Starfall, friend. News of the rogue blades has already reached them, but Hajimi gathers the blades within their walls to protect them. He will not act."

The simple statement hit Koji hard, a punch that knocked the air out of him. "The blades refuse to help the Kingdom?"

Mari nodded, sympathy in her eyes. "Most, but some, like these before you, have committed to saving the Kingdom however they may."

He breathed deeply, trying to center himself. The world was worse than he thought, but there was still hope. Some still fought.

Koji's confusion had been so great he had momentarily forgotten about Asa. Feeling guilty, he looked around the room. Two dayblades were present. "Please, masters, will you help save my friend?"

An uncomfortable silence settled upon the space. The dayblade who had been playing chess looked up and spoke to Mari. "It could very well be a trap, my lady, a distraction to seep the energy away from our healers."

Mari seemed to be contemplating the same thing. Koji thought that whatever had happened in Starfall, it had made this group exceptionally suspicious.

Mari's answer was quick. "Perhaps, but if we start refusing aid, we are doing no one any good. Are you able to heal this woman, Jun?"

The dayblade stood up and walked toward Asa, putting his hand on her chest. He closed his eyes and was silent for a few moments. When he opened them again, urgency filled his voice. "It is worse than I thought. I believe I can, although her injuries are severe. The healing *will* drain me."

The decision was clearly Mari's to make, but Koji couldn't think of anything to say to persuade her.

"Do it."

As soon as Asa was gently taken from him, Koji bowed down deeply to Mari. "Thank you very much; we are in your debt."

She waved away the gratitude. "Save your thanks until your friend is better. Until then, we have food and warmth to provide. Will you join us?"

Chapter 11

Asa dreamed.

At least, her awareness felt like a dream, but it was also as real as anything she'd ever done.

She wandered the space that hovered between waking and sleeping, not sure what was true and what was not. She heard voices and laughter, but all she saw was Koji, his concerned face close to hers.

Her less lucid moments were filled with blood-soaked memories. The people she had failed to protect, from the day she had learned her father had died to today. The lives of so many were on her hands.

Asa had fought Koji before in the streets of Haven. Then again with Juro in the fields. Both times she had been defeated, but both times, she had thought the battle was close.

Then she saw him fight the three nightblades in River's End.

He was so fast and so strong. Had that been a dream as well? The pain felt real, but the situation hadn't.

Asa wasn't nearly as deadly as Koji. She wasn't nearly as strong or as fast. Every time they'd dueled, he'd played with her, but that didn't make her angry. She was glad he had spared her.

When she came to, she was in a world entirely different than the one she had been in before. She wasn't cold or tied to a post. She didn't have to watch as bodies were carried away and burned. Instead, she was in a warm tent, the soft sounds of voices in the background. She tried to move, but a gentle yet firm hand held her down. Tracing the line of the arm, she saw it belonged to Koji, his face worried.

"Jun says you should rest. You aren't strong enough yet to be up and moving around. You'll be fine, though. He healed you."

Asa figured the questions could come later. For now, she was simply grateful to be awake and alive, and that surprised her. She had thought she was ready to die, that there was nothing left to live for.

The pain of what had happened hit her again. She doubled over, tears pouring down her face. She hadn't been able to save them. How could she live with herself knowing what had happened?

An arm wrapped itself around her quivering shoulders, and she slid comfortably into Koji's embrace. They didn't say anything but just sat there, Koji letting Asa cry about what had happened.

Eventually the tears subsided, but she needed to tell her story. Someone else needed to know what had happened, needed to know how she felt. In hushed whispers so as not to disturb the rest of the tent, she told her story, from seeing Koji assassinate Shin to finding a place where she felt welcome. She forced the story out, pushing the words away as though they were poison.

When she was done, she cried again until she felt empty. She fell asleep in Koji's arms.

When she awoke again, the tent was the controlled chaos of a camp being taken down. The blades moved with a quick and silent efficiency, packing gear with the ease of those who had performed the task hundreds of times. Koji told her a storm had passed and they were on the move again. Lacking any better plans, Koji had volunteered them to accompany the party. Asa didn't mind. She had asked about Starfall, but Koji shook his head. There was no help to be found there.

She was given a horse and warm clothes, and she was already feeling much better. The party moved at a walking pace, in no rush to get anywhere. Asa and Koji remained near the rear of the small column.

Up front, the woman named Mari argued with Jun, the dayblade. He had to be a man of no small talents to have revived Asa.

She thought they looked like a motley group. Most wore the blue attire of House Kita, but the uniforms fit poorly if one looked closely enough. They huddled deep in their uniforms against the cold. Some forces even a blade couldn't overcome.

They started a fire that night, and Mari came and sat down next to Asa. The blade bowed to the lady. "Koji tells me you are the one who made the decision to save me. Thank you very much."

"You're welcome. How do you feel?"

"Not quite whole yet, but better."

Mari paused, then asked another question. "Do you stand for the Kingdom or against it?"

Asa scoffed, the query feeling absurd to her. After all she had been through, she didn't care at all for politics. Mari looked hurt, and Asa was reminded of something Kiyoshi had once told her. At the time, she had thought his statement a pleasant and naive ideal. Now, though, she wondered if it might be the wisest thing she'd heard.

"I don't care one way or another about the Kingdom." Mari looked upset, and Asa rushed to finish her point. "The Kingdom is only useful so long as it protects the people it rules. If it does, then yes, I'll support the Kingdom. Otherwise, may it rot in pieces. All that matters is that people can be safe and live their lives as best they can."

Mari sat there silently, speaking only after she'd carefully considered Asa's words. "Thank you, Asa. I'd never thought of the matter quite that way. I, too, think about the people, but I've always thought the only way to keep them safe was by maintaining the stability of the Kingdom. Perhaps that's not the only way." Her voice was thoughtful.

Despite not knowing Mari well, Asa liked her. She was direct, and her inner strength was apparent. Koji had explained how Mari had earned the service of the blades who surrounded them, and Asa could now see why. She wasn't sure she was ready to take anyone's orders yet, but if she were, Mari seemed as good a choice as any other.

———

The most obvious challenge facing the small group was that Mari was clearly directionless. One morning matters came to a head, and they didn't even tear down camp, staying in one place until they decided on a clear course of action. Mari had been heading back toward her brother, but Jun had asked her several times to rethink that decision, and finally Mari acquiesced.

Asa collected bits and pieces of information from the assembled blades. Mari had come to Starfall to seek an alliance. The request was far outside the bounds of tradition, but the Kingdom was in a precarious position, and Mari had made a strong case. Although she had been rejected, it seemed that when the small group had coalesced around her, she reverted to her original plan, thinking to go to Hiromi with the blades.

Asa saw Jun's point of view clearly. She had already watched a similar story play out, and she knew how the tale ended. A small group of blades joining a lord without the blessing of the council? Such an action would both infuriate and inspire the other lords, who would also seek to recruit blades to their cause. Asa had little doubt such attempts were already under way. Mari's return to her brother would add legitimacy to these actions, and all would be lost. Either the council aligned with a single lord or none at all. Any path between those options would spell the certain doom of the Kingdom.

Mari had been stubborn, but she eventually heard the blades out. Her willingness to change her mind was testament to her character, but they were left with the problem of what to do. Koji suggested an answer that sparked debate.

"We could return to River's End and destroy the rogue blades before they gather more to their cause."

The blades loved Koji's suggestion. Word of what had happened at River's End had spread throughout the party, and the hatred they all felt for those blades and their actions burned as hot as the sun. Koji's suggestion was direct and decisive, characteristics the blades appreciated.

Mari, although she shared a portion of the blades' anger, was more reasonable. She pointed out that her party was outnumbered by the rogue blades. Failure, or anything less than an amazing success, would end whatever they decided to accomplish.

Koji, however, was persuasive. He was willing to take most of the risk on his own shoulders. He would be the point of the spear. His voice was strong and confident, and he outlined a plan for attack that almost had the blades running for their horses. Even Asa admitted the plan was bold. Everything would depend on Koji, but the young blade seemed eager for the challenge. Having seen the full extent of his skill, Asa was less worried than some of the others. Koji was the best nightblade she had ever seen.

Eventually Mari capitulated. She did so with disappointment written on her features but also with a measure of grace.

River's End was less than a half-day's ride away, so the decision was made to launch the attack early in the morning. They decided to pack up camp and move closer to the river. Several blades, led by Koji, went to find a boat for the attack.

That evening the group sat around the fire, eating and telling stories. Asa had never been part of a larger group of blades. She'd traveled with her master at times, but her need for revenge had always set her apart. She was used to traveling alone, the wide-open spaces and narrow city alleys hers and hers alone.

Her mind buzzed with thoughts, moving from one to the other like a bee among flowers. She couldn't forget or push aside the memories of her actions in River's End. She had acted rightly, but no amount of bathing would wash away her guilt. Revenge was forefront in her mind, but from experience she knew even that wouldn't end the anger and disgust she felt. She wondered if anything could.

There was a comfort, though, in being among companions. For one, she didn't have to hide who or what she was. Traveling alone, she had often traveled incognito. She didn't like the stares and attention she received when she wore her black robes, so more often than not her weapons were hidden and robes packed away.

The other blades weren't wearing their robes today, either. They had shed the blue uniforms of House Kita and replaced them with regular traveling clothes. For what they were about to do, they didn't want anyone making connections back to Mari. As Asa looked around, she saw the companions were well provided for, so long as they weren't forced to fit into borrowed uniforms. With so much time spent on the road, blades valued gear that would last. Their personal robes and coats were thick. Most wore leather boots, but three or four of the hardiest, Mari included, wore only raised sandals.

The stories ranged from the mundane to the mystical, from the everyday to the epic. Some of the stories rang of truth. Others might not have happened but contained a moral all the same. Asa's mind and body slowly relaxed, and she was surprised to find that she was enjoying herself.

Jun told a story that was a variation on one of Asa's favorites.

"Long ago there was a nightblade who had settled in a small village. He married a beautiful woman he fell in love with and tried his hand as a farmer growing rice."

Asa let out a small smile. In legends, blades and civilians intermingled freely. She had never known such a time, but more than once, when she had been younger, she had longed for it. Today such things never happened. Well, almost, she thought, the memory of one unique man coming to her.

Jun continued. "The blade was nothing special as a farmer. The crops grew, but the family did not prosper. Likewise, with his attention divided, his swordsmanship also did not improve.

"One day he came upon a white fox whose leg appeared to be broken. The blade, who had a kind heart, offered to bring the fox to a nearby dayblade for healing.

"As soon as he offered, the fox stood up and walked, and the man saw that the fox had five tails.

"The fox said, 'For your kindness I will bring about all that you desire.'

"The cycles passed, and the fox's promise came true. The rice in the field multiplied, the man had three strong children, and students came from across the Kingdom to study the sword under the famous master.

"Much time passed, until one day the man came across a cat injured in the road. Now the man had no time for such distractions. He hurried on, only to be stopped by a voice behind him. He turned and saw a white five-tailed fox where the cat had once been."

Jun's voice deepened as he imitated the fox. "'For a kindness long ago, I have protected and guided your fields and your hands. For your ignorance, I shall withdraw my magic.'

"The blade tried to make amends, but it was too late. As was foretold, his crops were eaten by locusts, his children weakened and were on the verge of death, and rumors spread that he wasn't able to block a single cut with his sword.

"Several moons later, the man heard the wailing of an injured cat outside his house. The night was late, and the man was bitter, and he thought at first of throwing a stone at the feline to get it to leave. But when he saw the cat with the broken leg, he thought of his own children, weakened, and bent down to care for it.

"As he did, his eyes were opened, and he saw he held the five-tailed fox in his arms.

"'You will always receive that which you put out into the world,' the fox said as he disappeared from sight.

"The blade wasn't sure what the next day would bring, but he went to bed that night contented."

Mari came over and sat next to Asa. The lady was clearly distraught, but Asa was in too good a mood to try to pry the reason out of her. She was enjoying the story. Jun told the tale differently than she had heard before, but the heart of the fable was the same. As soon as Jun finished, with the blade returned to his former glory, his lesson forever learned, she turned to the lady of House Kita. "Does something trouble you, Lady Mari?"

"Asa, you've seen terrible things happen, right?" Mari asked.

Asa flinched from the memory of her sword flashing down twice. "Yes."

"I've never ordered people to kill one another. The thought is troubling to me."

Asa studied the lady, the younger sister of a man she'd watched die. The fact that Koji had killed her brother hadn't come up yet. Asa figured he would tell her when and if he was ready. Mari was strong, there was no doubt of that, but she hadn't been raised as a warrior.

"Death is a part of life."

"True, but that doesn't mean I need to command it. Who am I to have such power over the course of a person's life, to determine when it should end? The blades at River's End have done wrong, but who am I to judge their punishment?"

The lady looked like she was going to continue. Asa guessed these thoughts had been running through her mind since the decision had been made to assault the village.

"Who are you not to do whatever is necessary to save your people?"

The answer shocked Mari into temporary silence.

"What do you mean?"

"I will not pretend to understand what it means to live the life of nobility. But life is about balance, and to those who have been given much, much should be required. You were born with a responsibility to your people. If you do nothing, these blades will be a threat beyond comprehension. Thus your path is clear."

"But must it require violence?"

"Maybe not, but I can think of no other way. Can you?"

Mari shook her head, a deep sorrow on her face.

"Do not think in terms of right and wrong. You will drive yourself mad, and none of us know how the Great Cycle moves through our lives. Ask instead if you are doing the best you can and be satisfied with nothing less."

Mari gave Asa a slight bow. She said nothing in return, but Asa could see her turning ideas over in her head.

Asa wasn't much interested in Mari's plight. She was eager for the morning sun and the chance to bring justice to those who had killed Daiki and Ayano.

———

Asa couldn't recall the last time she had been on a boat. Cycles ago she had taken one from the Northern Sea upstream for several days. The travel hadn't been particularly quick, but she had some time between assignments, and the captain had promised a relaxing journey. The journey had been pleasant, filled with breezy sunny days and calm currents, but Asa had decided there was little special about riding on the water.

Nothing today changed her mind. The blades had found a decent rowboat for their assault, just barely large enough for the entire group. They were all there except for Koji. Mari sat in the back, protected by the blades and Takahiro. Together they sat, cramped and eager to fight, if for no better reason than to get off the boat and be able to stretch their limbs.

Mari's presence had been argued, but she had won easily. The lady of House Kita argued that she would not become a leader who sent others to fight where she wouldn't go. If they were going on her command, she would share the risk. The look in her eyes and the tone of her voice made it immediately clear she'd accept no arguments, but Asa was still surprised when the blades capitulated. Takahiro had promised he would remain close by, guarding her in the conflict.

The boat traveled downstream toward River's End, the current carrying them along. The river was hardly swift but moved fast enough so that the snow and ice covering the earth couldn't quite get a foothold. The only noises heard were the soft creak of the boat and the muted sound of the tiller gently directing the water behind them.

Asa had volunteered to travel with Koji on his part of the mission, but he had wanted to go alone. None of the blades were sure of the wisdom of the decision, but Koji's unshakable confidence eventually convinced them. Even with his skill, Asa wasn't sure how he would triumph if too many blades reached him at once, but he had been insistent, and after her rescue, she wondered if her presence would just hold him back.

Asa's doubts and worries dissolved as they approached the village. She extended her sense, easily able to sense the blades inside River's End. She couldn't be sure at this distance, but fewer blades seemed to be present than she remembered. Perhaps not more than a dozen. If true, Mari's forces were barely outnumbered.

Asa sensed the light of the gift die out beyond the borders of the village. For those with the sense, others with the gift felt like bright pinpoints of light. When one who was sense-gifted died, it was as though the world got just a little darker each time. The world dimmed again. It could only mean that Koji, approaching River's End from the land, had killed a patrolling pair. Asa was surprised the deaths had come so close together.

When Asa and her companions turned the corner of the river and River's End came into view for the first time, they saw a village in confusion. Blades ran back and forth, disorganized as a group could be. As Asa watched, one group of blades rushed forward to defend the docks but then ran away toward Koji's line of movement. No one seemed to be in charge of organizing the defenses.

Asa shook her head in amazement. It had only been a few days since Koji had killed Akane and rescued her. In that time, the entire collection of blades seemed to have fallen apart without a strong hand to guide them. Had their discipline been so lax to begin with?

Jun decided they should ground just outside the village. They could land at the docks, but Jun didn't want to give the defenders a natural choke point.

They grounded the boat on an uncontested section of land a few hundred paces from the outskirts of River's End. Mari commanded eleven blades. With herself, Asa, and Takahiro, that made fourteen people total.

In preparing for the battle, they had decided to shed tradition. The idea had been Jun's. Despite being a dayblade, he had been a part of enough skirmishes to have a solid grasp on basic battlefield strategy. Asa had been dubious, but Jun had the most experience in battles. The others had followed and contributed what expertise they could.

Blades most often fought in pairs, but Jun had organized them in groups of four. Takahiro and Mari made their own two-person group, protected by the other three squads. Asa hadn't been sure how she felt about the idea, especially coming from a dayblade, but as the blades from the village attacked, the older man's wisdom immediately became apparent.

The village's defense wasn't coordinated. Blades came out, seemingly at random, attacking in the pairs they were no doubt used to. As each pair met a group of four, the battle was already decided.

Asa had taken the point for her group, and their first conflict was over almost before it began. A pair of blades charged them. Asa stepped toward the first of the two, her short sword easily blocking the cut. Behind her, another blade stepped in, his steel sliding between the ribs of Asa's opponent. The remaining blade, now alone against all four of Asa's group, died quickly.

With a few moments to breathe, Asa threw out her sense and felt another pair of blades die on the other side of the village. Koji couldn't be stopped. Their assault was going better than they could have imagined.

But the enterprise was going to get more difficult. The remaining defenders had figured out that running out to meet their attackers wasn't working. Whoever was in command was rallying them in the center of the village, the same small clearing where Asa had been forced to kill Daiki and Ayano.

After regrouping, Mari, Jun, Asa, and the other blades approached the village. Each group distanced itself from the others, attempting to assault the center from different directions. They moved slowly, ensuring that they didn't walk into any traps. It was difficult to fight against the impulse to charge now that their blood was crashing through their bodies, the familiar surge of energy that came from combat. They outnumbered their opponents now, and all Asa wanted to do was wade into the thick of battle and be done with it. Looking at her companions, she knew they felt the same. Still, their discipline held.

Before the two sides could meet, Koji tore into the center of River's End, a force of nature. Though outnumbered seven to one, he didn't seem to mind in the least. Even having seen him fight multiple opponents before, Asa realized she still underestimated his true skill.

He was so fast. His sword was a blur, and even gifted with the sense, Asa could barely keep up with Koji. Against seven he still might have lost, but the rest of his companions were close enough to seize on the advantage his arrival provided.

The battle was ferocious. The rogue blades seemed to know they would be shown no quarter and fought with unflinching fury. Without Koji, the battle might have turned out differently. But he was a force, a power that couldn't be contained. The blade was everywhere, his steel slashing in the early morning sunlight.

Asa found herself in a one-on-one fight with a rogue nightblade. Her opponent had already been wounded and wasn't moving fast, but he was putting all his strength into every attack. Asa dodged once but couldn't respond as another enemy stabbed weakly at her. She kept backpedaling, forced to block her opponent's next strike.

She blocked the cut a little later than she would have liked. The power put into the attack knocked her sword off to the side, leaving her completely vulnerable. Time seemed to slow down. She saw the gleam of satisfaction in her enemy's eyes.

The moment was only a heartbeat long, but the flood of emotions Asa felt made it seem like a lifetime. Anger quickly replaced despair. Anger that once again, she hadn't been strong enough to make a difference.

Koji's blade seemed to come from nowhere, snaking in from the corner of Asa's vision. His blade pierced her opponent's neck, a cut that even in the moment seemed impossible to Asa. Koji gave her a look of disdain, and then he was gone, a blur of death on the battlefield.

The battle was over moments later. The outcome had not been in question, but Asa was surprised by how successful they had been. One of their party had received a deep cut, but Jun and another dayblade were already busy healing the wound. Beyond that, they hadn't suffered anything beyond a few scratches. She couldn't believe it.

The reason was obvious, and everyone understood. Koji had shown them a talent none of them could have imagined. Asa was still in shock. To think she had one time tried to duel him single-handedly. Soft congratulations were passed around, but everyone gave Koji space, scared of an ally with such power.

Asa exhaled a breath she hadn't realized she'd been holding.

———

That night Mari and her warriors made the decision to set up camp outside the village. After the battle, they had given the bodies of the rogues a proper ceremony, but still, none felt comfortable spending the night in the houses of River's End.

Their fire was burning brightly, wood from the village providing the companions more heat than they had enjoyed in several days. Despite their victory, the mood around the campfire was grim. Justice satisfied the blades but brought them no joy. Each would have much rather avoided the killing of their brothers and sisters.

For Asa, the emptiness was especially deep, reopening the same void she felt after her own personal revenge had been accomplished.

She couldn't help but think that everything was completely meaningless. She had spent her life trying to find and kill the man who had murdered her father and destroyed her family. That was done, yet she felt no peace. She had avenged the death of the couple who had welcomed her into their home and still felt no better.

As her thoughts dwelled on the past, Asa grew more frustrated. Memories of Koji's sword saving her replayed themselves in an endless loop. Eventually the scenes playing through her mind changed. She saw Juro dying at Koji's hand. She saw her sword as she took the lives of those who had offered her shelter.

As the memories played, she ground her teeth, anger surging. She hated being the one who needed to be saved, hated not being able to do more.

Koji had no such problems. After the battle, which he had won almost single-handedly, he had thrown himself into the task of cleaning up the village and helping dispose of the bodies. No one had done more to win the fight, and no one had done more to clean up afterward. The awe and fear the other blades had shown gradually turned to respect. Jun was still the voice of the party and Mari was the leader, but Koji had become the heart, a role he fell into naturally.

Asa had no such convictions. She had agreed to join the party for the raid on River's End, but that was only because she had needed to see justice served. Now, though, she wasn't certain about what she should do next.

Her thoughts were interrupted by Koji as he came and sat down next to her, a look of earnest concern on his face. He spoke softly so that their conversation could not be overheard. "Asa, are you all right?"

She gave him what she considered to be a very unconvincing smile. "No."

Koji didn't respond, giving her the space to explain herself further if she so wished. She tried to summarize her thoughts.

"Koji, after everything we've done here today, I still don't feel better. There's no joy in what we did, not even any satisfaction over an accomplished task. Part of me is glad that we brought justice to the villagers, but they've passed on to the Great Cycle, and I'm not sure they care. What do we do next?"

There was a prolonged silence as Koji thought through his answer. Asa was reminded of the first time they had met, and she had thought that perhaps he was stupid. Now, as before, she realized just how wrong that impression could be.

"I do not know about you, Asa, but I do not fight for the dead. I fight for the living."

The simple statement rocked Asa to her core. Her life flashed before her eyes: the day that she received the news of her father's death, her training as a nightblade, her evenings spent awake imagining the face of her father's killer. Could life be so simple?

As confused as Asa was, she wasn't able to reach a conclusion as Mari came and sat next to them.

She was direct and to the point. "I don't know what you two have planned next, but on behalf of all of us here, it would be my pleasure to invite you to join us."

Asa glanced over at the lady. Mari moved with grace and confidence, showing none of the hesitation she had the night before. Looking over at her, Asa couldn't tell Mari had just been part of a vicious battle. But how would she react if she knew that the man she was sitting next to had killed her brother, the lord of her house, and the woman next to him had failed to protect him? Would she still have the air of command she did now?

Asa pushed the thought aside. She needed to stop living in the past and think about the present. "Where will you go?"

Mari's voice was more certain than Asa had anticipated.

"We'll head to the south and west. I have an extensive network of shadows, and there are places I may go to get more information. My plan is to continue traveling through the Kingdom, trying to help however I'm able. With dayblades and nightblades, we can both heal and bring force to bear. I hope to do more of the former, but if the latter is necessary, so be it."

Asa had already liked Mari, but the determination in her voice was just the trigger that she needed to make her own decision.

Koji answered first. "It would be my pleasure to join you."

Mari nodded. If she was half the leader that Asa assumed she was, Koji's answer would come as no surprise.

Asa's answer was equally certain. "I have nothing but respect for what you are doing, Lady Mari, but I cannot join you at this time."

A raised eyebrow was Mari's only reaction.

Asa felt the need to explain herself. "You know little about me, my lady, but for most of my life, I was driven by revenge. Not long ago, I accomplished that revenge, but it brought me no peace. If anything, it has only brought me more doubt about who I am. In River's End, for the first time, I felt a measure of contentment I've not remembered in a long time. I don't know who I am without revenge, and until I decide that, I am more of a hindrance than a help to you. I must respectfully decline, although I hope the invitation remains open so that I may join you later."

Mari nodded. "I will not pretend to understand your reasons, but on my part, yes, the offer will remain open. We would always be delighted to have you."

With that, Mari stood up and left the two alone.

Koji looked at Asa. "I'm surprised. I thought that for sure you would join as well. Would you like me to join you?"

Asa felt nothing but heartfelt gratitude for Koji in that moment. Perhaps he didn't understand himself, but Asa recognized the importance of the question and the depth of the feelings it contained. She shook her head sadly. "While I would love nothing more than your company, I believe it's best if you continue with Mari. She's walking the same path that you wish to follow, and I would not have that taken away from you. Know that I will find you if and when I am able."

Koji didn't seem satisfied with the answer, but he accepted her reply. "Where will you go?"

Asa grinned at the foolishness of her decision. "I have a friend whom I need to see."

Chapter 12

Asa departed early the next morning. Mari would miss the nightblade, but she had other, more pressing concerns. Many days had passed since she'd left Hiromi to his war, and she needed information.

Mari hadn't lied when she spoke to Asa about her plans for the future, but she hadn't uttered the entire truth. She wouldn't admit it to any of the warriors who traveled at her side, but Mari maintained a secret hope that their force could be used to her brother's benefit. She understood she was biased, but if Hiromi could become the next king, she felt the Kingdom's future would be more secure.

She did plan to continue heading southwest, toward the ruins of Haven and the last location her brother had occupied. There were places she could stay where her network of shadows would get information to her. She had a weapon now, a group of blades willing to follow her. With information, she could wield that weapon with deadly precision, striking at the targets that would change the course of the war.

Her blades broke camp and traveled in the direction of an inn where Mari would find the news she sought. Most of her blades elected to set up a new camp about a league away from the inn, more comfortable in the plains than among people. Jun, Takahiro, and Koji accompanied her to the inn.

They remained there for two days while information made its way to her. Mari studied each piece of correspondence with a renewed focus. Most were small, square pieces of paper with the sealing wax broken, but some were notes of her own conversations and thoughts. She wasn't just collecting information anymore. She had a purpose and a design.

The news was both good and bad. Hiromi had won the first engagement with Katashi. Although reports were varied, Katashi had apparently pushed his troops too hard too fast. Hiromi's forces hadn't been as organized, but they'd been well rested and fed. Their father had always said an army fought better on a full stomach.

She should have been overjoyed by the news. A victory for their house was to be celebrated, but her heart refused. She told herself it was because she mourned the loss of so many lives, unwilling to admit she was entertaining the thought that if Katashi had won, the war might have ended almost as quickly as it started.

The bad news, which was bad no matter how one looked at it, was that the victory hadn't been decisive. The accounts Mari read, written in the dry, observational tones of professional shadows, could never do justice to the field of battle. But the numbers in front of her spoke volumes. Thousands dead on both sides. Katashi's forces had been reduced by more than two-thirds, but the story wasn't much better for Hiromi.

Her brother had lost more than half his men in the battle. They had driven Katashi back, but the price had been far too steep. Mari thought of the number of families who had lost a son or a husband in the past moon. If Hiromi wasn't careful, he would damage generations of families.

Mari considered all the information about the battle carefully, but none held her interest the way a short note did, written on an unremarkable square of paper of poor quality. The note was written in a small, precise hand, the writing of one of Hiromi's aides and one of Mari's most important shadows.

The note told her that her brother and his generals were considering retreating to their house lands for the winter. It was only early autumn, and in most cycles past, there would still be time to finish a campaign. But this autumn had remained cold. While snow this time of season wasn't unheard of, it never remained on the ground. A note from another of her contacts in their own lands reported that many of the mountain passes were already closed with snow. It seemed that winterlike weather had arrived early, and Hiromi and his generals recognized this.

Retreating for the season was the correct decision. Even though she hadn't been trained in warfare, Mari knew that well enough. Their army wasn't equipped for a winter campaign, and families needed their men back to finish whatever harvest hadn't been killed by the frost.

The tragedy was that because they would retreat, they were in for a longer war. With no decisive victor, the houses would each have the winter to regroup and plan strategies for the coming spring. Instead of an army from each house meeting haphazardly, each contingent would be able to bring its full strength to bear.

Mari wrote down all the information she deemed pertinent in her own hand in the code she had created for herself. The originals were thrown in the small fireplace in her room.

She didn't have a plan. From everything she had learned, there was no way for her small band to somehow alter the course of the Kingdom in a single stroke. But she needed to speak to her brother. Together, perhaps, they could plan for the upcoming war.

———

When Hiromi entered the tavern, Mari smiled. She and her blades had been on the road for another two days catching up with his army, and she had made sure that her letter got to him. All the same, she wasn't sure he would come. She didn't dare enter his camp, and convincing him to leave the protection of his army was no small risk. His guards would be outside, ensuring this secret rendezvous was protected.

Her smile was returned by looks of outrage and concern. Hiromi rushed to her table and sat down. "Mari! Where have you been?"

Mari opened her mouth to answer, but his series of questions continued, not giving her the space to answer. "Did you know that I've been worried sick about you? Do you know how terrifying it is to have your sister leave on the eve of battle with a cryptic note that may or may not be real? I feared that you had been taken hostage to be used against me. Please don't ever do anything like that ever again. You are the only family that I have left."

Mari couldn't help but be touched by her brother's concern. It was sometimes easy to forget that they were blood.

Seeing that her brother was finally going to give her a chance to speak, Mari responded. "I'm sorry, Brother. I didn't think that my departure would affect you the way that it has. Rest assured that I meant you no ill will, but I would never get my case heard in front of you. I needed to take action."

Hiromi looked as though he were about to explode, but then he gained control of himself and took a deep breath. His shoulders slumped. The man in front of Mari was no longer a lord but her younger brother once again. Mari reminded herself that he, too, was going through a struggle.

When he spoke again his voice was softer, but there was a hint of steel Mari hadn't noticed before. He had been blooded by warfare, and that could never be taken away. "I, too, am sorry for the way you've been treated. I was caught in a situation I wasn't prepared for, and you weren't helping. As much as we both wish that Juro was alive, he isn't, and I am now lord of our house. I cannot be questioned by my sister in front of my generals. You left me no choice."

Mari's voice was also gentle but firm. "And you left me no choice. I tried to tell you of my concerns in private, but you did not accept my invitations. I felt there was no other way to speak to you."

Hiromi met her gaze. "Well, then, it appears that we both acknowledge our mistakes. You must understand that I cannot let you back on my council, but I will make a promise to you that should you request my presence, I will always be available."

Mari had expected as much.

Her brother's face turned into one of curiosity, and Mari recognized the conversation had shifted. "So now, sister, you must tell me what you've been up to and why we are meeting here at a tavern outside my camp instead of inside it."

Mari almost regretted having to tell Hiromi the truth. They had just repaired their relationship, and she worried that she might destroy it all over again. Regardless, she had no choice. She needed her brother, now more than ever.

She took a deep breath. "I went on a mission to Starfall."

Hiromi's eyes, which moments ago had been warm, friendly, and concerned, suddenly turned cold. His expression was all that she had feared, and she rushed to explain before he could stand up and leave the room. "I knew that you would not approve, Brother, which was why I undertook the mission without telling you. I had hoped to offer an alliance to the blades with our house. With their help, you'd be able to win the war quickly and bring peace to the Kingdom once again."

She watched the war of emotions raging over her brother's face. She could see that more than anything else, he wanted to stand up and leave, never speaking to her again. But he had just told her that he would always be available to her; if not for his own word given just moments ago, Mari was certain he would already be gone. Eventually, his entire body shuddered as he took a deep, loud breath.

"You are beyond foolish, my sister. I don't know what could have possibly possessed you to think that such a course of action was reasonable. Have you forgotten so soon that it was the blades who killed our king? That the blades killed our own brother? That they plotted to rule this kingdom? If you weren't my own sister, I would have you executed for treason immediately. And to think that you did this with any connection to our house. You have brought nothing but disgrace and dishonor to our name."

Each statement was said quietly, but each with the force of a punch, and each felt exactly that way to Mari. She had expected that Hiromi wouldn't approve, but she had never anticipated this level of distrust or hate. Suddenly she realized just how wrong she had been about one fact: it was already too late for the blades. The damage had been done. The news and rumors had escalated to a point of no return. Her brother's feelings weren't rational. He simply loathed the blades. And if a lord hated the blades, his subjects would, too.

She realized there would be no reasoning with Hiromi. The look on his face said that even more clearly than his words.

Mari was stuck at a crossroads. She didn't want to lose her brother, but she didn't want to lose the blades, either.

Hiromi solved her problem for her. "I don't know what you have planned, Mari, or what you are thinking." He stood up from the table, his voice just loud enough for her to hear. "But end your foolish games and come home. You'll be welcome, and despite this madness, I will still consider your advice in the future of our house. But you need to come home now. The moon will be full in, what, twelve days? I can see from your face you are still involved in something. End it however you must. If you are back in Stonekeep by the full moon, all your transgressions will be forgiven. Otherwise, do not plan on coming back at all."

———

Her ride back to the blades' camp was a silent one, Mari completely lost in thought. How could the world be so wrong? Suddenly everyone seemed to be an enemy. If you didn't agree completely with one's worldview, you were an other, a traitor to your house, an evil person.

Hiromi's eyes had changed so quickly. The scene played through her mind repeatedly, and every time she shuddered at the memory. She understood his rage. If she found the blade who slew her brother, she would want to kill him, too.

The four rode into camp without a word. Takahiro, Jun, and Koji had all been inside the tavern guarding Mari when she met with her brother. They hadn't been close enough to hear the discussion, but they had seen enough to know it hadn't gone well. They didn't ask questions, giving her the space to reflect.

As they rode into camp, Takahiro took her horse without a word. Mari walked to the small fire in the center of the camp and sat, lost in thought.

The sun rose in the sky and started to fall, and still Mari made no move. At times her eyes were unfocused, staring into the ground in front of her, then they would focus and watch the blades around her.

Like most civilians, Mari hadn't spent a great deal of time around the blades. Traveling with the small group gave her new insights into the culture of the people who held such a unique status in the Kingdom.

Of the eleven blades traveling together, four were women. Three were dayblades. Jun was the oldest by far, with most of the rest appearing to be not much older than Mari. She wondered about that, curious if her group was representative of the blades. Or did the younger blades simply have more hope for the Kingdom?

What surprised her most, though, was how comfortable she had become around them. In her previous life, getting full sentences out of a blade was considered an achievement. In camp, surrounded by gifted peers, they weren't talkative exactly, but they spoke regularly.

Yet their dedication to their training set them apart. Mari knew from her studies that most blades lived to train, but seeing that in action was far different than she expected. If the group needed food, only one or two hunters would leave, the duty rotating among the blades. Once the food was procured, the group ignored hunting until the current supply was gone.

Instead, the nightblades seemed to divide their time between dueling with wooden swords and meditating. Even the dayblades would practice laying hands on one another. Mari had spent a little time among military units, where most energy was expended in trying to get soldiers to focus on the tasks at hand. Here, Mari thought they should rest more often.

On the road they moved differently as well. Most groups would have traveled in a tight pack. Not the blades. They detested being too close to one another too often. They spread out wide, casting a net with their gifts to prevent ambush. Even when they camped, the tents were more spread out from one another than those of average infantrymen.

Despite their oddities, Mari felt comfortable. Her heart no longer raced every time a nightblade spoke to her, and she had laughed around a campfire with them.

Her brother had made her choices clear. Either him or the blades, but it couldn't be both. She longed to return to Stonekeep, its familiar rock walls and steep walkways. But Mari couldn't shake the belief that she was meant to remain with the blades. If she accepted her brother's offer, he might hear her advice, but how often would he act on it? He was just as likely to ignore her guidance in favor of his own thoughts. With the blades, she could act, not just advise.

That night, around a campfire, Mari brought her problem to the group, as she felt they all deserved to know her challenge. She spoke of her conversation with Hiromi and told them about her fears, that the attitude toward the blades had gone too far.

The companions accepted her fears with surprising calmness. Mari had expected them to be distraught or concerned. Instead, she seemed to have simply confirmed something they had all feared. Jun said as much.

"Your concerns are well grounded, my lady. Like you, I wish they were untrue, but I'm afraid the attitude you've described is one we've seen all too often of late. If you were to spend a day wearing our robes, you, too, would understand. We are used to attention, but never fear, not like this. Even dayblades, who are best at healing, are shunned from villages, where our help could mean the difference between life and death. In the eyes of the people, we are not part of the world they live in."

Mari fought against the wave of helplessness that washed over her. "Then what can be done? I fear, not just for the blades, but for a Kingdom without the blades. One cannot survive without the other."

Silence greeted her question. She had hoped that one of them, at least, had an idea worth pursuing.

Eventually Takahiro broke the silence. "I don't know how to change the attitude of the Kingdom. Such work is well beyond my skill and experience. However, I believe that change happens one person at a time. That's something we can do. One person, one family, one village at a time. We can make people believe that a different future is possible. We can get people to believe in the blades again."

Mari looked at her guard, moved by the commitment in his voice. She appreciated his thought, but it wasn't what she was looking for. "You're speaking of the work of a lifetime."

Takahiro nodded, his passion getting the better of him. "Then it is good we have our entire lives still."

The comment snapped Mari out of her depressed reverie. He was right, of course. His idea wasn't the solution she wanted, but Takahiro had given them a path, and that was more than she was offering. As she glanced around the circle, she saw that the blades agreed with him. She couldn't help but smile. To her, Takahiro had been a confidant, a trusted guard, and an excellent swordsman. She had never thought of him as a leader. It was a mistake to underestimate your enemy, but it was also a mistake to underestimate your friends.

"Very well. It's decided then. We spend this winter serving the Kingdom. We will bring healing, and in places where that's not enough, we can provide strength. Together, we will spread a new message and work for a new day."

Blades were not known for cheering, but Mari was content with the satisfaction she saw in their eyes.

Jun cleared his throat. "My lady, there's something several of us have spoken about, and I believe it needs to be brought to your attention. All of us here know who you are, but if your actions become known, you could bring ruin to your family. Perhaps it would be wise if, from now on, you wore something to conceal your identity?"

Mari was ashamed she had never thought of that herself. If she walked this path and was captured or even if word got out, the revelation would be a convenient pretext for the other two lords to join forces against Hiromi. That was something she couldn't allow.

"You are right. From this night forward, I shall protect my identity."

Jun nodded in satisfaction, and the conversation turned to other, less weighty matters. Mari's attention drifted, her imagination filled with thoughts of Stonekeep. She would miss the place and would miss her brother more. But she was convinced that even if her actions weren't perfect, she was heading in the right direction. One step at a time, she would forge a better kingdom.

Chapter 13

The winter had been quiet, cold, and brutal. Koji and his compatriots may not have been fighting swarms of enemies, but Lady Mari kept them well occupied. In this harsh season, their real enemies weren't other men but the elements in the world.

Koji, in particular, felt that he had never worked as hard since he had originally trained as a nightblade cycles ago. Part of the work was his own doing. He was personally training harder than ever. There was much to do.

In the moons since Asa had departed, the number of blades under Mari's command had increased. Their group, originally about a dozen strong, now were more than fifty, with new people coming almost every day. Rumors of Mari's deeds were spreading. She had been as good as her word and better. The companions went from village to village, avoiding the large cities, doing what good they could.

As much as they were able, the dayblades did what healing they could without giving themselves away—not an easy task and not one they always succeeded at. More than once they had been run out of villages because their true identities had been discovered.

Every time, though, they left without casualties, and word of the companions' behavior and actions was spreading.

Just eight days ago they'd come into a village where an elder had been praying for their arrival.

Koji had ventured into the area initially. A lone nightblade always went first. More than once, the mood in a village had proven to be too volatile to risk. Not this time. Koji had entered and asked for the village elder. He had been escorted to the home of a local leader, but when he had come in, the elder was prostrated before his shrine to the Great Cycle.

When Koji told the elder he was with the Lady in White, the man burst into tears, telling him he had just been praying for exactly that. The village had been starving, and the local hunters hadn't been able to find food in the brutal weather. Koji wasn't comfortable with the elder's praise, but they had been welcomed with open arms into the village.

Mari had ridden in later that morning. Her traveling robes were white, as were the silk robes underneath. Though rarely seen, Mari had assumed the outfit as a costume, and few details were overlooked. Her hair was tied with white ribbon, and a matching veil covered her face.

Her choice had been controversial. For most, white symbolized death, but Mari claimed it represented the cleansing power of winter. She had her way, and now, whenever the blades rode into a village, they were led by the Lady in White.

That day had been exhausting, as they all were. No task was too big or too small. Dozens of freshly killed animals were carried in. Dayblades healed what illnesses they could. Jun sat down with the local medicine man and provided supplies and guidance on different mixtures. One or two of the younger blades played with the youth in the village.

Watching Mari was enough to give a person hope. Serving under her was what Koji thought life as a nightblade was supposed to be. For the first time, he felt like the skills he had worked so hard to develop were improving the world.

He wasn't the only one who felt that way. Since Mari's movement had begun, not a single blade had left. Everyone who started with her remained, and to Koji's knowledge, no one entertained any thoughts of departing. If anything, the blades in her service had become more fervent in their desire to serve.

The group's increased size came with its own share of difficulties. The one that was most obvious, occupying most of their time, was the procurement of food. The winter had been every bit as harsh as the autumn had foretold. The weather never warmed, not even for a few days. The air turned more frigid, the sharp wind tore through whatever clothing they had, and the snow seemed to get deeper every day.

Setting up the tents became more difficult in the snow. Often they stopped whenever they found small groves of trees that provided both shelter and less snow to dig through. They built the fires high as they prepared for sleep, and one of the primary duties of the night's watch was to ensure the blaze didn't burn out.

Though many of the nightblades struggled, Mari seemed to thrive. She wore less than most of the blades, yet seemed more comfortable. Many blades seemed to think it a sign of her resilience, but Koji saw only a woman who had grown up in the mountains.

Hunting was not a difficult task for a nightblade. When you knew where your prey was, much of the difficulty was alleviated. As trainees, hunting was one of the first tasks nightblades were expected to master.

Koji had never hunted in weather like this, however. Even if you could sense your prey, getting to it in the deep snow was another issue entirely. He lost track of the number of times he thought he was within range of a deer or rabbit only to lose the animal in the snow. No matter how good his condition, he wasn't as well adapted to the snow as the creatures of the forests and plains. Koji wasn't alone in this, either. They all struggled to hunt, and more often than not, Mari commanded that what food they had killed be given to the villages and farms they passed. Koji was more lean than he had ever been in his life.

Staying hidden was also more of a challenge the more people they moved with. It was one thing to hide a dozen people, but fifty was another matter entirely, and once they reached a hundred, another matter again. The question constantly arose about what to do with their swelling numbers, whether they should stay together or split up and spread out.

Koji believed they should split up. The advantages of traveling in a smaller group were too strong to ignore. They could move more quickly and evade detection more easily. They could feed themselves with greater ease, and the more they fanned out, the farther their message would carry. Koji had made his arguments known, but the final decision was Mari's.

He understood the argument about safety in numbers, but he didn't believe that safety was worth the price they would pay.

Koji did not envy Mari the decision she would have to make. He felt that it was one thing to play the hero when you had a group large enough to do some good but not so large as to pose a threat to the major forces in the world. If this growth continued, Mari would soon command a large and fiercely loyal contingent of blades, one of the largest ever assembled outside of Starfall.

When that happened, they would most certainly draw the attention of the lords, and then Mari's mettle would truly be tested. Would she fight? Would they run and hide? Would the flame of their beliefs, which had once burned so bright, fade out until even the wisps of smoke had disappeared? Koji didn't know the answer, but he was grateful that one was not required of him. He was more than content to serve as he was able.

Despite his comfort, Koji recognized that it was only a matter of time before decisions needed to be made. The time of reckoning was coming soon.

———

Koji woke up before the morning sun, as was his new custom. When he had been younger, he had never felt the need to be up early. He was often awake late into the night with his friends growing up, and he woke when he pleased.

He had soon outpaced his friends in the development of his swordsmanship, and it wasn't long before he wasn't invited to their evening outings. The exclusion had hurt, but Koji had focused his efforts on his training, growing ever stronger, outdistancing them even more. But his nightly habits had remained until recently.

He couldn't say why exactly. Waking up early felt right, and being able to see the sunrise in the morning had become one of the favorite parts of his day. The morning was a time of silence and possibility, a new day that hadn't yet unfolded.

That didn't mean Koji didn't fight to get out of his bedroll. He awoke most mornings with the covers pulled high over his head, cozy compared to the brisk air of the tent. After overcoming that first hurdle, he still had to leave the tent and step out into the crisp winter air, air so frigid his lashes stuck together if he closed his eyes for too long.

Koji dressed warmly and stepped outside his tent. Looking up, he saw no stars, but that had been true for the last three days. A soft breeze swept across the plains, but even that was cold enough to cut through the layers he wore.

Passing the night's watch, Koji wandered off away from the camp. What he was about to do was easier if no one was around.

He found a place where the ground was slightly depressed, providing a slim protection from the wind. Koji didn't necessarily seek comfort, but a little wouldn't hurt. Satisfied, he sat down and crossed his legs. He started by focusing on his breath, breathing in deeply, exhaling half, breathing in deeply again, and repeating the process. The technique was one he had been taught when he was young. It helped warm the body during cold weather, working here as it always had for him.

Once his breathing was settled, Koji attempted to meditate, to relax deeper into the gift he'd been given at birth. In training, he had never been a strong meditator, preferring action and movement. His ability with the sense was adequate, but as a nightblade, it was his greatest weakness. There were others who could sense much farther than he, others who could sense details in action he never could.

But at River's End, he had a revelation. The battle had started normally enough. He had killed the patrols as they had planned, but when he reached the center of the village, something had changed. He had fought at a level far beyond what he had thought he was capable of. Koji wasn't one for false modesty. He knew he was an excellent sword, but he had never fought that well.

Since the battle, Koji had been trying to recover that feeling, to understand what had happened. He had sparred with almost all the blades, often insisting they attack him in groups. The sensation never returned, causing him to question his memories of that day.

Although he had no answers, he had suspicions. Battle, by its nature, sharpened one's focus. Combined with the rage he had felt at those blades and their dishonorable behavior, he had fought in the perfect set of circumstances to maintain near-perfect focus. He hadn't actually been faster or stronger; he had only felt that way because he had used his gift better than he ever had before.

For more than a moon, he chased that suspicion, at times feeling tantalizingly close to the answers. There were moments when his reality shifted, when he knew what was going to happen long before he should have. Once he had known what cut to make against an opponent before the other blade even drew his weapon. He was on the right track, but every time he tasted success, he only wanted more.

The nightblade wished he had spent more time paying attention when he had been younger and his masters had been trying to demonstrate mental training techniques. He remembered a few basic strategies, and some of the blades in the camp had shown him others, but he was out of practice. Rebuilding the skill was almost physically challenging.

But Koji persisted. For a few moments he had experienced the next step in his evolution. Every morning, before the camp woke up, he would leave and meditate, seeking the new skill.

Eventually Koji opened his eyes and normalized his breathing. There had been hints today he was getting close, heartbeats where everything seemed to come into sharper focus. Yet no breakthrough came.

Koji stood up. He knew the sun had risen, but it was hard to tell. With the thick, ever-present clouds above, the only difference between dawn and daylight was how bright the gray clouds became. The weather was influencing the other blades as well. The camp atmosphere was quiet and somber. Mari would have to throw a celebration soon to keep spirits up.

As he wandered back toward the group, Koji was surprised to run into Jun, meditating in much the same way. As he neared, the dayblade opened his eyes, clearly not succeeding in his practice.

Driven by curiosity, Koji stopped. "Jun, when you meditate, what does it do for you?"

Jun frowned. "What does it do for you?"

Koji gave him a hint of a smile. "Not much, but my hope is that it makes me a better warrior." He almost left it at that, but he felt compelled to say more. Perhaps Jun would have some wisdom.

"When we fought at River's End, my gift was different. I could sense my opponents' moves farther in advance, and I could just sense *more*. I've been hoping that through meditation I can reconnect with that level of skill, but mostly I have failed."

Jun nodded thoughtfully. "Dayblades are similar. Our skill comes entirely from our use of the gift. We are always training to sense more intricate flows of energy inside the body. The better we do, the better we can manipulate those flows to heal others. I assume the same principle holds true for you as well."

Koji agreed. "I've never needed to worry before. I've always been strong enough and fast enough. But against other nightblades, skill with a sword is almost less important than being able to use my gift better than others."

Jun was thoughtful. "I will think on your problem, Koji. If anything comes to me, I will let you know."

Koji bowed slightly and left Jun in peace. Lost in thought, Koji meandered to his first task of the day: supervising training. After River's

End, he had been acknowledged by everyone to be the best sword in the group. As such, Koji had unofficially been given the role of supervising training. Like him, many blades focused on the development of their combat skills to the detriment of much else.

Koji couldn't have been put in charge of a more enthusiastic group. He had never taught anyone. Once he was granted the rank of master, he had much more interest in traveling the Kingdom and completing assignments than he did in teaching children how to fight. However, he was enjoying the process despite how much he stumbled and fell during his teaching.

His role also gave him the advantage of being able to train himself every day. Koji always wanted to try out original techniques and ideas. He practiced with forms he had learned were weak to see if there were advantages his own teachers had overlooked. On the days where his awareness shifted and became sharper, he experimented with stringing together cuts that would have opened him up to fatal wounds without the foreknowledge he possessed. He wanted to see if all the meditation he'd completed would have any effect. Acting as a trainer gave him new opportunities.

Their training area was nothing fancier than a small area outside the camp. When Koji arrived, Takahiro was in the circle with a nightblade who had recently been given the status of apprentice. A moon ago, Koji might have laughed. There were warriors, like Takahiro, who were convinced that even though they didn't have the gift, they could defeat a blade in an honest duel. Usually the nightblades considered them delusional and worth mocking. At one point, Takahiro had been the subject of many jests whispered among the blades.

For most nongifted warriors, a single severe beating was enough to teach them the foolishness of their beliefs. In rare cases, a second would have to be applied. Takahiro had been suffering daily beatings for more than a moon, and the soft mocking smiles had slowly become grunts of reluctant respect.

Koji was no different. He had shaken his head the first time one of the inexperienced nightblades pummeled the former head of Mari's guards. The blade had given no quarter, and none had been asked for. That was the way such lessons were taught. In a way, it was a mercy. Better that than suffer a delusion.

Koji had been entertained the next day, too. And the day after that. Eventually, though, it stopped being funny. Takahiro was a humble swordsman, and he was willing to get beaten by anyone in the name of progress. Even Koji had to admit the warrior had gotten much more skilled. Takahiro had become a respectable opponent, even for a blade. He wouldn't win, but that was an accident of birth, no fault of his own.

Regular soldiers could kill nightblades through sheer force of numbers. A small group could potentially accomplish the feat as well. Shin's nightblade-hunting groups of eight had been a good example.

Because a nightblade could sense what was about to happen, the only way to defeat one was to take away all the blade's options. So long as a single cut, block, or movement remained, a talented blade couldn't be brought down by civilians. Remove those options, and it could be done.

The lesson was one Takahiro had learned well. A single man fighting with only a sword had little chance of removing all options, but Takahiro did what he could. Koji watched with interest. The two were fighting with wooden swords, and Takahiro's opponent was known to have a hot head. The fight was closer than Koji thought it should be.

The nightblade launched an attack, all strong cuts. Takahiro danced back, and Koji fought the urge to shake his head. Against Takahiro, defense was a better idea. With the gift, the blade could have sensed any attack and responded immediately, ending the battle in one move. By attacking, the advantage was lost.

Takahiro stabbed out with his sword. The attempt was nothing but a bid for space, and it worked. The youth halted his advance for just a moment, giving Takahiro a little room to move. The blade realized his mistake and followed it up with another one, attacking again with fury.

Koji frowned. Had the guard angered the boy before they started? If the objective had been to make the blade attack wildly, it was working.

Takahiro slid backward again, coming right up against the edge of the ring, marked by a pile of snow. Koji's eyes narrowed as the blade came in yet again. This time, instead of dodging, Takahiro deflected the boy's sword, redirecting his attacker toward the edge of the ring. The nightblade didn't even seem to notice.

Koji's reality shifted, and he saw the moves he couldn't believe were about to happen. But they did. Takahiro sliced at the blade. The blade's instinct, which was correct, was to step back and to the side. But the blade wasn't paying attention to his surroundings, and his foot slid into the pile of snow marking the edge.

For just a moment, the blade was distracted, looking down at his foot. The moment lasted less than a heartbeat, all the time a warrior of Takahiro's skill needed. One more move, and the blade went down, clutching his stomach as Mari's guard drove his weapon into him.

A shocked silence fell upon the ring. Takahiro had earned the blades' respect, but he never should have beaten any of them. These blades were so proud of themselves, the idea of losing to a civilian was unimaginable. Everybody needed to focus less on self and more on the group.

Koji broke the tension. He stepped into the ring and bowed deeply to Takahiro. The guard's grin was as wide as his face. "Congratulations. It was well fought."

Takahiro bowed even deeper before helping the blade he had fought up. "Thank you. I have had good teachers these past moons."

The guard's modesty resonated with the blades. Perhaps they were upset one of their own had lost, but Takahiro set an example. He trained as hard as the most dedicated among them.

Koji picked up a wooden sword and swept open his hands. "Who shall it be today?"

Three volunteers stepped forward, eager to best him. No matter how the fights turned out, there were always those who would try again.

Ryan Kirk

Koji tried to find the sensation, the feeling of being far ahead of everyone else. Every day he took a different approach. Today he tried remaining calm, steadying his breath and focus. He had to find the strength he had in River's End.

At his signal, the fight began. The three didn't waste any time, coming in all at once, trying to close any avenue of escape he might have. Koji stepped to the side, making sure all three weren't getting to him at once.

Earlier in their association, Koji's simple moves might have worked. The nightblade he stepped toward would have continued his attack. Koji would deal with him and then move on to the next. Now they knew one another well, and the blade on Koji's right was no fool. She stepped back and away from Koji, avoiding a single duel in favor of a group effort.

For a few moments they danced around the ring. Koji attempted to isolate one of them, and they refused to be singled out. When he was certain he wouldn't catch one of them in a weak moment, Koji let them attack together.

He was faster, but against three blades in a confined space, there was only so much he could do. He deflected and dodged their blows as much as he was able, but they soon broke his defense.

Koji concentrated on remaining calm and focused. Suddenly everything shifted. Colors were just a bit more vibrant, the snow sparkling white, the wooden swords a rich brown. Koji sensed where the gap was going to be, the place where he could change the direction of the entire fight.

Without hesitation, he followed his instincts. He stepped right behind a vicious cut, and suddenly, without warning, he was no longer hemmed in by swords. He was among his opponents instead of in front of them. One blade acted as a human shield from the third. With a single move, Koji cut down two of the three. The colors dimmed, and Koji's sense returned to its normal state, but the temporary advantage was enough.

Koji finished the battle in a few moves, absently bowing to his opponents afterward. This wasn't the first time he had touched the altered state. He could brush against it, but he couldn't seem to stay there. As he stepped out of the ring to hearty congratulations from the assembled blades, Koji felt that he had failed again.

———

A few days later Takahiro summoned Koji into Mari's tent. When he stepped inside, he was surprised by the chilliness. They carried plenty of wood for fires, but Mari's was small, and Koji felt as though the interior was just barely warmer than outside.

Mari noticed his discomfort, and her eyes twinkled. "You're not from my house lands, are you?"

Koji shook his head. "No, I was born in the lands of House Amari."

Mari's grin faded as Koji named one of the now-enemies of her house. "If you had been born in the mountains, as I was, you would understand. This is pleasant to me. My brother, Juro, always told me that I was a child of winter. I much preferred the snow to the sun."

Koji's gut twisted as Juro's name came up, but Mari had another question on her mind.

"Tell me, Koji, you were born in Amari lands. Do you feel any loyalty to their house?"

Honestly, Koji had never really considered the question. He hadn't lived in Amari lands for many cycles, not since he was six and had been given to the blades for training. "No, none in particular. I was quite young when I was taken for training, too early to develop any attachment to a house."

Mari's eyes were unfocused as she considered the answer. "Do you think your other blades feel the same?"

Koji shrugged. "Loyalties are problematic, my lady. There are so many to choose from. Lords, ladies"—he gave a pointed glance at her—"the Kingdom, friends, family. Who's to say what causes one to choose any one over the other? I suspect there are almost as many loyalties among the blades as there are anywhere else."

"Hmm. Please don't call me 'my lady' anymore. I was never comfortable with titles, and I'm sure my brother has disowned me by now."

Koji didn't have anything to add, so he stood silently, waiting for Mari to tell him why she had summoned him. When she came out of her reverie, she looked him straight in the eye.

"I've decided to split up the party."

Koji approved of her decision but said nothing.

"The reason I've asked you here is because I've decided that my party, in particular, is going to be small. We're gaining notoriety, and I think it's best this way. If we're captured, we don't lose many people, and they'll be searching for me specifically."

She handed him a piece of paper, a wanted poster for the Lady in White, as Mari had come to be known.

He nodded appreciatively at the sum. "They do want your head. Traveling in a smaller group will be easier to conceal."

He was still surprised that for all the good they had done, the only reward Mari had received was a reward on her head. All for consorting with blades. The entire situation would be an entertaining story if Mari's life wasn't at risk.

Although Koji approved of her idea, he still wasn't sure why he had been summoned. Mari dispelled his confusion quickly.

"Koji, I would like you to be part of my group. Right now, I'm thinking it will be only me, Takahiro, Jun, and you."

The nightblade frowned. A tiny force. He had expected seven or eight at least. If they were attacked, they would be at a great disadvantage. Koji was good but still just one blade. But another question was even more pronounced in his mind.

"Why me, Mari? Wouldn't I be better suited for working with a group of blades?"

"Perhaps, but I have two simple reasons. The first is logistic. If I want to travel small but travel safe, I need the best, and from every account I've heard, that's you. Second, I trust you."

Koji wouldn't have felt more uncomfortable if Mari had thrown him in her tent's fire and stabbed him repeatedly with a knife. He opened his mouth to speak, to tell her the truth, but nothing came forth.

Mari watched him carefully. "You seem uncertain."

Koji stammered. "I am honored, Mari, but I don't know if I'm best suited to be so close to you."

Mari's eyes narrowed, and Koji was certain she could see into his heart to discover the secret lurking there.

Koji wasn't ashamed that he had slain Juro. He had been wronged by the lord and been well within his rights to revenge himself on the man who tried to kill him unjustly. He didn't want to hurt Mari, but he needed to tell her the truth.

He took a deep breath but still remained silent.

Mari pierced him with her stare, the only sound in the tent the one log crackling from the heat of the fire.

"I believe you are. There are going to be a few days of preparing and organizing, but be ready to leave soon."

With that, Koji's audience was at an end. He thought again about speaking, but the commitment he'd grasped only moments ago had wavered. He stepped out of the tent, the winter air feeling especially bleak.

Chapter 14

Asa was certain of one thing. She hated winter. She couldn't remember the last time she'd been warm. Vague memories of summer floated in her imagination, but every time she tried to hold on to one, a gust of icy wind stabbed through her clothing, and she was back in the present, freezing, miserable.

Finding her destination had been more challenging than she'd expected, mostly because the locale she thought was her destination had changed. At the first place she tried, she discovered the person she sought was already gone. Undeterred, Asa followed the directions given, wishing she only knew the land better. The area was one of rolling plains, and after a few days of travel, one hill in the land looked much the same as the next. Lacking a better knowledge of the land, she wished her directions had been clearer from the man who had given them to her.

She came over yet another rise, and suddenly her entire world changed. She cursed her luck. If she had come from any other direction, the house would have been much easier to find. The rise in the land sheltered the domicile from the wind on one side, and on the other, tall trees stood majestic, bending in the wind but not breaking.

The woods ran to the north and south, but Asa's vision of the forest had been blocked by the land. Had she come from any other direction, she would have been able to follow the tree line to her destination, probably saving her at least a day or two.

She extended her sense and felt three lives below. As soon as she felt them, doubt crashed against her heart.

She wasn't sure she should be here. Honestly, she wasn't even sure she was safe here. But she had nowhere else to turn.

Asa glanced back at the endless plains she had crossed. Maybe it would be better if she returned the way she had come? Her journey had been hard, but the difficulty paled in comparison to what she would face down there. Already her face burned with shame.

She stood there forever, studying the house in an attempt to delay her decision. It was a small house, once clearly run-down, now repaired in places. Firelight flickered in the low light of early evening, and at times Asa thought she could smell the scents of food cooking. Her stomach rumbled with desire.

The location of the house was excellent, sitting just inside the wood line, protected from the elements by the trees and hill. A casual traveler could probably walk fairly close in the daylight and never know the house was there. The location suited her friend as well as any place could.

Asa could sense him, down there with his wife and child. That by itself was reassuring. She was close enough that he would be able to sense her, and his natural inclination was to be invisible to the gift. If she could sense him, that was only because he willed it. A small gesture, but one that spoke volumes.

That gave Asa the courage to put one foot in front of the other. She carefully shuffled down the hill, afraid she'd slip and fall in the snow, embarrassing herself even further. She made it down to the bottom of the hill without incident.

Asa couldn't bring herself to trust, not completely. She kept her hands well away from her swords, but she proceeded cautiously, her sense extended, seeking a trap she couldn't see. Inside the house, her friend stirred from his place near the fire and came to the door.

Asa was about ten paces away from the door when it opened and Daisuke stepped out. Although his physical presence wasn't intimidating, even seeing him caused her heart to skip a beat and halt her progress. She tried to hide her fear to little success. She could still sense him, which was a good sign, but she wasn't stepping any closer. Not without an invite.

Daisuke crossed his arms, a war of emotions crossing over his usually frozen face. Asa kept her sense focused on him, prepared to run if he gave any indication of attacking.

A stranger meeting Daisuke might think nothing of him. He was of average height and size. His dark hair was cut short, and although his winter clothing hid all visible traces, his movement belied the strength of his limbs. If one didn't look in his eyes, he'd seem no more than a kind stranger. But he was probably one of the most dangerous men Asa knew. She didn't want to be his enemy, but there was a real chance she was.

The wind whipped between them. Asa didn't allow herself to react. Her eyes narrowed in focus, trying to get some indication of what Daisuke would do. If he attacked, she wouldn't have much warning. For his part, Daisuke was as still as a statue and just as expressive.

Finally, when Asa didn't think she could take it anymore, his eyes softened, and a smile broke out on his face, as though he was seeing a long-lost friend.

"Come in, Asa. You look like you're about to freeze. We've got hot food and a fire."

Asa released a breath, a wave of relief passing over her.

———

"How many trees are within ten paces?" Daisuke asked.

Asa paused as she attempted to count.

"Too slow, Asa. A moment, nothing more, that's all you'll ever have. If you aren't fully aware, you'll miss it."

Asa sighed. She'd heard this speech before. Several times already today, in fact. "What am I missing?" She tried to keep the exasperation out of her voice, but she failed miserably.

"Everything."

Daisuke also paused, and Asa knew he was about to launch into another tirade. He might be one of the most dangerous people alive, but he was a poor teacher by her estimation. When she was feeling charitable, she would acknowledge that what he was attempting to teach was difficult. He couldn't show her what to do. He couldn't demonstrate a technique. All he could do was explain, and she wasn't understanding.

Much of Daisuke's skill relied on an almost complete awareness of the environment. Asa had seen him in action several times, so she knew he lived what he taught. All the same, she had been training under him for a full moon, and she still didn't feel as though she had a quarter of the awareness he did.

"Asa, we've been over this. You know what you need to do. Discipline your mind. Where are you?"

"Here."

"And when are you?"

"Now."

He shook his head. "But you're not. Even now you're thinking about other ways to gain the skills you desire. There is only now, always. If you can do that, I will have little left to teach."

"You could teach me how to hide from the sense."

This time it was Daisuke's turn to sigh. He had told her repeatedly he didn't know how to teach the skill that made him so dangerous to nightblades. His invisibility had always been something he was able to do naturally. The answer didn't convince Asa, but Daisuke was insistent.

Asa knew that skill with the sense differed among blades, and there was no end of debate among scholars as to what was birthright versus training. She had always belonged to the camp that one's ability with the gift, once bestowed by birth, was entirely shaped by practice. Training—nothing else—was the reason some could sense farther than others or sense at a deeper level than others. If Daisuke could hide from other blades, she reasoned she could also learn. He disagreed.

"Come," he said. "Let's practice together." They sat down in the snow and closed their eyes. Asa let her sense expand, as did Daisuke. The point of the exercise was easy. He just wanted her to be aware of all things. The practice of the exercise was almost impossible. Asa wasn't sure how to fall into a relaxed state of awareness. She could only focus on one thing at a time.

Daisuke, on the other hand, seemed to know everything. At times she would ask him a question, and his answer was almost instantaneous. After most of the morning had passed this way, he stood up.

"Enough for now."

They walked through the forest, Daisuke again testing her awareness. They would do some light sparring, and then came more questions. His expectations were simple to state but impossible to achieve.

One time, between bouts of sparring, she asked him how he had trained. A sad smile came across his face. "Just like this."

"How long did it take you?"

"Several moons to grasp the basics. A lifetime to become as good as I am now."

"That's not a reassuring answer."

He gave a nonchalant shrug. "If it was easy to do, everyone would. This is how you become more dangerous to your opponents. You have to work harder than they will."

At times, Daisuke's pragmatism got on her nerves. Just once, she wanted him to give her some sort of inspirational talk, some sort of encouragement. But he never did. He always pushed everything back on her. She was free to leave whenever she wanted. If he asked her to complete a task she thought was ridiculous, she was welcome to refuse. Everything, both for good or ill, was on her shoulders.

Asa respected his consistency, but still he made her mad.

Asa most looked forward to late afternoon, the only time in the day when she felt as though she was making progress. She still remembered their first day out in the forest after her first warm meal and bed in days. She had taken a fighting stance, and Daisuke had looked at her with a question in his eyes and asked, "Don't you carry two swords?"

Asa had been confused. "Yes."

"Where's the other one?"

She looked down at the one short sword she held. "I left it in your house."

The answer confused Daisuke even more. "Why?"

She frowned. "No one has ever trained me with two. My former master used to call it a disgrace."

"You've trained all these cycles with a short blade to take advantage of your speed, and you don't fight with a second?"

Asa shook her head slowly. She had practiced some, in secret, but she didn't think she was very strong with two blades. The only time she'd tried the move in combat had been against Kiyoshi, when it had done her little good.

"Are you more concerned about honor or strength?"

Her answer was immediate. "Strength."

"Then go get your second sword."

Asa's life soon changed. Daisuke taught her the fundamentals of fighting with dual blades, and after she'd passed the initial challenge of manipulating two swords, she improved quickly. If she could sense Daisuke, she could beat him.

Today he hid himself from her sense. Some days he forced her to rely on sight and her skills with two swords, depriving her of the advantage of her gift. The daily battles were often even. His sense against her two blades made for fascinating exchanges.

She had been training under Daisuke for more than a moon. The sun was going down earlier at this time of year, but by the time it did, Asa was well exhausted from the day's training. She hadn't advanced her awareness nearly as far as she'd like, but her combative skills were progressing nicely.

She wasn't ready to leave, though. In her bones, she knew the storm was coming and that she'd have to be stronger yet.

———

Daisuke's small house contained four people but didn't feel crowded. To Asa, the environment felt comforting, like wrapping a thick blanket around herself in the coldest heart of winter. Daisuke and Keiko, his wife, slept in a small loft just big enough for a bed. Mika, their daughter, shared her room with Asa, an arrangement that delighted the precocious girl to no end.

One of Asa's small worries had been that Keiko wouldn't like having her as company. She was a jealous woman, and although Asa had no desire for Daisuke, the blade still remembered the glares she had received the first time they met in Haven before it burned.

There was no cause for concern. Keiko had welcomed her with open arms, as though she was a cherished friend and not someone she had only met once before.

The last time Asa had seen Daisuke's family, she had helped them escape from Haven. Those had been trying times, and guile and haste had been required to get them out. She was glad to see they were both doing well. Mika had now seen six cycles and looked as though she had doubled in size since Asa had last seen her.

Asa also noticed that at times Mika became almost invisible to her sense. The first time it had happened, Daisuke had been in the room, and he had shaken his head. Asa understood. Her own mother, after the death of her father, didn't want her to become a blade. After everything Daisuke had seen, it was little surprise he didn't want Mika to become involved in the life of her father.

An observer passing by would have seen nothing unusual about the meal that night. The four of them sat around the table, the bulk of the evening's entertainment coming from Mika's endless stream of questions. Asa answered as many as she could, but some of Mika's questions were challenging. She didn't want to tell Mika she met Daisuke in a heated battle against eight guards. She didn't know why the grass was green, and she certainly wasn't going to tell the girl how many men she'd kissed.

The entire time, Daisuke and Keiko exchanged loving glances and gentle smiles. Asa imagined that when she wasn't present, they were the target of all these questions. They were probably grateful for a short break.

The fire warmed the room, and Asa felt both body and mind relax as the evening wore on. The meal was simple but tasty, Keiko clearly proud that her cooking had improved in the past few moons. Asa wasn't sure, but she felt like she remembered Daisuke once saying he did most of the cooking when home.

Unbidden, memories of Asa's childhood returned to her. Her own family had sat around a table in the winter much like this. Growing up, she had loved winter on the farm. There were fewer chores to do, and the sunlight was shorter. They spent more time together as a family, sitting around the fire while Sachio, her father, told stories.

Some time had passed since she had thought of her family, and Asa realized that the sharp stabbing pain she usually felt was gone. There was still a constant ache, but the pain had diffused and become something else.

Asa turned to Daisuke during a short break in Mika's questioning. "Daisuke, do you know any good stories?"

Daisuke's grin was easy. "I do, but Keiko is the real storyteller in the family."

Mika clapped with excitement, and Asa repositioned herself to be more comfortable. Keiko thought for a moment and launched into a tale about a brave dragon who wanted to be human. Variations of the story were common throughout the Kingdom, but Asa had never heard one told half so well as Keiko's. Each character had a unique voice, and Keiko knew exactly when to pause for dramatic effect.

Asa fell completely into the world that Keiko's voice created. Inside the house it was no longer winter, but a lovely spring day. The world wasn't about to fall into chaos, and flying dragons existed and wanted to give up their strength and immortality to be human. Keiko finished her story, making Asa feel almost as sad as Mika looked.

For a single moment the world was perfect. Keiko relaxed comfortably into Daisuke's arms, and Mika was lost in the story world her mother had woven. Asa felt as though she hadn't a care in the world.

It couldn't last. His movement was subtle, but Asa sensed Daisuke tense. The action, slight as it was, snapped Asa out of the world of comfort and into the world they lived in. She focused her sense, pushing it out until she sensed what had gotten Daisuke's attention. Far away, at the edge of her ability, a group was gathered.

They weren't close enough yet to see the house and could miss it altogether depending on just how bad the weather was outside.

Keiko, in Daisuke's arms, felt the change in her husband and sat up. She looked at him inquisitively.

Daisuke gave her an unconvincing look. The group wasn't huge, but it wasn't small, either. Asa wasn't certain, but she counted about twenty. "Perhaps it's time for you to put Mika to bed," Daisuke said.

At just that moment, Mika yawned. "But, Father, I'm not tired!"

Daisuke replied, "No, you're not, young one. But look at your mother. She's worn out from a hard day of work. Maybe you could take her to your bed and help her go to sleep. Could you sing her a lullaby?"

Mika nodded vigorously as Keiko let out an exaggerated yawn. "Yes, Father. Are you going to sleep soon, too?"

Daisuke approached Mika and gave her a tight hug. "Of course. Asa and I are just going to go outside for a little bit. You know how your dad likes to train."

With that, Mika and Keiko went into one of the three sleeping rooms and shut the door. Asa and Daisuke threw on heavier clothes and went outside.

After the evening spent in the warmth of the hearth, stepping outside was like being stabbed with a hundred icy needles. Asa almost turned around and went back into the house, potential threats be cursed. She joined Daisuke in trudging up the hill, taking up a position near the top of the rise.

Off in the distance, she could see a few pinpricks of light, torches in the blackness of night. It wasn't snowing, but the wind was picking up snow and whipping icy flakes around, creating blizzard conditions even though the sky above them was clear.

Asa took a moment to be impressed by Daisuke yet again. He had been relaxed with his wife and daughter when he sensed the group, meaning he had extended his gift an incredible distance with little focus. As difficult as his training was proving, there was no doubt she was in the right place. If she could develop the same skills as Daisuke, she'd be powerful enough to create whatever change she wanted.

Her reverie was interrupted by Daisuke standing up. "Come, let's get closer to them. I don't sense that anyone is gifted among them."

Asa concurred, and together they walked toward the lights. If any of the other party had been gifted, the two blades would have been discovered. Daisuke could hide himself from the sense, but Asa couldn't.

The blowing snow and moonless night made the two nightblades invisible. They carried no fire, guided only by their sense and Daisuke's knowledge of the area. They stopped about two hundred paces away from the party in the direction they were traveling. Daisuke and Asa both lay down, covering themselves with snow. They wouldn't have long to wait.

Eventually the band of soldiers passed in front of them. Their green uniforms marked them as Lord Isamu's, but they looked sorrowful in the driving snow. Their leader drove the men forward, his voice carrying to Asa's ears. He told them their destination was only a league away, and there they would have warmth and food.

She felt a brief flicker of pity for them. The only destination within a league was open prairie or forest. No nearby settlements existed to host soldiers. Even though the stars were visible above, their commander had led them far astray.

The infantrymen approached and trudged forward, some passing within twenty paces of Asa's hideout, none even remotely suspicious of her presence.

After the soldiers moved on, Asa and Daisuke rose from the snow. She looked to him for guidance.

"They mean us no harm, and if they continue through the night, they won't come any closer. We'll take no action."

That was good enough for Asa. She, too, preferred to avoid unnecessary bloodshed.

As they watched, though, the soldiers stopped and started setting up camp.

"Of course, they would," Daisuke said.

Asa felt as though she owed Daisuke, and she saw a chance to repay a small portion of her debt. "I'll take watch tonight if you like. Just to make sure they don't stumble upon your place."

He watched her for a moment, his face unreadable. He nodded. "Very well, thank you."

Just like that he turned around and started walking back toward his house.

Asa wasn't sure what made her call out. Perhaps it was the evening with his family. Perhaps it was that she knew they wouldn't be overheard. "Daisuke!"

He turned back to her.

"I can't tell you I'm sorry. I won't lie to you, and my feelings are too confused to say how I feel. But he was a good man, and I am sorry that I've caused you suffering."

Daisuke's eyes were harder than steel, and Asa worried she had gone too far. The wounds were still too fresh. In the entire time she'd been training with him, they'd never spoken about the fact she had killed Kiyoshi, the man who had sheltered and trained Daisuke since he was a child.

His eyes softened just a little. "He wasn't a good man. He was the best I've ever known."

With that, he spun quickly toward his house and walked away, the blowing snow causing him to vanish from sight.

Chapter 15

Mari heard the rustling of fabric outside her tent. "Come in."

Takahiro stepped in, looking grateful to be in the warm tent. "You sent for me?"

"I did. Can I offer you some drink?" A bottle of good wine had been given to them by a wealthy man whose child had been healed by Jun. Mari saw no reason why it should go to waste. To her surprise, Takahiro accepted. She had rarely seen him imbibe.

"How may I serve, Mari?"

Mari poured two cups. They didn't have proper wine cups on the road, but their dented travel cups worked just as well. She sniffed at the beverage, pleased with the fragrance it presented. Her first sip was delightful, and she fought a sudden urge to lie back and finish the entire bottle. She didn't think Jun drank at all, but Koji would be disappointed in not being allowed a taste.

"Mostly I need to talk."

Takahiro looked as though he'd been expecting as much. That was no surprise. Mari had called on him several times in the past half moon. Spring wasn't long away, and she would need to decide on a course of action.

"You've come no closer to a decision, then?"

Mari sat down and looked up at her closest friend. "No. Every direction seems fraught with peril. There are days when I wish this winter could last forever."

Her forces had continued to grow. Although communication had been slowed by the harsh weather, she estimated that she had almost two hundred blades under her command, spread throughout the Kingdom. Jun wanted to summon them all together in the spring, to hold a gathering where they would announce the next stage in their revolution. Mari had agreed to the idea, but she still had no idea how best to use the immense power she found herself in control of.

Attacking the armies of a lord was an option often spoken of in hushed whispers. Mari hated the idea of resorting to violence to achieve her ends, but she was in charge of a force made largely of warriors. Hunting on behalf of villages would only take them so far in solving the Kingdom's problems.

They needed to take a bold action. Her shadows had reported the lords already gathering up their armies. Katashi had been the first to summon his, long before the spring melted the snow and allowed the men to plant their fields. Hiromi and Isamu had no choice but to prepare as well. As soon as the weather turned, war would wash over the Kingdom, and Mari felt as though her small force was the only one that could stop the rising tide.

She didn't need to say any of this to Takahiro. He had been her counsel for as long as she could remember, and he knew her mind and situation as well as she did. She looked to him, begging him for answers.

He sipped at the wine, a smile spreading across his face. "This is very good."

Mari gave him an irritated look as she took another sip. He was right. The wine was full-bodied and fruity, yet not too sweet. The bottle was even better than she'd assumed.

He glanced at her over his cup and made a careful study of the tent.

"If you have something you want to say, say it."

He grimaced, as though he was forced to do something he found distasteful. "Have you considered stopping?"

She glared at him, but he had already begun and was determined to see his idea through. "When this all started, I was behind you. With a small group, we could wander around safely doing some good. I thought the danger was manageable. But this has grown into something beyond what I expected. I never imagined the blades would be so hungry to follow you. To follow anyone."

"So why should I quit?" Mari struggled to keep the anger out of her voice.

"Because the danger is becoming too great, and you don't have a vision for what you want to do. If only one of those was true, perhaps I'd be able to support you, but there's nothing to support."

Mari stood up and almost hit him. He saw the motion as she drew her arm back, but he didn't react. Though they were close, he was still hers to command, and if she decided to strike him, so be it.

She stopped herself before doing something she would regret. If Takahiro had made her that angry, it was because he was right. Her only goal had been to help as many people as she could. An idealistic goal, but vague and undefined. She needed something to work toward. Otherwise he was right. She didn't deserve the blades who followed her.

"What if my goal was to see the Kingdom at peace?"

Takahiro grimaced again, and again Mari almost struck him. There was no point being honest part of the time and hiding his feelings the rest. "Say it!"

"I know how this sounds, but I've been thinking about the matter. All of us have been trying to imagine how to put the Kingdom back together, to make things the way they used to be. I think, however, that's foolish. The lords will fight one another, and I don't believe even our force can stop that. Although we are changing the attitudes of the people in regard to the blades, there is still a great deal of enmity toward them."

Takahiro took a deep breath. "I don't think we can go back to the way things used to be. We have to find a new way forward. We have to imagine a better future."

At first, Mari didn't want to consider his words. His ideas were rotten and bitter to taste. But like eating sour food when she was a child, Mari forced herself to think about what he had said. All she longed for were days past. What Takahiro said was just as true for her as it was for the Kingdom.

She had ignored her brother's final offer and had no doubt he knew who the Lady in White was. Stonekeep and its thick, comforting walls could be closed to her forever.

Mari sat back down and sipped silently at her wine. "Thank you."

She didn't have the courage to say any more, but nothing else was required. Takahiro knew her mind. "I am sorry to be the bearer of difficult ideas, but it is my duty to protect you, including from yourself."

"I don't suppose you have any ideas for a new future, do you?"

Takahiro finished his wine. "I am but a lowly soldier, my lady. That honor falls to you."

———

Mari knew that the situation was already bad in the Kingdom and was only going to get worse. As she had feared in autumn, there wasn't enough food, and there were too many mouths to feed.

The four companions were in yet another village. Mari had been to so many she had lost track of their names. They had gone incognito, as had been their habit since separating into smaller groups. Being recognized when you were traveling with dozens of nightblades was one risk. Being recognized when you had only one was far more dangerous. Better to scout the land first before revealing her true identity. As such, she was dressed in simple traveling clothes today, with no white visible.

When she had first heard she was known as the Lady in White, she had been surprised. She had chosen the costume as a symbol, but she had never expected it to spawn a title that spread from village to village before her. Names and legends had power, and she had come to recognize that her idea might live beyond her.

This village was larger than many they had visited, a hub of local commerce, which was why they had come. While Koji's hunting fed them all, the body and heart longed for more than just meat cooked over a fire.

Some of the shops were still open. Mari imagined the ones that were closed had run out of supplies. Those that remained sold goods at exorbitant prices. She was certain people worked for days for less money than she had spent on rice and a few spices.

If there was one resource Mari still possessed, it was her money. She had used a letter of credit to draw as many funds as she could before Hiromi froze her accounts. Since then they had traveled with saddlebags filled with gold. Mari often considered giving it away, but she didn't possess enough wealth to change the reality that there wasn't enough food for everyone to survive the winter.

She stepped inside one last shop, her party more than happy to wait outside. Jun was arguing with Takahiro and Koji, a spirited philosophical debate on whether violence or medicine had changed the history of the Kingdom more. The shop sold ribbons, and Mari, in a rare mood, thought some simple fabric would be wonderful to tie back her hair, which seemed to be growing faster than it ever had before.

The woman inside was ancient and matronly, and Mari instantly felt at ease. She flashed the shopkeeper a smile, which was warmly returned. Mari browsed the ribbons, trying to find one that spoke to her. While she looked, she struck up a conversation. After the customary introductions, she asked how the village was faring under the difficult conditions.

The shopkeeper's answer was much more challenging than Mari expected. "We're doing well enough, so long as we don't get any unwanted guests."

Mari frowned. In a small town, they were guests, and the woman's comment was pointed. "Are you afraid they'll take too much food?"

The woman, who at first had seemed so kind, had taken on a hard and bitter edge. "You could say that. I'm afraid the Lady in White will come and take all our food, leaving us to starve."

Mari was taken aback. How had such rumors spread? Had some of her people overstepped the boundaries they had set? That had always been one of her greatest fears in sending people out in her name. She couldn't lead them all directly.

"I thought the Lady in White was trying to help the villages," she responded, forcing uncertainty into her voice.

"I don't know where you heard that, but we have it straight here in this village. We've heard how her people go around killing those who disagree with them and taking food from those who agree, sentencing them to death just as well. No. If she comes here, she'll be captured and executed for her crimes. To think, she does all of that with nightblades! Beyond horrible."

Mari had been fingering an ivory ribbon she thought would go well with her Lady in White outfit. Suddenly she wasn't very interested.

She was here, though, and would do anything to allay the older woman's clear suspicions. She chose a red ribbon and had the woman cut a length.

Mari stepped outside as quickly as she was able. She looked at her companions. "We need to get out of this village as quickly as we can."

They had left their horses in a stable on the outskirts of the area. None of her friends questioned her. They just turned and started walking out of the village the way they'd come. Koji and Takahiro were on alert, searching for any possible threats. Mari had a bad feeling.

Koji drew his blade with blinding speed. Mari didn't know what was happening, but she heard a soft sound of metal striking metal. Koji had turned to one side and looked like he was going to sprint away, but Takahiro yelled at him. "Koji! We need to protect Mari!"

The blade stood up straight, seeming confused. He was used to fighting, not guarding. Takahiro's instincts were right. The bodyguard yelled again, "We need to get out of here now. Run!"

Mari looked down and saw a slim needle sticking out of the snow. She recognized the shape as one designed to be used as a blow dart. Her mind put the pieces together as Takahiro grabbed hold of her and started running. What would have happened to her if Koji hadn't been with them?

They ran toward the stables, each of the homes of the village a shade of brown in Mari's vision. Everything seemed blurry, her eyes unwilling to focus. How close had she come to death?

Four men appeared at the stables, figures dressed as everyday villagers but who clearly didn't belong. Takahiro grabbed Mari's shoulder and brought her to a stop. Koji sprinted forward.

Mari had seen Koji fight before, but she didn't trust her memories. In her dreams, he moved as fast as lightning. As she watched him defend her, she realized that she had exaggerated his fighting only slightly.

His cuts were so fast she didn't see them. All her eyes caught was his sword flashing and reflecting light. For a few moments in time, Koji was in the heart of the four enemies, swords flashing all around him. No one could survive such an onslaught.

Then the battle was over, and the four men were on the ground, dead or bleeding out. Koji stood alone, unharmed.

Suddenly he darted off behind the stables. Another man was getting on a horse and trying to escape. Before he could get his mount turned around, Koji was there, leaping up and cutting him down with one graceful movement.

They had a few moments before the entire village was on them. The companions flipped over the bodies and examined them. Mari steeled herself, surprised when she recognized one of the men.

Takahiro heard her sharp intake of breath. "What's wrong?"

"I believe these are my brother's men."

Takahiro had been searching through their bags, throwing out food and trail supplies. He stopped and looked at the faces. "I think you're right. I recognize this man," he said as he pointed to the one Koji had killed first.

The realization almost knocked Mari to the ground. She had known that her brother would piece together who the Lady in White was. He knew she was traveling with blades, and there weren't many women in the Kingdom involved in that distinct activity. She had never considered that he himself might try to have her killed.

She could even see the reasoning now that her eyes had been opened. If her identity were discovered, it would be used against him. Blades were still considered outlaws, and traveling with them made you one as well. She could be used to discredit his claim to the throne.

But assassination? Despite everything, they were still blood.

Her eyes wandered over the bodies, and her thoughts wandered in circles. She watched as Takahiro went over the corpses, taking all the food he could find. Something tickled in the back of her mind, a half-formed idea. She tried to relax and let it continue, and when it did, she actually laughed. The plan was brilliant in its simplicity. She knew what she was going to do.

Takahiro looked at her, clearly worried the pressure was causing her to go mad. Mari turned to Jun, who was busy checking to ensure that Koji hadn't been wounded in the fight. "Summon everyone for the gathering. The time is now, and I know how to break the lords."

Chapter 16

Koji's mornings had become much more complicated in the past few days. After their ambush in the village, Mari had decided on her strategy. Even now, thinking back to that time, the blade had to smile to himself. Part of Mari's plan wasn't new at all. In fact, it was a fairly standard tenet in warfare. But the second half, that was something only Mari would have come up with.

Before the blades under her had separated, they had figured out a way to get messages back and forth. There was little need for the most part. Each small group was fairly independent, and Mari had made sure they knew that they had her trust. The messages were used mostly to pass along important intelligence.

The downside of the network was that it was slow. Mari and Jun set the date for as early as they dared but knew that by the time the message reached the farthest edges of the Kingdom, the blades who received it might not be able to return in time.

For Mari's plan to have the greatest effect, haste was of the essence. The winter was still biting cold, but the season couldn't last more than another two moons. They needed to be organized and moving before that happened.

Based on the logistics of the messages, Mari's party would be the first to arrive at the gathering location, a long, shallow valley in the territory of House Fujita. Koji was certain that if Lord Isamu knew what was happening on his own lands, he'd be furious. Fortunately, of all the lords, Isamu was the least aware of the events happening on his terrain. The position was also defensible in case the situation became desperate.

As more blades trickled in, Koji had to spend more time every morning to leave. With a tiny group, he didn't have to travel very far to be able to meditate clearly. As the gathering continued to grow, he needed to travel farther just to leave the boundaries of the camp and even farther to meditate in peace.

Mari was nearing the time when she would have to begin. Her shadows informed her that every lord was already moving, and there was a real possibility war would start before the snow had melted. Her forces had to be faster.

As was his custom, Koji sat in the snow and focused on his breath. Not long from now, this daily ritual would be difficult to follow. If Mari's plan succeeded, they would be on the move constantly, with little time to rest and be still.

His meditation worked for a while, his focus expanding to where it needed to be. The effort wasn't nearly enough. His quest to find clarity had been useless. His comfort with the sense had increased and he could push his gift farther than before, but in combat it was of no greater use.

Today, as with most days, his mind wandered. With so much happening, it was difficult for him to focus on his sense. Every time he redoubled his efforts, he became even more distracted.

One matter was the most distracting. Mari's plan had him commanding one of the large units that would be integral to her strategy. For a number of reasons, he felt uncomfortable with the idea, but he hadn't developed the courage to face her yet.

Finally, he quit. He stood up and drew his sword, running through the same practice he had completed almost every day since he had been a child. As his body slipped into the motions, his mind relaxed.

For a moment, his world shifted, the colors became more vivid, and he was in the state he so desperately sought. But in his next breath, the moment was gone.

Koji almost threw his sword to the ground in frustration. Mustering every scrap of control he had, he resisted the urge.

Barely controlling his frustration, Koji slammed his blade back in its sheath.

He wasn't sure what he needed to do to become better, but he knew he needed to speak to Mari before it was too late. The longer he waited, the worse the situation would become. Facing his fear, he turned back toward the tents.

———

One benefit of Koji's position was that he was quickly admitted to see Mari when he came. Takahiro was at the door, ensuring her time wasn't wasted by needless demands. Koji simply said he had something important to talk about and was let in.

Mari was again poring over papers, taking copious notes using a system he didn't understand. Koji knew how to read but was amazed by what Mari did with the ability.

Mari seemed to know almost everything of importance happening in the Kingdom. She knew where the various armies were, what villages were starving, and which were well fed. Koji suspected she even knew what was happening in Starfall, which meant blades were selling information on their own kind.

In a way, he supposed, Mari was a little like a blade. Their advantage came from the ability to take in heightened information about the world, to predict events happening just a little in the future. Mari did the same, although without the gift.

He waited for her to finish her notes. When she looked up, she smiled at him, and his heart broke. He admired Mari, perhaps more than anyone he had met. Following her had been the most honorable decision he had ever made. To know that his secret might discredit her, or even worse, bring her disapproval unto him, was almost more than he could bear. It reinforced his decision. This was the right thing to do. He stood up a little straighter and spoke.

"Mari, I do not think you should put me in command of one of the units you are creating."

For all the agony he had suffered over the past days debating what to do, getting the words out was surprisingly easy after he started.

Mari didn't respond, waiting for him to say more.

"Mari, serving under you has been an honor, but as a nightblade, my hands aren't clean. I'm afraid that if people ever find out the crimes I've committed, it would ruin our cause. If I am a mere warrior, you can disown me. But if I were a commander, you wouldn't have that chance. It's much safer to simply put me with a unit, probably not even your own."

She frowned at him. "I don't care what you've done in the past, Koji. Your work now is all that matters, and you've done great work. You've saved my life, and you've trained a number of nightblades. You've earned this."

"Thank you, Mari. But some crimes can't be washed away, and few people in this Kingdom possess the same tolerance you do."

Mari looked unconvinced. "If that is your only argument, I must disagree. Perhaps you don't feel worthy, for whatever reason. But I've been traveling with you for moons now. I've seen the way you train, and I've seen you kill. If anyone knows your heart and your character, it's me. There's no one I would rather trust with these blades."

Koji started to get exasperated. Mari would always be Mari, and that very consistency was one of the reasons he swore his sword to her. But the trait wasn't without drawbacks.

"That's not all, Mari."

She gazed at him expectantly, and for a moment, he almost told her that he had killed her brother and the king. But as he looked in her eyes, all he saw was kindness and trust.

"There's a difference between being a good warrior, or even being a good person, and being a good commander. I know that I'm a good warrior. There are some who are better but not many. But I am not a leader of blades. I have no grasp of battlefield strategy, and I hardly have the charisma to keep blades in line. The greatest service I can offer you is my ability to kill, not my ability to lead."

He wasn't sure if it was his argument or the tone of his voice that stopped Mari from objecting. She studied him, and Koji worried she would see the darkness of his past in his heart. For the longest time, she said nothing.

When she did speak, her voice was soft but strong. "You're sure about this?"

"Absolutely."

Koji could hear Mari's tent snapping in the breeze, but his eyes were only on her, wondering what she would decide.

"Very well. It's not the decision I would make, but I trust you with my life, Koji, and if you are certain about your feelings, I will replace you."

Koji bowed deeply to Mari and left, relieved that his request had been honored, terrified that he might be the one to break Mari's spirit.

A few days later, the time had come. Koji was ready. Since his self-imposed demotion, his status had been unusual. Because Mari still considered him a personal guard, he was still invited to meetings of the commanders, and his task list seemed to grow every day. Commander or not, Mari trusted him, which meant more to do.

He had been given his fair share of inquisitive stares when Mari announced he was being replaced. Of the three commanders, Koji had been considered the favorite by many. All Mari said was that he had requested to be reassigned. As curious as they might have been, none of the commanders inquired deeper, and Koji wasn't vocal about his misgivings.

Koji joined the other blades. From one perspective, this was still a small gathering. There were less than two hundred blades present, and as they huddled together against the cold, they didn't take up much space. Someone had found a wagon, and Mari climbed on top to speak to her audience.

Even though their numbers weren't impressive, their capability was great. Koji had tried to remember his history, but he didn't think a larger force of blades had ever been assembled outside of special festivals in Starfall.

Mari was conversing near the wagon with Jun, and while they waited, several of the blades near Koji fought for his attention. Their situation was dire, but the mood around the camp was strangely jubilant. The days had been filled with hunting, training, and fires that lasted long into the night. From the sounds Koji heard each night as he drifted off to sleep, quite a number of blades had fallen into couples while they waited for the gathering to become official.

A blade next to him, even younger than he was, spoke conspiratorially to him. "Koji, I know that you are able to talk to Mari whenever you want. Maybe you can convince her to hold a gathering, maybe during the next cycle?"

Koji chuckled softly. Truth be told, he wouldn't mind another gathering as well. It was relaxing to be in the company of blades, to be doing good for the Kingdom. He was still haunted by his demons, but his days were as content as he had ever remembered.

"I'll see. I can speak, but she doesn't always listen!"

The other blade was about to laugh but turned serious as Mari stepped up on the wagon.

The lady of House Kita was in her full Lady in White costume, her heavy robes making her seem larger. Although the platform was only a little higher than the surrounding area, Koji thought she towered over all the blades. Her spotless form stood out against the worn and motley collection of traveling clothes the warriors and healers wore.

The only change to Mari's outfit was the veil, conspicuously absent. Standing in the middle of the crowd, Koji could easily make out every facial feature, from the strong set of her jaw to the slight upturn of her mouth.

Koji couldn't hear a single murmur among the crowd. Mari's strong voice carried over the assembly.

"Brothers and sisters!"

Every eye was on her, but Mari didn't rush. As Koji looked at her, he knew she was the embodiment of what it meant to lead.

"First, I must thank you for all you have done for the Kingdom so far. The stories of the kindness and good you've done this winter— hunted and hated—will someday become the legends we tell our children. Of this, I'm sure.

"All of us know it is easy to be kind to a friend, but to serve those who live scared of you, that is a quality not many possess. But it is within all of you, and my words will never express my gratitude."

Mari paused and looked over the crowd. Koji felt a stirring of pride to know he was associated with blades of such honor.

"Our work is not yet done, though. For all the lives we have saved and all the good we have done, the Kingdom is still at war. Soon the snows will melt and the armies will march, and this ground, the ground that feeds our families, will be poisoned by the blood of friends.

"The lords do nothing to stop this. They fight for a throne, not for their people.

"We're going to teach them what comes next! We're going to show them that they can't starve their people to feed their armies!"

Despite the reserved nature of most blades, Mari's passion caused a cheer to break out in the crowd. Koji joined them.

"Although our strength is tremendous, I do not want to see unnecessary bloodshed. Our mission, as I see it, is to hit the armies of all the lords in such a way that they can't make war on one another.

"While they focus on their fronts, our groups of blades will tear them up from behind, hitting their supply lines."

A murmur went up from the crowd. There was no honor in taking a supply depot.

"I know what you must think," Mari said, "but our purpose is twofold. All of us have seen the waste the lords have left in their haste to prepare for battle. Across the Kingdom, families starve so the armies may march and fight. We take these supplies, not just to stop the armies, but to feed the people whom we've sworn to defend."

Koji wasn't sure he'd ever seen a crowd of any size change their minds so fast. They had all seen what was happening in the villages.

The winter had been one of the most brutal in memory. Each of the lords had made the decision that feeding their armies was more important than feeding their citizens. In most cases, the armies left a little behind, but never enough for the village to survive.

Mari would fix the problem. They would attack the supply points, take back the food and matériel, and return the goods to the people. Mari had planned a series of strikes against each lord, one after the other. The pace would be brutal, but her goal was no less than to entirely cripple the armies. In the best case, she could stop the war in its tracks and feed the people in the process.

When Koji had first heard her idea, he had been astounded. He loved the plan and had done everything he could to shape it into a feasible strategy. From the looks of the assembled blades, her idea resonated with them as well.

He knew how they felt.

Mari finished her speech.

"I know that many of you have sworn your swords to me, and for that, I am ever in your debt. Everything I do is for the Kingdom, but only because of the loyalty you have shown me.

"If I were a lord, I would command you to serve, but I am no lord. All I can do is ask. Do this for the Kingdom. Do this for me. If you are not comfortable, please feel free to leave the gathering whenever you feel called. I assure you, no one here will stop you from departing. Our mission will be difficult, and our lives will certainly be at risk. It is, as always, your decision to make."

With that, Mari bowed down deeply to the blades and stepped down from the wagon. Koji looked from face to face, and he knew no one was leaving.

Mari now had her own small army, ready to stop the war.

Chapter 17

The snow had yet to melt, but the signs of spring were promising. Asa and Daisuke had more daylight to train in, and although the days were still frosty, Asa could feel the extra warmth of the sun on her skin. Spring was growing closer every day, the winter a long journey almost over.

She stood alone in the plains, just outside the largest village they had ever trained in. Daisuke's house was a few days' walk from a few villages, most only a scattered collection of huts. This particular village was the largest within a three days' walk, holding perhaps fifty people.

It was her final test of a sort, even though Daisuke never said as much. Asa's fighting skills had improved considerably, her two-sword style developed to a point where she was eager to duel Koji again. She wasn't invincible, but she was much, much better.

The other skills Daisuke tried to teach her, though, were much more challenging. Those were the skills they tested here today: her ability with her gift, her awareness, and her focus. Although her dual-sword style was an incredible improvement, these were the skills that would make her truly powerful. She had seen Daisuke's skill, and although she still wasn't anywhere close to his ability, she believed she had improved.

Her test wasn't complex. The day was bright, and although it was cold, the people of the village were out of their houses, enjoying the sunlight as best they could. All Asa had to do was get from one end of the village to the other without being seen. Her test began the moment she reached the edge.

Calming her breath, she extended her sense, getting an understanding of the place. The fact she could reach her sense over the entire area was in itself an indicator of how much she had improved under Daisuke's strict discipline. After a while, Asa was sure of what she had already guessed: there would be no easy way through the village.

Daisuke stood on the other side, using his own gift to sense everything happening. Asa took a deep breath and started walking toward the village.

She stopped just on the outskirts, waiting for people to clear out of her way before she began. She had chosen a narrow backway through the buildings to avoid the most eyes. The path bent and turned between huts built closely together.

When Asa sensed her moment, she stepped forward. The first dozen paces were easy. She could sense that no one was nearby and the path was completely unobserved.

Her first challenge came after she had passed an intersection. Her sense, wandering throughout the area, detected someone stepping onto her route in an intersection in front of her. Asa started to backtrack, but her gift warned her that someone was standing next to the intersection she had just passed. She couldn't remain where she was, but either direction seemed to be a failure.

In the past, Asa would have tensed. Her mind would have raced, not finding any answers no matter how fast it worked. After several moons of training with Daisuke, her response was different. She focused on her breath, quickly expanding her awareness outward. There wasn't much time. The woman up ahead would see her in a few heartbeats.

Her sense, more refined, felt the man behind her lean against one of the huts, its wooden walls bending slightly under the pressure. Asa realized his back was toward the intersection. His posture indicated he wasn't leaving anytime soon, but if she moved quietly, she might be able to stand behind the man without him noticing her. Asa retreated, turning the corner and seeing his back. He was a bulky figure and not terribly observant. Asa slipped into his shadow, crouching a little.

The woman entered the path Asa had just been standing on. Now she had to trust luck. The intersection she hid near had three routes. If the woman chose Asa's route, there was nothing more she could do.

The pedestrian entered the intersection, and Asa held her breath. Possibly an elder of the village, the woman continued straight, never glancing in Asa's direction.

Before, Asa would have gotten back onto her first path as quickly as she could, but now she knew better. She kept her focus on her sense, planning her next moves. More people were walking near her original path. She'd be better served by choosing a different alleyway.

Asa stood up and snuck quietly away, paying attention to her footsteps to make sure she didn't make a noise that would attract the bulky fellow's interest.

Her next obstacle was a wide path that cut through the middle of the village. There was no way to avoid it, but here Asa had more luck. When she arrived, no one was looking at the space she needed to cross. With no time for hesitation, she darted across into a narrow passage on the other side.

From here she moved quickly. She was nearing the other side of the village when another danger presented itself. One person was in the passage behind her, around a corner for now but would see her in a few heartbeats. A crossing was in front of her, but two men were talking near it.

Asa scanned her surroundings. She smiled when she looked up at the roofs. Several in the area were flat, and her sense told her the buildings were currently unoccupied, the residents out enjoying the bright weather. She ran up to one, putting her foot high up on the wall and pushing up, letting her hands catch the edge of the roof. With one smooth motion she pulled herself up.

She rested for a few moments as the person who had been unintentionally following her passed below, completely oblivious that he had almost ended Asa's test. During her rest she glanced around, grinning from ear to ear when she saw that she could make it to the edge of the village on the rooftops.

Making sure not to be seen or heard, Asa leapt lightly from roof to roof, covering the last fifty paces of her task with no problem. She leapt with pride off the last roof, landing and rolling softly on the other side of the village, completely unseen.

Not long afterward, beaming, she walked up to Daisuke, whose face was as expressionless as always. He gave her the slightest of smiles as she approached.

"You did well. Not quite the ideal route, but an acceptable one. You kept your focus, used your imagination, and your ability with your gift is better than I've seen from you."

From Daisuke, that was high praise, and Asa flushed with pride.

"Come, let's have lunch. Then we can begin our journey back."

———

Asa was content. Her stomach was full, and her satisfaction at the completion of her test was deep. As they journeyed toward Daisuke's house, she noticed other subtle signs of spring. Here and there, a green blade of grass poked through the snow, and songbirds flitted around the blades' heads.

She wasn't sure the last time she had been so content. Her days were filled with effort and training, but she was happy to be learning under Daisuke. She loved making little Mika laugh, and she was surprised that she'd miss Keiko's company as well.

Daisuke, who always seemed to have a window to her thoughts, broke the companionable silence that had lasted between them. "It is perhaps not my place to ask, but I must. Have you put any thought toward what you will do next?"

There were layers to the question, and Asa understood them. Daisuke believed he had taught her everything he knew. She had nothing more to learn. That was not to say her skills couldn't improve further, but lack of knowledge was no longer the problem. Asa knew what she needed to do. Henceforth, improvement was more a matter of practice than of learning.

He was also asking what she would do with what he had taught her. With her belly full and Daisuke's inquiry opening the door, she finally worked up the courage to ask him the question that had pestered her since the day he'd let her into his house.

"I'm not sure. I do think about it often. But may I ask you something?"

Daisuke's silence passed for consent.

"When I came to your door, after what I did, why did you welcome me?"

His eyes were unfocused, as though he was seeing something far in the past. "My own feelings were mixed. I had long thought what I would do if our paths crossed again. Often I believed I would kill you."

The statement was simple and uttered without malice. Asa wasn't surprised, but it did hurt.

"Simply, though, I welcomed you because of Kiyoshi. Knowing what I know now, I think he saw to your heart better even than you did, and certainly better than I. His last request to me was that I train you as well as I was able. After . . ."

Daisuke's voice, normally steady, wavered. He took a deeper breath and continued.

"After he died, I couldn't fulfill the promise I made to him. I had enough respect for him not to kill you, even though I desperately desired to. When you found me, more than anything, it was his wish that made me bid you welcome."

Asa stopped and bowed deeply to him. He nodded silently, and they continued. For some time, Asa didn't trust herself to speak.

"What do you believe I should do?"

"I do not know. I am out of touch with the events of the day, familiar only with the general state of affairs. Both Kiyoshi and I would have the same ask, though—that you serve the people of the Kingdom as well as you are able."

The answer was too broad for Asa's taste. She had the same feeling but wasn't sure how that could best be accomplished.

She was surprised when Daisuke continued. "Know that I mean no malice in this, but once we return home, I will ask that you leave within a few days."

Asa felt like she had been kicked in the shin. Before she could think, she blurted out, "Why?"

Daisuke glanced at her and smiled gently, his expression surprisingly tender. "It is not because I want you out of my family's life. I'm sure that both Keiko and Mika would be more than happy to have you as our guest forever. You have become as close to us as Kiyoshi was, and that is no small feat. Even I admit that I wouldn't be opposed to your presence. You are a skilled warrior, and the home is easier to manage with you present.

"You will always be welcome with my family, and our door will always be open to you. But you are hiding, and I would be a poor teacher if I continued to let you do so."

Asa wanted to protest, but the words died before they could leave her lips. Claiming to be living with Daisuke to continue training was a half truth at best. While she was with him, there was no need to figure out what she lived for.

"I'm not sure what to do," Asa repeated.

Daisuke stopped walking and fixed her with a penetrating stare. "Why did you come to me?"

Asa was momentarily disoriented. "To get stronger."

"Why?"

"Because I want to prevent the people I care about from dying."
She thought of her family and Daiki and his strong-willed wife.

"You're a fool."

The words stung, but Asa could hear the affection behind them.
Nevertheless they upset her.

"Why is that wrong? Isn't that why you're out here, in the middle
of nowhere?"

Daisuke shook his head as though she was a child who didn't
understand the simplest explanations. "Part of why we are here is to
protect my family, yes. But the real reason is because we wanted to start
a new life together. Asa, no matter how strong you are, you can't prevent what comes to us all. Your purpose needs to be better than that."

"Your idea of 'protecting the Kingdom' is too vague."

"Then be specific. Serve one person or one village. Just serve. Even
if it's only one person at a time, you'll be making a difference in this
world, and that's all Kiyoshi or I could ask for."

Daisuke, like his mentor Kiyoshi, was one of the best people she
had ever met. His decision wasn't easy to accept, but it was right.

"May I stay a few more days and say my goodbyes to your family?"

"Of course. I would never deny you that."

Asa, not one given to self-expression, felt like running at Daisuke,
leaping at him, and wrapping him up in a tight embrace. For a moment,
she felt as though the feeling would overwhelm her. Then she got control of herself and gave him a small bow.

They continued toward his house in silence.

———

For the next few days, Asa tried to hold on to every moment with
Daisuke's family. She knew she had grown attached, but it was only
when their company was going to be taken away that she understood

just how close they had become. The moments slipped like sand through her fingers.

She and Mika played frequently in the woods behind the house. They imagined they were high ladies, fussing over their clothing and food. Asa hadn't expected to enjoy playing with the girl, as she had never had a chance to play when she was young and saw little need now. But Asa gradually softened, and although she couldn't throw herself into the imagined settings with the same enthusiasm as Daisuke's daughter, she took part without complaint.

Daisuke continued her training, although there was little to teach. Their training had become more practice now and less instruction. The time was still valuable, especially for Asa. She focused on Daisuke, intensely curious how a nightblade with such incredible skills lived. She watched how he went about his morning chores and observed how he interacted with his family. At times she was able to admit that she wanted what he had.

One morning Daisuke asked Asa to join him for a walk through the woods. As she often did, Mika asked if she could come along, and Asa was pleasantly surprised when Daisuke agreed. They walked in silence through the woods, soon coming into ancient forest where the trees had seen hundreds of cycles. Asa had passed through before but generally avoided the area.

The problem with old woods was that they weren't what they seemed. If one walked through them having only the regular five senses, one would hear only the silence suspended among the trees and footsteps underneath. The canopy overhead blocked most of the light, and even the height of day could seem like the depths of night. The forest almost seemed to be dead or dying.

With the gift, walking through old woods was an entirely different experience. You could sense the bugs and the critters that hid before your presence. The trees themselves, majestic in their age, gave off a powerful sensation, and the ground underfoot was alive with life.

Intertwining roots and burrowing animals and creeping insects lit up one's sense with a flood of information, like being in a city.

The difference between what a blade's normal senses said and what the gift said made going into the old woods a disconcerting experience. Asa had never enjoyed it.

Asa's best guess was that some human intuition, some hint of the gift, must reside in everyone, because very few people went into old forests. Sure, there were stories of mythical creatures that abducted children in the woods, but Asa suspected that was only an attempt to rationalize an underlying unease.

Daisuke was unusual in that he didn't seem to mind the thick trees and narrow paths. Like her father, Mika also seemed unaffected. They walked for most of the morning, going deeper and deeper into the woods. At times, their path became so dark Asa wished for a torch.

She watched the two of her hosts move and realized they had a destination in mind. Daisuke wasn't wandering or searching. He was moving directly for a place, a place deep in a forest few people dared enter even the outskirts of. Mika, from her carefree attitude and excitement, also seemed to know where they were going.

Eventually, they came to a small clearing. A very small hut appeared that looked as though it had only one room. Daisuke led the way in, and Asa saw her guess was correct. There were two beds set up and a very simple cooking arrangement. The hut had everything needed to live, but there was no extra space.

Asa ventured a guess. "You built this in case the worst comes to pass? A place to hide if events turn against you?"

Daisuke nodded.

He didn't have to say anything more. Asa understood the brilliance herself. They would be safe from any military units, and in the confined spaces around the hut, even if an entire group of soldiers attacked, Daisuke would be able to pick them off one by one.

Nightblades would suffer the same fate. The trees were thick and dense, and Daisuke couldn't be sensed. He could slay a group of blades with almost equal ease.

The only danger Daisuke faced here was if the entire forest burned down, but Asa didn't see that happening. Lumber was a precious commodity, and someone would have to be incredibly desperate to destroy the woods intentionally. Acts of nature were possible but unlikely.

Mika tugged at Asa's clothes. "This used to be a shrine, but my father turned the inside into a living space."

"I wanted to show you this place," Daisuke said. "There's no telling what's going to happen in the Kingdom in this cycle or even the next. My hope is that my home is spared, but I have plans in case it isn't. Here I can defend my family indefinitely. I want you to know where it is in case you need a place to return."

Asa felt a sadness grow in the pit of her stomach. She knew what it meant for Daisuke to show her the last place he had created for the safety of his loved ones. For him to trust her after the suffering she had caused him was almost too much to bear.

She bowed deeply to him. "Thank you."

As she straightened, a thought crossed her mind. "Daisuke, I'm sorry that I must ask, but how do I even find this place? I don't have the slightest clue where we are."

Daisuke chuckled. "Perhaps there is one last lesson I can teach."

He knelt down and indicated she should do the same. Asa followed his lead, smiling when Mika also squatted down. Daisuke showed the palm of his hand to Asa. "Place your hand on the ground and focus your sense beneath us."

Asa did as Daisuke asked, extending her sense down below. She couldn't remember ever having tried. In her experience, they had always focused on expanding their sense out, not down. She sensed the root system beneath, but that wasn't new to her, as she had felt its influence most of the morning.

She lifted her hand and looked at Daisuke. "I'm not sure what I'm supposed to be feeling."

"Can you sense the flow of energy through the roots?"

Asa frowned. She had never thought of trying such a feat. She replaced her hand, closed her eyes, and focused on expanding her sense. This time when she found the roots, she did as Daisuke asked. Surprisingly, there was a direction to the energy, toward the hut Daisuke had made.

Asa stood up. "What are you saying?"

"I believe there are lines of force that run through the world we live on, something I've pondered for many cycles. If you extend your sense at any point in these woods, you'll feel the flow of energy toward the hut. Focusing through your hands works as a start, but if you practice, you can feel life flowing beneath your feet as well. Locally, here, it all points toward the same place."

Asa felt as confused as when she first began nightblade training. "What does it mean?"

Daisuke shrugged. "I'm not sure. I just know it works. Practice. You'll be able to find the place again if you need to."

Asa accepted his reasoning, even if she didn't understand it. They worked on chores through the middle of the day, cleaning out the house and collecting firewood from downed branches.

The three made it back to Daisuke's by early evening, just in time for Keiko's meal, a simple dinner of rice and fish caught the day before from a nearby stream. Asa thought the food tasted particularly delicious, wondering if it was the cooking or the atmosphere that made every bite seem like a slice of pure pleasure.

As they neared the finish of the meal, Asa decided it was time to break the news. Without much warning she said, "Tomorrow I'm leaving. There's still work I must do."

Keiko wasn't surprised by the news. Asa had told her days ago, after coming back from the village, that she was planning on leaving soon.

Mika, though, was caught unprepared. Tears bubbled up in her eyes, and with a deep breath, she just barely managed to hold them in. "I thought you were going to stay here forever and we could be sisters."

Asa's heart was shredded by the girl's desire. She'd never had a sister, either. "I would like to, Mika, but I must go out and try to help other people in the Kingdom."

The girl wiped her tears and fixed Asa with a fierce look. "My father says that a nightblade goes around and makes sure the bad people can't hurt anyone. Is that what you are going to do?"

"Yes, that is what I'm going to do."

She didn't get a chance to say anything more. Mika continued, "And you'll promise you'll come back when you're done so we can be sisters?"

Asa would have rather faced one of the nightblade hunting units than Mika at that moment. She glanced at her parents, but although they gave Asa supportive looks, it was clear she was on her own. She approached Mika on her knees and, acting on an impulse, gave her a hug.

While holding the girl in a tight embrace, she said, "Mika, there is nothing I would rather do than stay here and be your sister." Surprising even herself, she found that she believed what she said. "But you know that what I do is dangerous. If I can, I will come back to you, but I might not."

The girl might have been young, but she understood. Asa broke off the embrace and glanced at Daisuke and Keiko again. Daisuke bowed his head the smallest amount, and Keiko had a single tear crawling down her left cheek.

They finished the meal in silence, and that night as they prepared for bed, Mika came into Asa's bedroom and snuggled next to her, falling asleep as Asa stared at the ceiling and told stories of the nightblades of legend.

She was up the next morning before Mika. It would be hard for the girl to wake up and have her gone, but Asa feared that if she waited, she wouldn't have the courage to leave.

She whispered a goodbye to Keiko, who embraced her tightly. Daisuke walked with her to the rise hiding the house. "You'll track Mari and join with her?"

"Yes." Since their return from the village, Asa had thought of little else. If she had to serve someone, she couldn't think of a better person.

Daisuke bowed to Asa. "It has been an honor having you. You are welcome anytime, and remember to practice the skills you've learned. And Asa?"

She looked at him expectantly.

"Whatever you end up doing, just remember to serve. It's not about you."

Asa nodded, and before she could change her mind, she turned and walked away, putting Daisuke and his family behind her.

Chapter 18

The snows were melting, and Mari was certain she was now the most wanted person in the entire Kingdom. Shadows from each of the house lands had come to her with posters calling for the capture of the Lady in White. The rewards were becoming enormous, almost enough to feed a city for a full moon.

The irony wasn't lost on Mari. Her strategy, such as it was, was working. Food and supplies were raided and stolen from the armies and brought back to the cities and villages they had come from. The Lady in White returned the people's money, but the lords would have to take it back to pay the sum they were promising for her capture.

When she had been a child, she had loved to imagine herself in a different world. She loved the walls of Stonekeep, but there were times when she wanted nothing more than to be on a horse out in the wild. At times, to feed her fancy, she imagined that she was a bandit queen, always on the run from those who would bring her to justice.

What would her childhood self say now if she saw how Mari lived? Her juvenile imagination had become her daily reality, but the reality was nowhere near as romantic as her dreams had been. The ground was wet and cold, and although her party's spirits were high, their conditions were miserable. They didn't dare spend more than a day or two in any single place. She traveled with more than fifty blades, always running, always pursued by the armies of Lord Isamu.

Her danger grew as her reputation did. Once, the Lady in White might have received indifference or perhaps a hesitant welcome. Now if she rode into a new place with her white costume, villagers bowed low to her.

Some days she realized that many citizens of the Kingdom had more loyalty to her than to the lords of the lands they lived on. At those moments, she considered shifting her aims and taking the Kingdom for herself. Wouldn't she be a wise and just queen?

As tempting as the idea often was, Mari never allowed it to linger. The Kingdom had never been ruled by a woman, and while the villagers were happy to hide her and deceive her pursuers, there was a vast difference between that and allowing a woman to rule.

A smaller voice in her head warned her of the temptation of power. Hiromi had been a good man, the type of man who would never consider sending assassins after his own blood. But power was insidious, worming its way under a person's honor. Her even entertaining the thought of usurping power from the lords who had a legitimate claim was proof enough of that.

Her best path was to stay the course she had originally set. War had been delayed for more than a moon as armies and lords struggled to figure out how to feed and supply their troops while at the same time preventing the rioting of their people. She had received reports that each cadre of blades was being pursued by part of an army, pulling necessary troops off the front lines of the battle.

Skirmishes still erupted between the houses, but Mari's actions had so far prevented the full war she feared. She wasn't sure how much longer her forces could continue. As their reputation grew, more troops were assigned to them, and the chase became more intense. Mari's group had almost been surrounded twice, but each time they had managed to find a way out thanks to the abilities of the gifted.

Mari worried that soon they would need to resort to violence to continue their mission. She dreaded the possibility but did the best she could to steel herself for the inevitable day. Better her blades kill a handful of soldiers than the world fall to war.

Mari's actions also moderated the attitude of the populace toward the blades. No doubt the fear and hate persisted, but a starving family accepted food no matter the source. The quality of the blades in her service was paramount to their success. If even one blade lashed out at a citizen, the story would be different. But her blades, so far, had answered hate with food supplies. Even if they were jeered, they continued serving.

Mari wasn't under the illusion that the blades were different than citizens in terms of temperament. There were blades who made wise and caring decisions and those who made rash and arrogant ones. But recently, she had seen the quality of people who came together for a cause. They had been given every opportunity and every reason to strike back in some villages but always held their temper.

Mari specifically remembered a larger village named Highfield. Her forces had brought in food recently liberated from Isamu's army and were passing it out on the outskirts of the village. From the back, a group of local youths threw heavy stones. The blades sensed the throws but couldn't dodge all the rocks. One hit a nightblade on the head as he dodged, causing blood to flow rapidly from the wound.

The blade had collapsed, and his son, another nightblade serving next to him, had immediately pushed through the crowd. Everyone started to scatter, afraid of the impending bloodshed. Even Mari feared the reputation she had worked so hard to cultivate would be destroyed.

But when the son reached the young men who had assaulted his father, he knelt in front of them and offered rice.

The incident had turned out well. The father was healed by a dayblade, and the youths were shamed in front of their entire community.

Not every experience was as positive as Highfield. Twice now they had had to leave the food at the edge of a village because no one would come out of their homes when the nightblades were present. The phenomenon was less common but still happened.

The process was agonizingly slow, but piece by piece, the blades were working toward Mari's goal. She only wondered if it would be enough.

———

Mari wandered through the camp one evening, completely exhausted. She had never been a warrior, but she had always been active, and this campaign was draining her. Around her, the blades were subdued, a hard day's ride putting them all in a quiet state.

Even tireless Takahiro was sitting silently around one of the fires they had started, waiting for his dinner to cook. Mari sat down next to him, his only response a small, guttural grunt.

She sighed and eventually stood up again. She was just as fatigued as anyone else, but she was restless, her mind unwilling to settle. Takahiro was in command of this group, but her mind kept racing over the future, trying to see the next step. No matter how she wrestled with the problem, no solution came to her.

When Asa rode into camp, the entire gathering came alive. Some of the blades knew Asa better than others, but she was a change and a welcome one at that.

She pulled her horse to a stop and slid smoothly down from the saddle. Mari frowned and looked at the brand on the mount. It had been stolen from Isamu's army.

The nightblade followed Mari's gaze. "I figured the loss of one horse wouldn't bother them much."

Another blade came up and offered to take care of the horse. Asa gratefully accepted, and Mari invited Asa to come to her tent. Mari wasn't sure what it was about Asa that she liked so much, but she was grateful beyond measure to see her face.

Mari prepared some tea, and the women knelt to face each other. Asa, surprisingly, spoke first. "You all look as though you've been training all day in the sun. Some of those blades seem ready to pass out where they stand."

Mari nodded. "We have been on the run for a moon now, and it requires tremendous sacrifice."

Asa sipped from her cup, giving Mari a slight bow of appreciation for the drink. "Word of your deeds is spreading fast. I passed no fewer than three villages where the Lady in White was all that was spoken of. To most, you are a hero, but to some, a traitor."

This wasn't surprising to Mari, although she did feel a slight pain that some would consider her a traitor.

She didn't say anything. None of this was for public recognition, and it did no good to complain.

The two women sipped their tea. Mari, as host, had the responsibility to continue the conversation, but she suffered a moment of doubt. Why had she called Asa to her tent? They weren't that close.

But there was something about Asa that Mari couldn't put her finger on, a feature even more pronounced now than it had been in the past. Mari decided to plunge forward.

"Asa, I'm frustrated and worried for the blades and for the Kingdom."

Mari had Asa's full attention, but the nightblade didn't respond.

The lady struggled to find the right words. "We're doing well. We are the dam in the river, but we are weak, and when we break, the war will flood the Kingdom. I need the cooperation of a lord."

Asa bent her head forward slightly to acknowledge Mari's problem. "You don't think your brother would listen to you?"

Mari laughed. Asa had been gone when the attack happened. "He tried to have me assassinated."

Asa frowned. "So?"

The nightblade's response startled Mari. She stopped laughing and shook her head, trying to be certain of Asa's words. It took a few moments to do so, but Asa's face clearly indicated the question.

"If someone tries to kill you, they aren't very likely to listen to you."

"Why not?"

Mari bunched up her face, perplexed by Asa's attitude.

The blade replied, "I assume your brother found out about your alliance with a group of blades?"

Mari nodded.

"If word of your actions and identity spread, he'd lose the war before it ever began. Ordering your death was a cold but rational action, right?"

Mari exhaled loudly. Yes, she supposed Asa was right.

"Is there another better suited to hear your plans for the Kingdom?"

Mari considered her options, limited as they were. Katashi would never hear her, and Isamu, well, Isamu wasn't fit to be king. Hiromi already knew what Mari was doing, so if he did ally himself with her, it would be with full knowledge of her secrets. Hiromi was her best option. She shook her head.

"Then it seems to me your choice is clear, even if unpleasant. You must speak with your brother."

Mari disagreed again. "Even if you're right, there's no way I can get to him. He's one of the most well-defended people in the Kingdom right now, and I am under threat of death."

Asa smiled. "Then it's good I decided to come. I will escort you to him."

Mari's heart pounded in her chest. To talk and complain was one act. To sneak into an army encampment, possibly kill guards, and meet secretly with her brother was an entirely different act. She couldn't.

But Asa sat in front of her, calmly sipping tea and looking expectantly as though she was waiting for Mari to tell her when they were going to leave. Mari set down her tea and paced the small tent, regretting she'd let the daring nightblade in.

The worst part was, Asa was right. If Mari's only hope was speaking to a lord, her brother was the best choice, and if that was true, she would have to try. The alternative was fighting a slowly losing battle until her companions broke and died.

She stopped pacing and knelt again, staring Asa straight in the eye. "Can you get me to him?"

Asa didn't respond immediately, considering factors she didn't bother sharing with Mari. "I believe I can. Nothing is certain, of course, but I believe so."

Mari wasn't sure why she was listening. Walking into that camp was no different than committing suicide, except suicide was probably quicker and less painful.

But she was already risking her life every day. She didn't think of the danger when she was protected by one of the largest gatherings of nightblades ever, but the fact remained. Asa was forcing her to live up to her ideals.

Before Mari could stop herself, she said, "Very well. I will need to prepare my commanders for my absence, but we will leave in the next few days."

Asa bowed as she sipped the last of her tea. "Thank you for the wonderful drink, my lady. I look forward to our time on the road together."

Chapter 19

Koji watched as their commander, a nightblade named Ikko, sketched out the supply depot the blades were about to attack. Even before Ikko spoke, Koji knew that the strategy they were using now wouldn't work forever. Here they experienced far more defenses, far more troops, and far better placement than they had encountered before. They might be blades, but their enemies were not fools.

Almost a hundred guards surrounded the supply depot, which itself had been built on a foothill that overlooked the area for a league in every direction. The scouts sent in earlier reported that patrols were regular and alert.

When the campaign, if that was what it could be called, had started, the blades hadn't fought much in the way of opposition. The supply lines had been guarded, of course, but the troops hadn't been seasoned or well trained. They were the dregs of the army, so far below the skill of the nightblades as to be a joke.

No longer. Mari's campaign had brought reinforcements, some of the best from the front. These were men who took pride in being soldiers, who trained every day in the hope of becoming officers.

Individually they posed little threat to the blades, but together, they were a force to be reckoned with. The missions were getting more challenging. If the blades didn't switch their approach, they would soon be overwhelmed.

Ikko broke down the plan, such as it was. Koji was grateful, again, that Mari had heeded his request not to be put in charge. As he listened, their commander brought up point after point, simple facts that Koji would have forgotten.

Koji occupied a place of honor among the group he traveled with. He was widely recognized as the best sword in the group and practiced diligently so the position wasn't taken away. Whenever a plan was made, he was in the heart of the battle and wouldn't have it any other way.

Ikko's plan was to attack at night with a direct charge up the foothill. It wasn't a complex plan, which Koji appreciated, but he worried that the blades were starting to attempt more than they could handle. The soldiers at the top would see them coming. They would have archers and some fortifications. Who knew what else was up there?

Worse, Koji and the group didn't have the time to better strategize. A pursuit troop was hard on their heels, and everyone figured they'd catch up in another day or two. They needed to strike now or risk being cornered.

Koji would lead the main force up the path that wound to the top. Two other small groups would attempt flanking maneuvers, but Koji and his team would handle the brunt of the counteroffensive.

Everything would have been easier if they'd been allowed to kill the guards. Unfortunately that had been one principle Mari had been adamant about. If the nightblades started killing guards, even for a good reason, all the goodwill they had worked so hard to develop would be lost.

So far there hadn't been any deaths on either side of the combat, but Koji was beginning to believe that was more luck than anything else. As the odds continued to stack against the blades, they would either have to kill or die in their attempts to complete their missions.

The commander looked up at his warriors, his silent expression welcoming questions. There were none.

"Very well," he said. "Get what rest you can. We will begin our attack soon."

———

As had become custom, Koji led the main force up the hill. The supply depot had originally been a collection of four huts that had been reinforced. They were in the mountainous lands of House Kita, and stone was plentiful. Between the terrain and the heavy walls of the huts, the supplies were quite defendable.

Koji and his troops discovered that quickly enough. As predicted, they were spotted long before they got to the huts. The alarm was raised, and the guards formed a strong perimeter, using boulders to hide from arrows that never came.

Arrows shot down, though. Koji figured there had to be at least two squads of archers up top, and he was close enough to be able to sense them pulling back their bowstrings. He squatted underneath his short round shield, feeling the impacts as the arrows dug into his protection.

Nightblades rarely carried shields, but after a few assaults, the precaution had been deemed necessary. While the practice was distasteful to many, it was one of the reasons Ikko could claim that none of his blades had been killed.

Their progress was slow, much slower than Koji would have preferred. The path was full of loose rock, and with nothing but the dim light of the moon to guide their footsteps, the blades couldn't move too quickly. And crouching down to protect themselves while arrows clattered all around didn't speed up the process.

The team's challenges were just beginning. Up above, Koji heard a sound that seemed like a giant was groaning. The groan went silent, and then a small trickle of stones became a booming echo. Koji's mind, used to the sounds of battle, froze, completely unable to comprehend what was happening. Was the world splitting apart above him?

He looked up in time to see a giant shadow, darker than the night, hurtling toward him. Without thought, Koji threw himself to the side, avoiding the shadow and whatever evil it represented.

Behind him, in the space he'd just vacated, a boulder crashed down the hillside, crushing two nightblades behind him, the sounds of their shattering bones echoing in Koji's ears. A third nightblade, a woman, was spun around like a child's plaything as the boulder struck her side on its way down the mountain.

More groans and more cracks. Koji looked up to see if any new shadows grew above him.

He was awed, just for a moment, by the sight.

From his position on his stomach, chin against the earth, all he could see above the hillside was the glittering multitude of stars, each one twinkling with life against his sight.

Boulders crashed to each side of him. The nightblades were too slow to react; they couldn't understand what was happening. They couldn't sense boulders, and in one brilliant move, their greatest advantage had been reduced to nothing.

Koji thought he yelled but couldn't hear his own voice.

More blades, people he had befriended and fought by for moons, were suddenly gone.

Koji tried to remember what he knew about the hilltop. House Kita's forces couldn't have that many boulders up there. Hugging the ground would do no good. The blades were still targets for the archers, and what defense they had been putting up with their shields was in complete disarray as they searched for boulders.

Koji got to his feet and charged up the path. He was less than a hundred paces from the top, but every step was agonizingly slow. Running uphill after everything he had endured took almost all his strength. His legs were on fire as he crested the top and leapt into battle, already tired.

Plenty of spears and swords waited for him. He sensed the strikes and the cuts, abandoning his shield as three spears pierced it in one moment. Sliding in the smallest of gaps, Koji lashed out with his wooden sword, his cuts as quick as he could make them. He had no time to do anything but cut and dodge, cut and dodge.

He didn't find the same clarity he had before, but he was still a powerful force, single-handedly pushing into the line of soldiers. One spear cut through his upper left arm. A sword gently caressed the outside of his thigh, drawing a trickle of hot blood in the cool evening air. He brought down soldier after soldier, but fighting alone, a cut would eventually get through that stopped his heart.

Two other nightblades crested the ridge, aided by the distraction Koji had created. Immediately he could feel the pressure against him relent as the guards turned their attention to other threats.

Koji was happy to remind his opponents of just how much of a threat he was. Now that he had aid, he pushed himself even harder, sowing as much confusion in the ranks as he could. The blades had taken losses, but he was certain he could turn this battle around.

More nightblades crested the ridge. Slowly the tide of the battle was turning.

Koji's perspective changed again when two of his cuts were easily deflected by a third party. He spun to his side, expecting to find a skilled swordsman.

He wasn't expecting to face a nightblade, cold steel in hand.

The woman's face seemed somehow familiar, as though from moments half-remembered. Why did he recognize her?

Her blade flickered in the moonlight, and his sense lit up with possibilities. Suddenly he remembered. Not her name, but where he had encountered her before.

She had been a master back when he had been a student. He had watched her duel before he was allowed to do the same. She had been skilled.

His memories were accurate. Her blade flashed all around him, testing his defense, forcing him to give up more ground than he desired. Much more, and she'd have him on the hillside, poor footing the end of him.

She wasn't fighting with a wooden sword.

Koji earned a small reprieve when another blade, one fighting with Koji, rushed in. That duel was over in two moves, a long red line drawn across Koji's rescuer's chest. But the sacrifice gave Koji a chance to get grounded, to find his bearings in the middle of chaos.

When she came at him again, he was ready. He shifted as he sensed her attacks, his own sword darting in whenever he felt he had a chance of striking her. He wanted to draw his real sword. The battle had already been unfair. She had been waiting at the top while boulders had killed Koji's friends.

So long as Mari lived, though, he had sworn his obedience. As much as he desired to draw and match steel against steel, he would not. He would not disappoint her.

His legs and focus were tired, and she was almost as fast as anyone he'd ever met. Fresh, perhaps he was faster, but he hadn't felt energized in some time.

Koji's foot slipped, and he fell, his opponent's blade all around him. He didn't have time to think. He just rolled, crashing into someone and bringing them to their knees.

His entire world was a tangle of arms and legs and steel. He felt something pierce his abdomen, but it didn't cut deeply, fortunately. Koji made it back to his feet somehow, coming face-to-face with his attacker.

Her strike was fast, and Koji's reality shifted. He could sense her attack, could see as her weight shifted, preparing for the cut she believed would be fatal. In his mind's eye, every action and reaction unfolded, and he knew exactly where he needed to be.

His response wasn't perfect. Her strike sliced deep into his stomach, the side already wounded by the previous stab. Koji found himself inside her guard, his own sword snapping around and crashing against her skull. She had started to react, had started to move backward, but his blow still knocked her to the ground unconscious.

Exhausted and bloody, Koji kept trudging forward. For a few moments his blades had lost momentum. More must have happened, but Koji had lost track of the fight in the midst of his own struggle for survival. The battle had turned again. He slapped away a final assailant as his group finally claimed control of the hilltop.

By far, it had been their bloodiest encounter. Koji wasn't sure, but he guessed at least a third of the blades who had started the mission weren't present. Some might have been injured below but were still alive. Koji hoped that was the case.

He slumped to the ground and closed his eyes to rest, bloody but victorious.

———

After the dayblades had finished healing him, Koji turned his attention to the nightblade who had almost killed him. She was slim but had certainly been strong. She was older than him, maybe by almost twenty cycles.

Koji took her weapons and waited for her to come to. When he got tired of waiting, he poured some water over her face. She sputtered and sat up, taking in her surroundings before acting.

Her eyes fixed on his. "You didn't kill me."

"We're trying to avoid bloodshed."

Koji's statement was laced with meaning. They had taken the hill without killing a single soldier. The nightblade who had attacked Koji had a younger blade under her wing, and even the boy hadn't been killed. But Koji and the blades he traveled with had lost several friends. They were sure of eight so far, but the number would grow once the sun rose over the horizon.

To her credit, the nightblade didn't argue morality with him. She shifted her weight subtly, and Koji's sword flashed to her throat faster than she could move. He wasn't injured anymore, and while he was exhausted, he was still fast.

Koji had decided not to restrain the nightblade in any way, trusting instead his own sense and speed. Without her weapons, he was fairly certain there wasn't anything she could do against him. He saw that he had made his point. Her body relaxed.

"What will you do with me?" she asked.

"Nothing."

She raised a questioning eyebrow at that, clearly not trusting his answer. Her belief or disbelief didn't bother him much.

"Once we finish loading all the supplies, we'll be off. If you really want to leave in a hurry, I suppose I can escort you out of here and return your weapons to you when I'm sure you won't harm any of us. It makes no difference to me."

She eyed him warily. "Aren't you afraid I'll spread word of what happened here? That I'll lead them to you?"

He shrugged, too bone-weary to fight. "There's a unit tasked with trying to hunt us down about a hard day's ride behind us. I can't give you a horse, unfortunately, but you're welcome to join them if you wish. They've been following us for a while, and I expect you'd be able to find them easily enough."

Even though she didn't seem to believe his answer, the blade didn't challenge him anymore. She couldn't provide any aid to the unit unless a battle was imminent, and the group of blades he was with was doing everything to avoid more conflict.

Koji did have one question for her. "How could you do it?"

"Do what? Plan the defense of the hill?"

He looked at the warrior with fresh anger in his eyes. His mind spun as he realized a truth. She had told House Kita's soldiers how to defend the depot, how to make the target the most costly to take. If anyone was responsible for the death of his friends, it was her.

His voice, cold and hard, didn't waver. "No. Betray your people. Betray the Kingdom."

The nightblade looked at him for a moment and then actually snickered. "You believe that, don't you?"

He was too angry to be confused.

"Open your eyes. There's no more Kingdom. There are three houses, and that's it. And the blades? Beyond the Lady in White, they aren't doing anything. They're hiding behind the walls of Starfall, Hajimi hoping that if they just lie low long enough, everything will blow over, and the world will return to normal. But that chance is long gone. It was gone the moment Shin died."

Koji felt the old familiar feeling of shame lodge deep in his gut. He didn't accept the woman's statement, but it was the deepest cut she could have made.

"I was born and raised in the lands of House Kita. His general, Kyo, offered me a position, with land and servants. Who would I be to refuse such an offer? Better live and prosper than suffer and die."

Koji supposed that in a way, he understood what the other nightblade was saying. Every part of it made him sick, but he understood.

He didn't want to have this conversation any longer. He stood up, the disgust obvious in his eyes. "If you want to leave, let me know. Otherwise, don't move. I will kill you without hesitation."

She saw the glare in his eyes and didn't question his look. She seemed to sink inside herself as Koji stalked off, eager to do anything that would get his mind off the dishonorable blade.

———

If fighting was the worst part of his mission, delivering the food and supplies they liberated was Koji's favorite part. They rode into town proudly, black robes fluttering in the breeze of a beautiful spring day.

They had been on the road so long it seemed like all the villages were the same. This one had its own flavor, of course, but was still so similar to all the rest. The houses were in need of repair, the healthy and robust men of the village recruited for the army and gone far too long. Koji took it all in: the roofs with tiles missing, the support beams bent or broken, the wood warped or cracked. Most of the homes had started their lives as glorified huts, and the harsh winter and heavy snows hadn't done them any favors.

As the blades rode in, they were greeted by women, children, and the elders of the village. Everyone was too skinny, without even the tiniest amount of fat. Skin hung from bones. The village, like so many before them, was dying.

Koji was grateful he didn't need to lead the way or converse with village elders. He was born a warrior, and being friendly to those who once sought his death didn't come naturally.

He knew that if not for Mari, they would still be hunted for wearing their black robes. They might have the better part of an army on their tail, but thanks to her, they didn't have everyone trying to betray them or turn them in. These people seemed grateful to have the blades here.

They should be. Koji and his group carried enough food to feed the villagers for an entire moon. Hopefully it would be enough to last until the earliest parts of the harvest could be gathered. Regardless, as was their custom, the blades planned to leave everything behind.

After Ikko spoke a few words with a village elder, he gave them all the sign to dismount and begin unloading the food.

Koji dismounted with all the rest, looking forward to a break from the saddle. One of the most problematic challenges of being pursued was saddle sores. He was certain that he'd soon have a permanent bend to his knees.

The villagers started to crowd around, the emotion visible in their faces. Although Koji had watched this scene play out time and time again, he still got emotional. These were people who had been left to perish by their lords. The very people who were supposed to be protected were those who suffered the brunt of the indignities from the soldiers. Koji was continually disgusted.

One old villager wept and told them it was the first time she'd eaten a full meal in two moons. A young woman, clearly with child, bowed her head all the way to the ground, not getting up until Koji gently lifted her. Children treasured every grain of rice, a tremendous departure from the natural wish to play with their food.

Koji relaxed into the scene, breathing deeply and simply observing. This was as close as he ever came to believing that he had made the right choice in becoming a nightblade. This was what he had envisioned. He enjoyed the laughter of the children and the animated voices of the adults speaking with one another.

Another woman approached him. She was attractive, and Koji was reminded again that he hadn't been with anyone for many moons. She offered him a cup of sake, which he gratefully accepted.

The liquor warmed his body even more than the spring sun. He struck up an easy conversation with the woman, who turned out to be married. Her husband had been called to war, and she was forced to tend to their farm on her own. She confessed that she thought she was going to die from starvation.

Just before Koji fell into a state of pure bliss and relaxation, he sensed a slight disturbance. His mood immediately shifted. In every village, there always had to be one. Why?

This one seemed fixated on him. Although he wasn't taking a straight line, the villager was working his way to Koji. The nightblade cracked open his eyes. As he had suspected, it was a boy who had seen no more than twelve cycles. They were always the ones who fell prey to the propaganda, the ones who envisioned themselves as heroes for killing a nightblade. When Koji was feeling charitable, he could understand. After all, as a child he too had wanted to be a hero.

But Koji wasn't feeling charitable today. Not after the sacrifice that had been made on behalf of this village and this child. No one else seemed to notice. The nightblades, like Koji, were relaxed and unaware of the danger in their midst. Koji sensed the intent, sensed the boy with his hand behind his back.

The boy covered the last five paces in a running leap. Koji lazily opened his eyes, grabbed the boy's wrist, which held a long and wicked-looking knife, and twisted. He came close to breaking the youth's arm but stopped just before.

The woman sitting next to Koji had fallen backward off the bench, completely surprised by the attack.

The boy yelled, not realizing the foolishness of his argument. "Let me go! You all deserve to die for killing the king!"

Koji didn't yell back but kept the pressure on the boy's arm through his wrist, holding him to the ground. "My friends died to bring you this food, boy."

For a moment, a tense tableau reigned. The youth, angry and delusional as he was, wouldn't listen to reason, and Koji needed a target for his frustration and loss.

The blade gathered himself first, letting the boy go. It would do no good to lecture him. He was just another example of a much larger disease.

The youth got to his feet, his eyes staring daggers into Koji's. "I will kill you all."

With that, he ran off, although not very far. Koji could still sense the boy's energetic presence when it stopped a few houses down.

He turned and helped the woman back up. She was clearly ashamed and looked as though she was going to turn away.

Koji, desperate for conversation, tried to reassure her. "It's fine. He did a very good job of hiding what he was about to do until the last moment. I was almost surprised as well."

The woman didn't seem to know what to say. "You are not what I expected you to be," she finally muttered.

Koji understood. He'd heard the sentiment before, but the woman continued. "You are all so . . . human."

Chapter 20

Asa had always considered herself well traveled. As a nightblade, she had crossed the Kingdom countless times, and although there had certainly been places where she'd been far more often than others, she tended to think there wasn't much she hadn't experienced.

One of those experiences she'd never had was seeing infantry on the move in wartime. She had come across encampments when the Kingdom was at peace, and while the sight was impressive, it paled in comparison to the army on the move with battle on its mind.

The tents were everywhere, and the men patrolled with three times as much frequency as usual. Asa had thought at first that perhaps she and Mari could walk into the camp as followers, but that seemed particularly unlikely now. Even if they made it in, they would attract all sorts of attention, and they'd never make it very far.

The camp was a busy hive of activity, and Asa wasn't sure how they were going to enter. Thanks to Mari, they had the blue uniforms of House Kita's army, but they would need more than just uniforms. The patrol patterns of the guards were easy to predict, but there were so many it was unlikely that any single mistake would give the women entry into the camp.

Even with Daisuke's training, sneaking into the heart of the enclosure would be a challenge. That challenge was the very reason they had left Takahiro behind despite his strenuous objections.

Mari's guard had argued that the Lady in White was wanted, not Mari. She could still walk into camp safely and approach Hiromi.

Mari had pushed back. Her brother had tried to have her assassinated. If she came in publicly, he would have no problem surrounding himself with appointments and guards and would likely set a bodyguard on her, not to protect her but to limit her movement.

They would have to rely on some combination of stealth and deception to reach Hiromi and hope it was enough. Takahiro had acquiesced eventually but had then insisted he accompany them.

Asa hadn't budged for a moment. Sneaking the two of them in was enough of a challenge. She wouldn't try with three.

Cursing, Takahiro had eventually given in, forced to remain with the unit Mari had been traveling with.

More than once, Asa doubted her decision to help the lady. She could be living on her own, surviving peacefully by hunting in the woods. What foolish sense of duty had led her to this point? Memories of Kiyoshi, Daisuke, Daiki, and Ayano were all that tied her to this idea of serving a cause.

Despite her doubts, she remained. This was the path she had decided to walk. She couldn't leave until she had at least made the attempt.

The two hid in the rocks overlooking the encampment. One part of their task had been made easy: Mari's supply raids had forced the camp to stay in one place for quite a few days. The women had made the journey faster than Asa had envisioned. Mari's determination had played a role there, too. Whenever Asa thought to call a stop for the day, the lady pushed them harder.

Mari was studying Asa studying the camp, a smirk on her face. "I thought you said you could do this."

"I thought you said we didn't have a choice," Asa shot back.

Mari shook her head sadly. "No, we really don't. This is as good a chance as any we are likely to have."

Asa almost told her that it wasn't much of a chance, but she already knew that. No point in stating what was blindingly obvious.

The sun started to go down, but Asa still required more time before she dared to try infiltrating the camp. They crouched down into their hiding place and pulled out food. Asa devoured her portion, hungry from another day on the trail. Mari's discipline was better.

"Asa, I don't know that I've ever had the courage to ask, but what motivated you to join my cause?"

Asa struggled for the answer she wasn't sure of. "You protect the people."

Mari wasn't satisfied. "Yes, but I mean really, why do you do it? What drives you? Why are you willing to risk your life to go down into that camp with me?"

In an uncharacteristic moment, Asa decided to tell her a short version of her life.

"When I was younger, I was obsessed with revenge. My father was killed by a nightblade, and I spent most of my adult life tracking him down. It was why I had trained in the first place. I was successful, but revenge . . ." She fought for the right words and failed. "Revenge didn't bring me any peace, and it didn't right any wrongs. I ended up questioning myself and what I had done. Since then, I haven't felt at ease. Strangely, I feel almost like I need to complete the work of the man I killed."

Asa's voice drifted off, her thoughts wandering the passages of memory.

Eventually she continued. "Simply put, I think that serving you is as close as I can get to what I'm supposed to be doing right now. I don't have any good answer, unfortunately."

Mari smiled. "You're not alone. I think that no one really has any idea about the meaning of our lives. We all pretend. We make plans and discuss our beliefs as though we've found an answer, but I think most are just guessing. I'm leading a cadre of nightblades, yet I'm not half as certain as I must act."

In most people, such a confession of weakness would have bothered Asa. But not from Mari. She spoke earnestly, not seeking sympathy so much as just stating a fact. Not for the first time, Asa wished that Mari could become the new ruler of the Kingdom.

As the sun set, the two women huddled next to each other. The spring nights, especially in the mountains, got cold, and staying together kept them warm until it was time to move.

They both took turns napping. Asa didn't want to leave until deep into the night, so they had time. Asa fell asleep first, with Mari waking her when the moon was high in the sky. Mari slept until Asa thought the time was right.

She nudged Mari awake.

"It's time to go."

———

The first part of the trip was simple enough. They picked their way down the dark mountainside, Mari leading the way. Asa was slightly ashamed, but Mari was more experienced in the mountains, and her footing was much better than the blade's.

From there they passed close to the outskirts of the camp. The land was uneven and rugged, near the end of one of the many mountain ranges in Mari's land. This gave them the advantage as they approached, but eventually they couldn't sneak anymore.

Asa decided a simple approach was best. There was no way to sneak into camp, so they were forced to walk in. The two came as close as they dared to the perimeter and hid in a clump of tall grass. Asa waited until the shift changed.

Several groups of guards converged on one spot to listen to commands from a unit officer. Asa used her sense, and when she was sure no one was looking in their direction, she stood up with Mari and simply joined the group. When it split, Mari and Asa followed a contingent of guards going into the camp. As soon as they could, they separated from that group, now entirely in the camp.

Asa paused and took a deep breath. Her heart had been pounding. She couldn't fight off an entire army. Not even Koji was that good.

They were soon ready to go. From here, the mission was more straightforward. Hiromi's tents were near the center of the camp, so they would need to head in that direction. At first, that wouldn't be a problem. On the outer edges of the camp, they could walk freely without being questioned. But the closer they got to Hiromi, the more guards would be present.

Asa decided straightforward was best, so they began by walking directly into the heart of the camp. With their hoods up and uniforms on, no one questioned them, just as Asa expected.

After a few hundred paces, though, she broke off a main path and started walking behind the tents. She figured they were starting to get close enough that they might be stopped.

She flashed back to the village with Daisuke. This was the same task, just with much higher stakes. Turning around, she told Mari to be silent and be right behind her, no matter what she did. She calmed her breath, focused on her sense, and started moving.

The task was easy enough to begin. No one was walking between the tents at this time of night, so most of Asa's awareness was spent making sure the two women weren't making noise. Once they had to stop for a few moments when a soldier came out to relieve himself behind his tent.

After a section of tents was finished, they came upon the real challenge. There were still several rows of tents to go, and the area was crawling with people despite the late hour. Mari leaned over and whispered softly in Asa's ear. "He might still be awake with his generals. If nothing else, he is a dedicated commander."

Asa hoped she wasn't right. Mari needed to talk to Hiromi alone if Asa was understanding correctly. If they came into the tent and a general was still there, their entire cause would be defeated.

But first they needed to get there. Asa extended her sense and tracked people, not searching for holes. One of Daisuke's first lessons to her had been to turn her mind off when trying to use stealth. Aiming to predict patterns consciously always worked out poorly. Better to trust intuition and instincts.

Which was exactly what they did. Asa didn't seek an opening so much as wait for one to appear. Eventually it did, and they moved quickly, Mari staying less than a step behind Asa the entire way.

The opening shifted and moved, but Asa was in her element now. She stopped and pushed Mari down behind a tent as a guard peered over toward them. She crawled right behind another guard as he was talking to a fellow soldier. At one point she drew her knife and cut a small hole in the bottom of an empty tent, ushering Mari inside first.

The entire time, Mari didn't complain, which Asa found impressive considering she had every right to be making this journey on foot in the middle of the day. She simply followed, trusting Asa's lead. So far, she was incredibly grateful for Mari's attentiveness.

They reached the end of the line of tents, leaving nothing but a final empty space between their location and Hiromi's tent. Asa used her sense to search the area, but for the moment at least, they were safe.

But Hiromi wasn't alone in his tent. Another man was there.

Originally Asa had planned to go through the front of the tent. That plan was destroyed by the presence of two stationary sentries. Asa could deal with them quickly if she needed to, but she wouldn't know what to do with the unconscious bodies. If she left the bodies out, they would be discovered in short order, but if she brought the unconscious guards into the tent, their absence would be noted just as quickly.

There weren't many patrolling guards here, though. Asa didn't know why exactly. Maybe they thought their perimeter secure? The two intruders could just go to an unguarded side of the tent and cut their way in. Asa studied her surroundings again, ensuring no one would observe them.

They crept forward on hands and knees, moving as quickly as possible. They crouched in a shadow cast by Hiromi's tent. Asa pulled a knife out and slowly went to work, cutting an opening through the fabric, her actions as silent as the night itself.

Each moment was agonizing, as Asa was afraid someone would approach. Since they were covered only by shadow, even a half-alert guard would see them.

Finally, the aperture was big enough, and Asa held it open as Mari crawled silently inside. For just a moment, Asa reflected that this was an awful lot of work to talk with a little brother.

Asa followed Mari in, coming into the middle of a heated discussion between Hiromi and an older man, who must have been one of the lord's generals.

"My lord," the older man was saying, a hint of despair in his voice, "I agree with everything you say, but it simply can't be done! We don't possess the forces necessary to accomplish every goal. If we are going to pursue this war, we need to decide on our objectives and be willing to risk the rest."

The two women had found a dark corner of the tent, and the two men, absorbed in their argument, had no idea they had company. Asa was ready to stand up and introduce herself with her sword, but Mari held her back.

Hiromi paced the tent, and Asa got the impression she was looking at an overgrown child, sullen and temperamental. This was the lord Mari chose to believe in? Even at a glance, Asa could tell Mari was twice the leader than this fool.

He returned to a table near the center of the tent, lit by one of the few candles in the space. He stabbed his finger at the map. "Let's look at this one piece at a time. You're saying that if I commit any more forces to pursuing my sister, one of our fronts is guaranteed to collapse?"

The commander agreed. "You are stretched too thin as it is. Even if you stopped this pursuit of your sister and reassigned all your troops to a single front, you'd still only have one strong front. The other would still be weaker than I would like."

Hiromi's pointed finger became a fist that smashed into the table again. "General Kyo, you keep telling me that you need more men, but where are there more to get? It's my understanding we've already recruited every able-bodied man in the land."

Kyo cleared his throat. "As we've discussed, my lord, you could increase the range of people who are recruited. Boys who are excited to serve, and even older men who still have a fire for your house. Your call would be answered."

Mari turned to Asa and indicated her time had come. She stood up and entered the light.

Kyo's reaction was immediate, and Asa had to give the old general some respect. His sword was coming out of its sheath, but Asa had sensed the movement before it began. She shot from her hiding place, putting one hand on the hilt of his weapon and slamming it back into the sheath. Asa brought her knee up with all the force she could summon and drove it between Kyo's legs, leaving him a collapsed mess on the floor.

Mari spoke softly, her voice still filling the tent with a comfortable sense of command. "Perhaps, younger brother, I can help you with your problem."

———

Asa took up position near the entrance to the tent, close to Kyo. The general had eventually worked his way to his feet, wary of the blade and her speed. Fortunately, they hadn't made enough noise to attract the attention of the guards outside. Asa's positioning was clear, though. If he made so much as a squeak, he would be the first to die.

Kyo still looked as though he was going to throw up, which pleased Asa. If he was busy dealing with his own queasiness, he wouldn't be thinking about ways to make her life miserable.

Hiromi and Mari stood near each other, not quite nose to nose but far too close for casual conversation. They spoke in whispers, but Asa could still hear them clearly. She thought about warning Mari to keep her voice down, but the two siblings were in a world Asa couldn't breach. So she stood guard and hoped for the best.

Mari poked her finger into Hiromi's chest, pushing hard. She was a little taller than her brother, and she definitely held the power in the room. She had, after all, come with a nightblade.

"You tried to kill me!" she whisper-shouted.

Hiromi backpedaled, and Asa almost laughed at the sight of one of the mightiest people in the Kingdom being intimidated by his older sister. He looked like he wanted to escape, but Asa blocked the entrance.

"You allied with the blades." His response was flustered and uncertain, almost as though he'd never realized the extent of his order.

"So?" Mari's voice was furious, and if words could wound, Hiromi would have been bleeding to death on the floor.

Finally, Hiromi found a little of his spine and straightened up. Asa took note, and she saw the flicker in Mari's eyes that indicated she noticed as well.

"So! How can you even say that? Have you already forgotten it was the blades who killed our brother?"

Mari's entire posture changed, and although Asa could sense what was about to happen, she still watched in disbelief as Mari grabbed her brother's clothes, swept his legs up, and slammed him to the ground. Asa had no idea Mari knew anything about defense or fighting.

The lord was on the ground, staring up at Mari, shock on his face.

"Grow up! You're lord of this house now, and you can't make decisions based on personal vendettas. You would watch the entire Kingdom burn just to get revenge for Juro's death?"

Something Mari said was exactly what Hiromi needed to hear. The fight went out of him, and he relaxed on his back, taking deep, convulsing breaths. His sister collapsed to her knees next to him.

"I'm sorry, and I miss Juro every morning when I wake up. If I ever find the nightblade who murdered him, I will kill him, too. But this is bigger. The Kingdom needs to come first. You haven't seen how the people are suffering."

The tent fell silent as the two siblings both came to terms with their emotions. Asa glanced over at Kyo and saw a look of stony anger on the man's face. She frowned. He was part of another element at play, another perspective she wasn't seeing. But then her attention was diverted as Mari helped Hiromi up to his feet.

Mari drifted over to the table where her brother and Kyo had been debating strategy. Small figures stood on the map, inscribed with symbols representing everything from unit strength to allegiance, but Asa hadn't paid the display much attention.

Mari frowned as she looked at the map. She pointed at a set of pieces. "Is that true? Why are they there?"

Hiromi nodded. "They are marching on Starfall."

Asa thought Mari was going to send her brother crashing to the ground again.

"Hiromi, how could you?"

Confused, Asa stepped forward so she could read the inscriptions on the pieces. With her back to the general, he acted immediately, standing up and starting to draw his sword.

Asa had never let her sense wander from him, though. Her own draw was faster, and without looking, her sword was at his neck, forcing him back down to his knees. Most of her attention was drawn to the map in front of her. She understood why Mari had been so angry.

244

Katashi had invaded the lands of House Kita, heading toward Starfall. Hiromi's troops were nowhere to be found.

"Brother, you are more foolish than I had ever considered. You let enemy troops onto house land!"

"Yes! Don't you see the brilliance of the plan? Kyo and I thought of it together. Katashi attacks Starfall, a city filled with blades. The forces will destroy one another, and we can come in and deal with the remnants. Then my forces will have the upper hand, and the Kingdom will be mine."

Mari's eyes were wide. "Do you even hear yourself? Why do you trust Katashi? You haven't even left troops between him and Stonekeep. What if he walks right past Starfall and attacks our home?"

The look in Hiromi's eyes made it clear he hadn't even considered the possibility. Kyo fidgeted behind Asa, and she fixed him with a hard stare. The general knew more but remained silent. What was he thinking?

Hiromi's defense was feeble. "Katashi wouldn't dare. He is a lord, and if he was so foolish, it would be all the justification I would need to get Isamu to ally with us."

Asa had never seen Mari roll her eyes, but she did now, as if she thought the sky itself might provide answers to dealing with her brother. "Think, Hiromi! If Katashi is in an advantageous position against House Kita, why would Isamu ally with us? When you want to win, you ally with the strongest power, not the weakest."

Hiromi looked taken aback. Asa knew little about strategy and less about politics, but Mari's words rang true. How had Hiromi become so misguided?

"Well, then, what do you propose, Sister?" Hiromi's tone was still defiant, but at least he was asking the question.

"The same action I've always proposed. We need to ally ourselves with Starfall. They are willing to work with you. You need only to support them."

"No! I'm not going to ally with the people who murdered my brother!" Hiromi's voice was petulant and weak.

Mari glared at her brother, getting right in his face. "Do you have the strength to win this war on your own?"

Kyo spoke up. "You do, my lord. We've spoken about this."

Mari's glare never broke. "Look at the map and tell me the truth."

The general was about to speak again, but Asa pressed her blade against his throat. She could see the indecision on Hiromi's face. Perhaps the lord had received poor advice. Perhaps he was victim to his own anger over his brother's death. But he wasn't a fool. For a moment, Asa saw the leader Hiromi could be as he was forced to face facts.

This was the moment Mari's campaign came down to. Would her brother see reason or not?

The tent was silent, but Asa thought she could have cut the tension in the room with her sword.

Hiromi's response was surprisingly strong. "No."

Mari didn't gloat, but her voice turned from steel to silk. "I know how you feel about whoever killed our brother. When this chaos has passed, we need to find that blade and bring him to justice. But I want to see you as king, Brother, and that means we need to win this war. The only way to ensure that is to ally with the blades."

Hiromi still looked as though he wasn't convinced, but Mari knew just what to say.

"Brother, remember, if you become monarch, you get to decide how the blades live. You will make the laws that govern them. You can make sure that what happened to Juro never happens again. But you must become king first."

Asa wasn't sure what part of Mari's argument convinced Hiromi, but she saw the moment his face changed. The blade's stomach turned over. Although she was glad they had found an ally here, a man whose opinion could be so easily manipulated was a danger.

"You're right, Sister."

Mari went over to the map and looked it over. "Can we make it to Starfall before Katashi?"

Hiromi glanced over at Kyo, and Asa realized just how little the lord knew about his own troops.

"I do not think so, my lord," the general answered.

Asa took a glance at the map. The forces seemed almost equidistant. Katashi would have no reason to hurry his troops. "Why not? If you make haste and ride hard, there seems to be no reason not to."

Hiromi was nodding as he looked at the map. "Yes, we are almost as close. If we hurry, maybe . . ." His voice trailed off as he waited for Kyo to confirm his half-formed thought.

The general stood up and shuffled toward the map, keeping a hate-filled eye on Asa. He studied the map for a moment and seemed to be thinking about the problem. Asa felt as though he was trying to cover something up.

"Perhaps I was mistaken," he admitted. "We aren't too far from Starfall. The nightblade is right. If we prepare and leave at first light, making all haste, we can probably beat Katashi there. The troops will be exhausted and in no state to fight, however."

Mari didn't seem bothered. "That's not a problem. Creating an alliance with Hajimi shouldn't take long. The groundwork has already been laid. Then, with the blades at our back, we can negotiate a peace with Katashi. Isamu will follow suit. There will be no more need for this war." The relief in her voice was almost physical.

Asa considered the statement. The plan was as good as any if war was to be avoided. There were many ways it could go wrong, but if most of the pieces could be made to fit, Mari might have her peace.

Unfortunately, Asa's opinion mattered not at all. It was still Hiromi who held the fate of the Kingdom in his hands.

"I agree," he said.

Mari actually embraced him. Asa chuckled as he initially flinched away in fear.

He looked around the table. "Let's end this war."

———

The sun had yet to rise, but the time since their meeting with Hiromi had been busy. Mari had asked for paper and ink and became consumed with composing letters. Asa used the opportunity to close her eyes. She didn't dare sleep with so much happening around them, but she could still rest.

For the first time in many moons, Asa felt as though there was a chance for the land. Maybe, just maybe, they could put everything behind them, and the Kingdom could return to normalcy. She hated to hope and be disappointed, but it was hard not to hope around Mari.

She opened her eyes when Mari stood up and stretched. The lady beckoned for Asa to follow, and she did. Together they left the camp, this time out in the open. Many of the troops recognized Mari and bowed deferentially. Asa wondered how they would act if they knew their beloved lady was also the Lady in White.

Asa assumed Mari wanted to be out of hearing range, and she was right. Once Mari was certain they were alone, she turned and handed a pile of letters to Asa. The nightblade stared at them in her hands, confused.

"Your next mission."

Asa frowned.

"I hope that this will work," she explained, gesturing back to the camp and her brother, "but I can't risk everything on a single approach. In those letters are the orders for everyone moving forward. The longest is for Jun, who I assume will take my place if anything happens to me.

I've explained everything I can, giving my advice for possible scenarios, but it will be up to all of you to fix this broken Kingdom if I fail."

Asa didn't like the way Mari was speaking, sounding as though she didn't expect to succeed.

Mari seemed to read her mind. "Don't worry. I'll do everything I can."

"I should come with you."

Mari shook her head. "No. There's too much risk. We can't travel with a nightblade, as much as I'd like to. Moving forward, our deceptions need to stop. I will no longer be the Lady in White, and you will no longer be my servant." She glanced over at Asa's new serving costume, brought in overnight on Mari's orders to provide an excuse for the blade's presence, a grin on her face.

Asa wanted to be reassuring, but it wasn't her nature. The challenges facing Mari were substantial. "You'll succeed."

"I hope so. I am worried, though. Once I knew almost everything of importance in this Kingdom, but messages are getting to me too slowly. I didn't know Katashi had crossed the river and invaded our house's land. Even my own brother's mind is more a mystery to me now than ever before. What else don't I know?"

Asa didn't have any answers.

Mari took a deep and slow breath. "It doesn't matter, though, not really. All that really matters is peace, and this is our best hope. Take the letters to the group wandering the Kita lands. They'll be the closest, and then the message can spread from there. I'm summoning everyone to Starfall, to play whatever role they may. I think . . ." She paused. "I think the fate of the Kingdom might be decided there."

Asa bowed. "If you believe so. Regardless, I will track the party and deliver your words as fast as I can."

Mari bowed slightly to Asa. "Thank you. I can't tell you how much this all means to me. Go in safety, and may the Great Cycle bless you."

Chapter 21

Family, Mari thought, was a puzzling concept. For most of your life, you got to choose, at least to some degree, whom you spent your time with. You chose servants, friends, and lovers. But family you were stuck with, and it was family that was always closest to you.

Of course, she had known Hiromi since he had been born. She had only seen four cycles at the time but had been old enough to be excited for another addition to the family. Juro, once her closest friend and playmate, was busy focusing on learning how to be a warrior and rule the lands. He considered himself too important for her.

At first, the bond between Hiromi and Mari had been strong. Neither was concerned about issues of inheritance when they were young, and they played together almost every day between their lessons.

Mari wasn't sure when that had changed. In her memory, it felt as though one day they had been almost tied together, and the next they had nothing in common.

Mari tended to believe the rift had developed when Hiromi had figured out she was a girl. Of course, he had always known she was a girl, but one day, when he had been about eight, he seemed to realize what being a girl meant. Juro trained in war while Mari learned to dance. Hiromi idolized his older brother, the sibling so often praised by their parents for his excellent progress. Mari became his sister, nothing more than an annoyance, an obstacle to his own development.

Once he began training with swords, he no longer played with Mari, and the two had drifted apart. Consequently, Mari and Juro became slightly closer. Hiromi's temperament had always been a little different than theirs. His mind changed more quickly, and his passions inflamed faster, with more fluidity.

But as well as she knew Hiromi, Mari felt as though she didn't really know him at all. Who was the man her younger brother had become? She still thought of him in the framework of when she had known him best, back when he was little.

But that did him no justice. Like anyone, he had been shaped by a lifetime of experiences both big and small. Judging him as she had as a child wasn't fair anymore. He was now a grown man and her lord, although she still struggled to think of him in those terms.

On the ride to Starfall, she tried to remedy the situation, to talk with her brother and understand his mind. Her efforts were met with mixed success. At times, she was rewarded handsomely. They would speak of his beliefs and fears, and she would learn more about Hiromi in one morning than she had known in entire cycles of their lives together.

She knew that he hated the blades but made the connection through their conversation that he had always desired to be one. He wanted to be a good leader and inspire his troops, but he spent so much time thinking about how to inspire them that he did little of the actual necessary work. Perhaps the most important fact she learned was that he wasn't confident in the face of his fears.

That was a subject that Mari knew about. She and Juro had often discussed it late at night, and she had experienced the same fear first-hand the past couple of moons. Leading, whether it be a village, a group of blades, or one of the great houses, was a privilege. But it was also a terrifying responsibility to shoulder. Life and death rode on your decisions, and not deciding often seemed easier.

Mari felt the fear. She had felt it when she started leading the blades. She felt it even when she sent Asa away. At night, the fear often kept her awake.

But a leader had to find her way beyond the fear. Mari's path was acceptance. She believed she was doing her best, and nothing more could be asked. The consequences would be what they were.

Hiromi hadn't found his way yet. As they rode, he spoke about his sleepless nights, his endless pursuit of advice from others in an attempt to make the correct decision. A part of him knew he was becoming too reliant on his advisers, but he lacked the courage to accept the full responsibility of his orders.

Gently, Mari tried to give him advice and guidance on their journey, but her words were usually shunned. Just as she'd judged him based on their childhood experiences, he judged her the same. She wasn't someone who had single-handedly led a group of blades to prevent full-scale war; she was just his older sister, who wasn't allowed to train with swords.

On the third day of their ride, Mari came to a realization, one that had been a long time coming. If she had to choose an ideal lord to follow, she didn't think it would be Hiromi. Yes, she still thought he was the best of the three lords to choose from, but that wasn't saying much. Katashi was far too devious and Isamu too inept.

She wanted more from the man she looked up to as lord. She wanted him to be confident in his decisions. Her ideal leader had a vision for his lands, something specific they could all agree on. Hiromi had none of these traits.

But that was the other reason why family was puzzling. Despite all his shortcomings, she still loved him. They were riding into a dangerous situation together, and if something were to happen to Hiromi, Mari would be devastated. She didn't question that for a moment. What did it mean to care for someone deeply but not like the person they were? The question troubled her far more than it should have.

A day away from Starfall, the siblings broke away from the main army, traveling with only the hundred guards that comprised Hiromi's honor guard, some of the best warriors in their lands. For the second time in less than a cycle, the walls of Starfall rose to greet Mari.

———

Everything felt so similar and yet different. She visited the same chambers, but this time the assembly was much smaller. In fact, the only gifted present were the Council of the Blades. The stands, once filled with blades eager to listen to her, were now empty. Mari found it eerie to be in such a massive space with so few people.

On her first visit, she had felt almost claustrophobic with the number of blades packed into the benches that surrounded the hall. Now she wished that any of those sturdy wooden benches had someone sitting on them. She hadn't noticed on her first visit, but in the hall of the council, the seat of power for the blades, no decorations adorned the walls. Not a single painting or scroll hung from the pristine white surfaces.

The lack of spectators had nothing to do with the number of people in Starfall, as there were still a few hundred blades in the city. And yet Mari didn't think the city was as crowded as it had been on her last visit. But it was hard to know, and harder still to trust that her memory of those days was accurate.

The room was quiet because the meeting had been declared private. Hajimi hadn't given any reason, but Mari suspected it was because the situation was getting out of control, even in Starfall. Most blades spent their days wandering through the Kingdom. They rarely settled in one place for long. For all of them to be gathered here must have been a strain.

As Hiromi and she had walked the streets, she could see the divisions among the blades and wondered how much longer Hajimi would be able to keep everything together. They had passed more than one heated argument in the streets, and Mari herself caused disruption. She was recognized from her last visit, and some blades came and welcomed her warmly while others threw their hoods over their heads and turned their backs.

The blades seemed just as fractured as the citizens of the Kingdom. Some called for an end to the war. Others called for an alliance with this house or that. Mari had even heard some proclaiming it was time to leave the Kingdom altogether.

The differences didn't surprise her. She had come to understand the blades were just as individualized as any other citizen, but her brother was astounded. His demeanor, which had been hopeful for most of the journey, had soured quickly.

"How are we supposed to get them to align with us if they can't even agree with one another?" he asked glumly.

Mari didn't have any easy answers for her brother. She didn't know how Hajimi would use his power to unite the blades, but she had to trust that he had the ability. Otherwise their very last hope was lost.

Mari assumed the situation was delicate enough that Hajimi didn't need prying eyes or public opinion influencing the decision of the council.

Hajimi bowed to Mari when the siblings entered. "Lady Mari, it is good to see you again. You have been busy since our last visit."

Mari returned Hajimi's bow. She was slightly surprised he, too, knew of her activities. She worried her secret wasn't as safe as she'd once thought. Mentioning her previous visit did her no favors, either, as Hiromi glared at her, reminded of when her traitorous behavior began.

Hajimi bowed to Hiromi as well, but Mari noticed the bow wasn't as deep. Hiromi did as well but contained his anger. Mari had to give him credit for that much at least. The meeting wasn't getting off to the start she had hoped for.

The head of the Council of the Blades motioned for Hiromi to begin. He did, starting with the problems facing the Kingdom.

After a while, Hajimi waved his hand. "Lord Hiromi, while I appreciate your efforts, please know that we are just as aware of what is happening in the Kingdom as you. If you are here, let us get to the real point of your visit."

Even Mari was taken aback. Hajimi was being unquestionably rude, which was unlike him. In Mari's previous encounters with the blade master, he had been perfectly respectful.

Then she understood. Hajimi was, in his own way, testing her brother. Mari wasn't sure she saw the need but realized she didn't see the situation the same way he would. Hajimi was the guardian for all the blades. If they were going to ally with any lord, the agreement had to go deeper than just the terms. Hajimi had to know the type of man he was dealing with. Mari knew that the two hadn't met for many cycles. That was why he continued to push.

Hiromi appeared as though he was about to walk straight out of the room, but at the last moment, he seemed to change his mind.

"Very well. I have come to offer terms of an alliance between the blades and my house. I realize such an offer is unusual, but the times seem to demand it. Only together can we stop the war that threatens our Kingdom."

Hajimi nodded. "Noble words, indeed. What are your terms?"

Mari squinted, studying Hajimi closely. He seemed an entirely different man than the one she remembered. How much of his behavior was a test for her brother, and how much was him being worn down by the endless siege of hatred directed at the blades? His stony face gave nothing away. Had he already allied with another house?

Hiromi sketched the outline of his terms.

"I propose an alliance of forces between the blades and those of House Kita. While this is unprecedented, the situation is as well. To address possible concerns, this agreement would be in force only until

I am officially recognized as the new king, at which time we will draw a new agreement between the Kingdom and the blades."

Hiromi paused, his eyes studying the council's expressionless faces.

"Although I do not know what form this final agreement will take, I am willing to consider returning many of the rights that had once been taken from the blades."

That had been a point of contention between the siblings. On the journey, Mari had argued that an entirely new system was needed, but to that he wouldn't listen. Hiromi was willing to be generous, to a point, but he wasn't willing to consider remaking a system that had worked well for so long.

Hajimi seemed skeptical but allowed Hiromi to continue until the lord was finished. When her brother was done, Hajimi's first question was difficult. "What about the census?"

This had caused the worst argument between the siblings. Mari knew from her conversations with the blades how much they hated the census. But to her brother, getting rid of the census was the equivalent of giving up one's last line of defense.

The heart of the problem was the nature of how the census was conducted. The people of the Kingdom had been counted for almost as long as records had been kept, but the census for civilians only counted families, not individuals. After Two Falls, King Masaki had decided that the blades were too dangerous not to be counted individually. Every blade had to be registered and, if they set up permanent lodgings outside of Starfall, had to report as such to the local authorities or be executed for treason.

Hiromi stood firm. "It would remain in place. There is no harm in being counted."

Hajimi countered. "There is every danger in being counted. Removing the census requirements would indicate to me that you trust the blades and aren't simply seeking to use us for our strength."

Hiromi's answer was weak. "It's not about trust. It's about planning and knowing what resources are available and what resources need to be available."

Mari winced. Hajimi wouldn't take kindly to being thought of as a resource. Everyone in the room knew the census was an issue of trust.

Hajimi spoke slowly, choosing his words with care. "As it stands, you don't make a compelling argument. If you truly wish to ally yourselves with us, I would ask one last question. All the houses have come to us. In truth, you are the last. Why you instead of them?"

The question clearly rattled Hiromi. He hadn't even considered the possibility the other houses had been there. Mari saw a different side. If the blades still hadn't allied themselves with a house, it was because they had found the other lords wanting. Hiromi saw a threat, but Mari knew that Hajimi had given her brother one last opportunity.

Her brother's answer surprised and impressed her. "I do not believe in comparing one house against another. Like any ruler, I have my weaknesses and my strengths. Yes, I am asking you to help my house, but I am not asking you to help me. I am asking you to fulfill the duty you once had to the Kingdom."

Hajimi nodded. "That is a good answer. Many would follow a leader who truly believed thus." He shot a pointed glance at Mari. "Are you certain about the census?" he asked Hiromi.

Hiromi was about to speak but thought better of it. Mari could see his mind was racing, but it was not her place to tell him what to do, not here, not now.

"Perhaps some agreement can be reached. I would, for example, be willing to consider a self-reported census, or perhaps even a census of blades only in active service. I am willing to bend but not break."

Hajimi stroked his beard, considering the lord's answer. He glanced from council member to council member. "I believe, at least, Lord Hiromi, you have given us something to discuss. You understand, of course, that a decision cannot be made today."

Hiromi looked as though he had just found out a loved one had died. "With all due respect, Hajimi, enemies will be at your gates soon. Haste is necessary."

Hajimi's smile said that he was well aware of the situation and that he was well aware that it was Hiromi himself who had allowed Katashi's forces to advance.

"Yes, but haste must be balanced by consideration. I assure you, you will be summoned as soon as a decision is reached."

The response wasn't enough for Hiromi but would have to be. Mari sympathized with her brother. But the blades would not be moved by more argument. They needed enough time to decide.

Mari took the lead, hoping her brother wouldn't be too greatly angered. "Your consideration is all we could ask for. You have our gratitude."

Hajimi gave Mari a knowing smile, and the two siblings left to await their fate.

———

In her brother's tent two days later, Mari couldn't help but laugh at Hiromi. After everything they had been through, he was still acting like a young child.

A memory came to Mari, as distinct as though it had happened a few heartbeats ago. The three siblings were much younger, and Juro was still alive, proud as always. The memory caused her heart to ache, but she breathed into the discomfort, allowing the sorrow to wash over her and disappear like a wave.

She didn't remember what the event had been for. The wedding of a noble, perhaps? A feast for a general leaving the army? No matter. Juro was walking around, as stiff as a sword, waiting for his sister and brother to hurry. Mari was also ready, her pure white robes beautiful, making her happy.

Hiromi had been the problem. Their father had a small uniform made for his youngest son, and the silk fabric fit too tightly over the growing boy. Hiromi wasn't pleased, but he couldn't make a fuss because their father was in the next room. None of them envied a punishment for displeasing their father on such an important day.

So Hiromi had launched a silent rebellion, stomping all over the floor and crossing his arms as tightly to his chest as he could. Not too much unlike today, Mari thought with a sad smile.

Hiromi didn't manifest anger today. Instead, he was nervous and worried, exhibiting the same behaviors he had so long ago.

So much had already gone their way. One more hurdle, and Mari knew her mission would be over. Hajimi and the council had accepted the terms set by Hiromi. The agreement had taken another day of bargaining, but the document had been signed and sealed. Mari carried a copy with her for their next meeting.

Sister and brother were back, outside the walls of Starfall, camped to the east of the city with their army. On the other side of Starfall, to the west, sat Katashi and his army, newly arrived.

The other lord had agreed to meet with Hiromi and Mari prior to launching his attack. Hiromi faced the last and most daunting task he had yet undertaken. He was going to announce to Katashi that his people had made an alliance with the blades and that the blades backed him as the new king.

Katashi could take one of two paths. The siblings hoped he would capitulate and realize he had been beaten. Any lord backed by the blades had far more strength than the other two. Fighting on would be hopeless. The terms of peace would no doubt be difficult, but Mari was confident they could negotiate something that worked for all.

Katashi could also, of course, refuse. If so, Hiromi and Hajimi had agreed to attack his army, destroying it between them. That prospect was certainly less than ideal but, if required, a sacrifice they were willing to make.

Either way, after the negotiations, Hiromi would make news of the alliance with the blades public. There would be pushback, but Mari hoped the Lady in White had created enough goodwill among the people for the agreement to be accepted.

She didn't delude herself. Cycles of work were still left to be done, but if she and Hiromi could prevent full-scale war, the sacrifice was more than worth it. They just needed to get Katashi to agree. The siblings assumed he would at least require to be second in line to the throne, a concession they were willing to make.

Finally, Mari convinced Hiromi he was ready. They mounted their horses with General Kyo and their honor guard and left. They'd struggled to find an ideal place to hold the meeting. They weren't foolish enough to wander into Katashi's camp, and he didn't trust House Kita, either. Starfall had been proposed, but Mari had never thought that would be accepted, either.

Instead, they rode to a location within sight of both armies and Starfall, a grassy area about half a league from the main gates to the south of the city. Both lords approached with nothing more than their honor guards traveling under a flag of peace.

Mari, like her brother, was nervous. It wasn't that warm yet, but she could see the beads of sweat on his forehead.

They rode slowly, each lost in thought. The late spring day was promising to be a hot one. All the clouds had burned away, and Mari was looking forward to the shade of the tent they were to meet under.

The two rode until they were about fifty paces away from the tent, and then they dismounted, their honor guard protecting them. Hiromi looked like he was about to adjust his uniform one last time but then thought better of it and walked toward the meeting place. Mari followed a few paces behind her brother.

Katashi was already there, sprawled comfortably on the grass. His posture was decidedly informal, and Mari wondered what message he was trying to send. Either way, the lord didn't look like he had a care in the world. He might as well have been out for a picnic for all the worry he displayed. The difference between him and Hiromi, who stood so stiffly it looked as though his uniform was frozen solid, couldn't have been more clear.

Mari hadn't seen Katashi since they had been children at court, but his presence made her nervous. He was immaculately groomed, not a single long hair out of place, all of it tied tightly back. His silk robes, the same deep red as the color of his house, were pristine, as though dust itself was afraid of the man. Even though the day was hot, not a single bead of sweat could be seen anywhere on him. His face was thin and beardless, and although there wasn't a single aspect of his appearance that lent credence to Mari's emotion, she was disgusted by him.

The lord of House Amari had sharp eyes that moved slowly, doubtless taking in every tiny detail of the scene before him. A smile crept onto his face, but Mari trusted the smile even less than she had trusted him before. He was nothing but lies.

"Welcome, welcome. It is good to see you here, Hiromi. Mari, I haven't seen you for several cycles. Your beauty makes even this afternoon seem dull by comparison."

Mari couldn't help herself. His words said one thing, but she heard something entirely different. She had a sudden urge to bathe, shaking her head slightly. She needed to push away such thoughts. They did Hiromi no good, and he might very well need her help.

Hiromi bowed and sat, trying to look as comfortable as Katashi and failing miserably. Mari clenched her fists. Her brother should be in control of this situation, but he wasn't.

Katashi continued. "I wanted to thank you, Hiromi, for allowing me to attack Starfall. It will not be an easy task, but my best generals have been trying to solve the problem of the city for many cycles, and I think we have a plan guaranteed to succeed."

Mari considered the statement, the first thing he said that had the ring of truth to it. Katashi was as manipulative as his late brother, but he was no fool. If he intended to attack Starfall, he had to have a plan. But Mari had no idea what it could be.

Katashi stopped as though he'd just realized he had forgotten something. "Where are my manners? You must be as parched as I am. We must have some food and drink!" He clapped his hands, and two chests were brought forward. Several of Katashi's honor guard pulled out light refreshments, wine, and water.

Mari was caught off guard. What was Katashi planning? On the surface, everything seemed so genuine, so kind, but she couldn't bring herself to trust him.

When they didn't partake of the food offered, Katashi snorted. "I'm not going to poison you on the eve of our victory. You've let my army into your land. We're allies!" To prove his point, he grabbed some food and ate and drank the wine. It wasn't a guarantee against poison, but it was a start. Hiromi, not the fool, called one of his guards and had him test the victuals and drink. When the guard didn't die, Hiromi dug in hungrily.

Mari was less eager to eat, but nevertheless picked at a small plate while Katashi continued, his voice lower and more serious.

"I've noticed, of course, that you haven't come alone." With a hand filled with a small rice ball, he gestured out toward the gathered army of House Kita. "This concerns me. Do you seek to aid me?"

With that, they had come to the heart of the matter. Hiromi couldn't lie but was awkward and unprepared. Mari wondered how he would handle the situation.

She had never been more proud of her brother than she was in that moment. Hiromi sat up straight and acted every bit the lord he was. "I come today to demand your surrender. The blades have allied themselves with me, and I will sit on the throne."

Katashi didn't look nearly as surprised as Mari thought he should be. He continued eating his food, his eyes studying everything.

He sighed. A strange panic filled her being.

"I am sorry to hear that. I truly had hoped that together we might rid ourselves of the blades that plague our land. Instead, you've befriended them. What did you offer them?"

Hiromi shook his head. What he had offered was no part of this conversation. "Nothing more than is their right. Do you yield?"

Katashi laughed, and Mari knew, deep in her bones, that something was dreadfully wrong. Perhaps Katashi wasn't surprised. She could understand that. She could understand most of his act. But they were supposed to have him at an advantage, and he was every bit as comfortable as he had been before. She looked around, wondering what the source of his confidence could be. Nothing seemed out of the ordinary, and she thought that perhaps he was the best performer she had ever met.

His next answer surprised her even more. "Very well. I suppose there is nothing to be done then. I don't agree with what you're doing, Hiromi, but I can't fault your ambition. What terms are you prepared to offer?"

Even Mari didn't know what to make of what was happening. Hiromi, seemingly oblivious to how wrong the situation was, launched right into his terms as though he accepted Katashi's surrender. Mari forced herself not to spin around but to look carefully. It was difficult to see beyond the rows of guards surrounding them, but Mari didn't see any additional troops approaching.

To all appearances, Katashi would indeed surrender to Hiromi. Part of her heard them arguing over terms, but the entire event was surreal. Katashi was smiling, as though he was part of a joke no one else understood. Mari looked around again, but still nothing was happening out of the ordinary.

Her brother's voice broke through her trance. "We are agreed, then?"

Katashi nodded, and the scribe who was present furiously wrote out the terms and presented them for both lords to examine. Mari felt a sinking feeling in her stomach. This was supposed to be their shining moment, the completion of all her dreams. Her brother was going to take the throne. But all she wanted to do was grab Hiromi and run away with him to someplace where all of this was nothing but a nightmare.

Both lords agreed to the terms, and Katashi insisted Hiromi sign them first. He did, turning the paper toward Katashi to make the peace official. Katashi looked at it, laughed again, and ripped it to shreds.

Mari was stunned, even though this was what she had expected all along. Katashi's behavior was so rude as to almost be unimaginable. Hiromi looked up at the other lord, confusion all over his face.

It was the last expression he ever used.

In the blink of an eye, Katashi drew his sword and slashed Hiromi's throat. Blood spilled everywhere as Mari's brother's body, its life pumping from him, collapsed in front of her.

Mari needed a few heartbeats to process what was happening. They had come under a flag of peace. Katashi still wore the same lazy grin.

Nothing had changed, except that his red silks were covered in blood, and her brother was dead.

Mari opened her mouth to wail, noticing the presence at her side too late.

An arm wrapped around her throat and pulled tight, cutting off her scream and her breath.

Confused, Mari thrashed about. She had been trained for this but hadn't been expecting an attack. Her assailant pulled harder, lifting her off the ground as her feet kicked helplessly.

Black dots swarmed the edges of her vision, darkening her sight with amazing rapidity.

She looked at Katashi but didn't want her last sight to be of him. She looked down at her brother, that look of surprise now permanently on his face. A movement from Katashi caught her eye, and the pressure on her throat was abruptly eased.

Mari collapsed to the grass, noticing part of her body had landed in her brother's blood, spreading throughout the tent. She gasped for air, hoping a scream would bring attention. What had happened to their honor guard?

Movement caught her eye again. Katashi stood up and disrobed, displaying a body that had clearly been through cycles of hard training. She had never known his skill with a sword. He reached to one of his guards, who handed him a clean robe.

Just as her reason began to return, he gave an order. "Bind and gag her before she screams."

Panicked, Mari tried to scream before it was too late. But a wad of cloth was stuffed in her mouth before she could let out a sound, and a thin rope was wrapped around her head several times to ensure it stayed in.

Before she knew what had happened, her arms were bound tightly behind her, and her ankles were lashed together. Everything was happening too fast.

She focused on her surroundings, trying to breathe through her nose, trying to understand. What about their honor guard? She looked behind the tent, where all her guards were standing still as if the treaty had been signed. Kyo was far closer than she had expected and was right behind her. When had he broken ranks with the guard? Was he coming to rescue her?

As she was being picked up, Mari saw Kyo bowing to Katashi.

"Well done, Lord Kyo. With your help, we will rid the world of blades and begin again, the right way."

Kyo bowed again, and Mari was tossed in one of the chests, her world going black as they slammed the lid shut.

Chapter 22

Nothing had been the same since the battle for the hilltop. Ikko's blades had continued on, choosing a few smaller supply caches to remind the army they were still a threat, but the task had become much harder. Armies were slow to react, but when they did, life became far more challenging. Supply chains were well guarded now, and although Koji lacked a complete picture of troop movements, forces seemed to be consolidating for a big push. That meant even more people guarding the supplies.

Koji still traveled with more than twenty blades, but the hilltop had changed them. A cadre of well-prepared soldiers had reminded them that they weren't immortal, that they died just the same as anyone else. In battle, confidence was everything, and their confidence had been shaken.

Even Koji, normally sure in his abilities, experienced doubt. No matter how magnificent he was with a sword, there wasn't much he could do against a falling boulder. He had experienced, for one of the few times in his life, the limits of his abilities. He wasn't pleased.

Not only had the battle shaken the blades' confidence in themselves; it had shaken their confidence in their entire mission. They had lost almost a third of their companions in one attack, and they weren't being replaced. All knew they were holding back the surge of war, but they were just beginning to realize that simple attrition would eventually cause them to fail.

When Asa found her fellow warriors, the presence of another nightblade seemed to light a fire underneath them all, but none more so than Koji. She was still in his thoughts daily, and seeing her ride toward them lifted his spirits.

She went directly to Koji, dropping nimbly off her horse and approaching him. There was a single moment of awkwardness, and then Asa embraced him. Koji couldn't have been more surprised if the sun had disappeared. He returned her embrace, glad to see her again.

They broke apart, and Asa looked up at him. "It's good to see you again, Koji. There's much to talk about, but I need to meet with your commander first."

Before he could reply, she was gone. Koji watched as she walked away, truly enamored for the first time in his life.

He watched as Asa and Ikko spoke, Asa dropping a large pile of letters in his arms. They talked for some time, but Koji found that he had a hard time looking away.

When Asa came back, Koji would have sworn there was a glow about her. She sat down next to him, and they looked out on the scene before them.

Despite the difficult traveling conditions, Koji had to admit the lands of House Kita were some of the most gorgeous he'd ever seen. He'd been in the area before but had never really paid much attention to the silent, imposing majesty of the mountains.

Koji's question was burning. "What happened to you?"

Asa's smile was soft but genuine. "I'm not sure myself. Do you ever feel like you're doing the right thing? That everything seems to make sense?"

Koji did understand. For the first time in his life, he felt as though he was fighting for something that mattered. He gestured toward his commander's tent. "What's happening?"

"A chance for peace. I left Mari not too many days ago. She convinced her brother to ally with the blades."

Asa continued to tell him what Mari had planned. Koji was shocked to hear that Starfall might be under attack soon.

They were interrupted by Koji's commander shouting orders. Koji didn't want to ride anymore, but perhaps their journey was almost at an end. Wearily they climbed back onto their mounts and turned toward Starfall as per Mari's last orders. He hoped that soon it would all be over.

———

Koji could sense they were close even before they could see Starfall. With so many of the gifted enclosed in such a small space, it was impossible not to sense the life energy. The group rode forward warily, making sure to avoid whatever patrols wandered the area around the city.

Eventually they came to a place where they could look upon the city, and Koji was amazed. He was sure he had never seen so many people at once. On each side of the city, an army was encamped, and Starfall itself was still ablaze with the energy of hundreds of lives.

His spirits had been buoyed by the past few days with Asa. The road had been hard and long, but if her news was true, hope was alive, which he hadn't dared to feel in a long time. All the fighting and struggle could finally be over.

When he saw the situation below them, his heart sank faster than a stone thrown in a river. They had known what they were going to see. Asa had told them that Hiromi was going to march his army to Starfall to be a countering force against Katashi's. But hearing something was going to happen and seeing it in front of you were as different as night and day.

Koji saw a situation ripe to explode. He could take in the sight of both armies without even having to move his eyes. They were far less than a day's march apart, much too close for comfort. Even a few soldiers too drunk for their own good could ignite the war. He desperately hoped that Mari knew what she was doing.

The blades had arrived near dusk and made the decision to set up camp away from the excitement below. They were still fugitives and didn't want to try for Starfall when it was surrounded by soldiers. Asa would try to find Mari the next day and get a better idea of their next steps.

Koji awoke in the early morning as the very first hints of the sun started to peek above the horizon. He rolled over and tried to go back to sleep, but something was off, something he couldn't place right away.

Uncertain, he pushed himself up and looked around, bleary-eyed. The rest of their group was still asleep, and his sense told him that no one else was nearby. But he couldn't shake the feeling something was amiss.

He turned and looked down toward Starfall, immediately seeing the problem. Both armies had moved even closer to the city, each just outside of bow range. So far, nothing had happened, but the coordinated movements were ominous. Koji woke the rest of the group to grumbles and moans, but they all went silent when they saw what was happening.

The blades were far enough away that the advance of the armies could barely be heard, almost like a thunderstorm far on the horizon, a distant, continuous rumble. But they noticed when the early morning sky was blackened by clouds of arrows.

When the first wave happened, Koji almost fell backward. There were so many arrows it seemed impossible that anyone could live underneath the onslaught. Black smoke trailed behind, and Koji knew they were fire arrows, designed to kill and burn.

The second wave was just as orderly as the first, a tremendous mass all released at once. The black streaks of fire burned over the walls of Starfall, thousands of death's messengers rushing to their destination.

The response from Starfall was weak. A few scattered arrows were returned, but nothing else. The walls were almost as silent as if the city was deserted.

The lack of reaction from the home of the blades was disappointing, but Koji wasn't surprised. Despite the walls, Starfall hadn't been built to withstand a coordinated siege. The city held no catapults, no boiling cauldrons of pitch to dump upon invaders. Blades despised siege engines and tactics, finding honor and glory only in personal combat.

That rigidity, combined with the belief that no one would dare attack the city, would be the end of them.

The belief wasn't hard to fathom. In their entire recorded past, Starfall had never been attacked. The mythology surrounding the blades and their historic role in the Kingdom had guaranteed their safety. But now the Kingdom had changed faster than the blades' worldview.

Koji gazed in horror as the scene unfolded below, the deadly beauty of the massed arrows turning his beloved Starfall into a grave.

He turned his attention from the arrows to the city itself. Not every arrow started a fire, but not every one had to. Koji could see dozens of fires already, and more seemed to become visible every moment he watched.

Koji looked around at the other blades assembled. "We need to help them," he said.

Asa glanced up at him, her eyes red with anger and sorrow. "How? There's not many of us, and thousands of them. If we attack, all we'll earn is our own deaths."

Koji's anger erupted. "We have to do something! I refuse to sit here while our home is burned before our eyes."

The group seemed to agree with him, but none moved. Even in his anger, Koji knew Asa was right.

The thought led to another. What had happened to Mari? How was it that the person who held all their hopes was letting the attack happen?

Two explanations came immediately to mind. Either Mari was a captive of her brother's, or she had betrayed them all. Koji absolutely refused to believe the latter possibility, but either way, they needed to get to her. Now he had a focus.

His thoughts were interrupted by a change in events below. The massive gates of Starfall swung open, and a group of nightblades, about fifty strong by Koji's estimation, attacked Lord Katashi's army.

Immediately Koji thought of joining forces with the blades from the city, but his half-formed plans were dashed before he could even begin to make them a reality. Hundreds of bowmen turned their sights from the city to the charging blades, and the air was thick with incoming arrows.

Many of the blades had the foresight to bring shields, but even they couldn't defend against the sheer volume sent against them. Many of the nightblades fell in the attempt. Of those who survived, some were brought down by spears at the front lines. The few who made it through caused chaos in the ranks, but from his vantage point, he watched the disturbances fade as the blades were brought down one at a time.

Koji cursed in anger, kicking at the ground.

He focused on what he could do. "We need to get to Mari," he said.

That drew their attention. Finding their leader was a manageable task. The party started toward their gear, but Koji held them up.

"No, it's better that a small group go than a large one. We've seen what happens when the blades attack an army. Better to rely on stealth. I assume she's being held captive among her people."

Asa volunteered to join him. The two of them combined would be enough.

They both donned the uniforms of House Kita. Asa's was hooded so she wouldn't draw attention for being a woman. Asa spoke a final word to the commander before they left.

She answered Koji's unspoken question as they started down. "I suggested that he start trying to find all the blades in the area. Once Mari's letters make it through, more will be coming this way, and it's better if they're stopped before they arrive."

Koji didn't say what was on his mind. By the time any more of Mari's units arrived, it would be far too late. This siege would last at most a few more days, and the other groups would take longer than that to arrive. The fight was over before it had even begun.

———

They made it to the outskirts of the encampment with little difficulty. In the chaos of battle, troops were moving everywhere, and blending in was easy. Koji didn't expect to have any problems until he and Asa were actually in the camp.

She insisted on leading the way once they were among the tents. Koji didn't argue, electing instead to follow her on her winding path. He was confused at first, but as they got deeper into the camp, Koji realized he hadn't seen another person since they broke the perimeter. He looked at Asa with a new respect. She was guiding them well, keeping track of far more than he had ever attempted to.

Asa's face was set with focus, and Koji decided not to compliment her on her skill. He just followed, growing more and more impressed as the small changes in their direction and speed kept them from detection.

Her gift was no small feat. Even in the midst of battle, the camp was crawling with people. Some soldiers seemed to be patrolling; others were clearly messengers, sprinting back and forth with commands. As the duo got closer to the center of the camp, more guards were present. The gaps in attention got smaller, and Koji wasn't certain how much longer Asa could prevent detection.

She kept pushing forward. Time was an enemy, and Koji understood that at some point, they would switch from stealth to force. He remained ready to draw.

The moment came soon. Eventually Asa broke through the final line of tents surrounding the center ring. A wide gap was there, full of so many troops there was no getting through. Asa stepped boldly into the open, pretending they belonged. Her ruse didn't work. They were almost immediately stopped by a pair of guards.

Asa stepped forward, blocking Koji's easy cut before he could draw.

She pulled out a sheet of paper, on which Koji could plainly see Mari's seal. The guard looked at it, looked at Asa, and looked at the paper again.

Everything happened in the blink of an eye. Both Asa and Koji sensed that the guard was about to yell. Less than a heartbeat after that, Koji sensed Asa going for her sword. The die had been cast.

Asa's cut was clean, slicing across the man's throat and cutting off his scream before it could leave his lips. Koji's was no less perfect, killing the guard's partner in one stroke. Despite the seriousness of their situation, Koji was impressed. Together, the two of them felt unstoppable.

Another pair of guards was on them in an instant. Koji watched in fascination as Asa drew a second, short sword. She dealt with both guards in less than a heartbeat, one of her swords blocking an attack while the other made deadly cuts.

Asa sprinted toward the center tent, slicing it wide open and leaping through. Koji followed a moment later.

His eyes adjusted after a few moments. There were a few people inside, but no one was fighting, not yet. He looked around. There, beside Asa, was another woman who resembled Mari but certainly wasn't their leader. Koji blinked, thinking he was hallucinating. Asa had her head cocked to the side, like she was trying to understand something she'd never seen before.

A whole group of guards burst through the tent, and battle commenced. Koji slipped between the enemy swords with ease, his own taking a life whenever it cut, his movements smooth and controlled.

In the corner of his vision, Asa was no less impressive. Koji had never seen a real two-sword style before, and she was far more dangerous than the last time they had dueled. Asa kept deflecting and cutting, deflecting and cutting, slicing down any opponent who dared come near her.

They both knew that if they remained, it was only a matter of time before they fell.

Koji led the way, clearing a path to the front entrance of the tent. Asa followed close behind, and the two naturally fell into protecting the other's back. Once they were clear of the tent, Asa made a break for it. Koji felled one more guard and followed her.

Even though they had just been in the heat of battle, the look of calm focus on Asa's face was unmistakable. They ran through the camp, turning frequently, their pursuers always right behind them.

Step-by-step they increased the distance from their enemies. Asa cut down one poor guard who stumbled unintentionally into their path, but otherwise she kept them away from crowds. Koji's sense was the only warning he had when she stopped suddenly and cut a hole in a tent, ducking in.

He followed, and Asa grabbed the open flaps and held them shut. The solution was far from perfect, but Koji knew as he sensed the guards rush past that they didn't need perfect. He was about to speak to Asa when she reopened the cut in the tent and stepped back out.

The trick had earned them a few moments, but now the rest was up to her.

Koji wasn't sure how long the pursuit lasted. They walked in a crouch, stopping and then sprinting. Once more they hid in an abandoned tent. The call had gone out, and every guard in the camp was searching for them.

Throughout it all, Asa silently guided them, avoiding every patrol even as they passed just paces away. By the time they reached the outskirts of the camp and had snuck away, night was falling.

Once they were safe, Koji looked back at both the camp and Starfall behind it. His home was on fire, large portions of the city sending up tall plumes of smoke that merged with the evening sky. His heart was torn in two, every hope he had felt dashed. Something had happened to Mari, and Starfall had been taken completely by surprise.

Asa eventually came and stood next to him, their hands intertwining. Her voice was soft. "We need to find out what happened. We need to see how we can make this right."

Her words stirred some hope in him but not much. As he looked upon the burning city of blades, he wished he could share Asa's optimism.

Chapter 23

Off in the distance, Starfall burned. Asa stared at the sight with empty eyes. So much had burned in her life lately. Haven. Kiyoshi's body. Now Starfall.

She had never really thought of Starfall as home. It had always simply been the place she returned to. She was surprised to feel so sorrowful about its destruction. As she watched the fires burn, she realized it was because Starfall had always been a safe place, the calm for any storm in her life. If Starfall fell, blades would have nowhere left to live in peace.

From the distance, the fires looked like a campfire that gave no warmth. More than once Asa had started to reach out toward them, but she felt only the cool night air on her hands.

Koji sat next to her, honoring her silence. She was grateful for his strength and his respect. Now, more than ever, she needed something to hold on to.

Her memories danced along with the flames. She didn't understand what she had seen in that tent. At first glance, Mari had been there, but when her eyes adjusted, the figure hadn't been Mari. Just a woman who dressed in Mari's style of clothes.

Asa's head was spinning. She turned to Koji. "Do you understand what we saw in the tent?"

"That woman wasn't Mari."

At first Asa was tempted to shout. Of course, the woman wasn't Mari. Even she knew that. But Koji worked through problems differently. He focused on one step at a time, she reminded herself. He wasn't just stating the obvious; he was starting on the problem by beginning with what they knew.

"So who was she, and why was she there?"

He scratched at his bare chin. "I don't think who she is matters. But why she was there, that is the question."

"Maybe she was a servant?"

Koji shook his head. "Her clothes were those of a lady."

"A mistress of Hiromi's?"

"Perhaps, although the similarity to Mari's appearance raises disturbing questions."

Asa agreed, unwilling to name the option they both suspected. Koji spoke their fears out loud.

"My gut tells me that woman was there to look like Mari."

Asa thought so as well, but she couldn't understand why a double would be in place. When she had left, Mari and Hiromi seemed as though they were on good terms. Why would they need a double? Someone needed to convince others that Mari was still there. She said as much to Koji, who agreed.

Now he asked the question. "Who would need to convince House Kita that Mari was present?"

Asa discarded options quickly. Hiromi was an obvious answer, but that didn't sit right with her. He was the leader of his people and could say anything he desired. Using a double seemed unnecessarily complicated.

The only other answer was Katashi. Had the lords met? Asa wished they had arrived a few days sooner so they would have known what had happened. They needed more information—fast.

That night, Asa wasn't able to sleep. They were keeping a close watch on the camp, and a few of the blades in Koji's group had donned

Kita uniforms to see if they could learn more. Asa tossed and turned and kept extending her sense, waiting for the blades to return.

They didn't do so until the next morning. A bleary-eyed Asa had gotten little sleep, and their news made her stomach twist into knots. Peace existed between Houses Kita and Amari. Hiromi and Mari had met with Katashi two days ago and come up with the strategy to destroy the blades once and for all. However, the blades also reported that Hiromi had taken ill and that most of the orders seemed to be coming from General Kyo.

Knowing what the two siblings had intended to do, Asa feared the worst. Something had happened to Mari. Now that she had more information, her mind immediately started making connections. It had to be Kyo. She didn't have a shred of evidence, but she hadn't trusted him from the moment they met. He had betrayed the siblings somehow, which was why they needed a double for Mari. Kyo was truly in command, even though orders were seemingly coming from Hiromi.

Rage burned inside Asa. She stomped out to the edge of their camp and watched the second day of the siege. The house troops had no plans to enter the city, content to keep sending fire in to do their work for them. There were no longer waves of arrows but instead a continuous trickle of fire, the archers seemingly aiming for parts of the city at random.

Koji came and stood next to her. He had come to the same conclusions, she was sure. "What do you want to do?"

"I want to kill Kyo."

"Do you think they're still alive?"

That was Asa's most burning question as well. If Hiromi and Mari had survived whatever occurred, that needed to take priority. But Asa despaired. What were the odds that an enemy would leave a rival lord alive, especially if he already had control of the lord's army through a proxy?

She sighed. If there was any chance of Mari being alive, though, she had to try. She'd be somewhere in Katashi's camp.

"Do we have uniforms for House Amari?"

"Yes. We have all the houses. When do you want to leave?"

Asa studied the field of battle off in the distance. "Not during the day. We'll want the cover of night this time."

Koji frowned. "Do you worry that will be too late?"

"No. Starfall isn't going to fall today, no matter how much damage they might cause. And if Mari is alive, I can't see any reason why that would change soon. Better to have the cover of darkness. We won't survive a chase like we did yesterday. Our entry and exit need to be unnoticed."

Koji stood up and put his hand on her shoulder. "In that case, you should get some rest."

———

Sneaking into encampments was becoming an old trick for Asa. The more she practiced infiltrating supposedly secure locations, the more she realized how easy the task could be with the right training.

In the cover of dark they broke through Katashi's outer perimeters with ease. The patrols were scattered far and wide, and while they might have netted those without the sense, Asa and Koji avoided detection.

As usual, the challenge began as they got deeper into the camp. In the outer ranks, where the soldiers made their beds, no one questioned the duo. They wore the red uniforms of House Amari, and people milled about freely. Asa understood the lack of protection here. Even if they drew their swords and started cutting their way through the soldiers, the overall effect would be limited.

One drunk man almost blew their cover. Asa sensed him coming but paid him no mind. But when he saw Koji, he seemed to think they were long-lost partners. The intoxicated soldier yelled for all to gather, drawing far too much attention to them for their comfort.

Asa froze, unsure of what to do. Fortunately, Koji had no such problem. He put the man into a hold, cutting off the air from his throat until he passed out. The man was so drunk he barely resisted, thinking the entire attack was a joke until too late. Koji left the man passed out on the ground. Anyone passing by would smell the wine and draw their own conclusions.

As they approached the inner ring of tents that marked the shelter of the commanders and lord's servants, the two paused to consider their approach.

Koji whispered in her ear, "Do you have any idea where she would be?"

Asa almost shook her head, but then reconsidered. If she was a lord who had kidnapped a lady, what would she do? She would want to keep the lady close to her own tent. Otherwise there might be questions as to why the lord was wandering so far afield. But not in the lord's personal tent. If what Asa had seen was any indication, there would be a number of visitors coming through the tent, and unless the abduction was common knowledge, the risk of discovery was too great.

Such reasoning gave them a direction to go in and narrowed down their choices. She explained her deductions to Koji, who agreed.

Their objective, then, was the tents that made up the center of the encampment. Asa calmed her breath and extended her sense, preparing to lead the way.

Eventually a gap in the patrols opened, and Asa and Koji slipped through into the inner rings of tents. Asa hoped that once they got close enough to the center tents, they would be able to just sense Mari. She thought she had spent enough time with the lady to be able to identify her energy in a crowd.

They took their time working their way through the inner rings of tents. Asa made each move deliberately, tracking the patterns of the patrols as they shuffled around. Exercising her new skills came easier to her the more she practiced. In a space this crowded, she could still only throw out her sense a couple of dozen paces before she was overwhelmed with information, but that was a substantial improvement from before.

Koji had no problem following her lead. He acted like her shadow, never more than a pace behind, the couple moving almost as one. She supposed he was probably using his sense to know exactly when and where she was going to move.

Asa sank deeper into the awareness Daisuke had worked so hard to instill in her. Koji, for all his strength, couldn't throw out his sense as far as hers. In this crowd, so long as they remained incognito, their safety was in her hands.

Soon they reached the clearing that separated the inner ring of tents from the center circle. Here there were no patrols, just stationary guards protecting their lord. Asa didn't sense any way to sneak through undetected, so the two backtracked a few paces to reconsider.

They couldn't dodge patrols all night. No matter how good Asa was, eventually they would find themselves trapped. They needed to find a location where they could stop and try to use their sense to find Mari, a place where they wouldn't be discovered. Unfortunately, all the nearby tents were occupied, and a patrol wasn't far away.

Asa glanced around, uncertain. Without warning Koji, she silently cut a slit in one of the tents, sliding into the darkness.

Koji followed, his movement silent. They were in the tent of a unit commander, his soft snores filling the space. Asa whispered to Koji as softly as she could. She would search for Mari. He needed to make sure they were safe. He nodded, and she planted her hands against the earth, searching for the woman who held their hope in her hands.

Her sense extended, passing by those Asa knew couldn't be Mari. She explored the heart of the camp, sensing and discarding people one by one. Time had no meaning. But Mari was present, in a tent not far away. Asa tried to focus, but surrounded by people, Mari was at the limit of her range. Asa sensed activity around Mari, but the distance was too great to know exactly what was occurring.

Koji tapped on Asa's shoulder, bringing her immediately to the present. She opened her eyes and saw a light dancing outside the slit they had made in the commander's tent. She cursed. Some alert guard had discovered the cut and was investigating. Her sense came back to her as she focused.

Koji slid forward, slowly pulling out his knife. Asa glanced back at the commander, a shadow on a bed, still softly snoring. She also drew a knife, just to be prepared.

The slit opened, and the tent lit up, temporarily blinding Asa. The guard uttered a grunt of surprise when his torch lit Koji's face. Koji's arm snaked out and pulled the guard toward him, causing the torch to drop to the ground. The tent started to catch fire, and the commander woke up to Koji driving his knife into the guard's heart.

The commander didn't even have time to react. Asa spun on her knees and clamped her hand over his mouth, drawing a red line across his neck with her knife. She waited a few precious moments for his life to leave him, then focused on getting out of the fire.

Koji was already outside, two tents away, crouching in the shadows. The blaze would be both a benefit and a curse. It drew attention away from them but also alerted everyone that something was amiss in the camp.

Asa swore. They were going to have to move fast.

Chapter 24

In the darkness of the chest, Mari lost track of time. As soon as the lid had been sealed, she gave up fighting. No doubt Katashi had planned out the details of her abduction, and there would be little she could do to influence events at this stage. Far better to be as cooperative as possible and lure them into a false feeling of security.

They hadn't made cooperation easy. She had been locked in the chest for some time, her legs cramping and her body covered in sweat. Moving was impossible, and Katashi hadn't bothered to provide any ventilation. At times, she worried she would die from a lack of air.

Even though there wasn't a hint of light, Mari knew the chest had to be out in the sun. The walls were warm to the touch, pressed up against them as she was. Her body was contorted at an uncomfortable angle, and as time passed, the agony grew ever more painful.

Finally the chest was opened, and Mari breathed deeply through her nose. The light was blinding, even though she saw she was in a tent lit only by a handful of candles. She blinked away the tears that formed in her eyes.

Guards pulled her roughly out of the chest, sending needles of pain up and down her body. They tried to set her down on her feet but she collapsed, her muscles unwilling to respond to even the simplest of commands.

Mari hoped at least they would remove the gag and give her something to drink. Instead, one of the guards fitted an iron collar to her neck and chained her to the main support of the tent. Then they blew out the candles and left her in the dark.

Lacking any better options, Mari tried to get some rest. She didn't know what the future held, so she figured any sleep she could get would be beneficial. She soon found that being restrained and gagged was far from the easiest way to fall asleep, but eventually exhaustion took her.

She woke up to a man with a torch entering the tent. Groggily she opened her eyes, then came to full awareness when she saw it was Katashi. From the moment the flap of the tent was open, she saw that it was still evening or perhaps early morning. Regardless, she glared at him with all the anger she could muster, hoping perhaps her look would do what swords had not.

Katashi looked completely unfazed, just as he had during their sham peace negotiations. He still had the look of a manipulator who had thought of everything, a man who had predicted events and enjoyed the fruits of his planning.

Mari had enough sense not to jerk at her bonds. As much as the release might have been satisfying, it would do her no good. Katashi would never believe that she was demure, but if she could get him to presume she wasn't an immediate threat, she might have a chance. A knife was still hidden on her thigh.

He smiled as he knelt in front of her. "Lady Mari, I'm sorry that our meeting has to be under such circumstances. I don't know if you know this, but I've admired you from afar for many cycles."

His words confused Mari. He admired her? They hadn't seen each other since they were both young. That made little sense.

He clarified. "Of all the lords and ladies in the Kingdom, I've always felt that you and I were much the same. You, of course, had the misfortune of being born a lady in a land that gives women no power.

I was born the younger brother of a man who had all the makings of a leader with great longevity."

Mari didn't know where Katashi was leading with this, but she paid attention, trying to see if there was some way she could turn his words to her favor.

"Like me, you discovered a truth that few people understand. Real power doesn't come just from having command of armies. Power comes from information. With the right information, you can bend a person to your will, make them dance to your song, wouldn't you agree?"

Mari agreed that information was important, but she had always thought it was so one could make the best decisions. Manipulating people was a dishonorable, low use of the gift.

"I see that perhaps you don't agree. But let me prove it to you. By the time we are done, I will have convinced you to marry me, of your own free will."

Mari thought that nothing Katashi could have said would have surprised her, but she was clearly wrong. A proposal, if that's what this was, was the last thing she would have expected. It couldn't be real, couldn't be true.

Katashi smirked. "This will be entertaining. First, I'm sorry that I had to kill your brother. He seemed a decent lord, but he was interfering with my plan, and I couldn't allow that.

"I'm going to tell you a number of my beliefs, and this one is the first. I believe, with my whole heart, the Kingdom is better off without the blades. Now you may think this is because my older brother was killed by them, and perhaps that influences my view a little but not by much. There was no love lost between Shin and me, and I've felt this way for some time.

"The fact is, the blades make us weaker. We've relied on them for too long to balance the conflict among the great houses. But they're just as fallible as we are, and we've seen more and more of that in the past few cycles. They are strong, but relying on them makes us weak."

Throughout his little speech Katashi's eyes were always on Mari, and she had the feeling he could read and understand even the slightest twitch of her eye.

"I see that you agree or at least that you've entertained the same thought. That doesn't surprise me. You've always been one of the most intelligent people I've known.

"So the blades must be dealt with. Here we disagree. I know you were eager to see them reintegrate into society, but that was the weakness of kindness on your part. It may work for a while, but people so strong can't coexist with those much weaker. The bear doesn't befriend the deer, and the tiger doesn't keep company with mice. The only solution is to eliminate them and drive them out of our land.

"Now you can see why I had to kill your brother. I almost had him where I wanted him. Through General Kyo, he was ready to destroy them all. But then you happened by, changing his mind. You were always the wild card, Lady Mari."

The only thought running through Mari's mind was that if she hadn't convinced Hiromi to try to save the blades, he might still be alive. Had she caused his death, however inadvertently? The idea made her want to vomit into her gag.

"I will get to the point. Although I do admire you, I am driven by rationality, and I do not care if you live or die. However, my life would be much easier if you remained alive and decided to marry me. Then our houses could officially be joined, and this war would be as good as over. If you wished, you could continue to rule over your house lands as my queen.

"I know you will be trying to think of alternatives. You are a woman driven by honor, much like your older brother. You care less about what you want and more about what you think is *right*." He emphasized the final word like it was some sort of curse.

"I'll spare you the work. There are no alternatives. Kyo is in charge of your army now, and if you refuse my offer, he shall claim the lordship of your house, backed by me. No one will oppose him. The blades, for all their strength, are finished. A chain of events has begun that cannot be stopped, not even by me. Either you will die here, with no one being the wiser, or you can rule as my queen and do what good you will for your people. I care not."

Mari hated herself, but she believed him.

Katashi stood up. "Such decisions are not to be made lightly. I know you will want time to think about your future and the fate of your citizenry. Our assault on Starfall begins today. I will come to you when I am able, perhaps in a day or two once the blades are broken. At that time, I will expect an answer. Until then, I will make sure you are fed and given water. But I must be clear: if you do anything that makes the guards suspicious, their orders aren't to doubt or ask questions. They will kill you immediately. If you say even a single word, they will kill you immediately. Do you understand?"

She did.

"Good. Oh, and one last thing," Katashi said. Mari's heart sank. She didn't believe for a moment this was anything but his final blow. "My network of shadows is better than yours. I know who killed your brother. The same nightblade who killed my own, something else we have in common. He is a young nightblade, very strong. His name is Koji."

———

For once, Mari was grateful that she was bound. Her restraints forced her to remain in one place. If not for them, she would have paced and kicked and stabbed at whatever she could.

Katashi had left without another word, leaving Mari to grapple with the information he had given her. She had no doubt he knew that she knew who Koji was.

Tears streamed down her face, and she writhed on the ground. She couldn't remember the last time she had lost control of herself, but rage and sorrow tore through her one after the other, each sensation filling the gap the last one left. She had trusted him! How could he have dared to serve her after what he had done?

If what Katashi said was true, Koji had set them on this path to war. Koji, who had killed her brother and left his corpse to freeze in the cold autumn air.

For some time she doubted the revelation. It was yet another trick by Katashi, an attempt to separate her from one of her strongest supporters. That was the real explanation.

But her heart knew the truth. It explained Koji's behavior the last time they had been together. That was why he had wanted to distance himself from her. That was why he didn't want to lead. If anyone found out Mari was the leader of the man who had slain the king, there would have been no hope for her or her movement.

She hated the truth. She raged against it and tried to forget. Hadn't he served her faithfully and done all her commands?

Or had he been a shadow? Katashi seemed to know everything.

Her mind raced in circles but kept returning to the same place. If she ever saw Koji again, she would kill him herself. She had never experienced a deeper cut of betrayal. He wouldn't just die; he would suffer for what he had done.

The sun rose, and as time passed, the sharp edge of her emotions faded. The pain was still there, a gaping hole she wasn't sure any revenge could fill.

Guards came in with breakfast and a basin. They were careful, as though she was a dangerous criminal who could somehow kill three trained and armed guards. She still had the long knife strapped to her thigh, but now wasn't the time to use it. Mari remembered the threats Katashi had made and was careful not to agitate the guards. She had a new purpose to live for now. They removed the gag, and Mari almost said thank you but stopped herself. She bowed slowly instead.

The guards didn't unbind her, instead feeding her themselves. Awkward and humiliated, Mari's anger grew even stronger than before. When the guards left, they didn't gag her again, but their looks were guarantee enough that she wouldn't make a sound.

Then there was Katashi. The very thought of him made her want to scream in frustration. His cool confidence infuriated her. But everything he'd said was rational and well articulated. She despised the idea of slaughtering the blades, but his vision seemed clear. He had a plan, and all she had ever been able to do was muddle forward like a fool.

She hated him, but his ideas wormed their way inside her mind, planting themselves and growing roots. He made her choices clear, and wasn't being alive better than being dead? So long as she was alive, she could make a change for her people.

Then the tears came again. She didn't want to think this way. Katashi brilliantly manipulated her with the promise of power, but she had no reason to trust his word. He betrayed everyone he came across, from her brother to General Kyo. Mari had no doubt that if she accepted the lord's offer, Kyo would be dead within a moon.

She thought back to the sham peace negotiations. If Katashi had simply killed her brother as soon as he had a chance, she might have felt differently. But he had dragged the meeting out, not even trying to convince Hiromi of his vision of a Kingdom without blades. Those weren't the actions of a rational man. Those were the actions of one who delighted in making others dance to his plans, just as Mari was now. They had been under a banner of peace.

The thought of Hiromi's death steeled her resolve. She wouldn't accept Katashi's offer. She would free herself and bring justice to the Kingdom, to all who had suffered.

All she needed to do was escape. The concept seemed as impossible now as it had before.

Mari decided to wait until an opportunity presented itself. Katashi had said he wouldn't return for a day or two, so she had time. Until then, she would act as her enemies expected, letting them think she was beaten.

She bowed to the three guards when they came in for the evening meal, and she didn't complain when they left her without bedding for the second night. Her sleep was poor, but every time she woke, she listened and waited for an opportunity.

The second full day of her captivity came and went, and her opportunity came that evening. She heard the guards speaking to one another. There were always three outside her tent, but one had been given orders to report to their commander. Only two would be guarding her for the evening. She decided it was as good a chance as she was ever going to have.

Her movements were slow and controlled. She didn't dare make any sound that would alert the soldiers outside, and she tried to work in such a way that if one of them peeked in, they wouldn't become suspicious.

Her first challenge was to get to the knife strapped to her thigh. As slowly as she could, she worked her hands down to her steel, bending and contorting until she could reach. Despite the agony of the position, Mari didn't let out so much as a sound. She worked the knife free, grateful that it slid out of its sheath without so much as a whisper.

Once she was sure she had the knife well in hand, she started working on cutting through the ropes that held her. She started with her wrists. As soon as they were free, she hoped everything else would come easily. The angles were all wrong, and she struggled to get enough leverage for the blade to cut through the rope.

Despite the fear of being discovered, she continued to work slowly. Doing so required every bit of discipline that she had. She kept glancing toward the tent opening, worried that a guard would choose just that moment to check on her.

She could feel the ropes around her wrists loosening, and with a soft snap, they pulled apart. Mari held her breath, terrified that the sound had been heard.

Once she was certain she was undetected, she moved very slowly. The chain attached to her collar tended to clink with motion, so she did everything she could to keep a steady amount of pressure on it.

With her wrists free, Mari could slice the rope around her ankles in a moment. Now her only problem was the collar around her neck. She wasn't sure how the collar was closed, and her only hope had been that it had been shut with some method she could undo now that her hands were free.

Working with the collar was the most delicate part of her escape thus far. Iron was noisier than rope, and keeping the collar and chain silent was enough to keep her occupied. Instead of trying to twist the collar around her neck, she held the collar steady while she turned, keeping the chain links from clinking.

She couldn't see what was below her neck, so she explored the clasp with her fingers. She silently cursed. There was no way of getting the collar off without a blacksmith's tools. Despair overwhelmed her, and for a few moments, she considered ending her own life.

But Mari refused to embrace such thoughts. She studied the chain, looking for weak links. The chance of finding one was slim, but it was better than nothing.

As she followed the chain, her eyes alighted on the other end of the link, where she had been attached to the central pole of the tent. Whoever had done that work hadn't been very thorough. The chain had just been wrapped around the pole three times and then a pin had been driven through three links to hold it in place. Restrained, there was no way she could have reached high enough to do anything, but now it would be a simple matter to remove the pin.

Mari did so, exercising care so as not to make any noise. She gently unwrapped the chain from the pole as though she was undressing a battle wound. Now she was free. But she assumed she was in the middle of the enemy camp, and carrying a significant length of chain with her would make her seem rather suspicious.

One step at a time. She had made progress. Before making her next move, Mari looked around the tent. As she expected, there weren't any convenient weapons simply lying around for her. All she had was her knife. It would have to be enough.

Mari wrapped the chain around her torso, which at least prevented it from making any noise. Satisfied she was as ready as she was ever going to be, Mari peeked out of the tent.

The two guards were there, backs to her, looking out on the camp beyond. As Mari had guessed, she was near the center.

Suddenly, not far away, in the tents that surrounded the heart of the camp, a fire burst to life. Everyone's attention was immediately grabbed, and Mari knew she'd never have a better chance than this.

She took just a few moments to calm her breath. Staying focused was going to be essential if she was going to survive.

Then she took her first life.

Her only thought as she emerged from the tent and slid her knife in between the ribs of the guard, straight to his heart, was that taking a life should never be so easy. Her hands moved almost of their own volition, pulling the knife out of the soldier and stabbing the second guard just as he turned.

Her second stab wasn't as precise as her first, but it was good enough to get the job done. She held on to the blade tightly, terrified of letting her only weapon slip from her grasp. As the second man turned, the knife sliced through organ after organ. The guard's death wasn't clean, but it would serve. Mari pulled the bloody knife from the sentry as he fell, standing frozen in shock as she looked upon her handiwork.

She looked up, trying to will her legs to move. Just then, two shadows in House Amari uniforms detached themselves from the tents across the way. Mari steeled herself. She hadn't even made it more than a few paces out of the tent where she'd been held captive.

Then one of the shadows threw off her hood and came into the light, and Mari realized she was looking at Asa and Koji, two of the last people she expected to see. She gripped the knife tighter, desperately wanting Koji to get closer so she could stab him as well.

The nightblades stopped in unison, and Mari cursed herself. Of course, they would be able to sense her intent. As strong as it was, she might as well have lit a warning beacon. Confusion was drawn across their faces. Asa took a step forward, moving slowly.

"Mari, we're here to rescue you." Asa looked around, as if making sure no one was nearby. "We can leave in the confusion, but we need to leave now."

Anger and reason conflicted in Mari's heart. She wanted to kill Koji, but she needed to survive. Her work was yet unfinished.

Slowly, she lowered the knife, sheathing it bloody against her thigh. The two nightblades still looked concerned, but together they turned around and started making their way out of the camp.

Chapter 25

Koji suffered two surprises in only a few moments. The first was that Mari had started her own escape, killing two guards in the process. Somehow this didn't sit well with Koji. In his eyes, Mari shouldn't have to kill. The act defiled her.

The second surprise was that she wanted to kill him. When he had sensed her intent, he almost doubted his gift. Reason quickly asserted itself, though. There was only one reason why her attitude toward him would have changed so quickly. She knew.

The knowledge rocked him, almost physically. The discovery of his actions had always been a possibility, but with every day that passed, he started to think the secret might never come to light.

Asa got them moving, Koji still trying to come to terms with what had just happened. He followed Asa as she acquired a uniform for Mari and stumbled behind them as Asa used her skills to get the trio out and away from the camp. Once they were safe, Mari turned on both of them, her face contorted by a barely contained anger.

What she said, though, caught Koji by surprise. "We need to kill Kyo. How many are with you?"

Asa gave Koji the first chance to respond, but when he didn't, she did. "Not enough, Mari. A few more than twenty is all."

"How many nightblades?"

"Twenty-one."

Koji knew it wasn't enough, not to take on an army. Mari didn't seem to care. "They will have to do. Are they still loyal? Will they follow on an impossible task?"

Koji answered, the first time he had spoken since they had met Mari in the camp. "To the end, my lady."

Mari fixed him with a furious stare, her eyes piercing into him, stripping away the layers of his personality until she reached the core of his being. Perhaps he imagined it, but he thought her eyes softened for a moment.

"Very well. Let's get to them and prepare. We'll ride at first light."

They made their way up to the camp where the blades were hidden away, watching the massacre below. Asa gathered all the gifted together, and Koji walked off and stood away, letting his thoughts run wild.

He sensed Asa behind him, supportive but not questioning. If he had something to say, he would say it. He didn't turn to look at her. "She knows."

There was nothing more for him to say. Asa had been there. Better than anyone else, she understood. "What will you do?"

That was the question. Mari had become more than just his commander over the past winter. She was hope. If she desired his death, he didn't see any more reason to live.

"Fight for her. Die for her, if I can."

He sensed Asa's posture shift. Though he couldn't see her, he knew how saddened she was by the answer.

"Then there's really nothing more, is there?"

Koji stared off into the distance. Asa, as usual, was right. His path was clear. Only one worry nagged at him.

"Do you think she'll understand?"

"Maybe. I don't know. She'll know your actions, though. You can't do more than that."

Koji took a deep, shuddering breath. There was nothing else. Reassured in his purpose, he followed Asa to the gathering of blades.

The two were the last to arrive, and Mari didn't waste any time in outlining her plan.

Most of it didn't surprise Koji, but a murmur of disapproval made the rounds when Mari told them all that she wanted to use wooden swords again.

Even her commander, who never questioned Mari, was surprised. "Mari, our mission is already dangerous enough. Not using real swords dooms any attempt we may make."

"I understand your concern, and I know how this sounds," she said. "But this is the heart of our work. This is why you followed me in the first place. I mean to make a new world. The victory will not be bloodless, but most of the troops down there are simply people trying to do their best. Some are professional soldiers; others are farmers and boys taken from their homes to fight for their lord. I only ask that you use wooden swords until we breach the perimeter of the honor guard. Then you may draw your steel and as much blood as you will. Those are the men who betrayed the trust of my family, and they will be repaid in kind."

Koji, as always, was impressed. Looking around the circle, he saw that her words had convinced a group of blades to become almost as nonviolent as you could be while still wielding a weapon. Seeing her inspiring the group once again reinforced his decision. He would do everything in his power to see her cause succeed.

After the gathering broke, Mari deliberately avoided Koji. He understood and didn't question. Asa had been right. He would allow his actions to speak for him.

———

When the sun rose the next morning, it rose on Mari, surrounded by her puny force, standing between the forces of House Kita and Starfall. They had crept into position before dawn. Mari understood the power of theater and planned to use it to full effect. On a long pole the banner of House Kita snapped in the early morning breeze, the sword and hammer, the symbols of her house, plain for everyone to see.

All except Mari were on foot, dressed in their traditional black and white robes. Koji felt calm and relaxed, excited to be wearing the clothes that marked him as a nightblade. In front of them was an army, thousands strong.

Mari's plan didn't have a bit of strategic reason. If Koji had planned the morning's assault, he would have dressed them all in the uniforms of House Kita, snuck into the ranks in pairs, and sown confusion throughout the army.

That wasn't Mari's aim. She wanted the army as her own, and whether or not she believed she could acquire command, she acted as though the result was already fated.

Koji eyed the ranks upon ranks of soldiers in front of them. Mari was counting on confusion, surprise, and her status with her people, all of which felt very thin to Koji, but he was willing to follow, to see where the day led.

He wasn't the only one. Despite the foolishness of the plan, every-one in Koji's group remained, each standing tall against a force that outnumbered them hundreds to one. Next to him, Asa was the other point of the spear. In her belt, in addition to her two short swords, she carried two sticks about half as thick as her wrist. She had wanted dual weapons for the upcoming fight, but no one had two wooden swords short enough. She had made do with the sticks.

Asa and Koji glanced at each other, but there wasn't much left to say. With a soft word from Mari, the entire group started walking toward the army. Their pace was slow and measured. Each of them left their weapons, even their wooden ones, in their belts.

As the blades neared, the front ranks of the army raised their spears, blocking their way. It was a problem but not nearly as much as if the archers had fired on them. A few stray arrows came forth, but most landed a safe distance away. The blades sidestepped the handful that were close. After the first few volleys, the attacks ceased, and Mari's group advanced unmolested.

Koji's eyes darted back and forth as he wondered how long their good fortune would hold. He could see the signal flags flying all across the formation, and he had little doubt commanders were being told to attack. Yet no one did, and Mari and her warriors continued closing the gap.

Mari softly called them to a stop about ten paces away from the tips of the spears. Koji struggled to draw in breath. The tension was thick, but still no one attacked. The nightblade almost wished someone would, just to break the tableau and give him a specific focus.

Mari let the front line take a good look at her face. Koji saw the points of the spears waver as their owners recognized the lady of the house they served. The last survivor of the three siblings spoke softly, and the nightblades resumed their approach, hands well away from their real and wooden swords, posing as little threat as possible.

Koji had thought the tension couldn't get any thicker, but now it was physical, like a solid wall he was trying to push through. The tips of the spears were ten paces away, five. He took another few steps, waiting at any moment for Mari to tell him to stop, but the order never came.

Unsure how to proceed, Koji decided to slide through the small gaps in the defense, shuffling forward awkwardly. He could see the fear and confusion written all over the faces of the spearmen. Sweat beaded down their foreheads, and their eyes darted back and forth as they waited for some order or command that would tell them what to do.

Koji and Asa passed the first rank, but they didn't attack. Koji could sense some of the spearmen turning, waiting for steel to cut into them from behind, but the attack never came. More nightblades, and eventually Mari, worked their way through the lowering spears, and the moment of tension began to fade.

Everything felt like a dream to Koji, and he dug his big toe into the ground until it hurt, just to make sure he wasn't still sleeping. Had they tried to charge, the wall of spears would have been the death of them.

As they walked, Koji started to hear the murmuring of the troops. "That's Lady Mari."

"Who's the woman that Kyo is with? I thought that was Lady Mari."

"Why is Lady Mari with nightblades?"

Most of the murmurs were confused. A few were angry. But no one attacked.

Mari and the blades continued working their way through the army, toward the center where Kyo and his honor guard sat. They passed through the ranks of spears and moved in among the infantry. Here there were paths to follow, separations drawn by the different units.

Koji was surprised by the variety of people who made up the army. There were those who were well armored and had weapons that shone in the early morning sun. Others carried farming implements and wore what could only charitably be called armor.

Now and then a shout would rise up, asking Mari what was happening. Her answer was short and always the same. "We've been betrayed."

They kept walking. Once a guard stepped in their way, begging for them to stop. Koji gently pushed him away, and they continued on.

Mari's plan worked better than they had any right to expect, though Koji never let down his guard. It would take only one person to ignite the pile of dry firewood they were standing on.

If they had one advantage in Mari's ridiculous plan, it was that they wore their robes. Everyone in the army knew they were facing nightblades. Koji guessed that knowledge saved their lives dozens of times on their approach. Fighting as one group against another provided an illusion of safety. But face-to-face, waiting for a single soldier to break ranks, many knew that to make the first cut against a nightblade was a death sentence.

A farmer broke ranks first. He charged at Koji with a scythe, wildly pushing away any soldier who stood in his way.

Koji didn't need his sense to see the attack coming and calmly drew his wooden sword. He ducked lightly under the swing of the scythe and snapped his sword against the side of the man's neck. The farmer collapsed in a heap. It was a single, isolated moment, but it broke the dam.

One by one they came, each soldier making an individual decision to attack. Many retreated to safer places in the lines, but some came. All the blades drew their weapons, and the battle began.

Despite the chaos around them, Koji felt peaceful, and the world became more vivid as everything became sharper and clearer. He knew where attacks were going to be far before they reached him. He flowed like water, moving forward, never resisting, always finding ways around his opponents.

If he died, he knew that it was in service to Mari and her vision. Koji believed, and he was willing to sacrifice everything for her. His gift responded to this clarity of purpose.

The feeling of power and strength was intoxicating. He was used to being strong and fast, but this was something else entirely. Not only was he able to keep track of his area but those of the other blades as well. If a blade seemed about to break under the assault, Koji would shift his position, reinforcing his companion.

At times his attention would wander over to Asa, and she seemed like an entirely different woman. Her two sticks danced intricate patterns around her opponents, breaking across them like the bow of a ship in water.

Despite the attack, the blades kept moving forward. Koji sensed the life go out of one of the gifted behind him. She had momentarily forgotten she was fighting with a wooden sword and tried to block a cut. The opponent's steel had gone clean through her sword and her torso.

They kept pushing. Every life was worth sacrificing if they made it to their goal, and they were close. Whenever Koji cleared himself even a bit of space, he looked to see how far away the ranks of Kyo's honor guard were.

Fifty paces.

Twenty.

Ten.

"Draw steel!" Mari shouted.

Koji sensed the next wave of the attack. He saw the brighter colors of the honor guard now within striking range. He heard the command from Kyo to kill Lady Mari.

The nightblade thrust his wooden sword deep into the stomach of a soldier who had charged him with madness in his eyes. That light went out completely as the soldier crumpled, Koji allowing him to take the sword with him.

Koji's real sword flashed out of its sheath, his hands gripping the hilt like a long-lost friend. Two quick cuts took the lives of two honor guards, and Koji stepped into the heart of the chaos.

He didn't try to understand what he was able to do. All that mattered was Mari. He kept moving and cutting, moving and cutting. Kyo's honor guard, supposedly the best nongifted swordsmen in his house lands, fell one after the other.

But there were a lot of them, and they worked well together. Koji made progress, but even he felt the momentum start to shift. The change was subtle, but what had once been an easy advance became a slog. One by one, the nightblades began to fall.

They were starting to tire. Most were in excellent condition, but combat was exhausting, and the toll would need to be paid. When it came to sharp steel, even a slight hesitation, a slight decrease in speed, could make the difference between life and death.

Koji pushed forward with renewed vigor, allowing himself to get cut off from his fellow blades. If he could attract enough attention, perhaps they'd be able to break the counterattack and breathe for a few moments.

His sense was all that kept him alive. Steel sang all around him, the air filled with swords hungry for his blood. Somehow he avoided the fatal cuts. But he wasn't unharmed.

His skin had been opened in a dozen places, cuts he had chosen to take in lieu of more dangerous strikes. His right leg had a deep gash, and although it held up under his weight, he couldn't leap the way he'd like. A hundred small cuts could be just as fatal as one deep one, and he was gradually succumbing to the sheer quantity of attacks.

Then Asa was there, just as bloody as him, her two short swords moving with incredible speed all the same. The entire battle around them shifted. They still had a chance.

Cuts rained down on them from every direction, but Asa's swords covered Koji's back. He focused on killing the honor guard, moving through them one by one.

He knew they weren't going to make it. Their progress through the crowd had almost been completely halted. Even though they had killed more than half the honor guard, those who were left would eventually triumph. But Koji didn't have to make their victory easy.

He was so focused on the battle ahead that he didn't sense the group of nightblades come up behind him and Asa. When the point of the spear had ground to a halt, it allowed the rest of the group to catch them. There weren't many left. Eight blades surrounded Mari, each bleeding from at least one wound.

Mari's voice somehow rose above the chaos of the battle. "Get me to Kyo! Nothing else matters!"

The reinforcements gave Koji the slimmest moment to look up and see where Kyo was. He was close, only about ten more paces. Those paces were filled with guards, but Koji would make that happen if it was the last thing he did.

Something shifted for him again, his world becoming almost unbearable in its intensity. Mari and her cause were everything, and the cause was close to completion. He turned to the group, taking a step back as a sword passed in front of him. "Mari! Get right behind me. The rest, to the sides!"

Mari obeyed, and the other nightblades fell into position around her.

Koji stepped into a new world.

His sword had always been like a lover to him. He knew exactly how it felt in his hands, how it sang when he cut just right. Every detail of the sword was etched in his memory. But it had never moved like it did that morning.

Koji felt like he was an observer in his own body, pulled and twisted by forces unseen. He knew where every cut was going to be, and he knew exactly where he needed to be at every moment.

When the first sword pierced his stomach, he didn't mind. By taking the strike, he opened up the last few paces between him and Kyo. Mari was right behind him, just barely protected by the remaining nightblades. Asa, in particular, kept her from harm from the sea of steel threatening to take her life.

Then Kyo was right in front of him, striking at him with his own weapon. Koji met steel with steel, swinging his own sword with all his might. The force of the impact drove the sword from Kyo's hands, and at that very same moment, all Koji's energy gave out. He collapsed before he could make the killing cut.

His back on the ground, looking up at the sky and the sword sticking out of his abdomen, Koji thought he'd done well. He saw Mari step over him, admired how fearless her face was at the end of it all. Mari's knife flashed out and sliced open Kyo's neck. It wasn't a clean cut, but it was effective, really all that mattered.

Koji closed his eyes and let shadow swallow him whole.

Chapter 26

Everything in Asa's life collapsed into a series of instants, memories inscribed upon her life forever. Koji knocking the sword from Kyo's hands, then collapsing into a heap, his eyes open but blank, a sword pointing straight up from his stomach. Mari's attack, taking the life from Kyo in one sweep of the arm. The general's flag falling to the ground, being replaced by Mari's.

Then Asa blinked, and life returned to normal. Confusion ran rampant, and while many of the honor guard had stopped fighting the moment their general was killed, there were a few who didn't seem to know or understand what had happened.

Asa's blades glimmered as they danced, taking life as they did. With her speed and two blades, no single opponent had a chance.

But she was beyond exhausted, shadow hovering at the edges of her vision. She had never fought this hard for this long before. If the attacks continued, she would fall, just as Koji had.

Mari's voice, strong and clear, overcame the fighting nearby. "Halt!"

One final swordsman came in, swinging at Asa. She deflected his cut with her left sword and reached out with her right, letting him impale himself on her steel.

He was the last fatality of the battle.

Asa looked around, nervous. No one was fighting, but everyone was on edge. The wrong move by one person would send everything spiraling out of control once more. Mari seemed to understand this, her voice ringing.

"We have been betrayed! You see me here, alive, the lady of House Kita. Do any still doubt?"

A soft murmur washed over the crowd. Mari had been well known, and her face was recognized. Asa watched as tension drained out of the bodies of many of the combatants. She looked around. Only three nightblades remained on their feet, and she was in the best condition of any of them. More than anything, she wanted to rush to Koji's side and see if he still lived, but she feared any sudden movement would doom them all. Mari's control was still too tenuous.

"Kyo watched as my noble brother Hiromi was murdered! He watched as I was taken hostage to be forced into a marriage with House Amari."

The feeling of the gathering changed again. Asa could almost sense the change in attitude. Confusion was fading, replaced by anger. The men here were loyal to their house, and any betrayal of the nobility was a betrayal to them all.

"Friends, I know many of us fear the blades and their power. But like us, they are people and citizens of our land. Two of them came and saved me from House Amari."

The mood shifted slightly, the people nearby uncertain how to take Mari's conciliatory tone.

"I do not know the answer to the blades, but I do know this: So long as I have any breath, I will not permit harm to come to any who call this land home. That includes the blades who live at Starfall."

The statement gained a mixed reaction. Asa tensed again, not willing to fight but aware she might not have a choice.

Mari showed no hesitation, no doubt. She stood there, tall and defiant, a woman seizing command of an army for the first time in the Kingdom's history. Asa was sure she would fail. The power and pull of history was too strong.

She was saved by a cry in the distance. "Look!"

Asa turned with everyone else, looking in the direction the shout had come from. Off in the distance, Katashi's armies were advancing, not on Starfall but on Mari's army. Asa frowned, unsure of why he would take such a bold risk.

Then she understood. He was no fool. He'd seen Mari's advance into her army. There was no way he would have missed her banner when it was raised. He believed that Mari had taken command. He would expect her to ally with Starfall, creating a force he couldn't fight. His only option was to divide and destroy before they could join.

The decision was exactly what Mari needed. The army, which had wavered back and forth, immediately came together under the threat of attack. Some certainly believed that Mari was their rightful commander, but Asa suspected many simply saw someone willing to take the lead. Often that was all it took.

Asa wondered if Mari had foreseen this turn of events. It seemed that way when the lady turned to her. "Asa, I have one last mission for you. You know Hajimi, correct?"

Asa nodded.

"I need you to go to Starfall and find him. Tell him we offer the blades safe shelter, at least for now, if they join us in our battle against Katashi. Tell them to wear their robes, and they will not be harmed by my forces. Can you do that?"

Asa looked across the field that was soon to become a killing ground. She glanced at Koji. Her heart demanded she stay by his side. "Will you find a dayblade for him?"

Mari looked down. "Let the Great Cycle take him."

Asa wouldn't accept that, and she stepped into Mari's face. "He gave everything he had to give you a chance to save your people."

Mari wasn't one to be easily intimidated. Not even by a nightblade. "He killed my brother."

"One act doesn't define a person. He's done nothing but sacrifice for you. He believes in you, and you're possibly the first person he's ever believed in. Don't prove his old self right."

With that, Asa stormed off to find a horse. She feared if she stayed any longer, she would draw her steel on Mari, and she couldn't live with that.

———

Asa's objective was simple, but fulfilling it would be anything but. Katashi's army was advancing, and from Asa's viewpoint, it looked as though a contingent of archers was continuing to do everything in their power to rain death down on the city.

Despite the chaos, Asa's thoughts kept returning to Koji. Her words to Mari echoed in her ears. "One act doesn't define a person."

It was the same argument Daisuke had made to her before she went to kill Kiyoshi.

Maybe she had been wrong. The idea had occurred to her hundreds of times since that fateful day, but never before had it settled over her heart the way it did today. She hoped Mari was strong enough to break the cycle of revenge and murder that ensnared her.

From her current position, Asa hoped she could approach one of the side gates to Starfall without attracting much attention. Once there, she was going to court consistent danger from the arrows above. There was no telling what she would find inside those walls.

After she found a horse, Asa rode as fast as the animal would gallop. She wasn't the best rider, and she felt like she was always on the edge of being tossed off the mount. If not for her feet firmly in the stirrups and her hands clutching the reins with all her strength, she almost certainly wouldn't have been able to keep her seat.

Unfortunately, Asa didn't move fast enough to entirely escape the attention of Katashi's army. He must have been looking for just such a messenger, because almost the moment she broke the ranks of Mari's army, several horsemen broke from Katashi's formation and rode to intercept her.

Asa pushed as hard as she could, but she soon knew she wasn't going to make it. Her enemies' horses were faster than her own and had a small advantage in distance. Nevertheless, she rode as fast as she could, hoping that perhaps a small party on the walls of Starfall would see what was happening and ride out to help her.

When the enemy cavalry got within bow range, arrows rose to greet her. She tried to judge the shafts as best she could, and she successfully evaded the first flight. The second flight landed all around her, one even tearing a small gash along her back. By the time the third flight came in, the distance was too close. Two arrows dug into her horse, sending the animal crashing to the ground.

Fortunately, Asa lost her seat before the collision with the ground and was thrown forward, tumbling end over end. She tried to push herself up, but her body refused to respond for a moment. There wasn't much more she could give. An arrow embedding itself in the grass next to her provided the motivation she needed.

With a heave, she shoved herself to her feet, looking around. Only four men were arrayed against her, but they were smart. None of them attempted to charge her, letting their horses trot around her in a circle, keeping their distance.

Asa didn't know what to do. She couldn't outrun a horse, and the men were wary and cautious. Her sense would warn her when someone was about to fire an arrow, but they all had full quivers and only needed her to make one mistake.

Lacking better options, Asa started running toward Starfall. The walls were still hundreds of paces away, but that was the only direction she could go. She had a slim hope one of the riders would let her get close to him, but the circle moved with her. They were patient.

Asa dodged one arrow and then another. She could sense as they drew back their bows, and if she shifted just as they released, their aim wouldn't be true. The game couldn't last for long, but it was the only one she could play.

She had made it about fifty paces when she saw the gates to Starfall open. She breathed a sigh of relief. Now at least there was a chance for her. Ten, then twenty nightblades charged out on horses, their yells carrying over the plains.

Another ten paces, and one of the arrows finally got her, lodging itself in her calf. Asa screamed in agony and fell, fire burning up her leg. The nightblades were off in the distance, still too far away to help. Another arrow, hastily loosed, drove into the same leg higher up. Asa shrieked again, the agony nearly unbearable.

She had to move. She needed to stay alive. With her good leg, she kicked the ground while she clawed with her arms, moving her body forward as another two arrows embedded themselves in the ground where she had just been, one grazing her good leg.

Crawling wouldn't be fast enough. She felt one of the riders fall to an arrow launched by a nightblade. She needed only a few more moments.

The riders made their decision. Two of them broke off and started galloping toward their army. The third remained, riding closer to Asa, sacrificing his own life for the killing shot. He drew back the bowstring, and Asa sensed him about to release.

She rolled, wailing as the shafts of the arrows dug into the grass beneath her, tearing deeply at skin and muscle. She could hear the twang of the bowstring as it was released, and an arrow dove deep into her chest, just missing her heart and puncturing a lung. She felt her own lifeblood gurgling as she tried to breathe.

Several arrows struck the rider at once, killing him and knocking him off his horse.

Asa was beyond the point of caring. The blackness that had lurked at the edge of her vision now closed in, and as a group of nightblades clustered around her, she couldn't tell where their robes began and where her vision ended.

———

Asa remembered only bits and pieces of the final leg of her journey to Starfall. The nightblades hadn't come prepared to carry the wounded, so they had picked her up and carried her, a process that was perhaps the most painful she'd ever lived through. Fire was replaced by stabbing needles, and every breath was a physical effort she didn't want to make.

When the shadow of the wall finally loomed over her, Asa wondered if she was going to die. It would have been pleasant to die in the shade. The day was nice and warm, and sleeping, even forever, had its appeal.

Then a kindly old face was close to hers. Asa couldn't hear what he was saying, but his eyes were calming. They were the sort of eyes that had seen many cycles of life and had obtained a wisdom few ever did.

Asa thought the man looked familiar, but her mind was wandering and she was having trouble focusing on any one thought.

Then it came to her.

He had been a librarian at the archives in Starfall. He had remained late one night just for her.

A sudden and overwhelming sadness came over her. So much of Starfall was on fire, and many of the papers in the library were irreplaceable. They had the history of the blades in them, and now they were gone, their past erased in an instant.

Then she felt a fresh agony, a surge of energy pouring through her body. Then three sharp, almost blinding pains as the arrows were removed from her calf and chest. She coughed up blood, and there were hands all over her. She saw another white robe and then another. Were three dayblades all trying to save her at the same time?

She must have lost consciousness for a while, but when she came to, she was propped up by a door, just inside a building. Outside she heard a soft thunking sound. She looked out at the road beyond the building, a flaming arrow quivering in the dirt. For a few moments she stared at the arrow, questioning why it was there. Then her memories returned, and she was seized by a momentary panic.

Strong hands held her calmly. "Easy now. You're as safe as you can be."

She hadn't even noticed the man next to her. She jumped slightly. The last person to surprise her that way had been Daisuke, but hiding from the sense was his special skill. Were there others like him?

As Asa's faculties returned, she realized she'd been so deeply unconscious she had lost touch with her gift. She took a deep breath and focused on reconnecting to the sense. Thankfully, within the space of a few heartbeats, her understanding of the space around her completely changed, the entire world lighting up with life and energy.

The man, the same dayblade from the library, offered her food, which she accepted. Being healed by dayblades was an exhausting experience, both for the dayblades and for the person being healed. As a young trainee, Asa had heard jokes about blades preferring to die rather than suffer through a healing, but she was grateful for every breath she took, even if her body felt as though it would collapse at any time.

She got right to the point in between bites of dried meat. "Where's Hajimi?"

"He's at the council hall. He's been trying to do what he can to keep us safe, but there's less and less that can be done."

"I need to go to him."

The dayblade's eyes roamed out of the doorway to the roads beyond. He looked like he was going to offer a warning but then thought better of it.

"You know the way?"

Asa nodded. Starfall wasn't that large as cities went. She remembered the way well enough.

The man stood up and went into the house, coming back with what appeared to be the lid of a pot. "We don't have much for shields around here, so we've been making do with what we can." He looked at the lid with a hint of remorse. "This is my last one. It's always been my favorite. It fits my pot well." With a last, somewhat longing glance, the man handed Asa the makeshift shield. She bowed deeply in thanks for everything he had done.

When she stepped out of the house, several things caught her attention. The first was that on the horizon, storm clouds were building. The second was that Starfall was a living, breathing nightmare.

For a few precious moments, she stood out in the open, mouth slightly agape at the scene before her, trying to understand how so much had changed since she was here last. To see the destruction Katashi had rained down on the city was beyond belief, beyond reason.

Buildings lay collapsed, burned to the ground all around. She couldn't sense many people, but those she could were hiding in the shadows of buildings, moving in quick sprints from hiding place to hiding place. Their caution was well warranted. Arrows were seemingly everywhere, and even a quick glance revealed blades who hadn't made it to the next shelter, their bodies slowly rotting in the heat of the day.

The sight reminded Asa to take shelter underneath the potlid. She did so just as another wave of arrows plummeted near her. None came close enough to be dangerous, but she tracked the angle of their flight so that she knew the best direction to hold her meager protection.

Off to the side, where the most recent volley had landed, a fire slowly grew across the ruins of what had once been a house.

Asa shook her head, focusing on what she had come here to do. She needed to get as many blades out of Starfall as soon as she could.

She walked quickly, unwilling to run and trip over an arrow, or worse, a body. Her eyes searched the sky, giving her a little warning for when she needed to find shelter. Her potlid quickly collected two arrows, and she silently thanked the kind librarian once again.

Every corner revealed a new horror. No escape from the sights was possible. In one street two young blades had died next to each other holding hands. In another, a half-burned corpse hadn't quite made it out of a house before flames had collapsed the building. Another nightblade had received a fatal arrow through her chest, still clutching a pail of water.

Even if she closed her eyes, the horror was still inescapable. The air was rank with the smell of burned and rotted flesh. Wails of agony mixed with those of grief. When she tried to shut out the smell and breathe through her mouth, the acrid taste of the smoke overwhelmed her. How could this have happened?

Asa couldn't help but wonder if for all their strength, the blades had been caught nearly unaware, confident no one would dare attack their sanctuary. The destruction seemed nearly absolute. Once in a while she would sense a group of blades, hiding someplace she couldn't see. These small groups gave her hope. They had been dealt a blow, but they weren't done for, not yet.

More than anything, Asa wanted to close her eyes. She had never romanticized war, but this was beyond the worst she imagined. This was a massacre. That anyone could come to a place to do this to another befuddled her. She was by no means a pacifist, but there was no honor in this.

When she came to the hall of the council, her hopes were almost dashed completely. The building was a shell of its former glory, one of its walls completely collapsed, the roof sagging in where it hadn't been burned completely through. The hall was a broken monument to a time that seemed to have already passed.

Before she turned around, she extended her sense, finding a few lives left inside. She approached and stepped inside, checking the quality of the roof before putting her lid down. The hall was filled with light and shadow, bright sunlight streaming through the holes in the ceiling. The shadows, by contrast, were dark and impenetrable.

Asa could sense him, though, the man who was in charge of the blades. Several advisers were clustered around him, but they looked more like a group of elderly citizens cowering from a storm than the leaders of the most powerful people in the world.

Asa strode toward them, grateful her mission was almost at an end.

"Hajimi."

The man she addressed looked many cycles older than the leader who had promoted her and sent her on her last mission just over a cycle ago. There was still strength in his eyes, but she could see that his spirit had been broken. He held no more hope.

Until he saw her, recognition sparking in his eyes. "Asa?"

There was no time for pleasantries. Every moment more arrows came flying into the city, threatening the lives of the remaining inhabitants.

"You need to abandon Starfall."

He laughed, a maniacal edge to the sound. "There is no place for us to run to, Asa. Our walls are surrounded by enemies, and everyone seems to have brought enough arrows for several wars. We haven't the strength to break through."

"You don't need to. Lady Mari has seized control of the army from House Kita. She guarantees you safe passage and the promise of negotiations so long as you assist her forces against Katashi."

Hajimi considered the meaning of her words, testing their authenticity. "So Lady Mari went and took over an army. A step up from the Lady in White."

Asa had worried she would have to negotiate or do something to convince Hajimi, but no such methods were needed.

"We must prepare the evacuation then," Hajimi said.

Just then another nightblade found her way into the hall. "Sir! House Amari has launched an attack against the walls. House Kita is also advancing, but they are farther back."

In a moment, Hajimi stood up straight and regained the fire in his spirit. "We need to buy time for the evacuation. Summon all able nightblades to the main gate. All others will retreat to House Kita's forces."

Asa couldn't imagine fighting again, but the choice wasn't hers to make.

———

The streets were strangely quiet, soft raindrops the only sound except for the occasional boom coming from the gates of the city. A handful of archers were on the wall, but most nightblades stayed below, hiding from the occasional arrows that still shot overhead. Katashi's archers were far better than the blades, so the decision had been made not to hold the walls. On the ground, the nightblades were deadlier, and their purpose wasn't to defeat the invaders but to hold them back. No point risking lives in a meaningless defense.

The near silence gave Asa a few moments to reflect. Despite the danger, she couldn't remember a time when she had felt more whole. Fighting to protect her fellow blades, and in turn fighting to protect Mari, calmed her in a way her quest for revenge never did. She never thought she would fight in service of another, but now that she was, she realized she had been wrong.

Was it Koji who had spoken about finding a purpose greater than yourself? She didn't remember, but the words rang true. When she had been tracking Osamu for all those cycles, she had claimed it was for her family. Now she knew that had been a lie. Her family was dead, part of the Great Cycle and whatever lay beyond the veil of everyone's final journey. Osamu had been for her, always had been.

But now she knew how insignificant she was in the way of the world. For all her strength, when her life ended, she would still be just one person among countless. By taking part in Mari's campaign, she had the chance to become something more, to change the lives of thousands. That, by itself, was worth the cost of her life.

The storm above intensified as the gates finally broke.

Their strategy, such as it was, was only to keep the invaders occupied and distracted. Hajimi was leading the evacuation, and their guiding principle was to get as many people out alive as they could, including the nightblades defending the main gate. They were to fight as long as they could before escaping.

There was one short breath of silence after the gates crashed to the ground, one moment of peace before the final storm overtook them all.

Then the streets filled with soldiers from House Amari, lines of spearmen leading the way. Asa had found a roof with a small shelter from arrows near the gate and hazarded a few peeks over the edge. The blades had assumed the soldiers would lead with a few ranks of spears, so no one stood in front of the advancing army. All of them hid in side alleys or on rooftops like Asa.

After the spears had passed, Asa sensed the first nightblades enter the fray. That was her cue. She drew her swords, thinking one last time about Koji and hoping he was still alive. He would have been a tremendous asset here.

Asa sprinted from her cover and leapt off the roof, crashing into at least four soldiers. The jump hadn't been high, thankfully, but they all still went down in a pile of limbs and steel. Fortunately Asa was on top of the pile, and she found her feet as the soldiers around her started to react.

If not for Daisuke's training, she never would have survived. But his obsession with developing one's gift and his insistence she learn how to fight with two swords saved her life. A hastily aimed cut came down at her head, but her right hand came up to deflect the strike as her left cut at the soldier's leg, sending him collapsing to the ground.

She kept her sense contained, focusing only on the life within a spear's reach, but thanks to her training, she was able to keep track of everything happening in that small space. She thrust out her hips as a soldier tried to stab her from the side, allowing the blade to pass behind her as she danced away.

Life became a continuous string of encounters, Asa's skill keeping her alive.

She deflected one stab to the side, forcing a soldier to drive his sword into his friend.

She slid under the slice of another soldier, her own sword cutting deep across his stomach as she passed.

A spear came at her from one of the front ranks, but Asa spun and cut through the wood. She kicked the falling spearpoint at her assailants, disappointed it didn't kill anyone but pleased it distracted two soldiers for a moment.

Despite her efforts, numbers were still a problem. There were hundreds of soldiers and only a few dozen nightblades. Her actions were drawing more and more attention, and if she wanted to live, she needed to retreat.

As the soldiers started to converge, Asa went low, staying close to the ground and cutting at legs. The strategy was a final gift from Daisuke, who reminded her that most troops trained only at higher heights. Fighting low to the ground was awkward for most swordsmen. Asa was already smaller than most soldiers, so the strategy was ideal.

She fought toward an alley, hoping it wouldn't fill up with soldiers before she got there.

Fortune was on her side, and she made it to the alley with only a few shallow cuts for her troubles. Once inside she sheathed her weapons, switching to a full sprint. She cursed as she sensed soldiers nearing the other end of the passage.

Her mind didn't panic, instead working its way through possibilities. Finding one, she bounced off the crumbling remains of one building onto the roof of another. She leapt across an alley, trying to lose any pursuers.

A few streets over, she heard a shout and turned toward it. A slender dayblade was there, surrounded by three men armed with spears. They were advancing steadily, but their backs were to her. She drew her swords and leapt off the roof, cutting down two of the spearmen as she passed them. Keeping her feet, she turned and cut at the remaining soldier, deflecting his long spear and getting inside his guard easily.

As the final soldier fell, the dayblade was still rooted in place, unused to combat. Asa turned and yelled, "Run!" Her shout succeeded in breaking his trance, and he turned and ran toward the gate.

Asa extended her sense, her stomach sinking as she realized how quickly Katashi's troops were proceeding through the city. Their defense might have slowed the army, but not for long. She was well behind enemy lines, and if she wanted to escape herself, she needed to get moving.

Nearby, she thought she sensed a glimmer of another person with the gift. Like a candle about to go out, the gift seemed to flicker. Moving silently, Asa went toward the blade.

After all that she had seen, she wasn't sure anything else could break her heart, but the scene in front of her did. A wizened man in white robes was dying, deep cuts through his torso and legs. From the amount of blood surrounding him, Asa was surprised he still lived. He was the blade she had sensed.

Next to him was a young girl who hadn't seen more than fourteen cycles. She was dressed in the black robes of a nightblade, but her gift was weak, so weak Asa almost didn't notice it. She approached, using her sense to ensure no one was nearby.

The dayblade smiled weakly. "Thank you for coming," he coughed. Blood spurted out of his mouth with every syllable.

Asa didn't know what to say but knelt in front of the man.

"It's too late for me," he said, "but this is my granddaughter, Junko, and I'd like you to get her out of here."

Once, Asa might not have accepted. When her purpose in life was to find and kill Osamu, her own survival was paramount. Today she barely hesitated. She bowed to the blade and stood up. Soldiers were coming. This section of the city had been entirely overrun.

Junko was unwilling to leave the dayblade. Asa gave them a few moments, but time was their enemy. She grabbed the girl's arm. "We don't have much time. If you honor your grandfather, say goodbye, and let's go." Her voice was firm, but she tried to keep the truth from sounding harsher than it was.

They weren't going to be fast enough. Two soldiers turned the corner, and Asa was on them without hesitation. If they escaped and brought more soldiers, the chance of the two nightblades escaping was zero. She slid in the mud, cutting low on both soldiers, bringing them to the ground.

When she stood up, the girl seemed to be in shock. Her grandfather was dead, and Asa was running out of patience.

Asa came up to her. "Your choice. Either leave with me or die here, but I need to go."

Junko came out of her stupor as Asa looked around for an escape route. Their best bet seemed the rooftops. There were too many soldiers to fight through on the ground.

Asa pushed the girl up onto a roof and then climbed up herself as the rain continued to fall. Using a combination of her sense and sight, Asa guided them toward the gate, hoping it would still be open by the time they got there.

Rooftop by rooftop, Asa got them closer, often crouching and waiting for a soldier to turn his back. Junko was weaker than Asa, so she had to find narrow gaps to jump whenever she could. Occasionally they had to get down from the roof, cross a road, then climb back up.

The going was slow, but eventually they reached what passed as the front lines, just a few dozen paces away from the final gate. Asa peered at the girl, who looked as though she wasn't willing to run through the horror of combat in front of them. Asa locked eyes with her.

"Are you a nightblade?"

The girl nodded.

"Then act like one. All you need to do is get to the gate and run to the army out there. You'll be protected."

Junko didn't seem to be any more convinced, but Asa could see her limbs get in position for the jump. Asa nodded, and they dropped off the safety of the rooftop. The battle almost immediately engulfed them, and Asa's swords were everywhere. The girl drew her own sword, but she wasn't very fast. Asa blocked a cut coming at the girl and then killed the soldier who made it.

Distracted, Asa almost missed a cut coming at her. The girl didn't, though. She blocked it for Asa, and then the older nightblade cut down the assailant. Asa gave the girl a quick bow of thanks and then pushed her toward the gate. Junko hesitated only for a moment and then ran.

Asa fought with the remaining nightblades, her strikes slowing down as exhaustion took its inevitable toll. They kept giving up ground, hoping for any more blades to come to the gate. It wasn't long, though, before they realized there would be no more survivors. Asa and Junko had been among the last. Their orders unspoken, the nightblades gave up ground even more readily, soon being pushed out of the gate, out of their city, and to the open space beyond.

Then Asa realized they were in trouble. Katashi's soldiers kept pushing through the gate, intent on killing every nightblade they could. The blades couldn't simply turn and run but instead were out in the open. Katashi's troops were starting to surround the nightblades who had fought so hard to protect the evacuation.

Asa had just enough time to sigh in resignation. She had succeeded in her mission, but this was still the final day she would draw breath. There was no escaping the waves of soldiers pouring out of the gate after them.

Asa took a deep breath and prepared for her final battle. She was ready.

When the first arrows landed, Asa thought that Katashi's archers were firing on his own troops. Only one or two soldiers fell in that first volley, but everyone paused for a moment to look into the sky, confusion evident on all faces.

Asa's vision was suddenly crowded by the black streaks that signified death at the end of their journey. They fell all around the group of nightblades, killing another dozen of Katashi's men.

Asa stared, uncertain how to feel. As reason reasserted itself, she traced the flight of the arrows and saw the wave of troops wearing blue uniforms advancing in an orderly manner.

Mari. Mari was coming to save them.

The arrows continued to fall, now in a disorganized, chaotic manner. But they were no less deadly.

Katashi's troops reacted more quickly than Asa did. They broke ranks and fled back to the walls of Starfall, seeking protection wherever they might. Almost half fell to Mari's archers before they could reach safety, arrows piercing them mercilessly in the back.

For what seemed like forever, Asa simply watched, her mind understanding what was happening, her body unable to react. She had been ready to die, but apparently it wouldn't be today.

She was completely exhausted. Asa sat on her knees, wanting nothing more than to sleep for most of a moon. The rain poured down, and the sky was almost as dark as night.

She was alive, but Starfall was no more.

Chapter 27

After the blades evacuated Starfall, the battle was over.

Katashi, devious and blinded by hatred as he was, was no fool. More than two hundred blades had made it out of the city, survivors of the short-lived but terrible siege. With Mari's forces reinforced by the blades, Katashi knew there was no chance of victory in battle. His troops immediately retreated to their original lines, and once the storm passed, the soldiers who had taken Starfall set a torch to what little remained as they left.

Several commanders and blades had urged Mari to attack Katashi's forces, but she held back. The damage had been done. Starfall was gone. She had no doubt Katashi was organizing his retreat, and she didn't think they would capture him if they tried.

Instead, Mari ordered that the focus be put on the survivors. Dayblades went around healing soldiers who would accept their help, and they made believers out of many in her army.

She looked out over the ruins of Starfall with a heavy heart. She knew that this was the beginning of a new age. The Kingdom, even though it still existed in name, was no more. The blades were now homeless, and despite the efforts of the Lady in White, much fear still surrounded them.

Mari didn't know the way forward. Her control of the army was tenuous at best, and she had to balance the expectations of blades, soldiers, and civilians alike. All she knew was that she had to try. Her house depended on her.

She missed Takahiro. Her guard was coming with his contingent of blades, but they hadn't been in time for the siege or its aftermath. His pragmatic worldview and honest opinions were needed more than ever. A few more days, she reminded herself, and she would be able to count on his advice once again.

If she didn't know what to do, she did know what principles she wanted to govern by. She had sent a notice to all commanders of the army and to the blades. A half moon from now, they would decide if she should lead them.

The idea had come from Takashi's works, the secret tome she had carried with her since she had begun this journey. The people had a right to choose, and she didn't want people serving her who didn't want to.

She had one final task to set aside before she could turn her full attention to her people. She dreaded the confrontation but couldn't put it off forever. With a sigh, she turned away from the sight of Starfall and headed toward her camp.

———

Mari entered the tent cautiously, even though she knew both residents sensed her approach. A gentle entrance still somehow seemed appropriate.

Asa and Koji had shared the tent since the siege of Starfall. Mari had her suspicions about their relationship but didn't say anything. Her own relationship with the two had been tense, to say the least. Despite what Mari had said to Asa before she left, she had allowed some of the first dayblades who came into their camp to heal Koji.

Although she hadn't talked with anyone directly, she'd heard rumors that Koji had come as close to death as you could. Word of his deeds had spread. The young nightblade had a monumental reputation to live up to now. Too many had seen him fight, and at times Mari thought perhaps Koji was even more respected than she.

Asa offered her tea, and Mari accepted. The three sat around a table, Koji's movements slower than those of an old man. From how he looked, Mari assumed he had a long journey of healing ahead of him.

They sat in silence, the two nightblades clearly waiting for her to speak.

She still wasn't sure what she wanted to say. Rationally she knew that where she was today was as much a result of the work of these two nightblades as anyone else. They had proven their loyalty with blood and actions.

But she wanted to kill Koji. She imagined driving a sword into his bandaged torso and reopening his wounds, twisting the blade as she did. She wanted his death to be slow.

Juro had been a good leader and a great brother. She wanted him back.

With blinding speed, Koji drew his sword out of his sheath. Mari jumped. She was grateful she hadn't been holding her tea, or it would have spilled all over her.

Without a word, Koji slowly turned the sword around and laid it on the table between them, the sharp edge of the blade pointed toward him.

Mari stared at the steel that had killed her brother, visions of grabbing the sword and taking Koji's head filling her sight.

He bowed down in front of her, giving her exactly the opportunity she desired.

Even though Koji didn't say a word, his meaning was perfectly clear. He was willing to give everything to serve Mari. She had seen that herself and couldn't deny it. If she wanted his life, it was hers to take.

Mari stood and picked up Koji's sword, testing the weight in her hands.

The lady glanced over at Asa, who sat sipping her tea, calm and composed. Only her eyes gave her away, slowly filling with tears.

How had they gotten here? How had she earned the ability to take the lives of such warriors without them fighting back?

Mari stepped to Koji's side. She raised the sword above her head, preparing the strike.

Asa closed her eyes, pushing the tears out. Then she reopened them and kept them focused.

Mari hesitated, the sword high in the air. Killing Koji was just, her right as a ruler.

She brought the sword down.

Gently.

Mari put the sword back on the table and knelt. She picked up her tea and sipped. She wasn't sure she'd ever tasted a better cup.

Asa smiled at her, and when Koji came back up, his own eyes were filled with water.

Both nightblades bowed down to her, their foreheads to the floor. It had to be painful for Koji, but he persisted. After they had both held the pose for a long time, they sat back up.

Mari didn't have the words. She hadn't forgiven Koji. But this was a start. She smiled, a weight lifted off her shoulders, and she received matching grins in return.

She didn't trust herself to say anything. She finished her tea and stood up, giving them each a short bow. Then she left the tent.

If they were going to build a better world, it started now.

ACKNOWLEDGMENTS

A novel is always a massive undertaking, and this one is no different. A tremendous team came together to make this possible, and they have my eternal gratitude.

Many thanks to Adrienne, who brought this whole story to life. Thanks also to Jason for making sure the production ran smoothly, which makes my life substantially easier. I suspect both do more behind the scenes than I'll ever know.

Everyone who has edited this book has made it far better than I could on my own. Thanks to Clarence for his insight and wisdom, and to Jill and Cheri for their sharp eyes and wonderful comments. Any mistakes that remain in this work are solely my own.

A great thanks to everyone else at 47North who had a hand in the production of this book and that I didn't get to interact with directly. Whether it's cover design, interior design, marketing, or any of the other tasks that go into making these words into novels, every detail matters. Thank you.

Finally, thanks to my friends and family for allowing me to hide in the basement for hours on end to write these books. I couldn't do it without you.

With gratitude,
Ryan

ABOUT THE AUTHOR

Ryan Kirk is the author of the Nightblade series of fantasy novels and its prequel series, Blades of the Fallen. He is the founder of Waterstone Media and was an English teacher and nonprofit consultant before diving into writing full-time in 2015. For more information about Ryan, visit his website at www.waterstonemedia.net.